THREE IN THE BUSH

- THE MENOPAUSE YEARS

DISCLAIMER

The sequel "Three in The Bush - The Menopause Years", would never have been written had it not been for the practice book, "One In The Bush", and for that alone I am exceptionally grateful. The girls are back in town only older and wiser…..maybe, only time will tell.

This story is still extremely childlike, has colourful language, its coarse, and at times possibly controversial, yet hopefully provocative and provoking all in good measure. If you feel that you may have a mild sensitivity or you're unable to control your ego, some or any of the above statements of facts may be irritating so may I be bold enough to suggest that this book is not for you. This is not a judgement call, you understand, it's a warning of sorts. You know yourself better than I do to decide as to whether to continue reading or not. Think of it like the flashing amber on a traffic light, proceed with caution.
It is a tongue-in-cheek romp that follows the exploits and adventures of three older 'girls' as they reunite Down Under to celebrate their 50th birthdays. It is a tale of the dreaded menopause, redemption, growth, personal evolution, camaraderie, love, and friendship.

The intention behind writing the last book was primarily for others, to hear, evoke, and create laughter in whatever form that takes. When we laugh, we give ourselves over to the immediacy of the present moment, which in turn permits us to relax and let go of any tension. Laughter can help open our eyes to previously unnoticed absurdities that can make life seem less serious - the Platypus is the perfect example of this. However, this book "Three In The Bush - The Menopause Years" has been written entirely for me. If you pick it up and get something from it, great, but that is and has never been my intention. When we laugh, there is only a pure, unadulterated release, space and joy are created as a side effect. I loved writing this story, and it made me laugh out loud, so for this reason, I make no apologies to the reader who finds it offensive - you take responsibility for how you wish to respond or react to this book. Your views on my experience are wasted, believe me. If, however, you feel drawn to "Three In The Bush - The Menopause Years" in some way, or you feel the need for some witty banter, light-hearted entertainment, and some laugh-out-loud moments, then "Keep Clam and Carry on Reading".
I have changed the names of some people in this book as I would like to maintain their anonymity. I have also changed the names of some of the

more challenging characters as I have accepted their apologies, forgiven them of any wrongdoing, and am no longer as pissed off with them as I once was, nor do I want to embarrass them or their descendants. They may also be stronger than me and might want to beat me to a bloody pulp. The names of the horrible characters have not been changed, so if you recognise yourself in this category then you need to change, not me. All other characters, stories, and events in this book, even those based on real people, places, and bad behaviours, are entirely fictional. The secret to this creation is knowing exactly how to hide my sources... hopefully. This book may ruffle a few feathers, revealing something in the reader that needs to be addressed, but in my defence, I was menopausal when I wrote this book, but it did teach me not to write for safety, it can be very 'dangerous' to do that. This is a manifestation of a fun adventure, maybe you can also find that inner childlike genie that we all have, only some are just hiding very, very well.

"If there's A book that you want to read, but it hasn't been written yet, then you must be the one to write it" - Toni Morrison

I'm a storyteller, and this is the story I'm telling. Settle in, and make yourself comfortable on the back of its wings. Ready? Away we go.

To my husband Chris, our children Estelle and Cael, and my fabulous Besties, without whom this book would never have been completed.

Lights, Camera, Action

PROLOGUE

Jules

Here's me, I'm back, back in the room. Even behind my crepey lids, something doesn't feel quite right, my entire body is tingling, my eyes are sealed, crusty sleepies, seeping through reluctant slits. I'd put my finger on it if I could, but I can't quite feel my arms yet. Best I try to gauge what's going on out there before I actually open them. I can sense some leftover makeup I don't wear keeping my eyes shut, making them impenetrable to the outside world. Oh oh, I might be in a bit of trouble here. The trick now is to forget the big picture, to settle in and focus on one thing before jumping in and immediately opening them. Pause Jules, take a breath, you need to be more prepared for whatever 'delights' await you out there before you wrestle them apart. What have we got so far; my cheek, entire left side body, buttocks, and thighs are pressing heavily down on what feels like a cold, hard, concrete-textured surface. My nostrils involuntarily permit the dank, putrid heavy air, weighted down with notes of alcohol and human emission, mingling on the imperceptible stagnant currents. My tongue is harder than Mike Tyson is in the ring, and drier than a camel's anal sphincter in a sandstorm. Saliva has leaked out, and puddled under my face, mixing with the grime and crud already present on the floor. Hopefully, saliva is all that it is, these days involuntary discharge can come fast and furious from every anatomical opening known to man or beast. No control of the rajin symptom streams that accompany the dreaded me no pause. Auditory fine-tuning allows me to pick up the dulcet tones of someone snuffling, wheezing, and snoring somewhere out there, sounds like a pig. Ange is definitely here with me, I'd recognise her snorts anywhere, even though she tells me she doesn't, right now she's snoring, must be Lesley grunting. Other than a faint tick-tock and a clinking sound, it's eerily still. Why am I on the floor? No blankets, pillow, comforter, hot water bottle, or cuddly toy. Nothing. Nada. Nought. Okay Jules, brace yourself, get those big girl panties ready for the big reality reveal, whatever is going on out there, can't be any worse than what we tell ourselves. After three.......it's counterproductive and overwhelming to think what's lying in wait out there, come on, breathe Jules, breathe, focus exclusively on this breath, only this one. This is my breath in, this is my breath out, it'll help avoid and dislodge any sneaky, intimidating, sticky, negative thoughts that keep trying to gatecrash my headspace. Here goes, on the count of three again, in for a penny, in for a pounding…one… breath, nothing ventured, nothing gained, two…here I come, ready…or not… eyes open wide, here's me world, I'm back, back in the room, far too impatient to wait.

Directly opposite me in the far left corner, an undulating living, breathing bundle of tabloids rises, then falls, phew, Lesley is here. I can't really tell though, opposite me, a tiny, single metal camp-like bed is fixed to the back wall, and a sleeping back swells, sniffles, wheezes, and farts simultaneously, emitting unseeable whiffs from one orifice or another, hard to tell what's coming from where. That's a relief, at least Ange is also here. From this angle, her highly sought-after, curly, dyed voluminous auburn locks, much admired, adored, and desired by men, women, and children alike, not only for its colour, high gloss, smooth texture, but for the immaculate tapered tips. It's much shinier than I remember, odds are Lesley and her beloved hairbrush must have had something to do with it. The somewhat familiar, golden hair threads, mingle with the unwanted, inevitable, age-related grey streaks, poking out from beneath the cloak of her tendrils, spilling out and over a wafer-thin, lumpy, stained 'mattress', and I use that word loosely, more like a giant, gently used, fanny pad. Getting old can really suck, especially when we try hard to cling to an image from the past that has long since left the whippersnapper station. Ange pays an arm and a leg to unrealistically recapture the carbon copy of her youth and would have an apoplectic fit if she could see the out-of-control elderly hairs I can clearly see from here, and that's without my long-distance glasses on. Where are they, I wonder? I'm not wearing them, or am I? I wear my readers on my head, and my prescription ones on a rope chain around my neck. Well, that's when I can remember which is which and where I have put them. 9/10 I get it wrong anyway... Alcohol may have played his part in all this because when I drink, I lose things like my bra, glasses, any sense of modesty, dignity, and control of my bladder.

The heads of her overpaid stylists will roll if she ever does find those grey hairs. They can only hide from us for so long you, one minute there's only one, next there's a warren of them, and they don't just confine their brazen breeding to the head either. We need to accept age gracefully, not reluctantly, thankfully she's here, so that must be Lesley over there in the corner, at least we're all here together, but where? Where are we? What do we have? One flimsy bed, a slit of a window with unnecessary bars, not even Ange could fit her scrawny arse through them, a stone floor, three stark walls, the fourth being more bars. BARS? Stainless steel grillage bars. Not the usual kind we are accustomed to, we're talking about the ones used to keep people out of or IN. We're in a feckin jail cell. Oh well, c'est lavvy, I've been in worse states, so I got this one, I really have, I've got this, just need to bend my top leg up towards my chest, inch the other one up slowly under it, then maybe, just maybe I can get up on all fours. Thank the lard for yoga, and dogging. But I tell you what, this menopause malarkey can be a real challenge.

Were we at a fair, a concert, a pub, or something, because the flashing green ankle bracelet would certainly indicate a win of some sort, maybe an exclusive nightclub entry band. It's not totally unattractive, I might keep it, it distracts from my fluid-filled arthritic ankle joint. Ahhh, another one of the many, many joys to add to the jubilations of the dreaded me no pause.

Time to check in with everyone, not sure I'm quite ready to be vertical though, easier to slowly inch my way doggy style toward Ange. If I gently, gently shake her awake, we can begin to piece the jail cell puzzle back together. My memory isn't quite what it used to be, another charming characteristic of age, two minds are better than one, Ange boasts her recollection is still intact, but as we know, memories are malleable and I frequently hear her tell a very different version to the same, but intrinsically different story to the tale I tell. I'll get to Lesley shortly, no point waking them both. Oh me what a pickle we're in. I wonder what happened? I don't have a scooby doo. Not a doo, do I scoob, not a one. There's an unattainable, unretrievable, totally forgettable void filling my empty thought station above. Ange has always boasted that she has a better memory than most, maybe when she was 12 she did, but I reckon that as she Adam Antly refuses 50, it's not quite what it used to be. Nothing ever is. She often tells me that memory loss comes with age and that she's categorically, emphatically, not old, let alone 50. She'll let me know in 10 years' time.

The manky pallet recently vacated by the previous occupant envelops and engulfs her tiny, frail, lanky frame, but don't let that fool anyone, they don't call her a pit bull in pearls for nothing. The mattress reveals its true gory, not-so-secret stains, no need for a blue light to tell its story. Forensics would have a field day with some of those novel cultures growing on and through the disgusting fabrics.

There's something uncharacteristically cathartic poking, prodding, and jabbing her boney back. 'Tis a very fine line between trying to rouse her and wanting to punch the living daylights out of the tattooed shoulder butterfly pupating from beneath the auburn cocoon, emerging more as a tired, jaded moth tramp stamp, rather than the original blue emperor it once was. Flitting and fluttering on the puckered, empty loose skin between her scrawny blades, the once vibrant wings faded, dull, almost transparent, wrinkled, and deformed. Beautiful actually, once young and full of life, now empty. Any joie de vivre it once had has been sucked dry. A tad more aggression is required, after all, it is Ange we're talking about, a delightful, yet demanding law unto only herself. She can have her chauffeur drive an actual saint to distraction, she can put the F in ear, be aggressive, impatient, scary, rude, intimidating, a little insecure, selfish, sarcastic, and funny, very, very funny, but enough of her good sides, even her bad self is funny. I love her, but right now, I don't, she needs to wake up and help me figure out why we're in the slammer. You know the old-fashioned ones like you see in the movies, iron metal bars on the front wall, perpendicular to Ange's alligator peep toe sandals, her highly polished manicured toes more than peeping out from the gaping toe hole, positively, actively clawing an escape route from their totally age-inappropriate confinement. I give up. I'll leave her to it for a bit longer and see if there's anything I can actually remember.

The cold metal frame of the bed presses across my back. Think. Think Jules, come on. Why are we here? How did we get here? Look around. A metal barred door to my left, paint peeling, worn down from the absorption from decades of constant pleading, anger, fear, and hatred. The door unlocks from the other side, a small rectangular barred window high on the back wall to my right, above Lesley, broadcasting the impartial unfolding of the outer world, permitting daylight to enter between their vertical bars. The hues of breaking dawn bouncing on their vapours. Dust fairies pirouetting with the unseen tears and hopes of past residents, each pixie surfing a unique vibrational path on the visibly expanding beam of light. Lesley is hiding under it all, sandwiched between being buried under some rough insubstantial blanket, and sheets made from torn local tabloid newspapers. A metal honey bucket and a kid's sink are in the other corner, the caged overhead ceiling light flickering its tormented Morse code feeble light, no competition for the presence of daylight effortlessly taking centre stage in the confined space. The first sounds of dawn dance their way inside, laughing kookaburras, a cock or two, yahooing babblers, delicate trills, and a variety of active and very vocal singers sharing the same expanse, filling the cell with a warming, pleasant atmosphere. At least I know we're still in The Bush, no mistaking that birdsong. Faint footsteps echo in the walkway, increasing in volume, enticing the tapestry of Australia's natural fauna to a one-sided battle, already won. I bet this is a place for the hormonally insane.

There is nothing more confining than the prison we don't know we're in - Shakespeare

BRRRING.. BRING ..BRING...BRING ..

Jules

Heavy plods trudge their way down the hallway towards me, increasing its weary volume the closer they get. Hopefully someone coming to free us.

"OY SHEILA?"

Is this my tinder date? Is it a he? she? I can't really tell as he/she/it/they/them is behind the wrought iron bars, and shaking my mobile phone at me.

...BRRRING...

"OY Sheila? I'm not your private secretary, I shouldn't be doing this at all you know, but your pal's phone won't stop ringing, so, please come and take the call."

BRIING..... BRRRING, BRING.....

"Hurry up, someone keeps calling your friend, Jules's phone."

Interesting. I am Jules. Maybe another piece to this puzzle. The thot plickens.

"Jules's phone you say? How do you know who's phone it is?"

"Cos it says on the back of the case, "It may be tempting to take me, but I belong to Jules, give me back please", now stop trying to be a smart arse and take the phone."

BRRRING..

"It's from someone called "Knobber." "

"Knobber?? Oh my gawd, why didn't you say that in the first place, give it here will you."

BRING... BRING...

"No, you come over here to me, I'm not coming in there. Your mate Jules isn't here, so you might as well answer her phone, no skin off my nose if you don't want to take it."

"What do you mean Jules isn't here?"

Briiing

"She's not going to be able to answer any calls for a very, very long time I'm afraid, I hate to be the one to tell you, but your mate Jules is in BIG trouble, the only cell she'll be getting is a jail cell. You and your pals here will get to protest your innocence when you appear in front of Judge Crooks later. Now take the bloody phone before I change my mind. "Knobber" is very persistent and determined to chat to someone, and you'll do Lesley."

"Lesley? You called me Lesley?"

Wait what?

Briiing

"That's the name they booked you in under last night, not that you'd remember, now hurry up will you before I change my mind, and hang up on them."

"No…don't do that. Give it here."

Brrring, briiing

"Hello?"

"Hey Jools, at last, I've been trying to call you for ages."

There's no mistaking his voice, there's only one person I have in my contacts under that nom de plume, he's not even a real knobber, not now at least, not ever really, but Ange got hold of my phone one day and I've never got round to changing it back to Mikey, Lesley's lovely husband, Mikey, or My key as I call him. Lard only knows what my name is in certain address books. Sam has me down as "Birth Giver" for instance, but not to be mistaken for hostility or even resentment, there's a beautiful ebb and flow of pure unadulterated love between me and my only child. I have him down as "favourite sun", it makes us both smile. "Knobber" is the nickname Ange gave him many years ago when he came out of the surf at Bondage Beach wearing a pair of pale blue lolly bags, clutching a limp, sodden box of milk tray chocolates to give to Lesley, pretending to be, you know who, what's his name? 007 dude, not Sean, not Pierce, one of the other ones. No mind, it'll come back if it's meant to. Should have been a romantic moment between them both, and everyone else there watching the proposal unfold, it would have been perfect had it not been spoiled by Ange whispering in my ear;

"Knobber."

"No Jools, it's me, Mikey."

Darn, I must have used my outside voice.

"Is this a good time to chat Jools? Lesley's usually up with the birds, the feathered kind, not you and Angy, phnar phnar. I'm hoping she might be out walking."

"Jailbirds?"

"All birds, you know Lesley, she loves the dawn chorus, you must have heard her morning trill, if you haven't already, you will. She calls it her morning "thrill", always makes me smile, Jools. Sunrise is her favourite time of day, so I thought she'd be her usual up and at em, bouncy self."

"Lesley?"

If they think I'm Lesley, which I'm not, then maybe that's not her over there in the corner, but if it is her, then who am I? Apparently, Jules is elsewhere. Very confusing.

"No, it's me, Jools."

"S'mee who?"

"Not Smee...ME."

"Me who?"

"This is beginning to sound like a bad knock-knock joke. Me, Mikey."

"Mikey who?"

"My key doesn't work, help me out here will you? Phnar, phnar, you fall for it everytime Jools."

"Ahhh, Mikey????........ As in Mikey???.... MY KEY?? Sorry, there's a whole lot to take in right about now. I'm not quite with it yet."

"The one and only, tall, dark and handsome... ha ha ha...not so dark these days, more like a well seasoned badger."

Breathe

"Okay, not so handsome, and just you wait, wrinkles will make a return some day, but still tall, slightly stoopid these days, but tall..ish, and I'll confess to being a wee bit of a "knobber" some of the time."

He heard

"Is this a bad time Jools? Is Lesley there?"

"As it turns out My key, she's still sleeping, so we'll have to whisper."

"Ha, ha, good, it was really you I wanted to chat with anyway, to make sure she still doesn't know anything about the surprise party. Does she?"

"I cannot for the life of me think of a bigger, more surprising shocker right now My key, remind me again, what party?" *"You tease you, it's all coming together beautifully at my end, all you have to do is have her on Bondi Beach at sunset, tonight."*

"TONIGHT? Blimey, that's come round quickly, where have the past few days gone?"

"Everything okay Jools? You still know the plan of A?"

"Yes, yes, I'm fine, what do you take me for My key, some middle aged, inept, ageing old hippie who smokes too much weed, loves psychobabble shite more than cannibals love having friends for dinner?"

"Now that you mention it, Jools."

"Look My key, no offence and as much as I'd like to continue chewing the fat with you, now is not the best time, I have to go and work on a few cryptic puzzles we set for each other. Besides, I'm still half asleep, having been rudely woken from my reveries to the jailbirds exercising their daily dawn drill. Not a spoiler alert, but I still need more beauty sleep."

"Ha Ha, you haven't told her, have you Jools? Does she suspect anything?"

"Suspect possibly, no, no, not a suspect, but maybe, she is totally absent, absent of any cunning party plans that you have come up with, she has no clue, well, not that I'm aware of anyway, but you know me, more than one glass of wine and it's a free world."

"I have absolutely no clue what you just said, does that mean you've told her?"

"No, I'd forgotten it already, so how could I tell her if I don't even remember myself."

"How will you remember to get her to the party tonight if you can't even remember it's on? This is why she calls you Dora."

"The Spanish quine with the monkey on her back? Maybe so, I have skills, they're multiplying and I'm losing my …. my…. What were we talking about? Seriously, what were we talking about?"

"Your memory Jools."

"Oh yeah, that's right. Look, I got this My key, trust me, I am Adam Ant that we will have her delivered safely to Bondage Beach tonight at sunset. Is that it in a seashell? Any other orders El Capitaino?"

"No worries, I trust you Jools. You and Angy are two of Lesley's oldest.."

"Look My key, I have to go, but I'll see you in 1 sleep."

"No, tonight..Jools..not 1.."

"Did you say 1 sleep? Tonight? My key, My key? One ? Two ? It's a bad line."

He's gone. Think. THINK Jules.

"Bloody amnesia."

"Pardon Jools, what's that?"
Bollocks, I thought I'd hung up on him.
"Sorry My key, I sneezed. One's a wish."
"You sound funny Jools, everything okay?"
"Sure, it's my 'cell' phone playing up that's all."
"Remember I want this to be a surprise."
"Guaranteed My key, life is full of surprises."
"Is she there with you?"
"She's so 'with us' My key, and I meant to say she's at the Monet Coffeehouse…. getting her Monet caffeine fix."
Shut up Jules.
"She doesn't drink coffee."
Told you!
"Getting it for Ange, you know how kind Lesley is My key…. and she'll be out walking off our very large dinner from last night."
Did we eat? Doesn't feel like it.
"I don't know about you, but I'm hungry enough to eat an entire kale, falafel, and cauliflower burger in a gluten free pumpkin seed bun with dairy free, coconut, cashew mayonnaise."
"Good to know Jools."

"Sorry, did I say that out loud, didn't mean to."
I can feel the bile and temperature rising.
"Let's round this up so you can escape off somewhere nice and enjoy your time together."
"Spooky My key, you literally took the words out of my mouth."
"Go do whatever you've all planned for the day, and if I know Lesley, and I do, then your day has already been micro-managed to the last second. I'm only calling to remind you of her 50th birthday surprise party, the emphasis on SURPRISE Jools. You really haven't told her have you?"
"Surprise? Every moment is a surprise My key, especially this one and as far as I'm aware, I'm still an unflinching, reinforced cell wall of courtesy and discretion."
"You've told her, haven't you Dora?"
It's Dory, but I do not have the strength or the will to take that particular malaprop of Lesley's up with him.
"Relax My key, by hook or Judge Crooks, we'll have her delivered safely."
"I trust you Jools…Angy not so much. You and Angy are two of Lesley's oldest and best, well you are, her Bezzie"
"Oldest you say? I'll have you know that I'm actually the youngest, and Ange, as she keeps telling us, is only 39 with 11 extra years of pure, contaminated experience, is the eldest."
I have to go and make sense of all this. If I'm not Jules then who the feck am I?
"Look My key, I have to go, feeling a bit cooped up, and ready to get the hell out of here. I'll see you later, it's a bad line, and I think I can hear her melodious humming having a twosome with rattling chains of all things. And the bars are definitely calling us. Better go before she catches us. I'll mark it in my diary. BYE."
Feck sake, that's all I need!

If feathers don't ruffle then nothing flies - Jessica Byrne

Constant use had not worn the ragged fabric of their friendship - Dorothy Parker

Wake Up

Jules

Ange's perfectly full, shiny, plucked, tucked, sucked, taut visage rolls slowly to face me, her permanent makeup still beautifully applied, her naturally tattooed rosebud-stained lips pulse in unison with the swell and fall of her ample synthetic breasts, rising like the morning sun in their plentiful glory, slipping as gracefully as the sunset. Pulsing their jellyfish matter from under her provocative purple bra, and familiar boob tube, unlike my two flappy, drained sacks which slide down either side of my chest like two squealing piglets trying to break free from a chewing-gum-coloured constraint. We can't win them all...or have the dosh to cheat at it either. She's gorgeous to look at, a real work of art, I'm tempted to touch her breasts, that would wake her out of dreams of booger slum fairies gyrating through her head. She turns away from me, exposing her practically bare arse, a feckin mahoosive red back spider peers out from beneath her dental floss thong. Her silk palazzo pants have rolled down to her hips and the cheeky wee blighter must have bravely snuck in during the night. If I flick it lightly and quickly, I might be able to get it off before it bites her, or I can slap it hard, squashing and killing it dead...SLAP... slap SLAP.

"Ange, you're awake."

"No shit Sherlock, being battered will do that to a sleeping beauty, FUCK SAKE Jules. That hurt."

"There was a very large red back spider, about to dig its lethal fangs into your inflated plump cheeky arse flesh Ange."

You're whale cum.

"Relax Trigger, that's just Alfie, my permanink tattoo, a constant reminder of a purely unselfish act committed by yours truly, and a gentle aide-memoire to those stood behind me to kiss my ass or I'll release my venom."

"I potentially saved your life from the real possibility of being poisoned by a real life red back spider, spookily similar to the one that bit Lesley's backside back in the day. Thankfully for you and me all I did was slap it, and not suck the venom out like you did. I can't remember diddly-squit, but the image of your face, knee deep in the crack of her arse, sucking it like a champagne flavoured lollipop, is as clear as crystal."

"Alfie's a souvenir of an occasion in which I put Lezzers in harm's way, and neglected to inform her that there was a nest of the venomous bastards and their babies residing under the outdoor, cludgie toilet seat."

"That was decades ago Ange, I can't believe you still carry the pain of that traumatic event in the form of a tattoo on your bahookie, the culprit of all things and of all the places, you choose your arse. Does she know you have this trophy reminder? I for one, and I know Lesley for sure, categorically do not blame you, we both see it as you saving her life actually, not putting her in harm's way, Take That. The greatest day, you saved her life, only after putting her in perilous danger though…joke! Let it go for feck sake, thinking all those negative thoughts is only going to add extra invisible weight to your svelte body."

"If your theory works Jules, then I'd be the size of a full house, furnished with stress, anxiety, and anger. You might be onto something. Imagine how I feel? It was my head firmly between her asscheeks, sucking the living daylight out of them. That image still scares me far more than any spider does. You'd better not have scarred me with all that slapping Jules, bordering on pleasant I won't lie."

"Not that you'd notice if that's what you mean Ange, only a huge, angry red palm imprint over a very flat, permanently dead, squashed spider, not so ready to bite another day."

"Fangs for that Jules. Boy, I haven't slept that well for years, what in gadz name did I take last night? Good shit whatever it was. Where the fuck are we? I don't remember getting home? Is this? Is this what I think it is? Furnishings, hygienic services, and cleanliness leave a lot to be desired, a hollow, musty cube of cold concrete, one way in, accessed by a key from the other side of an 800 lbs steel door with a wrought iron door. A tiny window, minimal natural sound or light. Day or night? No clue yet, faint zapping of flies in the distance, still in Australia then. Looks like every drunk tank I've been in all over the globe. Jules, I hate to be the bearer of bad news, but I believe we're in jail. My head is dirling, remind me why are we here again? I don't know whether I'm coming or going, isn't quite the penthouse suite at the Four Seasons I expected."

"I can give you more than 4 reasons as to why it's not Ange.

1. Wrought iron bars for doors as opposed to the ones we're used to leaning on.

2. The not so trendy steampunk, cement walls and floor.

3. Echoes of laughing guards, keys jangling from their belts

4.....”

"Alright, alright, alright Jules, you're hurting my head, I get the gist of it.”

"On the plus side my memory fails me.”

"THAT'S the plus side?”

"I'd rather be slathered in raspberry jam and put on a golf course to attract the flies away from the golfers, than go through the dizzying heights of menopause Ange, but here we are, best make the most of life despite its presence. The alternative doesn't appeal to me at this stage in my life.”

"I've told you before that I'm too young to have pause on men. Besides, some of the symptoms are more likely genetic, and not from the menopause. Let's face it, I'm a natural bitch, my mum was a bitch, so was her mum, all her sisters too and so on, maybe an excuse, but certainly not related to menopause.”

"The menopause bitch hairy fairy stole my figure, sleep, mood, libido, patience, eyesight, brain cells, political correctness and replaced me with a full beard, a moustache, a muffin top, bottom biceps, jowls, thighs, and cankles, and I have more wrinkles than the sharpeist of Shar Pei puppies.”

"I'd rather paint myself a hideous shade of pea-green and dance the tango in public than admit to my age.”

"Wrinkles are only evidence of laughter, good times, debauchery, and hedonism. I have them.”

"I didn't say I didn't have them Jules, they're surgically hidden under my hairline.”

"Thankfully beards are back in fashion Ange, some would say positively sexy, and I still have a smoking hot body, it's just disguised in the form of menopause.”

"What time is it? Or day even, what day is it? Look at me, but look at YOU! What's happened to you Jules?”

"I look like I've been through some kind of traumatic event, check the night sweats, day sweats and very likely urine deposits, hopefully mine, on my lovely new t-shirt that we bought from ...the...oh, oh, it's coming back Ange, we bought 3 Tshirts, different colours with Chinese characters on them when we stopped for petrol."

"I vaguely remember a gas station now that you mention it, but I hate to be the bearer of bad news Jules, that's not Chinese hieroglyphics, that's fancy lettering that clearly says, "Fuck YOU", or maybe "EWE", I can't really tell from this angle and all the soiled splatters."

"What a state I'm in, I must have had hot flushes, cold flushes, and I do feel clammy, clatty, itchy, you're bitchy and loud, my tits are droopy, and I could hook my nipples through my big toe and have an instant pair of trendy croc flip flaps. I have endless naps, desire for wine, coffee, chocolate, the odd joint, crabs, at all times of the day and/or night. My nipple impression is my phone ID, swiping my mobile under my top is easier to find than trying to remember a password. Boy, if only I had a dollar for everytime I forget my passwords, or get distracted ....you know what?"

"What Jules?"

" …. I quite fancy ice cream…."

"Mmm yes, what flavour would you have?"

"Dulce leche, with sprinkles on top. Those laughing guards down the corridor have to look after us, right, and that means they'll have to give us breakfast or something to snack on at the very least. Every cloud and all that Ange. What do you think? Ice cream and/or pancakes?"

"Have you ever watched "The Shawshank Redemption" or "Orange is The New Black" Jules? I doubt this is a jolly holiday camp serving fresh fruit salad sprinkled with anything, let alone granola, coconut yoghurt, matcha, spirulina, served over bulgar wheat pancakes and ice fucking cream Jules."

" I'd settle for porridge if pushed Ange, not the TV show, the Scottish breakfast made from oats."

"I know what fucking porridge is Jules, I haven't completely forgotten my roots, besides you've been in Australia for as long as I've lived in the USA, so stick that in your pipe and smoke it."

"That was a great show, remember? Porridge, the hilarious prison life of Fletcher, a criminal serving a five year sentence, striving to bide his time, shifting this way, that way, forward and back, trying to keep his head above water by treading the feck beneath the surface, refusing to be ground down by the prison system."

"We're not Fletcher and we're not criminals…are we Jules?"

"I can even remember the names of the actors, Ronnie Barker, Fulton Mackay, Richard Beckinsale, but I can not for the life of me remember why we're here. You?"

"I can't remember jackshit either, my memory fails me for some reason."

"WAIT...... No, nothing.Wait....no, I thought I had something...but, nope, there's this invisible field of darkness, an infinite void of nothing in my way, it's almost in my grasp, then ..poof..gone. One minute you see it, next minute...do you think drugs and alcohol were a factor?"

"Does the Pope shit in the woods Jules? Realistically though, we both know that Her Majesty over there in the corner wouldn't have been involved in any of that."

"That's just it, what if that's not Lesley. The guard thinks I'm Lesley, unless of course they have it wrong and that is her tucked up over there beneath a heavy blanket of narcotic consumption, and yesterday's tabloid news headlines. Now that really would be a turn up for the books would it not, if not a highly entertaining notion that, baby over there in the corner is the ring leader behind all this."

"I won't lie Jules, there's nothing I'd really enjoy more than knowing Lezzers got us into this mess."

"It must be a mistake though Ange, why would we be in a cell of all places, we're far too old for most incarcerable nonsense are we not? The last thing I remember is ... .nope...negative, zilch, some bastard has wiped any traces of my salvable memories?"

"That's a stretch, anyone having access to our memories would have their eyeballs scorched."

"I guess it comes with our age."

"Speak for yourself, you mean your age Jules, remember I'm at least a decade and change younger than both of you."

"Parts of you are that's for sure. I'll go and wake her up, she's allegedly the sensible married mother of 4 boys, 2 dogs, 0 cats, a grinny pig and a partridge in a pear tree. She's bound to have a handle on this, let's face it, not us. Let me centre myself first though, I need to muster the strength to get over there."

Friendship is a peculiar seed. No matter the season, the

weather, or the time of the day, when planted on a nourishing soul, it will always bear fruit - Clairel Estevez

Age is of no importance unless you're a cheese - Billie Burke

Not The First Time To Wake In A Strange Bed

Ange

That slap on my ass was much harder than I usually allow I might add, she doesn't know her own strength that one, and her somewhat lotus position beneath me, is more like a big ole lump of clay chucked on a potter's wheel, rather than the Buddha type posture one would envisage. Her coat, or is it the prison blanket? Hard to tell, her dress sense is and has always been questionable, somewhere between jumble and hippy haute, hammy downs. A child in adult clothing, a real-life, breathing, bone fide kidult. The Falsa rug she wears around her shoulders is a cross between a wigwam and a teepee; two tents go to war. Totally, unapologetically herself, valuing the opinions of others without preconception, I'm envious of her carefree, happy, eccentric ways, with all my embittered heart, unlike me who can be riled by most anyone who gets in my way. In our own very different ways, we are strong, warrior women, who give our power to no one. My intensity is more aggressive, her force is softer. Gentler. Easily and willingly shared. She appears less tense than I feel, that's the childlike aspect of her I guess, having fun, adventure, and acceptance in this life, including the bad bits. So much for the eye that never sleeps, my insomniatic, tattooed, botox peepholes have clearly been off duty, and I have completely missed how we have come to be surrounded by concrete walls, a single bed with questionable bedding. Thankfully my vaccines are all up to date, as there's no way I could have or would have slept on the floor like Jules or Lezzers. The back of an obese Aussie bloke swallowing a stool with his lardy ass heaves at the far end of the musty hallway. Somewhat reassuring to notice he's wearing some semblance of a police uniform, at least we can rule out being kidnapped by some axe-wielding psychopath and dumped unceremoniously in a basement of his remote cabin to be used and abused as his sex slaves. At least it's a legit jail...or so it seems. The blue heeler, or copper for the uneducated, seems nonplussed by our stirrings, this particular mutt looks like he's been amongst more than his fair share of the pedigree, Not your Chum, grub. His sizable gut is spewing over his tight, cinched waistband, spilling its wobbling gelatine contents over the constricting plastic belt. He's sitting at a desk, laughing at some video on his lap. I hope it's his phone he's playing with, can't really tell from this angle. His grey, spiked short back and side mullets, glint in the glimmer of sunlight edging its way in from the outside ....daytime. That's a start at least. Only nights, weeks, months, possibly years, I have to fill in the blankety blanks. I must admit though, when we decided on a reunion for Jules and Lezzer's 50th birthdays, I had expected the only bars we would be frequenting would be of the pub variety, not the ones of the caged variety. The flashing red exit light harmonising in direct contrast with the green one on Jules's ankle, never noticed she wore an ankle bracelet before, let alone a flashing one at that. It's not as ugly as her seashell, melon pip, pubic hair necklace though, which she prefers to the plastic landfill tat you get these days, her words, not mine. I gave her an Elsa Peretti, Tiffany, scorpion piece of jewellery years ago to smarten her up. Bet she probably threw it out with the trash, totally unaware as to its value. I don't fucking care. I prefer to wear platinum and blood diamonds. She looks like a dishevelled old humming hippie.

"Flashing exit sign Jules? That rings a bell somewhere in the deep, dark recess of my mind, there it is one second, snap, gone the next, slipping behind the cascading veil of infinite drug, and alcohol addled, indifferent brain fog, never to be seen again."

"Constant reminders of our age, not that we're getting older Ange, but just as we get a grip of life and begin to really appreciate it, it mentally slips away from us. Why did we not appreciate the body, the mind, the youth we had...oh wait we did...or at least many others did. Not something to be proud of."

"No point in crying over spilled gin and tonic Jules, however, on reflection, it would have been nice if one of them had stuck around a bit longer than a few more nights, or weeks at the very least, it's positively exhausting restarting every time, every fucking time, and they all turn out to be weak, sad, pathetic, needy men, clutching at some external gratification to fill some sad, lonely void in them, let's face it, why else would most of them have affairs."

"At the time, you thought that's what you wanted Ange, remember? Life may have other plans in mind for you, now all we have to do is relax, and trust that every moment is perfectly designed to match what we need. If we assume that every man is weak, needy, whatever, then that's exactly what we'll get reflected back. Careful what we tell ourselves. A belief is only ever a thought repeated over and over again."

"I'll tell you what I believe right now Jules, that Lezzers looks like a bag lady under the weight of all those grubby tabloid publications, covered in fake news, food stains, coffee marks, rising and falling with every breath throw. I also believe she'd be appalled by her very loud snoring, like a suckling pig squealing for a tipple, oops I mean nipple. Does she have sleep apnea?"

"Not that I'm aware of, I actually thought it was your snoring? Stop talking to me, I'm trying to tap into my higher self, see if that helps us. It can reveal thoughts, the good, the bad, the ugly, the beauty, but mostly of all, our truth."

Sounds like Jules is mumbling something like, "what weight am I? What weight am I?" That can't be right, fuck, my hearing's going now. Why can't I accept that I'm getting older like her? It SUCKS! Focus, Ange, come on, you got this, you can hear her, ssshhh, listen.

"Where am I? Ting. Where am I? Ting."

Ahhhhhhhhh, that's more like it. I can hear her just fine, see I'm not getting old, phew, saved by the bell she doesn't have. She must be trying to find herself again, she's been looking for herself for as long as I've known her, and that's a very, very long time. She's a great friend, very loyal. Accepts me at my very worst, which can be fairly often I won't lie, that's why I love her, not that I'd ever tell her that you understand, too touchy-feely for me, and living in the USA hasn't softened that resolve either, in fact, quite the opposite, it's driven me in the other direction of that insincere lovey dovey bullshit that spouts freely from many an American lip. "OOO, I LOVE your hair..lips, dress, lobotomy scar." Doesn't matter, they've been conditioned to say something nice and insincere to everyone they meet, whether they believe it or not, usually the latter. "We must get together" bullshit... eh, false, they'd rather stick hot needles in their eyes... "oo, that's sooo funny", then LAUGH fuckers, you have to look as if it were funny, don't get me wrong, you know when sentiments are authentic, or whether they're a crock of shit. Again usually the latter. Jules is the real all-singing, all-dancing deal though, she's authentic, almost to her detriment, even at her worst, she's one of the most compassionate, empathetic, kind people I know, and doesn't get embroiled in the drama of others. Maybe I should marry her. I'd say I'd like to be more like her, however, there's no way I could seriously wear patchouli, harem pants, leg warmers, a headband, and enough crystals to sink a battleship, not even for a joke. Lezzers, however, is a whole different matter, she gets my goat. She knows how to wind me up like some clockwork sex toy, always has done, not quite sure how she does it, but she can make me rabid at the first sign of a potential malaprop. I don't even know what it is, but she gets on my silicone tits in both their unique time zones, almost every time. My mother was my only other nemesis. My mother, also called Lesley funnily enough, was a complex, emotionally void, aggressive alcoholic, and a tricky customer indeed. She's now found a deep peaceful place for herself and others, me included and it's deep down alright, 6 feet deep down.

From Lezzers malaprops to her annoying, obsessive, compulsive, irritating habits, including frenetic hair brushing, not even exclusive to her own shiny locks, anyone within arms reach of her wooden, Mason Pearson extinct water buffalo bristle brush, gets stroked within an inch of their follicle life. She can have me rigid quicker than I can neck 6 tequila shots, and that's saying something. According to one of my therapists at The Hokey Cokey clinic, my reactions at the hands of Lezzers only reveal parts of me that need to be addressed and healed or some other bullshit like that. Bumping her gums about the things that make us feel bothered, and uncomfortable, that we can't metabolise emotionally. Dr Feelgood's, I kid you not, favorite thing to say is, if you can't feel it, then you can't heal it, seek a milder, kinder, more forgiving response over reactivity instead. Fuck that, the only lesson I've learned so far is that I want to smack Lezzers in her snuffling, snorting gub most of the time, if only she'd stop reminding me that I saved her life back in the hay day, which I did, but only after duress. She won't let me forget that we share the same blood either, which in her opinion, makes us practically siblings. That's not how transfusions work Lezzers. I have one sibling already and I don't care much for him either.

"What happened to us? What happened to us? mmmmmmmmmm, tiin gggg."

"Maybe you should get yourself over there Tinkerbell, I can't quite put my beautifully manicured finger on it, but there is something unfamiliar about that crumpled, heaving manky mass. Let's face facts here Jules, if Lezzer's was involved, we wouldn't be here, whatever has happened must be a mistake, there's absolutely no way she'd let anything get this far, everything is possible if it were only the two of us, but credit where credit's due, she'd always have her friends backs, so unless there was no drink, drugs, disco music, and a plethora of nubile young men, then there's nothing that could possibly have gone wrong."

"On the other hand Ange, maybe we're here because of drink, drugs, and disco music. Disco music? Scratch that, everyone loves disco music, who doesn't like a bop or five, it's happy, clappy stuff, not a direct shuttle to jail. There's no way on earth, wind and fire our dancing could get us into trouble, yours maybe, mine, not a chance in hell."

"Have you had lessons behind my back Jules?"

"The flashing cuff on our ankles doesn't help my groovy moves, you have one as well if you hadn't noticed."

"Excuses, excuses, look, watch this. I've taken barre classes for years, I can straighten my foot like a javelin, and ta da, my ankle bracelet can delicately slip right off, you might have more of a challenge getting yours over that inflated cankle of yours though. Have you sprained it?"

"Don't think so, but not totally beyond the realms of possibility. Tell me? How can I have a vagina drier than a parched camel with a dreuth on, and fluid filled ankles, bigger than your ego and not one drop in my parched honey pot where it is required the most."

"You're highly entertaining Jules, I'll give you that, your liberal disco moves are often mistaken for a Mexican jumping bean without the Mexican, the jump, or the bean, more of a dancer with ants in their pants, stripping off attire as you go."

"We all need to learn to be strippers Ange, removing the invisible, yet heavy layers of crap we've been lugging around for years, sometimes decades, and believe this, the body keeps the score. When people learn to say "maybe so", "maybe so", then they may notice they've been gripped by the same emotional issue forever. Carrying judgement, anger, fear, sadness with them, playing a game of tug of war between future and past, unaware of their body's scoreboard tallying the tension, pain, and suffering accumulated from past attachments. The best way sometimes to triumph at a game of tug of war is to let go of the rope, no winners, no losers, just right. The Goldilocks syndrome, not too tight, not too loose, just right."

"Feel free to Keep Clammy and strip all that bullshit away Jules, you'll be invisible in no time, just a big ole gobbledygook mass. What about this scenario, maybe there's a law against stripping, invisible or otherwise in this backwater place, and if you plausibly showed the entire town your camel toe, and cart horse dance moves, wearing your invisible nakedness, then that could explain why we're in this dump."

"Not just one camel either, the entire herd has shown up, and not a carthorse either, disco's more like this Ange. It's a glide, followed by a couple of shivers, followed up with some groovy quivers, like the feeling you get when you put a q tip in your ear. Glide. Slide. Cha Cha Cha, shake those intense exaltations of mind, body and feelings. An inner disco inferno, burn baby burn, burn that mother down, burn baby burn, disco inferno. Satisfaction comes with chains. I think maybe we're onto something here."

"There are probably laws in this neck of the woods against that type of unattractive display of motion Jules, …and as for the singing, if you can call it that."

"Harsh Ange, but fair. So we weren't at a disco then?"

"We could have been at a disco, my ears are still pulsing with the heavy beats of Saturday Night Fever or maybe a gunshot, was there a gunshot Jules? It won't have been a disco that got us locked up, no matter how bad your dancing and singing are. Was there a gun involved last night?"

"Only my guns, check these puppies out Ange."

"There's a time when admiring your flappy, loose, sail-like biceps, but this isn't one of them Jules."

"Let's look at what we have so far, three friends reuniting for some of their 50ths, they drive up the coast…..and there's a surprise party for Lesley back at Bondage Beach."

"Ssshhhh Jules."

"What?"

"It may have slipped your mind, but she's still over there Jules, she might look asleep, but she might also be wide awake, wouldn't put it past her to be lugging in, she can be sneaky like that."

"Perhaps that's more likely to be something you'd do Ange."

"Whateva Jules. At least we're all here together, right? Noone seems harmed in any way, right? We're safe…together…. just, well,….in prison. Not my first rodeo either, I've been in a jail before and this is pretty much how they all look; bars replacing open space, walls, floor, ceiling, encased in concrete smeared by a slimy cleaning agent mixed with human excrement and body fluid." "Sounds like an old pair of my underpants."

"Perhaps I still have jet lag, that's why I can't remember or I haven't yet had my daily medication. Speaking of such, where are my jujubes? When was the last time I had them? Where are my pills? Where are my fucking pills Jules?"

"Relax Ange, they're right there, where you'd expect them to be, and a whole lot more pert than mine are these days. I'll give you that, mine point south, grasping for the motherland, any day now, they'll achieve their goal."

"What?? What are you talking about Jules? Not nipples, MY PILLS! Where are MY PILLS?" "Ahhh, easy mistake, but yours do look amazing. I swear I was 18 the last time I had tits like that."

"Can you switch that blinking off, it's giving me a headache."

"I'm not sure I can Ange, it's on my cankle pretty tight."

"Fuck. You know what it is Jules, don't you? It's a criminal fitbit"

"Cool I've always wanted a fitbit, it would be criminal not to have one."

"Turn it off, the flashing green light is giving me a migraine."

"Hold on a wee minty Ange, I'm still trying to tap into my higher self here, see if that helps us out."

"Send me the link when you reach them. AGGGH, check out the mottled flesh on my smooth, tanned upper thighs?"

"Mortled? I bet we're getting closer to the truth right there Ange, we were mortled last night, bleezing drunk. That's why we're here."

"I said mottled, not mortled, although there's a distinct possibility we were pished. Look at the scorched rips on my silk palazzo pants will you."

"Pants? Very Amerkin of you Ange, we say trousers in these neck of the woods."

"Bully for you, my bare thighs look like a pair of slippery, bloated, mottled gray seals rippling through the gaping holes in both legs of my luxury silk palazzo TROUSERS. Happy?"

"No need to shout Ange, I can hear you just fine, unless you're ready to wake Lullaby Lesley.

"Look at my legs, will you Jules?"

"I have no occasion for such extravagance Ange."

"You may not believe this Jules, but being sexy isn't an extravagance, it's a necessity in my books, like you and all your presence bullshit, and just like these silk PANTS."

"I'm talking about the extravagance of having seals as pets Ange, not silk trousers which are pants, all I'm saying is that no amount of luxury can make us sexy if we don't feel sexy, we might think we're sexy, but better make sure it matches exactly how we feel, one chink in our thoughts, and bam, doubt sets in."

"I feel sexy, there you go. SEXY."

"Great, enjoy it while it lasts, Ange, because they come and go, like trains passing through a station. I personally don't feel the need to be sexy, as long as I get the occasional spring clean now and again, I'm sorted. My biggest thrill these days comes from chocolate, wine, hashish, disco dancing and Sam. I LOVE Sam."

"He's a great young man Jules, real credit to you, you should be one really proud mama, but he's your SON. Only I can feel sexy around him, you can't. I suppose being a single mum, you had to let your standards drop a lot."

"I'd do it all over again, Ange, in a heartbeat. You know I was heading to yoga the other week, and there was a frog at the side of the road, muttering to itself, I swear, there it was quite the thing, nattering away. When it saw me, it looked me directly in the eye and said, "if you pick me up and snog me like you mean it, I'll turn into the most amazing Adonis you have ever cast your beady blue over, we're talking the reflection of your physical and mental dreams, and we can have sex as often and as passionately as YOU like, so, I picked the wee fecker up and stuffed the cheeky croaker into my pocket and carried on my merry yogic way."

"Are you joking with me Jules? You turned down the chance of having the man of your dreams and more, so much more, and you squashed him in your pocket along with your usual crumpled, sticky tissues?"

"I know Ange, but at my age I'd rather have a talking frog."

"Booo haa ha. Why do I wear these ridiculous, hugely expensive pieces of age inappropriate palazzo pants anyway, whether they are all the rage in Milan, New York, The Bush, bum fuck nowhere, The

30

Outback, Australia. It took a gazillion worms to make them, and now they're ruined. I'll have to give them away now, would have been less hassle just to burn $5,000, do you want my hammy downs Jules? This is ridiculous, I need my pills, and a very loong, warm, deep, very bubbly, lavender infused bubble bath."

"Keep rubbing those mortled thighs like that, and The Genie from the damp, will appear Ange, either that or you'll spark a fire."

"Right now all I can think of is that I'm in a slumber party nightmare."

"You forgot to take your makeup off then Ange, aside from the permanent eyeliner, eyebrows and lipstick that is."

"I'll have you know that I'm wearing Rouge Allure Luminous Intense, Chanel's best red lipstick, it's creamy and silky, and it doesn't cake day or night, longing for every favorable cellfie occasion."

"Their lipsticks have no cellfie control either it seems and have bled into all the deep red crevices around the edges of...."

"Really? That's your take away from all this, that my lipstick has smeared like a big ole Toucan ink blot around my puckered rosebud lips, and not the fact that we're in a jail with no clue as to why or how we're here."

"I could do with two cans of beer right now, it must be 5 pm somewhere. Trust the process, that's what I say."

"Trust the processing more like, the quicker we're out of here, the sooner I get my medicine, you get a beer, and a leg shave. What are we gonna do? Tell me, what are we gonna do Jules?"

"I'll tell you what we're going to do, Ange, we're going to start with you taking your back off the wall, sit up nice and straight.... There's a reason we're here, and all we have to do in this moment is relax, and allow the solution to present itself, we need to take a breathe, recentre ourselves, settle down and open up to the tightness in our bodies that hold our truth."

"Right now is not the time to meditate Jules? Medicate, yes, but not meditate. By the way, didn't you have a bang?"

"I wish, oh you mean fringe, that's what you call them in Amerkin, and yes. Why Ange? "I don't want to be the one to state the obvious, but where is it Jules? Don't worry, be hairpy, the dearly departed bangs grow back."

"Where's my fringe Ange? I hate it when that happens, one minute you have a fringe, next minute you don't, kind of like the libido really, bang goes nothing. It's either been nicked, or it's slid down to join the other whiskers, bang on my chins. We have to get a handle on this, okay, now, let's relax..breathe.. and calm down."

"Am I the only one on this planet who gets infuriated when someone tells me to relax and calm down."

"Okay, settle in, allow the natural curve of your spine to be lifted and erect.."

"I could sure do with a bit of erect right about now Jules."

"Stacked easily, and gently, no compression, no crumpling in over your frontline."

"Perhaps it was a certain type of 'line' that got us here in the first place Jules, if they've taken the drug stash that accompanied me from The States, then I'll be really cross, I need them, even the legal ones. You make yourself comfortable down there Buddha, I'll unravel some of this selective amnesia, I wouldn't be in the slightest bit surprised if we were kidnapped, drugged by a sex trafficking gang, and kept as fuck gifts."

"Let's face it Ange, even if that's what we'd like, realistically that wouldn't be the case for a number of reasons:

1. I keep my weight on the higher side to avoid these encounters, makes kidnapping harder
2. Never mind feck gifts, they'd require forklifts to transport me in.
3. If they accidentally mistook us for a commodity, then we're in a return to sender holding pen"
4. I think…."

"Alright already, I hear you loud and clear Jules, you always say it's not what you think, but right now, in this very moment, I think you should put some pants on, it's bad enough looking at my scorched thighs poking through silk cloth, but to see your pair of unrestrained thippos rolling around is too much for anyone at any time in the day, so can we kick this off by finding you something to put on."

"Where are my harems? Why am I only wearing undies?"

"Oh, is that what they are? I thought maybe it was a new line in torture, close your legs for fuck sake Jules, I can see your bush, and quite frankly I'm not surprised you have no partner, there are a couple of chimpanzees going ape between your inner thighs. When was the last time you shaved?"

"The other day, I think Ange, why?"

"I'm not talking about your face ye eejit, I'm talking about your bikini line."

"1. I'd have to be wearing a bikini for that to be beneficial, and that ain't happening anytime soon, and

2. What's wrong with showcasing your personal primates with your Besties

3."

"That's your intention Jules, to showcase your silver backed gorilla to me?"

"A private viewing only for you Ange, and sleeping beauty over there. How special is that? Hmm?"

"And Crocodile Dundee down the hallway, and anyone else who happened to be injured in the events leading up to us being here, almost naked. Find something to put on you, I need to unsee the horror I've just witnessed, the last time I saw a state like that was kangaroo roadkill. Roadkill? Roadkill? Ring any bells?"

"What was I wearing? I was wearing my harem trousers under a moo moo I think."

"That's probably why you're not wearing anything, there are laws against harem pants as they're a danger to man/woman/she/he /it 's visual health."

"Speaking of visual health, the boob tube you're wearing is tiny, has it shrunk or something, is it for a baby?"

"Baaaaaaa, beauty is in the eye of the beholder Jules."

"One of the most liberating things about age Ange is when we realise that we're our very own beauty beholder, setting our very own guidelines, this power enables us to find beauty in the places and people where others have not been brave enough to look, inside ourselves."

"Really? Really Jules? You think this is the best time for a fucking teaching lesson? Make yourself useful and help me pull this waistband down a bit, the world is not quite ready for my 6 pack."

"The only 6 pack I'm interested in comes in the form of tins filled with gin and tonic. It's not budging Ange, can you maybe help out here. If we both pull, like a tug of war."

"My fingers are stuck, there's too much tension."

"Too tense?"

"A wigwam and a teepee tense, put some more effort into this Jules, I'm doing all the work, wait, is that a matching boob tube on the bed?"

"No, that looks like, yes, it is, a leg warmer, that must mean…you're wearing the matching one as a boob tube Ange."

"What! You think that's funny, who the fuck has legs this big? Are these yours? Get me out of it, I'm not wearing a fucking leg warmer as a top. Get it off me Jules."

"It's stuck, looks like you've swollen since putting it on. They must be pumping swell gel through the vents. Explains my cankles, that's why I wear leg warmers to hide the swelling."

"I can hardly breathe, it feels like I'm being swallowed whole by a boa constrictor. Every hair on my body is on high alert."

"Sod's law, or menopause? Some people lose hair all over their body while others, including me, seem to be growing it at an alarming rate, their coarse, white, firm camel resilient follicles, gaping from the pores on my chin, nostrils, ears, going totally rogue, surprisingly, the better behaved hair begins to thin and fall out. On the plus side I can now audition for Santa roles at our local amateur drama society. This ankle bracelet is heavy, I can barely lift my leg off the ground, what muscle group is being worked out? I lift weights, but this is more than my usual 1 pound I can tell you Ange."

"I shouldn't have been too eager to take mine off then, I do like a workout, usually with a fit young nubile personal trainer 'spotting' me"

"If it's a workout you wanted, then something's working, you're sweating."

"WHAT??? I am not fucking sweating Jules. I don't sweat. I cannot physically sweat."

"You may need to provide medical evidence of that in the future if required as it's dripping from the tip of your perfect rhinoplasty nose. Don't worry Ange, it's an age thing, it happens to the best of us."

"This has nothing to do with age Jules, if anything, I must have had a shower before coming in here, and didn't get round to drying myself properly. Besides, I've had most of my sweat glands removed."

"Blimey, your body must hold on to all that waste and toxins then, enough of this nonsense, let's get down to business now, relax and try to piece this mental, fragmented memory puzzle together. What do you remember about last Ange?

"Hmmm, let me think, you and Lezzers picked me up from Sydney airport in your faithful mount Volkswagen kombi van, Dirty Gertie Too. Lezzers let me sit in the front as my legs are longer than her stumpy ones, and we were off."

"Wait, remind me what day you arrived Ange?"

"I don't know Jules, July?"

"Not year, day. THINK Ange."

"I'm too exhaustipated to think."

"Exhaustipated?"

"I really don't give a shit Jules."

"Wait, what if this isn't a criminal fitbit Ange, or a homing pigeon device, how do we know it's not a bomb…omg! I'm wearing a bomb."

"What are the chances that these blue heelers of the bush would strap bombs on the cankles of two, not so elderly citizens? Zero chances, more likely we're being held captive for ransom, I'm worth a considerable amount of dosh you know Jules."

"We're more like Thelma and Louise than Patty Hearst. These distractions aren't helping us Ange, a little less conversation, a little more deep breaths. Sit quietly, and allow your boney arse to be here, fully here, present in this moment, I have a comfy backside, it's a great place for me to sit. Close our eyes if we can, and connect with that inner realm of thought, feeling and energy, gradually allowing all that crap, held in the form of tension and stress, to dissolve and fade back to the external world from which they came. Notice that if you're being distracted by thoughts, or noises from Snuffy Lesley Annie in the corner, or Constable Dribble down the hall playing angry birds, then know that all that crap is pure bollocks, those bitches of judgement, opinion, criticism, doubt can only get under our skin if we permit them entry. If we find our mind being lured into the future or trawled back to the past, don't be too concerned, recognise that it's all horseshit, we're here now, with our inner stillness and those 'hormonal cows' can't get to us. Take a breath and breathe out the all too familiar faecal flow, absorbed from the behaviours of others. When we find ourselves tempted back into thinking and thoughts around our own life's shit show, then bring our attention to what's on our mind, and say feck that, not on my watch, and feel the blood curling cocksuckers float on the murky river of shite as it leaves the body, leaving us completely relaxed and free of thought. Lower the inner gangplank and let all their nonsense spew out and further away from us, on their own flowing, shitty wee path. Breathe in energy, breathe out all that accumulated residue gleaned from the garbage of others, and as we rest on the out breathe, feel that "feck that" feeling, and watch all those tense pricks fall overboard into the deep, dark, heavy waters of life's squalls, from which they came, leaving us at peace in the safety of our own created drama. Appreciate the silence that comes with untethering our perceptions of others. Breathing every day, keeps death at bay. When ready, gently open the eyes."

"As lovely as that was, and I use that word loosely, we're still no closer to solving any of this Jules."

"No need for the wobbly bottom lip Ange…. THE WOBBLY BOTTOM LIP… sound familiar Ange, The wobbly bottom? And breathe, almost there. The bundle in the corner isn't moving much, the mouth is a gaping chasm of stunning porcelain veneers, and there's no mistaking the same Chanel rouge allure that has stained her botox-plumped lips. I'm not aware of Lesley having Botox, she has a natural, beautiful, relatively wrinkle-free complexion. The cheeks vibrate with each incoming snore and outgoing flatulence. The guard called me Lesley, if he thinks I'm her which I'm clearly not, then who's that over there? Can't be Jules, cos that's me. That's not Lesley, Ange. Feck, where's Lesley? Blimey, I don't think that's Lesley over there Ange, and if it's not, then she might be in very real trouble, or, collecting our bail money, either way, we have to get out of here now."

"Wait, a minute, what? That's not Lezzers over there?"

"I don't think so."

"What do you mean? Then where is she, and who the fuck is that? Where the fuck is she Jules? There's no one else in here, she's certainly not hiding under the bed, she's twice the width of it, so would be easily spotted."

"Nope, she's not here Ange, we have this single, deluxe cell all to ourselves. A perfect threesome, one of us being a complete stranger."

"She may even be dead for all we know Jules. No, no, that wouldn't be right, you'll have to tell Mikey, I couldn't be the bearer of that kind of news, now if she had an affair or switched teams, then I probably could, but not this, not brown bread."

"What are you doing Ange? You're telling yourself a story that hasn't even happened and it's already beginning to bother you. We are all only the sum total of the stories we tell ourselves, she's not brown bread or dead, she's not, I won't have it."

"I know what I am doing, Jules. My eyes are wide open, it's a habit I have of getting myself all worked up over something that is very likely never going to hopefully EVER be the case. Lezzers and I may have our differences, but I wouldn't want her dead, she's practically family as far as I'm concerned."

"The blood transfusion?"

"More like extended family Jules."

"Oooooh, got it. You still haven't told her, have you?"

"There hasn't been a right time Jules, and I haven't quite decided anything anyway."

"Yes, you have that's why you're here isn't it, and why you're so tetchy and on edge."

"I need something small and effective enough to take that edge off, and it's not her. Where are my drugs?"

"If we could just find a way to tell ourselves what has happened and how to get out of this mess. Or at the very least, try and remember HOW we got here? Anything? More importantly, we have to find Lesley."

"No, it's all a very well disguised, heavily shrouded cavity, cloaked under a cloud of alcohol and narcotics."

"And Tim Tams.. you have eaten a fair few of those, a mere observation of someone who doesn't eat."

"They're part of my five daily C'S a day I'll have you know Jules: Cocoa, caffeine, coke, chocolate, cocaine, cocktails."

"That's 6."

"Even better."

"This isn't helping Ange, stop distracting me, do you remember anymore than me? Why is she not with us? Why didn't we all stick together as planned ? Why did we separate?"

"First things first, we need a clear head for this, where's my paraphernalia bag?"

"I'd be very surprised if you get that back Ange."

"Watch and learn Jules."

"Ange, before we get out of 'dodge', let's take a moment in silence to see if we can't tap back into the events that brought us to this place. No good jumping to reactivity straight away, won't help us or Lesley."

"How far back are we going to go, Jules? Do we have time to do that? Surely all events and experiences we encounter in life lead us to this moment as you bleat on about incessantly."

"You're going to be like Scarlett O'Hara if you're not careful Ange, we all need to learn how to untie ourselves from what is preventing our growth, the choices we make determine our life. It's not what you think..it's not what you think Ange. We don't learn or grow much by giving any credence to thoughts. Go beyond the stories created DECADES ago about ..whatever.. doesn't really matter, life gives us plenty opportunities to see where we're stuck in the mud, and I've known you long enough to tell that you're stuck."

"Frankly my dear I don't give a damn."

"Exactly, like the lotus flower, we too have the ability to rise from the mud, bloom out of darkness and radiate our sparkle in the world. Our thoughts should be like a parachute for the body, mind and breathe, works best when they're open."

"Lezzers isn't as ….seasonally savvy as we are Jules."

"Precisely, everyone has been here at some stage, and I do mean everyone..sticky, gnarley, challenging situations, believe it or not, Michelle Visage or whoever that is over there in the corner, has experienced life's tempests, but by the look of her clothes, she's been surfing life's waves on a luxury private charter yacht, not a handmade flimsy raft like most of us."

"You digress…again Jules."

"From what?"

"I'm surprised to be the one to say…eh…Lezzers, Nursie, Lesley!"

"Shhhhh Ange, close your eyes, and take a breath, find the natural rhythm, and pace, the one that serves you best in this moment, and ride the back of each in-breath and out-breath."

"Don't get me wrong Jules, I am motivated in some small way to do this with you, but maybe I do need medication first. Do you happen to have an, I'm in a fucking jail cell with amnesia, get me the fuck out of here breath mantra meditation? Maybe try an Ommm, mani, pedi, pedi, mani. Mantra.."

"I'm so forgetful, but only when it comes to birthdays, anniversaries, and why we're in jail. The only thing you seem to forget are your past sexual conquests, excluding Lesley's lovely father in law, Richard that is."

"Bloody hell, here we go again, this bullshit is real, I think I'm losing the plot. Come on Jules, pull yourself together. Focus on the task at hand."

"One step at a time sweet Hezeus. Okay, back in the room. There's only one thing for it. Meditation. Come on Ange, join me."

"Again? You think med fucking tation is what we need right now? Your priorities are skeewiff, medication yes, there is no amount of meditation that's going to help find her. Before I lose my shit Jules, you must have your Maharaji va gina on speed dial, get them to work their magic."

"Shhhhh, close your eyes, and take a breath. I can handle this. Relax and release. I can handle this. Relax and release..I can handle this. Relax and release......OMG Ange, we need to get out of here. Lesley is in real danger, and it might be our fault."

"No shit Sherlock. Wait what? Our fault? Don't just sit there, do something."

"Don't just do something, sit here Ange"

"Are you out of your mind Jules, meditation is not the answer, now or ever."

"We're not meditating, come sit here on the floor, I have a cunning plan to get us out of here and take this show on the road, but we do need to get out of here now Ange before it's too late for the Big surprise. GUARD. GUARD. Ange, get down on the floor now. Lesley needs us, so we have to get out of here. GUARD GUARD. GUARD GUARD we have a medical emergency here, my friend needs her medication. Leave this with me Ange, roll with it. GUARD."

Difficult people are the best teachers - Pema Chodron

The Other Day

Lesley

I am beyond excited, I don't quite know what to do with myself, dishwasher emptied, ironing done, plants watered, lists for Mikey and The Boys ready, freezer, fridge, pantry stocked to the gunnels, Robbie's football kit washed, pressed and on his stair for his game tomorrow. Deano's hockey kit is ready for Thursday's game and on his step. Mikey, Jonno, and Frankie's stairs are full of clean, pressed clothes, all they have to do is bend over, pick them up, and transport them to their rooms. Shouldn't be too difficult I hear you say. You'd think! Still training Deano to actually put them away in the wardrobe or drawers and not to dump them on the floor, undoing all my hard work in the process. The others, well, not Robbie. I still do his. He's my baby, he's not quite ready to do it for himself yet. Mikey does tell me that I mother him too much, but that's what I am, a mother. He's going to be a teenager on his birthday, and then I might not even get the chance to brush his hair. That'll be a sad day, I love brushing their hair, seeing the clean, shiny glisten and glow under the gentle bristle strokes. Where was I? Yes, clothes, stairs, tick. More often than not though, yours truly, muggins here, ends up doing it herself and putting them away, I'd call in sick, but I'm a stay-at-home mum, so no excuses there, hung up my nursing angel wings when the boys came along, and I double dare anyone to ask me what I do all day, they'll have their words to play with, that's what. Half the time I feel like I'm running an insane asylum, the other half I feel like I belong in one.

If packing were an Olympic sport, not only would I qualify, I'd win gold. With my endurance, strength, determination, and Marks & Spencer knickers, I'm definitely a main contender. If they gave out badges, then I'd be more top-heavy than I already am, breastfeeding 4 big, strong, healthy boys has taken its toll on my mammaries and memories. I crack myself up. Angy has always said that if packing were a drinking game, then she'd win for sure, but I think that's because she fills every nook and cranny, and not just her case, with legal and very likely, illegal drug and alcohol paraphernalia. Not that I'm judging her you understand, but you'd think she'd know better at our age, maybe I'm wrong and should err on the side of caution, perhaps she's changed, although tigers don't change their spots and all that. If packing were a drinking game though, I'd be bladdered by now, 22 articles of clothing are not too much for a couple of nights away with one's Bezzies, you can never be too sure what each situation requires, and as I'm usually sporting athletic wear, without the sport or the athletics, I still like to be comfortable, besides I can't be seen wearing the same thing twice as Angy needs no additional fodder to make me the butt of her jokes. What do they say? One's mean, two is meaner, and three is the meanest, and I'm always on the receiving end of the meanest. She considers it to be playful banter, but she's not the victim, bullies rarely are, but now, I'm older, wiser, and ready for her.

I am so looking forward to this, a few days away from the usual, mundane daily grind, keen to be an adult again. I feel a bit anxious to see Angy though, I won't lie, she can be very intimidating, and her confidence can be really scary, her bite is definitely worse than her bark, however, there's a soft side to her, albeit buried deep, deep beneath the layers of her personal identification. She does prefer to have a tight rein on her emotions, not giving so much as an inch, to loosen her grip on them, which could ultimately work in her favour, and give her free rein to vulnerability. It's not easy to forget how she made me feel all those years ago when I was unsure of myself and full of doubt. I still can be, but I'm much more prepared than I was to manage her when she tries to entice those feelings back to the surface. Bring it on I say, am I really ready though? Och well, if I'm not, I'm sure she'll give me ample opportunities to show me when I get ticked off, only time will tell, I'm a grown, married woman of 4 boys. I've handled a whole lot scarier than her, like confessing to Jonno's headmistress, Ms. Erable, that he was the ringleader and mastermind behind the viral game, "Blow Me", the condom game where a very willing participant slips a condom over one's head, covering eyes and nose, leaving mouth to breathe, a completely safe game as far as I can tell, and I should know, I'm the retired nurse. The willing member,s'cuse the pun, blows said johnny, not to be mistaken with my boy, Jonno you understand, using nostril breath alone until the prophylactic is at its full lofty, airy carbon-monoxide-filled capacity, not dissimilar to one of those giant vertical windsocks you see outside second hand car dealers showrooms, before bursting their unnatural rubber sheath, and vegan contents, spraying caution to the winds. The only obvious mark left is the latex halo ring around said members' foreheads. Not sure where he learned the game, but I do recall Jools and Angy playing it all the time when we were younger, and it did them no harm, not that you can tell anyway. Besides, if they had a halo it would have slipped already and choked them. Angy does have a way of drawing attention to the insecurities of others, she's actually the perfect teacher for me when you think about it. I tell my boys that all the time; if someone provokes a reaction, ask them if it was meant as a putdown. Usually, and thankfully, if nothing else, it makes the one volleying the shots think about what they've said or done. Ask yourself 3 questions before reacting A) Is it true? B) If yes, is there anything you can do to fix it? And C) Can you continue to live your life despite 'its' presence? I'm a wife and mother with loads of accomplishments under my belt, so I am totally able to handle her, I hope. I'm actually really excited to see her, she's fun, and although she takes no prisoners, I guess it's all a front to protect her from something she's kept under lock and key, carefully tucked away for years. That's often the case with antagonists, easier to snuff someone else's light out, so theirs glows brighter. The older you get, the more candles, the brighter the glow. Does that all sound mean, I'll give her the benefit of the doubt when I see her. I see Jools on heydays and holidays only, but she's busy, and with Mikey and The Boys, I don't have time for much else either. This is going to be brilliant, I can't wait. Imagine after all these years, the three of us are having a reunion to celebrate our 50th...almost as soon as Jools gets here, that is, I know she's not late, but she knew I'd be up to high dough, so today of all days, you'd think she'd be early.

A few nights only, The Three Amigas are back together, Thelma Louise..and..? Who was the third person again? No mind, I feel more complete, when we're all in the same room, like the perfect party, true friends are never really apart though are they? Maybe in distance, but never from the heart centre. Angy is too busy living her best life in New York to be keeping up with an uninteresting wee Scottish-born, suburban, vanilla housewife like me I'm sure. I bet she schmoozes within the social circles of the rich, most prominent, well-known, celebrity figures of New York's finest, which must be fun, I won't lie. I wonder who the most famous person she's met is. Mikey tells me all the time that if my spending is anything to go by, anyone would think we were meant to be born rich. I can't even remember what it is she does, which is shocking really, but you can blame it on the pregnant, baby, children, teenager, and now peri menopausal/menopausal brain. Something to do with gardening I believe, must make good money though as she travels on a private plane. I hope it's nothing illegal. A few bits and pieces in your packing is nothing compared to a full plane full of weed for sale. Shirley not. No, she wouldn't, Jools would have told me if she was one of those drug donkeys.

A couple of years ago when we were all invited to my father-in-law, Richard's 70th on Hamilton Island. He has a beautiful house there, and for whatever reason, she was there. I thought my wedding was a one-night stand, but clearly not. Bit of a bone of contention there, I still can't believe she slept with Mikey's DAD of all people at our wedding, I know it was decades ago, but she shouldn't have, it was one of the only days in my life that should have been all about me, and not your bridesmaid shagging your father in law in the rowing boat down on the lake. The very same boat that was for mine and Mikey's departing honeymoon wave, but no, it turns out that on my special day, it was all about her. The wedding party, even to this day, still talks about what they witnessed, thankfully Mikey and I didn't see any of it as we were changing into our going away gear. Even Mikey's great, great auntie Mabel had to watch them trying to stand up fully naked in the boat and explain themselves to the gathering group, falling into the water for further drama, in the process. For decades now, it's all anyone ever talks about, stories and visuals of them together, naked, entwined, giggling and wet, playing on a constant loop in my mind movie theatre cinema. When I think of it, that's the only place either of them will ever find lasting commitment, in my mind, and my mind only, in my humble opinion that is. It does tickle me when I'm feeling particularly naughty to think how it would be if she were my wicked stepmother-in-law, now that would be funny, she'd be totally distorted over that one. Me calling her Mumsy, or some combination of step-mum-in-law, maybe Slumsy, now that would be the perfect revenge. Although my mother used to tell me that revenge is like returning to the horse that kicked you. I don't think she's in a drug carousel though, maybe it's something to do with sales, possibly at a garden centre? She might own it for all I know. I've tried to ask Jools, but she never seems sure herself, so I let it go years ago. I'll ask her myself when I see her shortly. Hurry up Jools, I'm going to get piles sitting on this cold wall waiting patiently outside my own wee house, have I got time for a quick pee? Plenty of time, she's not due for another 30 minutes, but I'm ready. I wonder if Angy's flying here on her private plane, now that would be fun, I'm sure she'd let me sit in the cock seat if I ask nicely. I'm not sure I'd like to fly in it though, imagine all the carbon monoxide footprints filling the air and your lungs, if we were all doing it, what a mess we'd be in, not that commercial airlines are much better, guilt is only diluted by the masses.

I think I'll stick to this land down under, don't feel the need to fly anywhere else, it's all right here, right now, all's well, happy and healthy in the LaLa land of Lesley.

She should be here any minute now, where is she, what's taking her so long? Have I got time to double-check all my honey-do lists again? Yes, yes I do, boys list of chores - check, Mikey's chore list - check. Dogs - sorted. Oooo, I can't wait a couple of days without having to think about anyone or anything other than little ole me. My needs are usually so far down the list, it's not even funny, this break is my break, and no one can tell me otherwise. I'm leaving everything, and I do mean everything at home, my iPad, laptop, phone, retainer, lubricant, vibrator, totally uncontactable, me that is, not my rampant rabbit. Unless anyone needs me that is, then they can call Jools, they've all got her no. if they need it, and I can always call them from her phone, which I know I will, keep it on my terms though, not a free for all or they'd be calling me every 5 minutes. Jools has already told me she's screening my calls, she says they are all more than capable of finding the matching sock, the iron, the jam, the sink, and the dishwasher as well as the next man, without me. She's right as usual, but it's MY job, it's my role, being their mum, a wife. It's who I am. Plain and simple. I'm not plain and simple, my life is. Basic. Vanilla, no hidden extras, they still need me as much as I need them. It works for us, and I love my life here in Australia with Mikey and my boys, it can be hallyracket and chaotic, but I wouldn't have it any other way, maybe dial the hormonal landslides down a notch or 10, that would certainly help the mental and physical well-being of everyone concerned. I don't want or need to be anywhere else other than right here, right now, I don't need to be defined as a nurse, I'll take mother, wife, and/or friend first. I bet Angy doesn't call me Nursie anymore, I bet she still calls me her other favourite, "Lezzers". It used to wind me up because I knew she was trying to get a rise out of me, but now I can taste my words before I spit them out, most of the time that is, but those menopausal monsters can be very persuasive, the non-menopausal me wouldn't behave like that, so if there's a problem, take it up with her, that's what I say. Where is Jools? She knows how anxious and impatient I get waiting. Punctuality is next to godliness and all that, I bet she'll blame her clapped-out rust bucket of a VW Kombi van, "Dirty Gertie 2". I'd understand if it was the original van, as in Dirty Gertie, the one that Jools and Angy bought all those years ago when we first came to Australia for our gap year. They actually drove it all over Australia to find me. Can you believe that?

ME! Changed everything. I had left them in Sydney and their childish, dangerous ways, and they came looking for little old me. I'll never forget seeing their dusty wee facies appear before me in the middle of The Bush. I have no idea, even to this day, how they actually found me in the remotest part of The Northern Territory, I must remember to ask them sometime. More importantly Angy saved my life, not once, but twice. I wouldn't have any of this if she hadn't. I often enjoy my Gratitude spot, a reminder to be thankful for everything and everyone I have in my life. It's not that hard to find, but most people struggle to nurture, let alone find their G spot. Almost 30 years on, Mikey and I are married, 4 big, strapping loons, Jools, is well Jools, single mum of the handsome Sam, an independent, travelling 26 yr old. Lovely and kind, just like Jools. She is always positive, upbeat, fun, authentic, and transparent, aside when she's not that is, but what you see is what you get, a rare breed indeed these days. I bet she still partakes in alternative recreational habits, maybe that's why she's always so chill, unlike Angy, who takes more than her fair share of narcotics and is so wired…that's not a judgement you understand, a mere opinion from my point of view that's all, not my place to criticise the choices of others, or tell them how they should behave, but surely you grow out of certain behaviours, like drugs, excessive drinking and sleeping around. I mean at our age it gets a bit old. Come on Jools, where the hell are you? It's not funny any longer, she can be so irresponsible at times, it's how they behaved throughout their teens, 20's, 30's, and 40's, Shirley they've grown up now we're all about to turn 50.

I promised Mikey I wouldn't say anything as it's none of my business, but Angy has never actually apologised to me for sleeping with Richard, on top of that, on my actual wedding day. When Mikey and I had our first dance to the Bay City Rollers, she was apparently dancing her very own Shag-a-lang in the men's toilets, before heading to the boat house for the grand finale. It's not like there weren't plenty of other available single men there, but she chose Mikey's DAD of all people. Technically he's single, but just because he's a widow, doesn't give her an excuse to sleep with him. Anyhoo, it's fine, water under the bridge and all that, I probably won't mention it, what she does is up to her. Mikey did let slip recently that she still visits him when she's in town. He lives on Hamilton Island! On the Whitsundays, you can't just pop in for a cup of tea when you're "in town". The nearest International airport is in Brisbane, which is, like 1000 km away, so it's not like she just pops in. I bet she pollutes our Aussie air with her private plane fumes. Now, Lesley, that was so uncalled for, Mikey says she uses it mainly for "work" clients. Is she a client? Golly gosh, the penny has dropped, it all makes sense now, all the secrecy, the giggles behind closed doors, and as usual I'm the last to not only suspect but to actually know this stuff. She's maybe a high-class escort. I still feel mortified that it was consummated on the same night as our wedding, and it was only brought to my attention later when a member of the wedding party confessed to finding them in the rowing boat they were about to decorate for mine and Mikey's moonlight bon voyage sail. If I'd known she'd been shagging in it, I'm not sure I'd have been quite so jolly waving to everyone as Mikey rowed me away. I should have known it was happening right beneath my nose. Anyhoo, enough of that, I'm not wasting any more energy on that. I've tried asking Jools, but she's not interested in the entertainment of others, or so she says, but where's the fun in that I ask myself. I bet she still watches Neighbours like I religiously do though, and it's full of drama.

Come on Jools, come ooon, we only have an hour to get across town, and although it's not too busy this early in the morning, you just never know what precautions you need to take. Angy should land in 30 mins according to her schedule, so we still have plenty of time. If she can be that accurate to her arrival, then it must be a private plane. Flying in on the toxic, expensive wings of her own flying 'broom'. Oh, that wasn't necessary Lesley, you know better. Mum used to always say, "Think of something nice to say, but don't say it". That doesn't sound right. "Don't just think of something that's not nice, say it." No..What is it again? I'll ask Jools. I am not the mean girl here.

WHERE IS SHE?

Not surprised she's almost late, not that she technically is yet, but if she was, then it wouldn't come as a huge surprise, she's never in a rush, and gets wherever in her own slow, and steady mode. I wish I could be on Angy's plane right now and whisked off to our reunion batch in the sun with a wee penis colada in one hand and a good book in the other. Mmmmmmm. If only the Dr Who's turdis was the real thing.

Now it's irritating me, where is she? By the time I've gone inside to get my phone to call her, she'll be here. Relax Lesley, they'll be fine without you. Relax Lesley. They'll survive, it's only for a few sleeps after all, that's nothing in the big scheme of things, NOTHING. I haven't had 3 minutes to myself in the last few decades, let alone a day or two to myself, away time with my Bezzies. Where's Mikey? He said he was coming out to say goodbye. Maybe he's waiting till Jools arrives, not wanting to wait on the pavement with me, scared what the nosey neighbours will think and all that.

Many people die at twenty five, but aren't buried until they are seventy five - Benjamin Franklin

If you are irritated by every rub, how will your mirror be polished - Rumi

Life is better with friends

Jules

"TOOT TOOT. TOOT TOOT. LESLEY Here's me!! WOOOHOOOOO Lesley….. WOOOOOOOOO"

"SSHHHH, will you Jools. You'll wake the neighbours."

"Could be worse Lesley, I could be using the horn, besides who's looking at me anyway, and if they are, they're probably thinking how lovely that Lesley has a friend coming to pick her up. Come on you old bag, we don't have all day, gie's a bosie quine, long time no squeeze, glad yer head still fits ever so snuggly into my ample booze-swam."

"Och, behave ye wee scallywag, you'll mess my hair."

"Mess your hair? We both know that's not possible Lesley, every follicle has its rightful pride and place on your perfectly manicured head, each one knows first hand not to get blown out of line, or it'll be groomed within an inch of its root by your barbaric boar bristle brush. Blimey, that's a mouthful right there."

"Wheesht, come on let's get going before I lose my will to party like a rockstar. I've been packed and ready and up and at 'em since 3 am."

"Relax Suzi Quatro, I need to say hello to My key before we go."

"Must you Jools, he'll only hold us up."

"Hi My key. We were just talking about you."

"All bad I hope Jools phnar, phnar."

"Aye, you wish Big Boy. You look well My key."

"Hey Ducks, be a dear and stick my weekend bag somewhere in the back of Dirty Gertie Two will you. Is there any room in this van of yours, Jools, it's full of black plastic bin bags with god only knows what in them, what are they for? I hope it's not rubbish."

"No, taking the clean fancy dress attire from the amateur dram society I belong to back from the laundrette. Pile them in the back My key, plenty of room back there for another black plastic bag or two, that you may or may not have if you get my drift."

"10/4 good buddy, read you loud and clear Jools, Mikey over and out."

"What are you pair wittering on about, come on Ducks, hurry up, put my bag under that seat, we need to get going. Angy will be landing soon, and we have to be there in time to greet her."

"I am more than happy to stick your weekend bag filled with a few nights glorious, peaceful sleeps worth of clothes, accessories and the kitchen sink, anywhere you like Ducks, that's the kind of husband I am."

"Thanks My key, it might be easier strapping it on the roof rack though, leaving more space inside for us. I swear these VW kombi vans get smaller and smaller, or maybe I'm getting bigger and bigger? Answers on a postcard only. If in the unlikely event that one of us misbehaves, then it'll be the roof rack spacious penthouse for them, and I don't mean you My key, that open air suite is only reserved for myself and/or Lesley, but more likely Ange."

"Refreshing yet somewhat intimidating to hear she hasn't changed much Jools."

"Relax Ducks, she'll be fine I'm sure, now back to me, I'm a modest packer as you both well know, like a well oiled packing machine, so put my relatively small bag under the passenger seat, leave the roof rack to Angy's full corsage. "

"I believe it's cortege Ducks, but who am I to correct you, only your husband, however they are two very different things, one is a train of attendants, which I believe is the one you mean, the other is a bouquet of flowers worn as a corsage at a funeral. Unless you're going to a funeral, then it's a cortege, I'm kidding, no need to look so horrified, we know she's going to have a camel train of luggage that will scare the living daylights out of the average human being. My suggestion, Ducks, is that you put your bag wherever you like and stick to your guns no matter what she tries to tell you. You know what she's like."

"I thought we were only going for a couple of nights, hence my weekend bag. How long is she coming for Jools?"

"Who knows with her Lesley, but guaranteed she's prepared for every possible, conceivable, inevitable outcome."

"That's a different ball gown all together Jools, now I'm wondering if there's something else I should have packed, maybe a cocktail dress, do you think she'll have a cocktail dress, you know me, I like all my ducks in a row, I like to have my i's stroked and my t's dotted. The bottom line here Jools, is that the 3 muskrats are going to be back together for the first time in years, so I need to be prepared for every occasion."

"Lesley, the only cocktail I want is the one that comes shaken, stirred, laced with gin, poured over ice and tells me I can dance, now stop fretting and let My key give you a leggy up to the passenger seat. Dirty Gertie Too awaits, do you need a step ladder?"

"Very funny Jools, I feel like a social hand grenade. The butterflies in my tummy feel more like gunpowder, there's enough heat and gas in my rapidly expanding body, and given the right environment is going to produce an explosive force. I can be a real pocket rocket when I want to be, can't I Ducks?"

"Try keeping the pin in for a tad longer will you Lesley? Maybe the climax? You don't want to suffer from premature explosions."

"No premature expolsions here Jools, no matter what Lesley says, phnar, phnar."

"Good to know My key, and incase you were wondering, the bungee rope on the roof doubles as restraints if you were in the slightest bit concerned for the well being of your precious pocket missile."

"I've not packed too many precious items, just a few dresses, shoes, bags etc."

"As long as my precious cargo of booze is protected Lesley, then we're all good in the garden of Edam."

"That's a given Jools, now hurry up Ducks, let's say goodbye, we need to be off, we can't be late to get Angy, and there's a few Honey Do chores you might want to take a look at."

"Believe me Ducks, I'm going as fast as I can, not that I'm desperate to get you out of here so I can rush and get all my Honey do sports catch ups. Love you, have fun, not too much, don't do anything I'd do, and you'll be just fine. Phnar, phnar."

"Bye, Ducks, make sure to wash your hands before doing the weeding, you never quite know what you touched back there. No offence Jools."

"None taken Lesley."

"Love you Ducks. Kiss the boys from me. Bye. love you."

"Au revoir My key, relax I got this, have fun with the boys, see you soon, nudge, nudge, wink wink."

"Nudge, nudge, wink, wink? Are you flirting with my man Jools?"

"Eh..no Lesley, breaking news, shock, alert, I'm not, now say your goodbyes you pair of Lovebirds, so we can be off from misery to happiness todaaaa aay."

"Right, that's enough Ducks, be off with you, you're holding us up. Jonno has an Aussie rule game after school, so remember to pick him up after Robbie's cubs, you'll have time to watch some of his games, he'd love to watch his big brother as .."

"Get your perfect Barbara Windsor/Dolly Parton, Minnie Mouse on speed bod, fully in here will ya Lesley."

"Pardon Jools? Who peed? Do you need to use the loo?"

"I went before I picked you up, depends how much I drink, I can be dry for minutes, do you need to go Lesley?"

"No shame in wearing Depends Jools, it comes to us all at some stage, I'm thankful my kegel exercises worked a charm, ain't that right Ducks, nudge, nudge, wink wink, besides I've been going every 5 minutes for the last 4 hours, so I think I'm running on empty, but that means nothing these days, I can still involuntary leak. 50 is just around the next bend, can't wait to see what it has in store for us, okay, bye, love you Ducks."

"Enjoy. Love you too Ducks, bye Jools, drive carefully, precious cargo and all that, and that's just the wine. Phnarr, phnar."

"Bye. Bye. Go on, off you pop. Drive Jools, just go. Boy, I never thought we'd get rid of him, I was contemplating decapitating his head with the window just to be rid of him, he'd have been quite happy to lean in and babble for hours, he's like an old wifie. Once he starts, he never stops, anyhoo, we're off now, how are you Jools? I like that you've embraced your age, you suit silver, the pewter curtain fringe sets off your blue eyes, you look like I'd expect, how's Sam?"

"Thank you, I think, and no longer a kid Lesley, in fact even as a 26 year old, he's more mature than I ever was, or am even. Living his best life, finished uni, trotting the globe with his trusty, faithful backpack."

"Like we did all those years ago, innocent, happy, curious and not at all jaded by life's lessons. Apples don't fall too far from the tree Jools."

"If he does absolutely nothing that we said, did, or do then he'll be alright Lesley."

"Speak for yourself, I was too busy nursing and pining for Mikey to be caught up in all that mischief. The naughtiest thing I ever did was put laxatives in Angy's wine."

"She doesn't need them these days Lesley, give her the wine and she'll talk shite for hours."

"I only did that as revenge for something I can't remember now. There must have been numerous occasions for vengeance though as I do recall finishing the bumper pack of 124 tablets. That's probably why she didn't smile much either, come to think of it, I must have overdosed on her."

"On the plus side Lesley, it gave her that get up and go feeling."

"Ha, can you believe we landed in this fair land almost 30 years ago, crazy to think of it not in minutes, moments, or months, but decades."

"Ange doesn't admit to being 30, let alone 50. I keep meaning to ask, but keep forgetting to, and I'm sure you've told me before, but why do you and My key call each other Ducks, it always quacks me up."

"I'm sure you know the story Jools, we've called each other that for a very, very long time. Not long after we got married it started, actually, he saved my life, you know, my shite in Nining armour. Remember? No? Can't believe I've never told you this story."

"Now I remember, you have told me Lesley, many, many times, my bad, I had a temporary blip that's all, put it down to the menopause. I can't be arsed with it all."

"I hear ya. You know what it's like these days, you forget what you were saying and doing most of the time, I do, I find myself halfway on my own staircase not knowing whether I was going up or coming down, anyhoo, where was I? Oh yes, Mikey and I were having an argument to the point of breakup, when he shouted "DUCK", so I did, and this golf ball, came out of nowhere, missed my head by millimetres, I swear, millimetres Jools, so Ducks became a thing of synchronicity with us. Funny thing though, we weren't anywhere near a golf course."

"Normally that would be a good thing that they missed, maybe it wasn't a golf ball, and they were reloading, or maybe there was a seagull overhead offloading and expelling the regurgerated contents of an entire fish and chip supper with a pickled onion and/or egg from it's annal jet engine. Although that would give your pet names for each other a very different ring to it." "I don't know Jools, I quite like the name 'Birdie'."

"Could be worse, the word Shite springs to my mind, that would make for a whole different story. Speaking of names, what do you prefer to be called these days? Nursie, Lesley, Lezzers?"

"I loved that you called me Nursie, everyone knew what I did, but these days, I prefer Lesley, plain and simple."

"Nothing plain and simple about you my dear."

"Ha ha right, I wonder what name Angy will use for me?"

"Brace yourself, she hasn't changed that much Lesley."

"Oh, you are awful Jools, but I like you. Shirley at our age, she will see all the childishness in name calling and will have moved on. Orrrrrrr, at least, if she hasn't, I have, it won't bother me, she can call me Lezzer's till the cow's come home, I shall remain an unshakeable ball of jelly."

"That's my girl, I was thinking you were mistaking her for someone else for a minty. She also won't admit to her own real age, even to herself let alone anyone else, so don't think about bringing up anything to do with being "OLD" on this trip, it could cause a riot... riotous laughter that is."

"Mutton dressed as mutton as my mum used to say God bless her soul."

"Be it on your own head if she hears you say that Lesley, aye Ange that is, not your poor dead mum, gawd rest her soul."

"I know, I know, I'm not the mean girl, I'm just so excited for this trip, I don't know what I'm saying half the time. I haven't been on a girls trip for what seems like forever."

"Four boys, a very handsome husband, 2 dogs, a grinny pig and a pear tree, would take up a lot of my time also."

"Hah, no granny pig, but a pair of trees, I was talked into that one. Do you still like Mars bars Jools, I have one for you somewhere in my bag."

"There's nothing better than a friend, unless it's a friend with chocolate."

"It's all good, I'm good, you're good, and I hope that Angy's good. It is what it is, Jools. It's fine, just fine."

"You can say that all you want Lesley, but unless it is felt in the trillions of cells in your body, then it is only ever going to be mental lip service, you have to feel the openness and space that comes with the freedom behind "it is what is is", and "it's fine". What are you still gripping on to, what are you willing to let go."

"I guess it's apprehension Jools, knowing that she's going to judge me and put me down."

"I'm sure it's not what you think, wait, actually it is, it's exactly what you think that it is Lesley, not the way reality actually is, only how you think it is, she is perhaps only a reflection of what you think of yourself."

"I think 50 is like underwear, it creeps up on you. Can you believe we've been in Australia for 30 years Jools, I'm sure I don't know how that happened. Memories can really take that out of you."

"All I know is that my back goes out more than I do these days."

A good friend is like a four - leaf clover; hard to find and lucky to have - Irish proverb

Time Flies When You're Having Fun

Jules

Cheesy peeps 50 eh? When did that happen? How did that happen? Without much resistance, Lesley's monotonous melody slips easily and gently to a different frequency, her voice, a pillion passenger to my awareness, the backdrop to my thinking for a change. It can be exhausting to actively listen to someone, whether they're wittering or not, interrupted only by our own mental take on things. Buys me some additional space to take that in, 30 years. 30 full, complete, thorough, lived years. That's almost a full three decades since we left Scotland behind, bright-eyed, innocent, obliviously hopeful, bushy-tailed, and wide-legged. Totally unaware of life's future adventures quivering in the wings of our awareness, ready to take a rightful place front and centre on our life's live stage performance, where only our bravest hero/heroine should exist. Honestly, I have no idea whether I can say hero or heroine without offending someone who prefers a different label and/or name for themselves, other than the ones given by some unintentional, external spokesperson. Still, a label is a label, no matter what you latch on to, a label's a label. Labels should be for products and wine bottles, simple as that, no need to pin them on to ourselves. Wouldn't life be so much easier if those who got offended by something we did or didn't say, did or didn't do, worked on that, just that, their shite, not ours? We've all got enough crap in our own lives without having to be worried about someone else messing with all that shit. Get back, and clean out your own stable first before meddling in others. We have the privilege to decide whether to join in the games being played, or not. Surely that's the ultimate bondage, letting someone else determine how we feel. There's power in keeping those prerogatives all to oneself. Choosing to watch the drama and antics of the playground as it unfolds from the safety and impartiality of the school gates. That's the most underestimated power move anyone can ever make, learning how to recognise when they've been caught hook, line, and sinker, dragged onto and into someone else's life's stage. Catch and release, they do not serve us. End of rant, but an Oscar-worthy red carpet performance, I might add.

Lesley was a real goodie two shoes, she only had eyes for My key, never strayed, never even eye fecked anyone else, well not as far as I'm aware. Who really knows all the facets of an individual, the different, unique pieces that make up our distinctive personal identity? Labels, imprinting, branding, and attachment to a mental pre-programmed conditioned precious database. Special and quaint only to us, hiding our truth behind the various masks and roles we wear, emotionally attached to some of life's past bittersweet human consumptions. Leaves a bad taste in the mouth, my advice? Listerine. We are after all only ever the sum total of our past experiences, and we meet every moment carrying the unnecessary, excess belongings of our beliefs and discernments into our outside world. By the time we notice how much imperceptible luggage we've not only accumulated but lugged around on a daily basis, we're old and have to dismantle and unravel all that shit, if we even remember it that is. Learn how to become a stripper, removing the additional layers and heaviness of self-doubt, fear, judgement, and opinions to expose creativity, and expansion, releasing the easy-going, happy self beneath the weight of the menopause monsters. I've stripped as much as I care to strip these days, reminding myself that I'm old, and flabby, ignoring any whispers that tell me I can't do something, even dance. Years ago when I was young and good enough, I didn't believe I could dance, too self aware to really relax and go with the flow. These days I rely on exactly those disco moves to keep me balanced. Effortless. I didn't appreciate any of it, any of it. Tch tch. Wasted on the youth. One of my favourite things to do is dance to the music being played in a restaurant as I'm being shown to my table, or going to the loo. I particularly enjoy eating in Indian, or Spanish places, nothing funnier than belly dancing to the loos, or flamencoing to the bar. The Paddy Ba is another good one. Totally get it these days, I didn't used to, but yeah, immaturity is wasted on whippersnappers. Speaking of wasted, that's how the three of us really began, two of us for sure. Backpacking. Mmm, backpacking won my heart.

"What the hell was that Jools?"

Her voice penetrates my reverie and scatters my story in all directions.

"Eh? What noise Lesley?"

"If I turn the music down, I might be able to see better."

"I prefer it turned up, so I can hear less."

"But, it was practically at full blast."

"So I can hear less Lesley."

"Listen Jools, it's stopped now, it was a low, steady, somewhat muffled growl, like a slow steady, train rumble."

"Maybe that's exactly what it was then Lesley."

"No, it came from inside, I'm sure of it."

"It came from inside you?" "No, silly billy, outside of me, but inside here, the van, Dirty Gertie Two, if that makes any sense. I'd swear on a pin drop it sounded like a train, I remember one time when me, Mikey and the boys, not sure if Robbie was there, he was though, we only didn't know it at the time, we had to wait for 9 months to meet him in person, as that night, he showed up as a twinkle in Mikey's eyes, a spring in his step, and a lopsided grin on his fizzog if you get my drift."

"I'd rather be slathered in honey and hung from a beehive than hold that image any longer Lesley"

"The boys were bathed and bedded sharp, we may even have forgotten to read their bedtime stories, plumping for the Singing Kettle's recording of The Train to Glasgow, instead. All we wanted to do was tear each other's clothes off. Och, those were the days Jools, daring and risky, these days I wish he'd wear more clothes, not less. That goes for me too by the way, he hasn't got exclusive ownership in that cover up department. There should be laws against the majority of men being topless though, especially when they're running, wouldn't you agree."

"Back on track Lesley, what has all this got to do with trains?" "Ah yes, trains, Mikey and I played Midnight Train to Georgia, not only to drown out the voice of Cilla singing to Mr McIver, but mainly to mask out any sounds, nudge, nudge, wink, wink from us. I'd like to say we played it on a loop all night, but once was enough if you're drinking in what I'm pouring. However, their music and Cilla played over and over all night long. Both of us spent and too exhausted to go turn it off."

"I wish I were drinking Lesley, might dislodge the visual of you and Glad eyes without his pips, shagging to the pace of a speeding train heading to Glasgow."

"What a night, The Singing Kettle - The Train To Glasgow booming from their rooms, on a continuous loop, we lay in the hall for hours, basking in the afterglow of Mr McIvor tooting his horn. Funny how I can forget what I had for breakfast, but I can still remember the words of that song. "And here is the driver Mr McIvor who drove the train to Glasgow, and here is the guard from Donibristle, who waved his flag and blew his whistle to tell the driver Mr McIvor to start the train to Glasgow. And here is the boy called Donal McBrain who came to the station to catch the train, and saw the guard from Donibristle, wave his flag and blow his whistle to tell the driver Mr McIvor to start the train to Glasgow." It doesn't take much to forget these days…My Mikey was just saying …."

Where was I? Back to me, oh yes, backpacking. Amazing what comes back, and staggering what leaves forever. It can be tiring trying to actively listen to someone, besides, I'm enjoying the daydreaming of my backpacking days, memories can be lovely places to revisit, just not all the time. I prefer the word backpacking over travelling because the mere notion of backpacking carries the essence of a somewhat nomadic lifestyle that differs entirely from that of tourism. For me, to backpack is to live on a certain budget, with only a couple of much-needed items. Only Ange really had the luxury of financial support in those days. She calls it her parental payoff. Lesley and I worked really hard to get here. Her more so than me. She's a real grafter, never asked anyone for anything, got where she is today on her own merits, found her North Star, and stuck to it. You do get used to moving from one place to another, not being stuck in the same place, at times with little to no planning or choice, sometimes that can be the fun, exciting part of the adventure when you allow it to be, otherwise it can be difficult and dangerous. You can take the girls out of Scotland, but not Scotland out of the girls and all that. Well, me and Ange, for sure. Lesley was and still is far more restrained than either of us two ever were or are. I don't necessarily think she's holier than thou, butter wouldn't melt in her mouth, kinda thing that either she or Ange thinks she is though..

One of the most beautiful things about backpacking is the fact that you get to choose the paths instead of the answers and shortcuts travelled by most people. To this day, not everyone understands the passion people have for living this nomadic, backpacking lifestyle. Lesley doesn't really understand why I bought Sam a backpack and an open-ended return ticket to Europe as a graduation present. He's found a place in the circle of life that suits him, for now that is, just happens to be 10,000 miles from here and me. He's happy. That alone makes me happy. We're only as unhappy as our unhappiest thoughts, as heavy as our heaviest emotions, and attachments to personal preferences, that we write for our reality screenplay. I would not be half the person I am, had it not been for all those meringues, I mean experiences, which have shaped and formed me. We're a combination of past circumstances, conditioning, and programming, now all we have to do is cast the weight of any limiting beliefs that we carry for ourselves and others, exposing the spacious, peaceful, harmonious essence hiding behind the veil of our 3-D stage curtains.

"Jools, there it goes again. Did you hear it that time?"

"Dirty Gertie Too has seen better days and occasionally grumbles her discontent from the bowels of her undercarriage. It's getting mighty stuffy in here, crank the window open a bit will you Lesley."

I think she must have farted, too embarrassed probably to admit to it, easier to help her out, and disguise it as a car problem. I totally get it, she doesn't have to be ashamed of any natural, involuntary whiffs of putrid emissions. I do it regularly, but usually cover it with a cough. No one ever notices, and if they do, I say nothing and let everyone blame everyone else. Especially at our age. Anything and everything can set off a bolt of bum air. I didn't even hear it, but I can certainly smell something, not wholly unpleasant though, like a big bowl of chicken fried rice..mmmm. Our own farts smell better than anyone else's don't you think? Eproctophilia is the term for when someone is sexually aroused by their own or someone else's flatulence. She can have this one. Ange for sure won't let her away with it though, it's all black or white with her, no middle ground, she sways from one pole to the opposite, never resting in the centre. She's always been that way, swinging from one extreme to the other. She was like that when we were backpacking, it was full on, mad, bad, and highly dangerous, but boy what a ride it was. Despite all its ups and downs though, it was an extremely joyful, rewarding time in my life. You get to meet plenty of other travellers, locals, and friends who begin as strangers, and end out as lovers and /or friends forever. Exploring new places, enjoying the freedom and acceptance that it brings, and the physical release it also carries when you are willing to let go of whatever is holding you back from being your absolute best self. An invisible backpack of sorts, roaming around the world in our own exploits, and endeavours, gleaning what we need to glean, picking up and packing on the weight of prejudice, perspicacity, and doubt, carefully tucking them into every conceivable gap in our inner, dark cavernous spaces, never to see the light of day again, until we're encouraged to react to someone or something that is. I traded my backpack for my invisible Mary Poppins medicine bag decades ago, it's now filled with lotions, potions, elixirs and fixers, tonics and histrionics, stories and glories, and a smattering of the peels of laughter. All carefully hand-picked from past situations from this fab adventure. Although I can forget what I was saying mid-sentence these days, I'm still able to reflect on what I've experienced in my relatively short 50 years here on this colourful spinning disco ball we call Earth.

"We own more than we need Lesley."

"Sorry Jools?" "No I apologise for interrupting you, but I was a way off in my own world. These days, if I don't say it as I think it, it disappears into an infinite void. Never to return."

"Och, not at all, I was twittering away about nothing and everything in particular. Personally, I've always been a hoarder, ever since I was a little kid. I have a difficult time throwing away things that I no longer need or even want. Consequently, I have accumulated clothes, toys, books, 'art', clay pots shaped like… maybe a dog, a turtle or a turd, and other useless sentimental things. Our house is bulging at the seams. Mikey says that one day all it's going to take is a huff and a puff and all its contents are going to spill and spew over the garden, pavement, and subdivision. He says that we've all been brainwashed to think that we need this stuff, in the belief that all these 'things' we desire or cling to, will give us permanent happiness."

"Yeah, true happiness isn't wrapped in material things. That's one of the liberating things about age, you get lighter the less you hold on to."

"Still learning that one. I remember that time Mikey…"

We learn the true meaning of impermanence on a much deeper level, we meet people who become our closest friends only to leave in a different direction after days or weeks, months, years, decades. We stay in places that become our home, then after a short time, we move to another new place, then another, and another. Our known reality, including the people we meet, becomes part of our comfortable, habitual daily tapestry, only for it to edge its spidery tendrils deep within the confines of our known 3-D realm, and just as we get comfortable, everything changes. At first, I used to struggle to let go of what I had become accustomed to, my norm, but I've learned not to take it all in like soup, ladle after ladle, preferring to use a slotted spoon instead, loosening the grip of attachment to a person, place or thing, appreciating the full enchilada in all its glory with each unseen mouthful. When we let go and trust where the universe is leading us, it's surprising to see that it actually guides us to where we are supposed to be, bringing us directly to situations and folk whom we are meant to meet on this grand romp. Every experience is perfectly designed to teach, energetically/emotionally, unleashing us from historic excess baggage, the challenging, difficult, knotty, uncomfortable life lessons. Learning how to shake that shit off in the process, so that no one or nothing in our outer world can do us harm, our job when we notice our reactions or lock into a negative pattern and/or habit is to pull the emergency brake on that express thought train before it completely derails. Slowing the wheels of life down, exposing the bigger picture, panning awareness further away from the original confining thought, changing every gawd darn thing. Now it all may seem terribly romantic, and fantastical, but things rarely go smoothly, infestations of bed bugs, fleas, language barriers, financial barriers, relationship barriers, health barriers, environmental barriers, mental barriers, sexually transmitted diseases-doesn't matter. Barriers. Same as everyone else really, the list could go on forever with what can go wrong during life's travels, including the long bus rides, intolerable smells, far worse than what's being fired out of Lesley, not to mention the incessant amount of people in small, tight, heavily populated places. But despite the difficulties, it can promote joy and pleasure, especially when we're at the age when we realise happiness is an inside job, and that there is not one single person, or experience out there that can complete or compete with that when we already know we're already whole. Outside factors are entirely neutral, the next moment only contains our personal preferences and prejudices that we're clueless to hauling across the threshold of every instant. Strip that away and it's a very clear, open, uncluttered centred space, likely the biggest most underestimated power move any one person can make in a split second. No preferences for outcomes. Have I said that already? It's all about acceptance, training yourself to see the good, the bad, the highs and lows of all life's dualities as another part of our experience. The detached spectator to our own , personal vista's actuality as it unfolds. We can all struggle trying to control how we want situations and others to look, sound, and be. Hoping that a certain someone or something can fill the subconscious binds of doubt, inadequacy, and shame, for example, avoiding doing the actual work that needs to be addressed, all that stored shite carried since childhood and beyond. The long distances travelled, fatigue, births, deaths, narrow-minded thoughts, agonising emotions, incidents, and people are all very much part of bumpy paths that lead us in a jiffy to being here. Here and now. Nowhere else to be. Now is all we have, own that and we have already won. Trains, boats, buses that don't arrive on schedule, overcrowded, constant stops, exchanging one full caboose for an equally cramped suffocating one. Guess what? We learn to survive and surf the squalls of life's challenges as they come in waves, one after another before cresting and breaking on, over and around us, riding the seafoam, not being dragged under, lost, caught and rolled in its turbulent watery barrel. Instead, we gracefully glide to the shore, not crashing, distressed, distracted, rotating in the submerged drum like a narcotic-fueled hamster on its wheel transporting us to a soggy grave. When we are faced with a situation that forces us to be strong, we learn to reunite our body and our minds using the energy of the breath as our inner global positioning system as it carves pathways throughout, penetrating tensions, compressions, tangles and tethers, stretching down and out along the length of our limbs. Each system of mind, body, and breath takes an equal share of our attention and our awareness. More often than not, our bodies and our breath are here, holding space, but our ignorant minds are taking the lion's share of our attention, onboard the mental thought, chatter train heading to the future reverting back to the past, speeding through the station of this moment, oblivious to the pressure, stress, itching, compressed muscles and spaces, sealing cracks with gorilla glue, and are not fully present enough to release the body's brakes. Sometimes, to be left with no other choice gives us strength and power we didn't know we even had. The good news is you don't have to go backpacking to experience life's great adventures, it's always on our doorsteps.

"I don't think she even likes me, Jools."

"What? Who Lesley?"

"Angy, I don't think she likes me, she's always rolling her eyes whenever I say something or not. You must have noticed, it's not like she tries to hide it."

"Lesley, don't take that personally, she doesn't like anyone very much. Including herself."

"Hmmm, I'm not so sure Jools, she comes across like she loves herself. I wonder if she still likes living in Uhmerica, and with Uhmericans, not sure I'd like that, I tell the boys all the time that they're Scottish born abroad, not Australian."

"What do you have against Australia and Australians Lesley?"

"Absolutely nothing, couldn't eat a whole one mind, seriously though, it's given us an incredible life. Wouldn't change a thing, I'm just, well, very patriotic to Scotland. I hardly notice the Aussie accent anymore, it doesn't bother me in the slightest these days. I love it here, and I love Angy even though she can be bristlier than a bristle brush."

"Again don't take that personally Lesley, she's bristly with lots of people. This is like Deja poo all over again."

"It's Vue Jools, even I know that."

"No, we've been over all this shite before Lesley, besties are more than just a comfort blanket, a trusty steed, they are a mirror/ reflection to all that we are, and all that we're not."

Shifting our consciousness beyond the trap of accents, language, colour, culture, religion, politics, nationality, shape, and size. Beyond the limiting belief systems branded on us by past experiences, casting our net of awareness out, snaring the billowing feelings that amazement and awe can transport when noticed. Like life, backpacking is an intense experience—it teaches us profound lessons that can open us up to the wonders and magnificence of our own role in our very own minute-by-minute reality show, let's face it who hasn't learned that just because correction fluid and blue tinted eye dew come in the same bottle, they do the same thing?

"I wonder if Angy still chases all those 'yummy' toy boys."

"Even old dogs chase cars they're never going to catch Lesley, besides she says all cats look 21 in the dark, could it be that, it's just an illusion. Imagination."

"Ha, good to hear she hasn't changed."

"The desire is still there, but the body has slowed down by default. I think she settles for the 'vehicles' that can keep up with her these days. My weekly exercise is to chase the ice cream van down, that keeps me going and has my sweat and saliva glands on high alert at the mere mention of Greensleeves, the first note has me activated and at the door."

"We can't live in the past Jools, you know, I always say that to Mikey, the past is the past, move on. No point in crying over spilled milk."

"The past was an opportunity to grow, learn, evolve, and learn what we need to learn. We all carry our own individual invisible plates across the doorstep of now, directly into the vast supper of this moment, a real smorgasbord of global dishes, each one filled to the brim with our personal data of opinions, prejudices, anger, fear, sadness, and we lay these full, heavy dishes on the table for everyone and everything to feast on, to be admired, judged, tasted, compared, enjoyed. What a banquet, everyone should try it just once. When you know, you know. You know?"

"I know, right. Och the amount we used to drink, well you pair more than me, glad I was taught the lesson of an easy pour when I was younger. I still enjoy the occasional tipple though, a creamy cocktail…mmmmmmmmmm."

"You know what Lesley, I can still manage to throw the occasional 85% proof liquid bucket down my gullet, only on the odd occasion, and that odd occasion coincides with Ange's arrival funnily enough."

"Och gaun and wheesht will you, you're one of those vegan types aren't you? You have to drink a 'special' vegan wine, no? Isinglass is derived from fish bladders and is used to clear white wines, like gelatin in ice cream. Also on the downside for vegans, wine can contain milk protein and egg whites. I'm sure there are plenty of self proclaimed vegans out there who quaff non vegan wine like it's pure fermented grape juice."

"How can you tell a vegan Lesley?""I don't know Jools, how can you tell a vegan?"

"Cos they keep feckin telling you, that's how."

"I've never tried vegan wine or non-alcoholic stuff, I mean what's the point? It's not as if wine really tastes that nice in the first place, it's got ethanol in it, so if Dirty Gertie Two runs out of petrol, you've got at least a month's supply of wine in the back there."

"Over my bed buddy Lesley, the only vessel filling up with my wine is our own vessel, Dirty Gertie Too goes dry. I am in more need of lubrication, I can assure you."

"Why do we even drink it if it's not good for us? I'll stick to my creamy cocktails thank you very much."

"A good ole porn cocktail always hits the right spot eh Lesley."

"Why is it called a Cocktail anyway? Who came up with that?"

"Someone who knew that absolutely no good story begins with a healthy salad. The origin of the cocktail is down to a mispronunciation of the French word for egg cup, coquetier pronounced in English, as cocktay."

"You just made that up Jools, maybe it began as a mispronunciation of the parrot, the 'cockortoo' "

"A cock or two you say, transports me immediately back to some fond, gently held memories of stories, people, places, stuff, come and gone."

"It's hard not to become too attached to stuff, we arrived on this fair land empty handed, and that's exactly the way we leave it, empty handed. A hearse doesn't come with the option of a roof rack. Mikey thinks that's a ridiculous saying, but he does laugh every time I say it, which means the world to me. I love hearing him laugh Jools. Although I'm a hoarder, I can also be quite ruthless when it comes to an annual decluttering. If it rests longer than a nanosecond, then it's out with the rubbish, usually Mikey and The Boys' things, not mine, or sentimental things. What's the point of hanging on to rubbish? Makes no sense. Drives me insane, I only keep things I know I'm going to need again or hang on to it, till it comes back in fashion."

"Brutal Lesley. You'd have a feel day in the back of Dirty Gertie Too."

"Alas, I left my hazmat suit at home, Jools, we do own more junk than we need. We've all been brainwashed to think that we need 'things' to make us happy."

"Easily satisfied with a double measure of 'sex on the beach', followed by a cock or two chasers."

"Tossing things out lightens the load Jools, aside from my bottom that is, it gets heavier by the second, I just have to look at a sausage roll these days, and bam, there it goes, slapped on to my buttocks and thighs, but I feel more content, grateful for the space the lack of material possessions creates. Tell me, why do you live…in …, let's face it, this clamped out, old volkswagen kombi rust bucket you call …home?"
"I resemble that remark Lesley, you can call me a clapped out, old rust bucket, but Gertie has been with me through thick and thin, my loyal,

somewhat reliable companion for years. I don't live here anyway, it just looks that way."

"I know you don't live, like, LIVE in her, but as near as damn it. You're always on the road, especially when you phone me you are anyway."

"I'm somewhat semi reliable, somewhat jaded, battered and bruised, but Gertie here has been my buddy on all these journeys, she's more of a passion wagon than I am these days."

"Nonsense, there's still juice in the old bird, and that's just you I'm talking about here Jools, and now you, me AND Angy get to enjoy the next adventure with her. YIPPEE."

"Careful what you wish for Lesley."

"I feel queasy, which is ridiculous, I'm a grown woman, she's my friend and I love her, but she makes me nervous, she's going to find me beige, vanilla, a dull, bored housewife, I know it."

"You'd be right if you KNEW it, but in the meantime, you don't and you're not, so shut up, and stop telling yourself that story, which you have totally made up out of absolutely nowhere, from absolutely nothing, it'll only have you bent out of shape."

"She still makes me feel this way. I was just telling Mikey…och, not important. Anyhoo, less of me, what about you? Not easy being a single mother at 24 and bringing Sam up like that?" "Sky, pluck, that really was a 180 degree change there Lesley. And "like that?" Ha, he had countless mothers, fathers, siblings, grandparents and poxy aunties like yourself and Ange. You forget, he grew up in Nimbin; nature, waterfalls, hippies, friends that become family, our blended framily, everything a Scottish transplant could dream of for their only child. He learned environmental initiatives, including sustainability and permaculture, cannabis counter-culture, grassroots political initiatives, and the practice of alternative social philosophies and the stunning hinterland backdrop supported each and every scenario. We were very lucky Lesley, and then at 18, I packed him off to uni and the dizzying lights of Sydney. He was fully prepared. He still is, and he's never looked back, he is a strong, independent, confident, and compassionate individual because of it. I am forever thankful to my past for teaching me how to authentically loosen my grip on expectations that I may have for him, letting him safely find his own sea legs. These days, it's often the reality that I lose my grip of. My framily call me Dory."

"I forget which one's which, is Dory the Spanish lass or the clownfish?"

"Jokers to the left, clowns to the right, I can juggle that's for sure, and it's neither Lesley."

"Four boys, volunteering, a husband, and a life, I must have come out of the womb without a view juggling."

"The fish that forgets everything is called Dory Lesley."

"I think it's Dora Jools, but no mind, I have no idea where you're going with that one."

"Let it go Darlene."

"Darlene?"

"The girl in the fish story Lesley?"

"If I'm not mistaken, and I rarely am, I think it's a boy, and a monkey called Boots. I'm a mother of 4 boys, I know my children's stories inside out I can tell you. Put me on mastermind, can you say that these days? What would you say instead? Mistress Mind? No mind? Nonmind?"

"Nomad, or just mad. I think they use " master" here as showing very great skill or proficiency, not as in a man who has people 'working' for him."

"Of course, silly me. How funny. Or it could be a wee fella."

"Eh?"

"A wee fella, you know, the title given for an underage male, aye master that is, not mind. Master."

"Possibly, but not on this occasion Lesley."

"Possibly not, anyway, I could……"

Blah, blah. blah…. The more I live, the less I plan. In fact, I have made no real plans for this trip, ignoring Ange's request to book the Four Seasons. There are plenty of places to stay, so we'll be good, rest assured though. Lesley here will have all her ducks in a row, i's dotted, t's stroked, rechecked, over and over again. What do I need to worry about? What could possibly go wrong? Life is full of uncertainty, and I like it that way on purpose, as I know we're going to be led to where we're supposed to be. In this way, the universe has never failed me.

"Remind me where we're staying again, Jools? You have got somewhere? Tell me you've booked something, you have booked something? There's no way Angy is going to leave it up to you, has she booked somewhere lovely? Has she told you? Is it a secret? Has she booked somewhere? You told me you were organising accommodation. You did that, didn't you?"

"Kinda Lesley."

"You're not suggesting that we all sleep in here are you?"

"What's wrong with Gertie Lesley? Hmmm? What are you saying here? Is my van not good enough for you? Ange and I lived in the original Dirty Gertie whilst on the road."

"When you were 21 I might add, we're all pushing or about to push 50, please tell me you're pulling my leg Jools. Och, stop teasing me, I saw that wink, you know what I mean though, I do like my creature comforts, I'm too long in the tooth to be sharing a confined space with you or Angy, I've planned this getaway mentally for months."

"Could be worse Lesley, I've had more than 3 people in here you know, sometimes one on top of each other, human bunk beds. Life may look like rainbows and unicorns, but things rarely go according to plan, so it's much easier on everyone concerned if we let go of expectations or personal preferences as to how we'd like the uncertainty of our future to be."

"That's one way of putting it, but I'd prefer to stick hot needles in my eyes than sleep here, no offence you understand, I just don't. Speaking of needles, did I tell you I'm thinking of laser eye treatment? It would make knitting so much easier, so I went....."

We face certain situations that could make some people upset or uncomfortable. Recently I burned my honey pot straddling a motorbike. I had to walk around like John Wayne for days, soothing aloe-vera-soaked fanny pads strapped to my inner thighs. Now, that may be embarrassing for some, but not me, the opinions of others on my condition does not buckle me in any way, other than the shape I was already in. Only yesterday, when I was cleaning and clearing out Dirty Gertie Too, preparing her for imminent criticisms and critiques, I found what I thought was an actual real-life scorpion corpse under the passenger seat, but it turned out to be the scorpion pendant Ange had given me as a gift one year, it came in a blue box and someone must have chucked it back there, okay, me to be fair, anyway, fascinating piece, like Lesley's bag which she's had for as long as I've known her.

"I love that you still use that timeless, beautiful, leather bag you inherited from your lovely mum Lesley."

"Did I ever tell you it was given to my mother on my granny's deathbed, soo it's really old and contains all the burdens, hopes, memories of so many fragments of full and fabulous former lives. It's battered, tattered, bruised and cracked, the ingrained stains are stamped in 'artistic' shapes and sizes, possibly red wine splodges. That would be me. Soup splats, probably Mikey, perfume sprays, definitely my mum, she was obsessed with spraying everything and everyone in her midst. I think I may have got some of my OCD tendons from her."

"Don't forget the coke trails…oops no, sorry that's my bag."

"The only coke stains I have on this bag Jools are from an exploding can sprayed by one of my delightful boys, and not in the saddle bags of one of those drug donkeys you read about."

"Incredible imprints and impressions stamping their secrets of the memories of the past. It's a real piece of art Lesley."

"Honestly, you'd think I never cleaned it out, look at this, receipts of purchases, returns, toothpicks, generational baby teeth, loose coins, a lipstick lid, various strands of hair, again generational, different lengths, shades, and ethnicity, blondish, that's me. I can't resist a good 'brush', no matter who, where or when, I'm always armed and ready to tame, and smooth the 'rowdiest' and unruliest of locks. Very few have escaped my strokes I can tell you Jools."

"Oooeser Missus, I have more bristles on my chin these days than you have in all your boar hair brushes put together. I was shocked to find a grey pube the other week."

"Och at our age it's to be expected, Jools."

"Not when it's on a fast food, falafel burger it's not Lesley."

"Look at this Jools, a crumpled tissue in various papier mache stages, a Kirby grip which hasn't been in circulation since the 50's, pens, blunt pencils, lead shrapnel, sticky notes of reminders never used. A collection of accumulated stuff deposited in the silk folds, crisp crumbs, somewhat wrapped, melted chocolate, ahhh here's your mars bar, and somewhere amongst other concealed folds always lurks a tic tac or two for some reason."

"That is so unlike you Lesley, everything else in your life has its squeaky clean, polished place, disinfected within an inch of its life, and I'm only talking about Mikey and the boys here."

"Ha, it's like my own junk drawer if you like."

"Like my junk van Lesley."

"Ha, yes, it's the only thing I am reluctant to ever clear out, Jools. I feel like I'm erasing a part of history that I don't care for, it's my treasure trove, and clutching it to my bosie brings me comfort, security I guess, yes, great comfort, and joy."

"I think it's a lovely story Lesley, a tangible reminder of love, love for a mother, a granny, and your boys. The places, people and things that the Old bag has experienced, I can tell you, and I'm not only talking about the lump of leather on your lap. "

"Ha! I know how it feels, memories gently worn away by circumstance, filled with attachments to the past, loved all these years, still carrying remnants of occasions in its glory hole, vintage makeup smeared in its wrinkles, fossilised sausage roll morsels, rowies, teething biscuits scattered on the granular, sandy bottom, here's the tic tac that has defied time, lodged against the now expired, rejected orange Starburst. Fabulous old bag."

"Steady, who are you calling old, you're an older bag."

"Only by weeks Jools."

"I love The Bag and the history it holds, reminds me a bit of us actually Lesley."

"Us? Classy, timeless, unique?"

"I'm thinking more along the lines of leathered, battered, bruised, tattered and splattered. Now that it's older though, it's softer than it was, not so rigid and tight, it's grown into itself, and old, it is old, very, very old, similar to you, me and Ange, bit knocked off centre by the beaten track, one or 3,846 battle scars to show for it."

"And the most beautiful people I know inside and out Jools. Speaking of "old bags", she'll be chomping at the bit waiting for us, bossing her entourage of bag handlers. I bet her luggage is like one of those tupperware parties for the rich and fabulous, where they all match, fit perfectly together, and manage to keep their contents intact."

"All the eager human drones, swarming after their queen, grateful for any handouts."

"Hopefully excluding her callous verbal ones Jools, besides you can't be a Queenbee if you're always behaving like a drone."

"Aye well, she is what she is, Lesley, we have to accept all the facets of a friend, including our perceived shortcomings that we may have for them, and not have exclusivity for the ones we prefer. A friend should be like your bag and your delightful jars of homemade Chicksmix, some good things, some bad, some downright unpalatable, but nonetheless, all in the same old bag and /or jar."

"I know, but I'm nervous. It's ridiculous how she makes me feel Jools"

"Only you can manage that one Lesley, learning how to be our own emotional baggage handler, it may be her fault that she provokes, but ultimately our responsibility to unknot oneself from her grip. That's our work, it's an inside job, when we're able to extricate ourselves from the mire hand delivered by events and mortals in our 3 d realm, then we'll learn to soar. How we feel is our prerogative, don't give that task to anyone else to handle, that's our work. Like stepping on a warm piece of gum on a hot day. It can take forever, if ever to extricate oneself from its bind. My advice? Don't stand on the fecking chuddy in the first place."

"You're so right Jools, I sometimes forget that she actually saved my life, I mean, that's HUGE, she actually saved my life, and for that I am eternally grateful, we are totally bondaged together through circumstance whether she likes it or not. Forever. Remember?"

"I may be peri, mani, pedi menopausal Lesley, but I'm not completely forgetful. It's one of those iconic events that should be framed, displayed on a memory board, and hung in a mental museum for all to enjoy. It has to be one of my Australia's Most Funniest Moments of all time, not at the actual time you were dying though. Years later. Years I tell you."

"I think it's hilarious Jools, and a cracker to tell at dinner parties, school socials and parent night outs. Not sure Angy shares it the way I do. Does she? Does she ever mention it? Probably not eh? You would though, it's a great survivor story. Does she?"

"I haven't heard her say anything in front of me, but that doesn't mean she doesn't see the humour in it, or maybe she carries it in the form of a mental memento trophy."

"You think she's embarrassed? Maybe that's exactly it. Humiliated even. Gosh I never thought of it that way before. But why? Makes sense though as she brushes it off with her perfectly manicured hands quicker than I am with a bristle brush after a bout of wind."

"Oooer missus, I knew it was you."

"I meant, wind, as in wind. You know what I meant Jools. Messes the hair."

"Hey, uncontrollable wind and leakages are part of the bumpy roads we travel. I thought it was Gertie's suspension, but at least her's is intact, unlike mine. Aggh, what the feck is that? Take it out of my face Lesley, I'm trying to drive here."

"See? It's a gift Mikey gave me, my souvenir."

"Is that what I think it is Lesley?" "Yes."

"Is it dead?"

"I'm not one to always state the obvious Jools, but it's been squashed and pressed between two scorching pieces of plastic and made into a work of art."

"I'd hardly call a laminated carcass of a red back spider on a keyring a work of art. It's BLACK, and huge. Come to think of it, just the way I like it."

"Said the actor to the bishop. The oldies are the goodies, don't you think Jools."

"Whatever you say. What are the hairy things around it? And I don't mean your lips."

"Och you, always the funny one. Well, it was in a nest of expired centipedes, so they were included. I know I'm predontic, but separating that tangled web, excuse the pun, was a stretch too far even for me. It's my reminder to always be grateful to her."

"100 percent of legs too far Lesley."

"I feel like I'm back in a school playground apprehensive as to what games she's going to play Jools, but excited nonetheless to see her."

"Relax Chook, no need to play any games in anyone else's playground other than your own, that is, safer to watch the games and drama of others from the school gates. If you don't want to be caught hook, line and sinker in her snare that is, or anyone else's for that matter, then learn how to catch and release. We all get exactly what we need, Lesley, not always what we want either. When we're faced with a situation that forces us to be strong, sometimes, to be left with no other choice gives us strength and power we didn't know we were blessed with. There is always someone or something put in our way to remind us that we're not fully stripped naked of all that emotional shite we wear."

"Speaking of naked, you know I've not really forgiven her for shagging Richard, on my actual wedding day. I mean, first off, who does that at their son's wedding. Took me years to survive that one at family celebrations, Jools. She made me feel like such a fool."

"The world is full of fools Lesley who never get it right, and I can tell you from the bottom of my heart that the story has been completely misinterpreted and exaggerated over the years, it took on arms and legs, like that key ring of yours, and is so over the top, it's just not true. Ask Ange yourself, but, keep in mind she has no clue people have been gossiping behind her back for years. There she is, the old bag, over there, herding a deceased leather herd."

"Is that really her?? I'm struggling to see past your pointed finger Jools, she looks like a cross between Audrey Hepburn, sandwiched between Goldie Hawn and Cher."

"Unlike me who's more like a baguette filled with bawdy heartburn, oldie prawn and flare."

No amount of anxiety makes any difference to anything that is going to happen - Alan Watts

Home Is A Feeling

Ange

As the NSW coastline expands towards me, a delightful wave of calm surges over and through me. We were innocent kids when we first stepped foot on this sacred land. Three Scottish girls taking the world on by the balls, so many years between then and now. So much has happened.

Sydney is one of the greatest harbourside cities in the world, alongside my other favourites of San Francisco, New York, Vancouver, Cape Town, Rio de Janeiro, London, and the dizzying heights of the good ole northern lights of Aberdeen. Sydney from the air on a clear day is a breathtaking treat, the harbour, with its dozens of inlets, is absolutely magnificent. The city skyline, the iconic Opera House, the Harbour Bridge are all equally impressive. It's an aquatic playground for Sydneysiders, with hundreds of miles of shoreline, scattered with unspoiled beaches, picturesque gardens, and pockets of natural bush. Speaking of bush, that's where we're apparently going to celebrate our reunion. Having friends like Jules and Lezzers, even with all their faults, is like coming home to a log fire and a comfy pair of slippers, nothing quite beats the familiarity and safety of true friends. What could possibly go wrong. I can't wait.

My body doesn't know whether it's coming or going, it is physically spent from leaving the Good Ole US 24 hours ago, arriving here in Sydney 48 hours later, missing a whole day somewhere across the flight path. How does that happen? 24 hours missing? Gone forever! Not the first time that's happened and I'm sure not the last. It was baltic when we left, minus 20 at least, a typical winter's New York, pitch dark, dreich day. JFK is one of the busiest terminals on the planet, and I'm still recovering from being around all those claustrophobia-inducing people, bustling about in their hidden, tight, impatient space. Terminal? I mean "TERMINAL"! Who was the bright spark that came up with that one? "TERMINAL" - a building that contains thousands of shit-scared, apprehensive, nervous flyers. Seriously look at it: "TERMINAL" in bold letters, welcoming the hoards of hopeful passengers into its gaping grip. FFS! The exact same word that means "ultimately leading to death", subliminally bombarding the subconscious psyche of their flying 'victims'. One would have thought that the main role of a terminal, in this case, would be to ensure the easy flow of passengers and their baggage; efficiently, orderly, meeting the needs of the airline operators. Perhaps calling the building "Skyspa", might be more soothing to calm the fear. It's why I often choose to fly privately, I don't have to deal with the great quaking unwashed. I only flew mainstream this time because it worked for me. Who notices the impact, the fear that these subliminal words have? I mean seriously, "TERMINAL", all that word creates is uncertainty and chaos in minds, risking life and limb as they climb aboard the 910,000 lbs piece of twisted metal steel, bound in certain parts by bog-standard tape and glue. Believe me. Tape and glue. Then up and away they all come and go, blazing their 460 mph streaks of uncertainty through the once deserted, but now cluttered sky. Uncertainty is a killer for most people, not me though, I'm as certain as I was as the day I was born. I wish. Apparently, it's okay to be vulnerable, the new black they say, not with me it's not, who the fuck wants to see anyone's vulnerabilities let alone mine, I don't like that feeling, too exposed for me, much easier not to show anyone that side. Keep that hidden under lock and key. I have some major decisions to be made in the next few days and unusually for me, I'm not sure what I'm going to do. Can anyone be sure of the outcomes of their choices, that they or anyone else make for that matter? There are trillions of nerves in the human body and some people seem to get on every single last one of mine. Lezzers can have me distorted at the drop of a hat, my mother, coincidentally called Lesley, used to be the only other person in this world that could wind me up like a clock, gad rest her pickled soul, she can't get to me so easily now. I don't know what it is, but Lezzers gets my goat, she does have the similar lack of listening traits that my mum had, maybe that's it, don't get me wrong here, I love her in that annoying faux 'sibling' way.

I hate this. It really boils down to me, doesn't it? Ugggh, what am I going to do? Only time will reveal the inevitable answers. Jules would be so proud of me for even getting this far, she's always the first to say, "If you never take the chance then you'll never know," and "If nothing changes, then nothing changes," and other bullshit like that. No point in spending any more time on that as there's nothing to tell or do until the time is right, or not. I do feel unusually giddy, bordering on nervous, what if it doesn't pan out the way I want? GRRRR, I NEVER second guess myself, but this is a life changer for me. FFS, get a grip, Angela. Relax. Where are my drugs? The other downside to fucking commercial travel is that I've had to stash my drugs in some very clever ingenious spaces, where only I can lay my hands on them. Like this old-fashioned candy string necklace, made up of Xanax, Tums, Ibuprofen, and Valium, and that's just for starters. One of the lovely perks of having a Premier 1 K status, is that you don't have to be around the frisson of the frightened travelling rabble all the time. You arrive at a private hangar, avoiding the main Terminal completely, and are escorted directly to a fully stocked lounge where you wait until the Captain comes to personally greet you and accompany you to your seat. As they should. Ridiculous amount of stupid money for this service. I have never paid for it, years of accumulating the points on someone else's dime, that's the best way to travel, none of this backpacking nonsense Jules has a penchant for. Fuck that for a game of soldiers, why would you when luxury travel is an option. I guarantee, none of the other 3 on board in the exclusive part of this plane actually had to part with their 'hard-earned' cash for the 'privilege' of a bed, spa, 100% attention, and flight bags filled with all sorts of goodies. Fizz is served before the cabins fill up with the optimistic pessimists, who are then unhappily restrained into seats too narrow for the scurviest of 10-year-olds. I suppose that's what you get when you can only afford the cheap seats. Thank the Log that my chum Farma Ceutical has kept me company for the 23 + hours of flying, literally from one side of the world to the other. A few flutes of decent champagne, not the garbage they serve in cattle class, a light meal served silver service style, more fizz, a couple more pills, a lie down under the eiderdown quilt they provide along with the silk loungewear, slippers, and aloe vera gel eye mask. Goodnight Vienna, hello Sydney.

I absolutely love it here. Sydney. I can already feel my shoulders dropping in sync with our landing, and if only I could naturally relax the hundreds of facial muscles gripping my loose epidermis from spilling its empty elastic, ruched, puckered folds, then I would, but the chemicals in beauty injections are binding and have prevented all natural contractions from happening. Not that it bothers me, I don't care whether I've been injected with the squeezed juicy extracts from an almost extinct gland of a living human animal. I don't care. I actually don't care. It works for me. Call me selfish. These procedures merely emphasise my tight poker face anyway, just the way I like it.

Now that I'm here, where are those little people to assist me with my bags? They should already be waiting, standing to attention as I clear customs. Good, they got the memo, there they are.

"Grab those bags and follow me, ALL of you. Come on, no dilly dallying, time is of the essence, I have a reunion to lead. Put all the baggage on the back of that guest service transport cart. Careful with those cases, they are probably worth more than your salaries combined. Thank you. Here you go. Now, run along and split this $100 between you, I don't have anything smaller. Now driver, oy, Bruce? Is that what your name tag says? You can't be serious? Your name really is Bruce? Only in Australia eh."

"Couldn't make it up Sheila, now where are you and this leather clad convoy heading?"

"Gate A, Terminal 1. And don't save the horses, I'm meeting two of my oldest, much older than me, chums, we haven't actually seen each other in person, all together for YEARS, so, mush, mush, I want to make sure I'm ready for the big meet, great, and greet. I was a mere child when we first landed on this fair land, and I can't wait to squeeze their squishy bodies, so, tally ho Bruce haste you not"

"Fair dinkum your Highness, My Queen."

"Bloody hell, does this mirror work Bruce? Can't be right though, look, there's a few more of these... these...."

"Wrinkles?"

"Agggh, how very dare you Bruce, I was about to say.... fairy strokes..."

"She must yield a very large wand, Love. You can't cheat age, fairy strokes indeed, bollocks to that, a wrinkle is a wrinkle end of, you can run, but you can't hide from the ravages of time. It's the only real tattoo of a full life lived worth having. Strokes of wisdom Sheila, that's what I say."

"I wouldn't say I'm as wise as this delusional mirror has portrayed me Bruce. Does appear that I've very much enjoyed being ravaged over time though."

There is no way I'm of the age my passport claims. I nearly died when the child customs officer declared it aloud to the waiting, fatigued, unwashed, drained, jet-lagged rabble, shuffling their way forward through customs like lambs to the slaughter. Bastard. Cheeky sod didn't seem in the slightest bit fazed, didn't flinch when I locked his clear unsullied eyeballs with my bloodshot ones, the no-nonsense legendary contemptuous glare, carried on his business like he'd said something plausible. The youngsters of today- no fucking backbone. I died once when I was 5 and my mum made me walk it off. Uggghhh, who says that? "the youngsters of today..."? Old people that's who, and I'm not old. He won't do it again, I can almost guarantee it. Young squirt. A mere reminder that some things are best swallowed. No doubt on some youth training scheme and not quite groomed on how to be intimidated by an unflinching fearless stare. It's cost me an arm, a leg, and facial paralysis to look this way, modern dermal fillers gorged with hyaluronic acid, saline-filled implants in different shapes and sizes with smooth, textured shells have entertained my lips, cheeks, breasts, butt, and vagina, and it's not going to be wasted on some prepubescent brat. A tonne of whale blubber has been pumped, sucked, inserted, and removed, this extra attention to detail better not have been in vain. I don't have many nerves left, but it's only fitting that I keep up with the latest rejuvenators, breast, lip, and cheeks upstairs and downstairs, including a vaginal augmentation. If I stopped it all now, it would all go to rat shit, a rerelease of Bagpuss and Pals.

I haven't seen Jules since I flew in on a secret squirrel assignment under the cloak of darkness last year, she's going to want to hear my decision for sure, but the truth is, I haven't made up my mind, my head is totally scrambled, slightly cracked, but a good egg deep down. The next few weeks will expose what needs to be exposed, giving me some clarity. Trust the process they tell you, but for the first time in my life, I'm doubting trusting the process. Why am I so resistant to this change? I'm usually such a black or white person, actually I'm entirely black. With shades of gray. .... ? No? I'm usually, almost right, most of the time. I can't help it if I work on a daily basis with a bunch of mainly testosterone-fueled buffoons, actually, I'm doing buffoons a disservice here, let's keep it as mainly a testosterone-fueled space filled with disposable species. I do not trust men. End of. If that's not the polar opposite stance from white then I don't know what is. What I'm trying to say is that I don't need a man to complete my life. Is it really complete though Angela? Would a relationship enhance what you already have in your life? Enrich? Smother? It must be so suffocating having a man full-time in life, the occasional sweep usually does the trick, but the rest of it sounds like too much effort. Get a grip of yourself, Angela. Settled then. Done and dusted, I can totally handle this without having to be the slightest bit broken open. No one gets to see my vulnerability, no one, not even me. Jules knows me better than most, that's for sure, she's been privy to the highs, lows, good, bad, mad, bad, and dangerous to know myself, my blessings, and shortcomings. She knows me inside out and still loves and accepts me, if only she knew the real me though, she might not be so giving with her love. She says it's only because she sees every moment as a blank canvas, a clean slate, fresh start, stretch fart, and that she's forgotten all the horrible things I've said and, or done to her and others. Listen to me, self-pitying old battleaxe, I sound pathetic. Let's reframe this, that's what to do. Reframe. Hear it all the time, or used to, especially when I worked for one of the biggest hedge fund businesses, not only in New York, but in the world. I started there not long after my gap year in Australia, almost, no, gosh yes, 30 years ago. My giddy aunt, 30 years? How has that even happened? So much packed in. I have fought every veneered tooth and platinum powdered dipped nail for everything, every dayum thing I have, and nobody can take that away from me, I've done it all by myself. On my tod, there may be some collateral damage and prisoners on my way up, but that has to happen. Candles have to be snuffed out in order for mine to shine, wouldn't you agree? It's all part of the power game you see, and I'm prepared and confident enough to make my own rules. I worked my way from the mailroom to junior analyst on Wall Street, via every bloody involuntary male room known to mankind. At that time, there were only a handful of females trying to forge a path in a very male-dominated stock market arena. You had to be tough, resilient, bare your teeth, claw, fight, and scratch if you wanted to go further up the dude chain, otherwise, you'd fall or be thrown by the wayside. Not everyone survives or is cut out for this cutthroat business, an abundance of male egos bouncing off each other, weak, inadequate egotistical armour lashing out in all directions. I've experienced my fair share of misogyny, sexism, bullshit, and desire from the men who were at the top but wanted to be under me. The powers that be would send you on all sorts of these motivating, transformative, "how to be a billionaire" courses, and I clawed my way out of the bowels of shredded paperwork, and by the time I reached my rightful place in the boardrooms, every single man that had tried to manipulate, control, and eye fuck me for their own greedy gains, had their genitalia impaled by my very own eye fuck daggers. Take that you egotistical sensitive, pathetic bastards. From there, it was only a hop, scotch, and a few jumps to hedge fund manager, portfolios director, and now CEO: chief executive fucking officer, the highest ranking person in the company, responsible for making all major decisions. Not too shabby for a Scottish lass from Aberdeen. I could give the reality show "Survivor" a run for its money. Never mind whining, how about, wine, wine, and more wine, that's what I need, but first I have more pressing matters on hand. Aside from the reunion, I am here for a very important, potentially life-changing meeting in Sydney next week.

"Come on Bruce, does this trolley thing not go any faster? I'd be quicker walking."

"That's a thought Sheila."

"Now, now, put your foot down and drive before I find myself 10 years older, and your tip decreasing."

"Ahhh, your 40th birthday reunion then?"

"I'll knock them in Bruce, you hit them over. Tip amount just increased."

"Shouldn't be allowed, check out that old rust bucket, pumping out clouds of carbon monoxide."

"That old rust bucket backfiring carbon monoxide just happens to be my sista from another mista, the other is her trusty steed, Dirty Gertie Too, the pigeon passenger is our friend Lesley, Lezzers to her fiends."

"I meant the van Sheila."

"No shit Sherlock, you're funny, I'll kill you last. Not as funny as her though, look she's deliberately driven past us, and pulled up alongside an old lady in a wheelchair instead of me. She'll be pretending it's me to Lezzers. Look, she's kangaroo jumping all over the place, when Dirty Gertie Too stops hopping, you can put my baggage in the back."

"Yes, your Highness."

Life is like jumping out of a plane without a parachute, only the last few seconds are fatal, but most people are scared to death the whole way down - Jonathan lockwood Huie

A Reunion Strengthens Connections Made Long Ago

Lesley

"Is that her? Jools? Audrey Hepburn with auburn hair, look, 11 o'clock. There? Jools? There, there, in the golf cart surrounded by leather? Look. You just hopped, Skippyed, and jumped by her. Please tell me that was her back there, and not this old dear in the wheelchair that you've pulled up alongside, if it is she's really let her standards down."

"Of all the airports in all the towns in all the world, you fly into mine Ange, come here you, you goygeous Amerkin human bean you."

"For Fuck Sake Jules, are you still driving this clapped out rusty piece of shit then?"

"No, I borrowed it especially for this very special, momentous occasion Ange."

"Good to see you, you old cow. I have a dreuth going on here, and am drier than my dead Aunt May on a good day."

"I feel Aunt May's pain Ange, and can match it with my very own dry camel's dingleberry that's been left out in the scorching sun without a drink for weeks."

"I distrust anyone and everyone who can go without a drink in hours, let alone weeks. You'd better have stocked those cheap, nasty, grubby little cabinets inside Dirty Gertie Too with something decent, and if I were you Jules, I'd see about the dingleberry before it takes the hump."

"Any kind of hump would be a bonus, not sure about the booze being "decent" Ange, but stocked non the less, besides, I can see there is no lack of plastic duty free bags amongst your very large, leather entourage. Planning on staying longer than a week are we? Is the plan to store the extra 523 pieces somewhere and only take a weekend bag with us?"

"It would have been irresponsible and out of character not to have packed for every eventuality Jules, I forgot to stop, that's all. I'm quite sure we'll find space, especially when we throw out some of the trash in there, no one is going to notice a couple of missing garbage bags, all my baggage is needed, you'll thank me later, I promise. Be honest, half the stuff in that van of yours is only fit for recycling … aye, recycling straight to the dump, that is. Speaking of bags, where is the wee munchkin? The blonde pocket rocket. There you are Sausage, bless you, hiding behind a wheelchair."

"I can't get out of Dirty Gertie Two."

"Too high Lezzers?"

"Och wheesht you, no, Jools parked so close to the curb that the wheelchair was in the way of the door, so I had to climb over the back to get out. Be there in a sec. You look fabulous, Angy, like Audrey Hepburn."

"And you look, you look just the same Lezzers, exactly the same, I would expect nothing more."

"Och silly me, what was I thinking Angy, I meant to say Audrey Hepburn's grandmother."

"Touche dahling, seriously though, where are your fucking wrinkles?"

"A balloon has no wrinkles, Angy, and using profanity isn't very lady-like."

"Well, neither is your moustache Lezzers."

"I can't help it if I'm a person who wants to be perfect Angy, but trapped in a body that doesn't."

"I'm a person who wants to stop after 2 drinks, but am in a large body that wants to be filled. Okay, you pair of dags, what am I, chopped liver? More like pickled liver spots, I spell 'liver', b.e. a. u. t. y, makes them so much more attractive."

"Your beauty spots Jules, give you more of a cheetah hide, not entirely unattractive, bleaching can fix it in no time."

"Then I'd be the cheater Ange, no point in pretending or masking it any other way than it is. Wanting it to be any different would only ruffle feathers. These beauty spots only come with age, what a privilege it is to have them."

"Don't say I didn't warn you Jules, when they all blend together, you'll look like a rhino. Speaking of rhino, I see you're still carting around that extinct water buffalo carcass you call a handbag Lezzers. Brings back memories for sure, I could smell it coming through customs."

"These days, that could be me, you're smelling Ange, if you get down my drift, and not Lesley's distinctive treasure chest. All I can smell is a delightful alcoholic aroma, wafting in delicate whiffs on the wings of a bouquet of grapes, twisted with notes of vanilla, meandering its contrails plucked from the crates of champagne I have in the back of Dirty Gertie. Only the very best for us. It's been a minute Laddies."

"Did you know that pickled liver is actually a delisake in some countries Angy? Jools?"

"Delicacy, Lezzers, it's delicacy, oh you almost had me there you cheeky mare, come here the pair of you, into the body of the kirk and give me another bosie, not too close, and be careful not to get any of that high street makeup on my silk blouse Lezzers."

"You haven't changed a bit Angy, not one bit, well, bits of you perhaps."

"Hard to tell, I bet, bits have been added, subtracted and erased Lezzers. It cost a gazillion dishonors to create this look. You know, when you've got it, you've got it, and you should flaunt it. Worth every dime Lezzers, every dime. Now, bring that shiny face carefully in, ….come, come here you … you tiny ….. thing. Alright already, that's enough, you can step back now."

"You do look fabulous as always Angy, you really do, even up close. I can hear the Uhmerkan drawl popping through. Say something else, so I can hear The Accent."

"Yo? S'up Biiitch?"

"That's a stretch too far, Angy. No need for the curse words."

"There are days Lezzers, when the supply of available curse words is insufficient enough to meet demands."

"I do hear a Scottish lilt here and there, but mainly Uhmerkan. I've always fancied one of those you know, you do make it sound cool Angy."

"Fancy A merkin, do you Lesley? The day is young, and I'm the genius in your lampervan, so your wish is my command."

"Don't be silly Jools, I'm happily married, you know that."

"What about Mikey, is he happily married, Lezzers? Joke. Stop trying to make everyone else happy anyway, you're not tequila. You both still have your Scottish accents, 35,000miles from your homeland, and hardly an Australian "but" between you. Right girlfriends, let's get this ball rolling shall we, want to be on the road and there before nightfall, so you two better have got all your psychobabble bullshit out of the way, yes? I'm talking directly to you here Jules, the only spirit I want to discuss, see, hear, and or feel in any shape or form better come in a crystal goblet with ice, and every time I hear the word "liberation", I shall consume a libation to drown and liberate my sorrows from both your higher bloody selves.Take that as the threat it is intended to be Jules. Lezzers? Would you be a deer, and get Bruce, I kid you not, the baggage whisperer, to look lively and finish up packing Dirty Gertie Too so we can begin our grand adventure. Tell him to put my bigger cases on the roof rack, everything else can squeeze inside the back beside you."

"What did your last slave die of Angy?"

"Disobedience, now come on, we need to get out of here. You won't mind sitting in the back Lezzers, your wee legs won't need folding the way my Elle McPherson legs do. Muchos."

"Yes, siiiir, duly noted."

"I love it when you say that word Ange, it makes me quiver all over. I got shivers, they're electrifying… say it all again…."

"Which word Jules, Liberation?"

"Nope."

"Libation?"

"Ooooo, yes, see? And I'm your chaufloosey, be afraid, very afraid. "

"I can always drive Jools if you'd prefer."

"Thank you for the offer Lesley, I'll defo keep it in mind, but for some reason the chair is stuck in one position, and it's a reach to the pedals for me as it is, but you never know, you'll be the first to know for sure, not trusting the non driver beside me with a car key let alone a car, that would be far more dangerous. Are you okay in the back?"

"Not sure, I got the choice, but yes, thank you for asking Jools, I'm fine, it's fine, it is what it is."

"Good. Get your legs properly in Lezzers and I'll slide your door shut shall I."

"Don't slam it too …"

The past has no power over the present moment - Eckhart Tolle

We're all just walking each other home - Ram Dass

Reunited And It Feels So Good

Ange

"There's no baggage left on the pavement Jules, so tally ho, safe in the knowledge there's no carcass left behind. Dirty Gertie Too's got her fair share of glory holes for me to fill with all my goodies, even the secret ones. We can safely leave Sydney behind in our liquid wake, go somewhere special to mark this unique experience, and nobody and nothing is going to dampen that for me."

"Why are you looking at me Ange? I'm not just any old nobody I'll have you know."

"And I'm not just any old nothing. That doesn't sound right, does it Angy?"

"I'm talking to both of you, let nothing get in the way of our celebrations, conviviality followed by comestibles, a melodious and timeless occasion where historic and hysterical, historical fiends rekindle and interwine."

"And laugh till we pee our pants …..if we haven't already done so, that is, at our age it happens at the mere mention of the word toilet. Blimey, there I go again."

"Enough Jules, my pelvic floor almost opened a few stitches, although leakages through peels of laughter is not a problem these days for me as I've had vaginoplasty and bladder augmentation"

"Cliterally the best Ange, and I'm not even taking the piss."

"I've never quite seen the point in a designer vagina, unless of course it's a necessary labiaplasty, you know when the lips can be seen beneath a skirt hem for instance. Oh I am sorry Angy, how insensitive of me. It's not my business you understand, and no judgement, but if that were me, which it's not thankfully, but if it were, I'd also have it done. Just saying."

"How do Australians begin foreplay Laddies?"

"I don't know Jules, how do Australians begin foreplay, maybe by going down on a waterslide without the water?"

"Or how about foreplay being one last chance to decide whether you want to sleep or not, being married all these years will do that to you."

"Brace yourself Sheilas, we're off. That's the answer."

"Bloody hell Jools, all four wheels actually left the tarmac back there, it scared the living daylights out of me, it practically lifted me off my seat, and I was buckled in. What was that loud bang as well, it sounded like a duck being stepped on."

"I heard it this time, Lesley. I thought it was you earlier."

"Me? I thought it was YOU Jools. That noise came from outside though, not inside, perhaps it was one of those speed bump things you get at airports, you certainly took off like every plane I've ever been in."

"Speaking of speed, can you lay your hands on a beautifully, personally stuffed powder blue bear Lezzers, it's in one of the cases?"

"There are a hundred cases back here Angy, not to mention the ones on the roof, and Shirley you can't think I'm going be climbing out there to find some Spade bear."

"Speed Lezzers, not spade, we're here to have fun, to relax, to chillax, get drunk, wasted, and shagged, not to dig a grave for ourselves."

"And, not necessarily in that order either Lesley, we both know Ange doesn't need a spade, her tongue is well equipped to dig her own grave."

"Speak for yourselves anyway, I'm more than happy to be away from the daily grind, Mikey and The Boys for a few days."

"We're all in agreement, there's absolutely no room for any smattering of spiritual talk, not one tiny morsel of enlightening nonsense. Jules? I mean it. The only spirit that I want to cross my lips is going to be the bottle of Louis X111 Cognac I have here as a giftage for our gorgeous chaufloosey, and pigeon passenger."

"She won't be drunk driving Angy. Will you Jools?"

"Before you get your panties in a twist Lezzers, I've seen her drive, so trust me when I tell you, she's a better driver impaired in some form or other. I'm taking my chances, it's far more relaxing if we both join her also, loosening the guy poles of that wigwam and teepee feeling."

"Well, I don't get it and I hope you're both joking, I've waited too long for this reunion to be staying in any tent, let alone someone else's native one, besides I want to remember what I can, when I can, how I can before I forget why. These days there's no guarantee of any of that, so I hope you're joking, besides you don't need alcohol to have fun."

"You don't need running shoes to run, or hair to have hairspray, but it helps. She's joking Lesley, we'll be staying somewhere lovely, somewhere special to mark this unique experience which is already soaring with buoyant banter, fun and frivolity. A timeless occasion."

"Enough Jules. I've been in the country long enough and known you far too long not to see where this conversation is heading. I know what you're doing."

"Qui Mwa? C'est non possible Ange. I have no idea what you're suggesting."

"I bet I know what you're incinerating here, Angy."

"It's insinuating Lezzers, insinuating."

"That's what I said, you must still have blocked flight ears, you were about to imply that she may say, it might be the last time we..blah, blah ...."

"That is entirely your interpretation of what I was about to say, Lezzers, not mine, but since YOU brought it up, it's true, you never know what's round the corner."

"Speaking of corners, Jools, please keep your eyes on the road, I'm a very nervous back seat passenger."

"Are we ready for a celebratory libation? Do the honours Lezzers, you'll find the duty free Champers somewhere. Pour us a drink so we can toast, and drink a cure to end all reunions."

"You won't really be wanting one will you Jools?"

"Put mine in a sippy cup Lesley, which you'll find above the sink. That way if I'm stopped for whatever reason. It's just a sippy cup. Upstairs for thinking, downstairs for dancing, and the middle for a fiddle de dum, fiddle de dee." "Genius Jules. A sippy cup. Don't know why no one, including the police, have thought about that before."

"It's not funny Jools, I hope you're both joking. Drink driving is so politically incorrect, let alone illegal, and I categorically have retired from any ridiculous notion to camp…anywhere… with anyone. I can easily stay somewhere else."

"Dirty Gertie will be free Lezzers, you could always bunk in here."

"My camping days are over, thank you very much, and as they say in your neck of the woods Angy, period. Not that I actually had many.

Camping trips, that is, not periods. Yet, thankfully I don't have them these days, menstruation replaced by menopause, involuntary power surges instead of the dreaded curse, anyhoo, a few nights camping away in someone's back garden, maybe a night or two with The Brownies, less so with the guides, and maybe one with…, too many critters for me, and nowhere to plug my hairdryer, it's not for me, although Mikey and The Boys have camped loads with their cubs, scouts, eagles thing, friends, groups, one thing or another."

"You must have had some lovely, peaceful, alone time to yourself then Lezzers."

"They weren't all away at the same time for your information Angy, besides, do you know how much preparation it takes to go camping BEFORE you actually go camping? And do you think Mikey and The Boys prepare for that? Nope, yours truly does. So, no, I won't be staying anywhere with flaps, thank you very much."

"Won't be with us then, wall to wall "flaps" these days...kidding Lezzers, it's a joke. Come on, loosen up."

"Ignore us Lesley, we're winding you up."

"Och, I know, it wouldn't be a reunion without me being the butt of all the jokes. Easy target and all that, and that is just fine by me, I'm excited to be here with two of my favourite people, here's your drinks, a wee one for you, mind Jools. You're the impregnated driver."

"Designated, Lezzers."

"Don't you start Angy, we both know that's exactly what I said and meant."

"Look out for the roundabouts Jules, according to this map, there's a few coming up just outside of the airport. We don't have them in NYC, so I'm preparing myself now by sculling this fabulous liquid offering, thank you Lezzers, so as not to spill a single drop later. At this rate though, I'll be terminal before we get out of the Terminal."

"Not the first or the last time I'm quite sure. Drinking without hearing the word liberation Ange? Changing the rules to suit yourself."

"Not at all Jules, I know you, better than you think, you manipulate the conversation, easily guiding the unsuspecting listening victim into your dull snares and promises of fucking liberation. I am too long in the perfect American cosmetic tooth department not to read you like a very,

very well worn book. All I'm doing is accruing fizz credit in advance of the inevitable."

"Fairy snuff Ange, and if it's a drinking game you want, then it's a drinking game you're going to get. I'll see your eye rolling and raise you my gobbledygook, let's see who gets rat arsed first shall we? Be prepared to drive shortly Lesley. Let's drink to that, cheers Laddies, and in the words of Rabbie Burns: "Here's to us, fa's as guid as us? Damn few, and they're all dead. Here's to the heath, the hills and the heather, the bonnet, the kilt, the plaid and the feather.."

"Here's to the heroes that Scotland may boast; may their names never die" That's the Highland man's toast, and they're all tattered, dead and buried with Lezzers's spade. Speaking of tattered Jules, what's with the blouse you're wearing? Looks like it's experienced night sweats, day sweats, urine sweats, wine sweats, drug sweats, caffeine sweats, even patchouli sweats."

"You're not wrong there Ange, the menopause is no fecking joke."

"She's not wrong there Angy, I try to eat something healthy. I've really tried that, but along comes Thanksgiving, Anzac day, Christmas, Boxing Day, Valentine, summer, Friday, or Tuesday and ruins it all for me. There are days that I feel like I can't catch a breath, and that I'm being wakeboarded."

"Waterboarding Lezzers."

"That's what I said Angy, besides they're similar, much and much the same thing, you know what I meant. The menopause is still no joke."

"I'm way too young for all that bullshit, Lezzers. I'll pause and just have the men please."

"I'll take the "pause" and have a cheese board please instead of the left over, discarded men thank you very much."

"I'd have a charred cuts board also Jools, speaking of cuts, what do they do with all the leftover bits that have been cut and removed from your face and body Angy? Do they recycle? Lovely luggage by the way."

"What? Ah, I hear what you're saying, Lezzers. Trying to be funny are we. Where do you think I got my matching leather cases from? And all this time here's me thinking it was crocodile hide, but now you mention it, I can see the 'freckles' "

"I knew it, it's a great way to recycle Angy, a bit disgusting, but good on you, and to think you have a problem with my wee cowhide bag."

"I know this may all seem plausible to your gullible mind Lezzers, but my matching baggage set is not made from mine or anyone else's discarded skin folds, other than Wally Gator's that is."

"Let's not rehash any of this Angy, you know what I meant, you're wasting your breath being so attached to correcting me, it's like water off a bucks back."

"Tch, you're mistaking me for someone else here, Lezzers, I have never really been particularly "attached" to anything you're saying."

"What is it you call someone who seems angry all the time Jools, I'd hate to get it wrong only to have MS Judgy, wudgy, fudgy pants here jump on me."

"A heliacal lemon."

"Me Lezzers? Bitter and twisted? Maybe in a dry martini, but it seems this is more like your horseshit, than mine. You're the one that's settled for a nice, comfy life, with a lovely, but let's face it, somewhat boring man, and four galloots of mankids, which admittedly must drive you absolutely fucking nuts to be surrounded by all that testosterone, sweat, 'hard' socks, unpredictability and moodiness. Besides, it takes one to know one right?"

"This is beginning to feel like I'm a voyeur on a second date, or an episode of the Germy Kill show at the very least, so stop squabbling the pair of you, honestly it's like sharing a confined space with siblings. In fact, it almost is! Blood sisters! Bite bitches! Chicks Mix!"

"YES, we are. That's it, we're more alike than you'd care to admit, Angy. That's why we're always bickering. You can pretend all you like, that we're not related, but deep down, you know we are."

"Only through a blood transfusion Lezzers, not sure how that holds up legally."

"But it's your blood coursing through my body, you risked your life, to save mine, if it wasn't for you, I wouldn't be here today. There'd be no Mikey, no Boys. You are a real gift to me whether you like it or not, never forget that. I owe you so much more than just one thing."

"Anyone would have done the same in my situation, Lezzers, but thank you, and if I ever need a debt repaid, I'll click my Jimmy Choo heels, and you can be with me faster than a speeding pullet."

"Bless you Angy, hopefully you won't need those Chimney Shoe heels anytime soon."

"And, poof, you can appear in a huff of smoke and save my life. How about that Lezzers? Date?"

"You know, I've never really been on a date. Like a real, live date, you know with an actual real live man, other than Mikey that is."

"What exactly do you mean Lezzers?"

"Mikey is my first, my one and only, anyhoo, enough of me."

"Only ever one Lezzers? It gets dull and terribly monotonous for me after a week or two, can't even begin to imagine the years of sexual purgatory with only one man, especially if you haven't 'trained' them adequately."

"I keep him very happy in bed thank you very much I'll have you know Angy, no complaints in that department."

"Oh, you mistake me here Lezzers, I wasn't talking about keeping him happy, I was talking about you being satisfied, hence why foreplay was invented by women, slow those stallions down a bit."

"Why are you huffing and puffing like the big bad wolf all of a sudden Lesley? You'll hyperventilate, and bring on one of your panic attacks if you're not careful, you do know she doesn't mean any of this codswallop."

"I do Jools, thank you."

"And you? Ange? Stop winding her up, and you, Lesley, stop letting her get to you and vice versa. It's like sharing a confined space with a pair of cridults."

"Cridults Jules? That's a new one on me."

"Critical adults who behave like petulant children. How do you get to this age without learning how to manage, handle and accept tricky friendships."

"Every little "tricky" thing I do is magic Jules. There's a witch in all of us, speaking of creepy, why are you wearing rubber gloves Lezzers?

They might help you keep those stickier situations clean, especially if Jules here is involved."

"They're my marigolds, Angy. I brought some with me..you know ....in case.."

"Incase of what exactly Lesley?"

"I thought I might clean DGT up a wee bit, you know a spot of dusting, tidying, cleaning, scrubbing, maybe organising a few cupboards....bleach. Give DGT a spa treatment, she's been neglected you know Jools. You carry on driving, and chatting, I'll find my van legs, and get to work. All those Pilates classes have helped stabilise my core."

"I know how you feel Lezzers, sitting here, moving rhythmically and N sync with the kangaroo jumps and varying speeds is helping my core no end also. I've been flying for days so when you're finished cleaning Dirty Gertie, be a deer and rub my shoulders will you. I have some Costa Brazil massage oil in my beauty bag under your seat."

"I don't even know what that is, but it sounds expensive, so never mind her shoulders Lesley, pour it directly into a crystal flute, then pour it down my parched throat, and if Gertie gets thirsty we can use the oil in her tank."

"It's a miracle oil Jules, and can put life back into most anything, anything I say, I've seen with my own eyes how this oil can bring the rustiest of 'vessels' back to life. Please feel free to try some, not that either of you need it, you seem alert on your own merits, no need for the extra. It costs me an arm, a leg and the contents of a freshly squeezed weasel's anal gland to get me to look this good. What do you use for your wrinkles Jules, on the back of your hands that is?"

"Snail serum and a bucket load of laughter. Each wrinkle is a deeply etched, entrenched, creased tattoo that has a story line running along the full length of the fine stripe, besides laughing doesn't cost me hardly anything."

"Something must have been fucking hysterical then Jules."

"How do you even collect snail seamen Jools? I can't believe you wear any sperm on your hands, let alone your face. Who has that job I wonder? How do they extract it?"

"Anyone that has a pair of bright pink rubber marigolds and 20/20 vision Lesley can have the job, you'll find the snail farm under the sink. Better have at it Lesley, give it a shotty, I'm beginning to feel a tad dry down under. Speaking of Down Under, can you believe it's been almost 30 years since we first arrived here? Who'd have thought, decades of shits, giggles, frolics, nonsense and laughter have taken us this far on its bountiful conveyer belt. We were so young, very young, innocent, although we didn't think it, we really were naive, bushy tailed, wide legged and usually legless."

"Speak for yourself Jools, remember I had Mikey."

"How could we forget, since you keep reminding us besides, he was 35,00 miles away. That was your chance, Lezzers."

"We all have to consume life's bitter and sweet morsels, accepting the choices we make from the good, the bad, the sad, ugly and indifferent squalls Laddies, the only things we should regret are the opportunities and risks we didn't take."

"Touchey Jools."

"It's Touche, Lezzers, touche."

"That's what I said, and you know it. I wouldn't change a thing, not one thing, I am who I am today because of all those moments, those choices. Like it or lump it, I couldn't and wouldn't change a thing even if I could. Would you Angy? Is there anything you'd change?"

"Maybe, maybe not, not sure about that one Lezzers, maybe the choices we make in this precise moment will be reflected in the form of future regrets. Not too late I suppose to begin my dream job of a karma delivery driver, how fun would that be?"

"We all arrived on this beautiful land all those years ago and boy did we grab it in both hands."

"Grabbed all the boys in both hands for sure Jules."

"Like I said Angy, not me, I didn't. I had Mikey."

"I can't say I regret anything Laddies, as every little thing I did and said, or not, was all part of my experiences, stuff it, it was my reality, and when I learned to accept all the feelings of guilt, shame, doubt, judgement for mainly myself, but others also, my life became easier. All of us are wearing our own invisible straight jackets, until by the grace of events, we can finally begin to un notch ourselves from the restraints, the contorted, squirmy feelings and their triggers. Age can be so liberating wouldn't you both agree? Apologies Ange, have another swig. If more people carried less judgement for themselves or others, then they'd learn to meet in that invisible, still, open, clear void that exists between all of us. If there's no anger carried, then nobody or nothing can anger us, shame etc, nope we can't be shamed, cos we're not carrying any, don't try anyone else's inadequacies on for size. You get the picture. Over the years, you have been my best teacher Ange, causing the most self reflection, I can't put my arthritic finger on it, but you bring out that mischievous, mad, bad and dangerous to know, rascal side in me. Sometimes when I'm with you, I think screw it all, I'm going to pack it all in and be a stripper. Then I remember I'm fat and can't dance."

"I feel quite hormonious today, like I'm on someone else's period. What do I bring out in both of you? There's naughtiness in everyone, Jools, my Robbie, for instance..."

"Are you saying it's my MY fault Jules? All those shenanigans and hedonistic highs, and lows were all my fault. Girrrrl, that halo has already slipped to your cankles."

"Fault? Hell no Ange, I absolutely love it when we get together, every miserable, fantastic, mischievous feckin moment of it. There are challenges that only come with age and pals for sure, some people can't shake their past, and the body keeps the score. Believe me the toxic barbs from our outer and inner realms can penetrate a heart, spreading vitriol, shame, shattering visions, dreams and goals. For instance, when I drink these days, I lose things like my bra, glasses, any sense of modesty and dignity and control of my bladder. When you're right brain, you see a fish, left brain a mermaid."

"What if I see neither Jules and I want to tear all that claptrap of yours into tiny pieces and force feed them back to you."

"Then you've bypassed peri, and gone straight to full blown menopausal Ange, but don't sweat, there are pills for that."

"Blah, blah, blah, yada, yada, yada, another libation please Lezzers. You were warned Jules. At this rate I'm going to be delightfully bladdered in record time. Don't be taken in by all this bullshit Lezzers, I love you too much to see you dragged into her warren full of gobbledygook dust bunnies. Speaking of dust bunnies, can you remove your humming carcass of a bag further away from me, somewhere we can't smell its putrid contents, the roof rack perhaps."

"It's not my bag that smells Angy…it's…it's…it's coming from one of YOUR dead leather remains you refer to as "baggage" actually."

"I highly doubt that my bags smell of rotten cheese… oh fuck wait… I brought some Pule cheese with me."

"PULL it out Lesley, and chuck it out the window will you Darl, a gift for the fur critters of the world, and relief for my singed nostril hairs. Anyone else have the same problem? My nostril hair is getting darker, thicker and blacker than a koala's pubes."

"Noooo, don't throw it out Lezzers, it's the most expensive cheese in the world because it's produced exclusively at Serbia's Zasavica Special Nature Reserve. It's made from the milk of an endangered Balkan donkey native to Serbia and Montenegro."

"That's why it smells so bad in here Laddies, it's been removed from an ass, not just any old ass either, an endangered donkey's ass no less. Hope it doesn't taste like it though. Cos it sure as hell smells like it? Not that I'd personally know, however, there have been times."

"If you say so Jules, let's find out shall we? Lezzers, would you be kind enough to do the honors again, she's driving and I'm navigating. The crackers are in the leather hamper."

"Lesley? You'll find some silverware and crockery in the cupboards below the sink with the snails."

"She's pulling your tiny leg Lezzers, everything you need is also in the hamper, exquisitely lined in green leather, hand stitched by the leather master whose hand skills are much sought after the world over. The one and only leatherman, Matthew Christian Payne, the leather meister to the world, and an absolute suede heart."

"I'm more surprised to hear that there's a sink somewhere in this van, than I am a snail farm. Is snail sperm really any better than any other kind? Probably made of the same consistency. It's difficult to see under the sink for the bushy, lush, green, aromatic flowering plant Jools."

"Mmmmm, that's like perfume to my nostrils, just the right amount of pungent terpenes; floral, earthy, fruity amounts all rolled into one fabulous olfactory delight. You don't like Lezzers?"

"I don't mind the smell too much if that's what you're asking Angy, you being in the whoreticultural industry you must be used to the aroma."

"You've devoted your best years preparing your Mikey and the rugrats for all of life's eventualities Lezzers; work, school, cubs, scouts, sports events and wet dreams, so you must be used to far worse stenches than a flowering plant from the family CannaBaceae."

"If that's your way of saying you love me, I'll take it."

"I wouldn't go quite that far, Lezzers, I just hate everyone else."

"Does that make you more of a dog or a cat person Angy."

"All I know for sure, Lezzers, is I'm not much of a people person."

I am not what happened to me, I am what I choose to become - C.G Jung

You can have a friend, one single friend, whose support is so fierce, so fabulously fierce, that you feel like there is an army behind you. Likewise, you can have many other friends, whose allegiance you are not entirely sure of. You can meet a new friend tomorrow who rocks into your life, rolls up and says, 'I am here for you.' And they actually truly are. Yet you have friends that you've known and loved for years who can't show up even for the best of times, never mind the worst. If you're really lucky you can have a few of the former, but one is all you really need. Friendship is not a numbers game, it's a game of instincts, trust yours - Donna Ashworth

Friendship Isn't A Numbers Game

Lesley

Was that meant to be funny? Was it a putdown? You never quite know with her, she's full of all those double entrees, those things that can be taken so many other ways. Honestly, the poor bag handler didn't know whether he was coming or going, and Angy kept referring to him as her "support worker". The cheek, he was the one that looked like he needed the support with all that leather weight lifting onto Dirty Gertie Two's roof rack he was doing. He really struggled to not only lift her cases but to find any space anywhere inside or on the outside of this tin can that they'd fit. I tossed a couple of rubbish bags out when we stopped, I mean, let's face it, no one will ever notice. Who needs 50 hair pieces, cigarette holders, and fans? No one, that's who! Well maybe the fans, we need those these days, glad I kept them. I'm sure Jools was taking them all to the dump anyway, I only helped her by lightening the load somewhat. What on earth can be in all these designer bags Angy has I wonder? Her life's possessions? Money? Maybe she carries cash everywhere. Shirley she can't have much more than this back in NYC? There's only one of her after all, unlike me, I have Mikey, The Boys, a fully furnished house, garage, shed, AND a storage unit. Stuff!! Too much stuff. Who am I trying to kid, though, she lives in a henhouse suite in New York probably filled with all sorts of lovely, lovely goodies, and luxurious expensive nick-nacks. Would I trade it for what I have? In a resting heartbeat. Joke, honestly though, not for all the coffee in China. Sounds terribly glamorous, but looks can be deceiving, and I bet she's lonely, and she's got a face on her like a well-slapped farmer's arse, excuse my language, but she does. She sure doesn't look happy, she's hardly cracked a smile since we pulled up, perhaps that's her resting, set face. Now I'm being unkind. My mum, bless her cotton socks, always used to say, "If you can't say anything nice, don't say anything at all." I'm not saying anything too unkind, just stating the truth and the obvious facts. I think she's maybe gone overboard in the cosmetic department and they've used cement as a filler.

"This is going to be so very different from 30, cough, cough years ago. Absolutely no more backpacking, slumming it, OR CAMPING for me these days. Me, Mikey and The Boys like to stay somewhere nice, clean sheets, breakfast buffet included and all that, a treat for me, but the usual kind of treatment the boys have come to know, love and want."

"I enjoy connecting with the people of this amazing, incredible land, that for me it's what permeates the greatest part of life. I love to engage with locals before sightseeing and exploring."

"I bet you bloody well do Jules, I also like the close encounters with a local or three."

"You get to meet the most diverse, fascinating people from all across the globe. Love goes beyond language. Some people don't even speak the same language we take for granted, no verbal means of communication whatsoever between us, but we cook together, eat together, exchange gifts."
"Bodily fluids Jules."

"Speak for yourself Angy, I don't and won't be exchanging anything, fluids or otherwise."

"Oh I was Lezzers, I was."

"And laugh, laugh so hard that the tears cascade down our inner thighs. Mind you, that's also not too hard these days, a cough, sneeze, giggle, a curb, an image of a toilet with the seat lid down, and/or the up can open that valve faster than a greased pig in a barbecue joint. One of the greatest presents one can give to another human being is their presence, an unwavering, genuine interest in someone or something else, regardless of language, religion, gender or nationality, besides, pure unadulterated, unwavering attention is so gawd darn sexy."

"I genuinely can't be assed getting to know, or feigning any interest in anyone new. The Four Seasons gives you that perfect anonymity. Noone bothers you, but please don't let me stop you. You connect all you like with the natives Jules, you'll find Lezzers, myself, a cabana, a drink or three n hand, somewhere deep in the bush."

"Now we're talking Angy, that's my type of tent?"

"How are the cocktails and hors d'oeuvres coming along Lezzers?"

"Horses d'oeuvres and a Screaming Orgasm coming up Angy."

"Bring it on. Been at least 10 hours since I had one of those."

"Och Angy, we all know you were on a plane 10 hours ago, and I'm sure they don't serve screaming orgasms."

"A mile high they do Lezzers."

"No!! You don't mean? Really? At your age? Who? WHY? I couldn't, oh I wouldn't. How? There's not enough room in those toilets for starters. You're yanking my chain, aren't you Angy?"

"Something was being yanked by the yank for sure Lesley. I'd be happy enough to rough it, an intense experience can teach profound spiritual lessons that can change us for the better you know."

"Do you know that's why I call her the exorcist Lezzers? Because she never leaves a party till all the spirits are gone, I see no point living as a nomad at any time of the day or night Jules, let alone on this particular, momentous, special occasion, but don't let us stop you, you fill your unkempt, gypsy Uggs."

"Trying it out once in a while might bring all of us to a deeper realisation about our lives and ourselves Ange, and don't think I haven't missed your eye rolling, they're going at it full pelt, like a Catherine wheel on speed. You owe me an entire round of drinks for that lot of eye rolling."

"Super, you fill your hobo heels with all that hippy tribe bullshit Jules, while I fill myself to the brim with the only spiritual lessons I genuinely need, which are coming in the form of Lezzer's Screaming Orgasms. Erase that last sentence, unless it's an image you want imprinted in your memory forever. I'll assume you found the Oval Swarovski Crystal vodka Lezzers."

It's not too bad in the back really, it's more like a doll's house than the back of a Volkswagen Kombi van, and I'm fine with that. I'm sure if I told her I got car sick, then she'd trade places, or Jools would make her. I can almost hear what they're saying, but these tiny mites in my ears bother me at times, and with all the other sounds going on, it's hard to decipher much of what they're saying. Better not really be mites in my ears. Can you imagine tiny mites in your ears, whistling in your drums? When I first started getting the ringing in my ears and they told me that's what I had, I didn't dare ask because what if there really were wee bugs making all that racket in my ear holes? It can be challenging at times, I won't lie, but no one needs to know, everyone is dealing with their own affairs. I guess that's why I like to twitter so much, makes me look more of a fool- or is it less of a fool- than having to ask someone to constantly repeat what they're saying. It gets embarrassing. No mind. It's rude not to listen properly, so I prefer to talk, takes the burden of asking someone to repeat themselves a hundred times, must be frustrating for them though, as I'm the one who can't hear, it's mortifying, that's what it is, or worse, I end up misinterpreting what's actually been said, or interrupting them because I can't hear they've not finished talking. It's definitely getting worse the older I get, or maybe I notice my faults more, or perhaps I'm more auditory selective than I used to be, just as well I'm a tough old bird. The back of DGT is bursting at the seams with jumbo, black plastic bags full to the brim with God only knows what. Jools must have been on her way to drop off some of this landfill tat before picking me up, but got unusually distracted, on her way there. NOT! What a lass. You know what though, I don't even care, I have waited months for this special occasion. It sometimes feels that I haven't had the chance to take a breath for decades, four boys, a husband, a job, a dog, a granny pig, a hamster, and three dead goldfish. Thankfully no partridge in a pair of trees. Yet. Don't speak too soon Lesley, when the cat's away and all that, who knows how many more animals are going to be added to the menage a trois while your back is turned? Running a home is categorically not easy. Fact. Over the years I have devoted years of my own blood, sweat, tears, advice, and acts of kindness for others, and these few days away with my old muckers are just what the doctor ordered. Mikey used to think I was a nymphomaniac, and couldn't get enough of me. These days, I'm more of a maniac and there are days I can't see him far enough. Boy, do I need this break.

"Cocktails are on their way, here you are Angy, Jools, a wee one for you."

"RIGHT. GO RIGHT Jules. RIGHT. GO RIGHT."

"Right it is Ange. Feck, did you see that? That car was heading straight for us, he missed us by a mosquito baw hair, but more importantly I didn't spill a drop from my sippy cup, my thighs are clasped round it, tighter than a camel's sphincter in a sandstorm, not one drop spilled, what a pro. Blimey, there's more cars heading for us. AGGAH What are they doing? Why are they driving towards us?"

"Don't panic Jools but I think we're on a roundabout, Angy said right, so you went right, right round a roundabout that is…the wrong way."

"To be fair Lezzers, it was an easy mistake, you can hardly tell it's a roundabout, the centre looks more like a forest, and we drive on the right in the good ole U S of A, so was momentarily confused, besides we hardly have any roundabouts as nobody knows how to use them properly."

"Look Laddies, if I take the next right, we should be back on the left, if that makes any sense. Thankfully no harm done eh. Everyone survive?"

"Well done Jules, nice manoeuvre there, handled like the pro you are, let's drink to that. Cheers Chumlettes."

"Slainte Laddies."

"I'm really sorry Angy, that sharp right took me by surprise, knocked me off my feet and some of your vitamins, medicine, drugs and tic tacs seem to have fallen out of one of your open bags."

"Firstly Lezzers, why was the bag open, having a nosey eh? Look, it's not a big deal, you're a nurse so put them back in their vials, before you do that though, can you pass me a sponge to clean the cocktail splash stain on my silk pantsuit, the very suit that makes most red hot blooded men pant. Pour some perrier on it first, that'll remove the tiny mark."

"Sure, here you go, your loyal wryness, but you're forgetting something, I'm not a nurse these days, my vial days are over, besides they're all muddled up together, the labels on the bottles are blurred slightly, so I can't read them, so I have no idea what goes where."

"Do you need my readers Lesley, they're a tad grubby and vile, but they do the trick. Here you go."

"Princess Fiona, Shrek and the wee ass, I hope these aren't readers, Jools, they're more like binoculars, I'm having a close encounter with the scars behind Angy's ear. I'll take my chances without them, thanks."

"Cheeky mare. Do you need them Ange? Readers, that is, not binoculars, you might find map reading easier if you're wearing something to optimise your vision."

"How very dare you Jules. Readers go hand in hand with getting older, and as you both know, that's not happening. I only choose glasses for their fabulous shapes, sizes, colors and styles, sounds like my men as well, insinuation otherwise is quite frankly insulting, and hurts me to my rotten core."

"Sorry to interrupt Angy, but how are you going to know what you're putting in your mouth if you can't read the labels?"

"Isn't that half the fun and excitement about putting something you're unsure of in your mouth Lezzers?"

"It's the anticipation of not knowing what's about to come Lesley, that's what it is."

"Makes sense I guess, but I'm far too controlling for that. I want to know exactly what I'm putting in my mouth, let alone in each vial. What if little hands were to get hold of these prescription drugs Angy."

"The only "prescription" that has been alluded to here Lezzers is the ones of the reading variety, and not the pharmaceutical type, those little "tic tacs" you have in your hands, pack a fair punch. Am I right or am I wrang Jules?"

"You're a doughnut, and I'm the meringue as always Ange, look, we're both mum's Lesley, so I'm quite sure that skill set comes with a very unique toolkit of thinking out of the box for putting them back in a box."

"You're so right Jools, let's think. Got it. Shape, size and colour code them, but if they're all tic tacs, does it matter? You always seem to get the best, most different sweeties, or candies as you call them in the states. I mean who came up with the idea of punch flavoured tic tacs. Genius. Bet they've made a fortune. Yuch, they're covered in hair from the floor well, hopefully from the hair pieces."

"They're working on the Margie Rita flavoured one, and the Screaming Orgasm tic tac as I drive Lesley."

"Shhhaaape, size, and color code them? For Fuck sake Lezzers, put them all back in the bottles will you, I'll sort it out later, call it a memory test if you like, but be a tootie patootie and brush off the pubes from the floor mats before you put them all back."

"What colour are they Lesley? Aye the hairs, not the tic tacs."

"It's not pubic hair if that's what you're asking Jools, too long, shiny, and dark."

"Phew, I was afraid they were mine; sparse, hardy, grey, dehydrated pubic bush fayre. Thank the Lard. Tell me Lesley why do you think I have all those merkins in the back."

"Bloody Nora, merkins? I thought they were hairpieces as in for your head Jools. I didn't realise they were for your pubic bald patch. Look, I'm an ask no questions, tell no lies gal, so I for one do not need to know any more, not my circus, not my merkins and all that, besides I've seen and done worse on the wards, you forget how funny hospitals can be, as well as sad, anyhoo, thankfully I still have my rubber gloves on. Can't wait to tell Mikey, he told me I wouldn't need them, but here we are not even 2 hours into our journey and I'm wearing them already. Can I be so rude as to ask why you had, oops I mean have so many merkins in the first place?"

"Glad you were wearing your marigolds when you touched them or didn't try one on Lesley, as I was taking them to the laundry after they were used by the entire cast in our recent pantomime, Babes in the Nude."

"Make sure there isn't one shiny or otherwise, single strand of anything that even remotely resembles anything pubic or otherwise anywhere near the tic tacs please Lezzers, I don't want my night's entertainment to be a game of Hairy Pharmaceutical Russian roulette, only without the Russian or the roulette, only the hair left to play with."

"Who are you trying to kid Ange, you're going to swallow, crush or snort them anyway which way, with or without a few pubic hairs, no harm done, look at me, I've ingested worse and I'm fighting fit, only a slight twitch in the left eye, the occasional limp…oh and I sweat and swear more than the average sailor, think of them as organic dental flossers."

"Since you put it like that, pass me a couple of the yellow and orange oblong shaped ones will you, take whatever you fancy first Lezzers."

"Those sound like the tequila sunrise flavoured ones, I'm driving, so I'll take a couple of the ones that look more like a regular, bog standard, un-tampered tic tac of some kind or other please Lesley."

"For all intensive porpoises girls, it's neither funny or clever to be your own farmerist. When it comes to real drugs, that should be left to the professionals to decide the quantities and combinations. It's irresponsible to just guess which one you fancy."

"I can only speak for myself here, Lezzers, so you don't have to worry your fluffy head any further over this, and believe me, I have been a professional drug guzzler for decades. Eyes on the road Jules, eyes forward. Where was I? Ah yes, after years and years of practice, I have the perfect, personally picked, chemically balanced psilocybin, hallucinogenic recipes known to man."

"They're already knocking me chemically off balance, the trees appear to be swimming, the road has melted and my hands are distorted. That's some wicked shit you have there Ange."

"You haven't taken any of the tic tacs yet Jules, Watch for the potootholle……..too late. Careful Jules, waaatccchhh, another...too late…again."

"It's my glasses. They must be dirty, can you take them off and clean them Ange."

"Hate to be the bearer of bad news Jules and tell you this dolly, but you're not wearing any."

"Where are my glasses? I'm sure I was wearing them."

"They're there in the folds of your…pantaloons? Bloomers? Harems? Whatever that kinda two legged tribal hammock you have wrapped around your waist is. Keep your hands on the wheel, and your eyes on the road, I'll get them for you. Almost got them. Help me out here Jules, unless you're enjoying me rummaging around in your folds, that is, move a bit to your left. There you go."

"Thank you Ange, I usually find I'm wearing them on my head. Aggh, that's worse, I can't see a bloody thing. These are my readers, where are my driving glasses?"

"Here put these on Jules."

"Thanks Ange, now, I don't want to alarm anyone here, but we have good news and there's bad news."

"We're going to hire a driver. Is the good news, the bad, he's not here yet?"

"Close but no sea ghar Ange."

"I don't have the patience or desire for this game Jules. I give up, just tell us."

"The good news is we appear to be holding course, no sharp bends, curvy corners, seems lovely and straight, just like us …most of the time."

"Seems Jules?"

"Yes, indeedy, the bad news is, I think my eyeballs were dislodged during the circus demonstration back there. My balance has been knocked off kilter. I can't see shit, it's a complete blackout."

"You have my prescription shades on Jools? You gave her my glasses Angy, take them off immediately, quickly, you'll get astigma wearing someone else's prescription. Please tell me you've got your chauffeur on speed dial Angy."

"I actually do Lezzers, but he's taking a much needed break in Costa Rica right about now."

"Look at that will you Laddies, they were round my neck all the time."

"I was joking, Angy, I don't really believe you have a chauffeur. Do You?"

"I have many, many appointments Lezzers, so I need someone to drive me to places, only chauffeurs and taxi drivers actually drive in NYC."

"I can see clearly now, thank you. I have glasses for every occasion; driving, telly, reading labels, rolling joints, plucking rogue hairs from their tight wee feckin burrows, even with the sharpest of tweezers, they can still escape me! But, these ones I'm wearing are my driving glasses, or not, but they work, everything looks sharp. For a moment I had a flashback to being back on the dodgems, and I was one of those kids who dodged the bumps of the other dodgems."

"I was always the one bumping Jules. Full on and as hard as I could. Nothing quite like a night of dodgems."

"I never really went on them, never quite saw the point really, I saw my fair share of whiplash in A & E. I liked the big Wheel though."

"Now that takes me back, nothing wrong with a few lashes of the whip now and again eh Lezzers."

"Loved the dodgems, haven't been on one in years, let's do that again sometime Laddies."

"I think we just did Jules."

"They don't have the same appeal as they did when I was a kid, I remember taking Sam to the fairground when he was 4 or 5, and the dodgems had shrunk, I could barely get my lardy arse alongside his skinny, tiny wee bottom. I had to let him drive as there was no room for the steering wheel in front of my enormous tits, that's for sure. He loved it though, especially the bumping. My neck however, not so much, cost me a fortune at the chiropractors. We were lucky back there though, there could have been much more damage done to this rusty, old, trusty old steed of mine, she'd fall to pieces, literally if she even got a whiff of a collision up her exhaust pipe."

"Can't believe you've still got this rusty, not so trusty, old banger of a tin can Jules."

"Old banger? Rusty, old tin can you say? Still going strong, she's perfect, I'll have you know Ange. Looked after me just fine. She looks after me better than I look after myself, if my body was a car, I would be trading it in for a newer, sleeker, shinier, younger model. My framework has an equal amount of bumps, dents, scratches, bruises and bashes, and my headlights are almost totally out of focus, my gearbox is seizing up, and it takes me hours to reach maximum speed. I regularly overheat for no apparent reason whatsoever and everytime I sneeze, cough, walk, hop, skip, jump or laugh, either my radiator leaks and/or my exhaust backfires. She has however escaped the delights of the menopause. This shit is real Laddies, I can tell you."

"I knew it was you backfiring Jools. Mikey and The Boys have put together a menopause jar in the kitchen which anyone can financially contribute towards if they've been in the near vicinity when I lose the plot, witnessing first hand that I need some time out. How do you think I'm paying for this trip? And that's only this week's takings."

"That's a great idea Lesley. Menopause Incentive Narcotic Jars: Minj for short. You're not alone I can tell you, financial contributions from others may well help relieve some of the symptoms. We could always start a menopause buskers movement, we'd make a fortune, the streets would be littered with menopausal maniacs shaking their tin cans. The Crap Band."

"My jar would be empty, there's no way I'm turning into a grumpy, dumpy, frumpy, old wifie like you two. I won't allow it, I have money to avoid such stuff."

"What do you mean turning Ange? It's heading your way, like it or not, it's coming because the alternative is even less appealing, believe me, quite literally breathtaking."

"If I ever get to the menopause stage, I'll drink myself into oblivion and sail through it."

"Isn't that what you already do, Ange? You could be through the other side from it all for all you know."

"Rest assured Jules, I'm not coming off any medications, or even cutting back slightly on alcohol so we can test your theory out. You never know what you're going to get, could be even worse than mad, bad and dangerous to know. I'm definitely not going to let myself stoop to these lower levels of acceptability. Unlike some of us. Just saying."

"Why do you always end your sentences with" Just saying" Angy?"

"Because dipshit is considered offensive in certain circles Lezzers."

"Do you mean me Angy? Is that what you're really saying? I wouldn't say I was frumpy, dumpy, yes, maybe slightly grumpy, and definitely old. You are talking about me aren't you?"

"Actually Lezzers, on this one occasion it wasn't about you, I was referring to my hammock wearing, Hamsa clad, hippy fiend of mine driving beside me here, or was I. I'm more like one of those classic sirens who grow gracefully like a fine wine."

"I'm more like aged milk these days, sour, lumpy and somewhat putrid smelling."

"I'll knock them in Jules, you hit them over."

If every single person who has liked you in your lifetime, were to light up on a map, it would create the most glittering beautiful network you could imagine. Throw in the strangers you've been kind to, the people you've made laugh, or inspired along the way and that star- bright network of you would be an impressive sight to behold. You're so much more than you think you are. You have done so much more than you realise. You're trailing a bright pathway that you don't even know about. What a ting. What a thing indeed.

Donna Ashworth

When You Have Crazy Friends, You Have Everything You Need

Lesley

How does she manage it? I went from excited to nervous to frustrated to anger in a nano, nano of a second. Now I feel like a right old, dumpy, frumpy, overweight, vanilla, decidedly grumpy suburban housewife. I know she didn't actually say it, but I can tell by the way her eyes move that's what she meant. Why am I crying? Stop it right now Lesley! Pull yourself together! Before she sees you. They've not noticed. I can't seem to say anything right, I end up looking like a silly school girl who knows nothing about overpriced, designer products or anything else other than everything related to health and education, I could talk forever on those matters. Mark my words, they sell the same stuff in Tar Jay, at a fraction of the price she probably pays for her stuff, I wonder if she has a personal stylist, that would be nice, ooo, or a chef, yes, that's what I'd like, it would make mealtimes so much more pleasant for everyone concerned. Her designer clothes are probably made in the same countries as mine, the same sweatshops, same ingredients, same 2-year-old fingers. Same. Different pretentious prices, that's all. I'm not sure she really listens to me or finds our friendship interesting or of any value. Shirley after all these years, she can accept me for the way I am, warts and all. It's not as if I'm asking anything of her either, just an indication that she knows I'm here and ready to be heard. Is that too much to ask for these days? I have enough of this selective ignoring at home and came away to get some reprise from it all. My validated points are being totally undervalued, even the funny ones, poof, dismissed by a verbal snap of contempt, reflecting the angry film of disgust and sarcasm stretched from ear to ear. I think they're her ears, maybe not. That's why she can't hear me properly, they might not be hers, given by some donor or other. Like I said, not my circus, not my merkins. I'm not going to get dragged into the mire of her dramas, I refuse to play her games, she is not going to suck me into her spectacles. She does look amazing, credit where credit's due, she looks superb in a very nipped, tucked, and plastic way, better and younger from a distance though, but amazing nonetheless. Although I can tell it's her, she looks shinier, tauter, thinner, more fake than I ever remember, and she still looks her 50-plus years, mutton dressed as mutton as my mother used to say. Listen to me? How horrible do I sound? Even if I didn't say it out loud, it's not nice to even think unkind thoughts, they cancel each other out and vice versa. She seems happy enough under that gruff exterior, I think, hard to tell. That's what I personally don't get, you have all these nips, tucks, sucks, trims, and seals for why? To make you look younger? I hate to be the bearer of bad news, but it doesn't work. I'm being serious here, it doesn't work, full stop. I'm a nurse and I know these things, your body is intended to age, it just is, you can't prevent it, and there's only one way to avoid any potential suffering that comes along with it, but it'll literally take your breath away. There are plenty of people 6ft under who'd trade places with me and my vanilla kneeples in a heartbeat. I'm happy with my lot, thankful for my Gspot that I get the chance to have droopy eyelids, boobs, a thinning smile, dry lips, arm sails, and flatulence. Not everyone gets to wear the naked gift of age, wearing the leftovers from emotional burdens as a hulking cumbersome cloak instead. The body keeps tally, some of us have heavier robes than others, but there's often extra emotional cargo in most of us. It's like we keep an emotional doggy bag from every circumstance we go through, and we always go back for seconds. What do you think would happen if only one woman, only one, told her truth? Her full, honest, authentic, brutal truth? Bearing her heart, story, and true essence for all to see. The whole world would rise to their feet and applause, that's what. Every single woman out there would get a standing ovulation, that's what. Eventually, with time, the weight of all life's events slips from our shoulders, like a slow-moving glacier, lightning the load somewhat, not physically in my case unfortunately, exchanging the heaviness for helium, lightening the load completely. I've stopped beating myself up about that one, I enjoy my food too much, every last, chocolatey, crispy, savoury morsel. Not all in one mouthful you understand, that would be plain greedy. There is a catch to shrugging the cloak off as we get older, our once shiny, vibrant, glossy, highly sought-after hair is exchanged for a frizzy, springy, peppered flaccid thatch. Drives me mad, costs a fortune to keep up with the root touch-ups and streaks. My hair's not so bad, it's blonde, so the grey looks more white. Angy doesn't appear to have many of the silver hairs, you can tell it's an expensive hair jobby she's had done, there's a difference between a salon box and a bought box don't you think? Jools doesn't seem to care about her natural Pepe le Pew hairstyle or her chubby cheek, hummy down clothes either for that matter, I don't know if she doesn't care, or is resolved with the way it is for her. I'm sure it hasn't been easy, like all of us I guess, we'd get an encore from the world for sure if they heard all our truths. Your body gives up, it just does, like a big old sack of tatties. Plop. Your mind, however, that's the bit you want to keep young. You don't want the shackles of cynicism, prejudice, or mental suffering that's for sure, it will transport you along life's converter belt faster than a toupee in a hurricane. What am I thinking? Silly Billy that I am. She must think I'm a right fool, I should laugh like my Robbie would have done, he's such a sweet boy, finds laughter and mischief in everyone and everything. I need to take a leaf out of his 12-year-old Oor Wullie annual. We miss out on keeping the intellect young when we spend too much time, money, and attention on trying to manipulate our body and mind into desired forms. Your unhappiness stems from the fact that conditions don't meet your expectations, so use that as the gift it is, and unwrap that sucker. Or not. Finding the childlike wonder and awe in everything, but keep in mind, everyone is hauling around 'stuff', and a smile from you might lighten the load on the miles of road. Smiles and miles have the same letters, funny that.

"You can roll a jobby in glitter, but it's still a jobby at the end of the day."

"What? What did you just say, Lezzers?"

Now she hears me. Damn, did I say it out loud? All of it? Some of it? Another annoying habit that comes with age, you think you're using an inside your headspace comment, but turns out you've said it out loud. Who knew? How very irritating.

"Asking about your job Angy. Is it all glitter and gussets?"

What does that even mean? Silly, silly. Maybe she didn't pick up on it?

"Glitter and gussets Lezzers?"

Fat chance, who am I trying to kid! Here goes. In for a penny, in for a pummeling!

"Yeah, she who leaves a trail of glitter in her gusset is never forgotten, or something like that. Come on Jools, help me out here. What wise words do you have to add to the saying?"

"Glitter is like herpes, if you get it, be prepared to have it forever, I had it once, I should know. Glitter in my foof that is, not herpes, that's my story and I'm not budging on that one, like I'm not going to budge, not one muscle am I going to budge when we get to the quiet, spacious, undisturbed, natural wilderness of the bush. Life would be so much simpler if we were carried along on the wings of glitter and glimmers in every situation, and not the triggers."

"I mean it Jools, we'd better not be camping, let alone glamping."

"Don't worry Lezzers, where you and I are going, we'll be experiencing four seasons in a glass, I can promise you that. Jules is free to fill her bush with glitter or anything else she sees fit or can fit."

"Like throwing a sausage up an alley. Only a few hours or to go, so, settle in for the ride, there's some bubbles in the esky, and a pre rolled, ready to be fired and inhaled in the glove compartment. Ange, would you care to do the honours?"

"Would you mind putting the fan on first please Jools, I don't want to take any of that stuff in, let alone reek of nasty, second hand fumes."

"Good idea Lezzers, point it towards me will you Jules, I'm addicted to secondhand drivers smoke, you won't reek anyway Lezzers, my lungs can sook up every last, escaping wisp, have no fear there."

"You're not partaking are you Jools?"

"Only the spliff Lesley, I won't drink anymore, and I'll stop texting, I find I spill and mis-spell it all too easily."

"I'm more than happy to drive Jools if that helps. I have my licence here with me, and I'm sure our family insurance covers me. Oh no, I dropped it, where did it go? I can't find it amongst all this stuff!!"

"Buckle in and keep clam back there, we'll find it when we stop, besides, like I said, I'm not sure your wee leggies would be able to reach the pedals, they're miles away from mine too."

"She only ever drives stoned Lezzers, and trust me when I say, it's preferable to the alternative. I'd be so bold as to say, it's better this way. Perhaps you should join us, then you might not notice she's been in first gear for the last 10 miles."

"Speaking of gear, let the fun and games begin. Spark her up Ange, and don't worry Lesley, I'll be just fine, Gertie and I have been together for many, many years, we know each other inside and out. Like an old married couple we are…"

"Like Drunk & Disorderly."

"Thanks for that Ange, we're ed Lesley, both a bit battered, beat up, and jaded with life's trials and errors, and I won't lie, there are times I'd trade her for a brand spanking new soft top, but then I remember that my loose skin would fly like an untethered sail even at 4 mph, like marshmallows, we stick together until one of us claps out. That right Ange?"

"More like the sticky pages in a porn mag Jules. Peas in a pod."

"We're all like vehicles, windscreen wipers on a rainy day, moving in sync with our eyeballs as they move this way, that way, forward and back. Even when our eyes are closed, we follow the inner narrative that we mentally dictate, typing out each word at a time, or we watch the imaginative mind movie we're projecting on the screens in our headspace. All we really want is to slow down, settle in for a full day or night of uninterrupted thought and sleep. But no, the express train of thought, just like wipers, speed full pelt through the mental station of this moment, carriages packed to the gunnels with projects, fantasies, regrets, rarely coming to rest. Menopause is the real deal. You're awake when you need to be asleep, and you're asleep when you need to be awake."

"Did you know the body needs a minimum of 5 hours, uninterrupted sleep to enhance your beauty."

"I sleep much, much more than that Lesley."

"Clearly not enough Jules, you still need more."

"I'm onboard a similar menopause train as Jools, I can be innocently making an alfalfa sprout and avocado crispbread for my lunch at 5pm, and cooking a tonne of mac n cheese for The Troops, and a sound, a smell, or someone says or does something, and I go crazy, binning the alfalfa sprout and avocado crispbread, inhaling all the pasta in one mouthful, meant for, 5 grown men boys, next minute I'm a blubbering spatula wielding, spanking maniac. And don't even get me started on full pelt, that's mostly gone, replaced by a dry, skinned, bald hide, scattered with the occasional sparse tufts of grey fluff. I do go back to being normal crazy from time to time."

"Not to brag Lesley, but I haven't had a mood swing, or hot flash in like, 7 minutes."

"Not me Lezzers, I'm smoother than Danny Zuko's slick pomp, but I can find myself on rare occasions, itchy, bitchy, psycho, mad, bad and dangerous to know."

"No changes for you then Ange."

"That's funny Jools, I'll take the grumpy and dumpy trait for sure."

"Nonsense Lezzers, you're always smiling."

"If you're happy and you know it, it's your meds."

"You know they say that married couples, like me and Mikey, live longer than singletons."

"Not a lot of people know this Lesley, but they're called sologamists. I'm a sologamist for instance, Monday to Friday only."

"I think you'll find it just seems longer Lezzers, for at least one of you anyway. I guess I'm, who am I kidding, what am I?"

"A hunter, gatherer Ange?"

"What would that make me? What would that make me? I have so many roles to pick from?"

"Maybe that's it Lezzers, maybe you're a No Body."

Who's she calling nobody? Is it just me or is she deliberately trying to make me feel bad? I am somebody. I'm somebody to lots of people. Mikey, The Boys. She used to put me down all those years ago and I thought the years of therapy, yoga, medication, meditation, and plastic surgery would strip at least some of those toxic barbs from her seams, softening the puckered, ruched edges. Clearly not, her ASStheticians must have cut out the nice, kind bits off instead of her unwanted parts. I'm not the Lezzers, the nursie, or even the Lesley that I was back then. So much filling between then and now, and not all of it sweet like a Victoria sponge cake, or a bed of roses, in fact at times it's been more like a doggy doo doo sandwich. Sometimes you need cake to make things feel better, even if they are in tiers.

"Giving you both the head's up, my bladder is no longer a sponge that can retain liquid until voluntarily expelled, I need advance before I laugh, sneeze, and/or cough. If they happen together, then we're all fecked, so tell me in advance if you plan to say something funny, then I can cross my legs and prepare my pelvic floor for the imminent pressure on my inadequate bladder. Thank the lard for shewees."

"Please tell me you're not using one right now Jules."

"Don't worry about me Ange, think of it this way, I'm really saving energy, I can do it all at the same time."

"I thought you got that loosey goosey bladder of yours nipped and tucked after Sam was born Jools."

"You had a nip and a truck Jules and didn't think to tell me, your bestie, and who's Sam? Kidding. Remind me, what age is he now?12?13?"

"26 Angy, same as my Jonno."

"Aggggghhh, bloody hell, those handsome wee blue eyed, curly blonde bop boys have finally reached my marketplace, and as it happens, I'm open for business. How terribly exciting, forbidden fruit. Love it."

"They prefer moist, juicy, fuzzy peaches to dry, gnarled, wrinkled prunes, I believe Ange."

"Thankfully my Jonno already has a girlfriend, hopefully that'll keep him out of your grubby little price racket?"

"Incorrect Lezzers, nothing is a) out of my price range and b) off limits. I'd be up for the challenge if I'm perfectly honest. Might even add it to my to do list."

"Over my dead body are you going to be my daughter in law Angy, I'd take you as step mother in law first, how does that sound eh?"

"Has a certain ring to it Lezzers, wouldn't you say, that je'n'as ce quoi, the perfect nom de plume, you can be my step mother in law anytime, a scareytale ending to end all scarey tales. Neither fairy, witch or wicked bitch, just right. I'd be one of the family Lezzers, could you handle that?"

"I wish you wouldn't tease me like this, Angy, he's an innocent young boy. Us sharing the same blood is family enough for me thank you very much."

"Exactly, but be careful what you wish for Lezzers, I could make it official, but when you know, it'll be no fun for me anymore."

"Stop it, Angy. La la la, I'm not listening."

She wouldn't dare. Would she? No, Shirley not. She wouldn't steep that low, or would she? I'd have her glittered gusset guts for garters. I can tell you. She's winding me up. She needs to go for men her own age, or older, not young boys like Jonno and Sam, that's plain wrong. He'd be scarred for life, although her being his teacher of sorts would put him in good stead for future partners. Stop it, Lesley, what are you saying? YUCK YUCK YUCK. That's your son you're talking about here and with her. She'd eat him alive. She mentioned it being on her "to-do" list, which is sick. As if going after my baby isn't sick enough!

"Call me shellfish as you'd say Lezzers, but a bladder leakage is only a great reminder that I haven't had to endure the birth and years of pain and suffering that follows childbirth that you two have experienced. Thankfully. So, to be honest no leakage trails slip from this tiny, tiny, minute, did I say, tight, moist little hole."

"It's an age thing also Ange, and if you'd not had that Vagi No Plasty, you'd see, sorry pee for yourself. All that means is that we can leave all the disco slut drops on the dance floor to you."

"I accept the challenge Jules. Bring on Boogie Wonderland."

"I'll bet not only earth, wind, fire, make an appearance Ange, but Tsunami Too."

"You both know I'm too Chic for that."

"Aww, I love all my boys, and wouldn't change any of the bladder leakage, sleepless nights, stretch miles, tears, laughter, love for anything in the world. Not even for Leo Dicaprio."

"COME ON Lezzers, Get real, I'd trade BOTH of you for him, even though an anagram for his name is "periodic anal odour", but who am I to judge lifestyles."

"You're too old for him though Angy, he likes them young, younger than even you claim to be"

"Let's feed him Robbie then Lezzers, how does that taste for you?"

"Stop it Angy. Don't get me wrong my boys do have their moments, couldn't eat a whole one, mind."

"Unlike Leo, I could eat him whole, including his glittery giblets."

"That's just being greedy now Ange. Shower me with the glitter at the very least."

"Speaking of eating a whole one, what ever happened to The Original, the one and only, for one night only, our very own surfie's passion wagon, Dirty Gertie, Jules?"

"After the FBI, CIA and Rupaul's drag show Down Under had finished with her, bits of her were stripped for evidence, and costumes, especially the rubber bits. She was incinerated and her ashes were turned into a casket made of gold and hand delivered to the metal junkyard in the sky, any discarded remnants were rolled into three cigarette papers with a roach, and smoked in her honour."

"Wow, Really? Och, you're winding me up Jools, aren't you? I can never tell with you, it could so easily be the truth. Remind me what the other name the pair of you had for Gertie? Not a passion wagon, something like that, but not."

"Fuck Truck."

"No need for that language Angy, besides it was something else."

"I think I should know Lezzers after all it was me and Jules that not only bought her, but lived in her when we travelled around Australia, looking for you I might add."

"I didn't even know you were looking for me, and if you hadn't been so mean, I wouldn't have left in the first place. I was quite happy being of service to the outback community thank you very much, and you only redeemed yourself by saving my life Angy...twice, once when you sucked the living daylights out of my derriere, and then when you gave me a life saving blood transfusion."

"Even after all these years, the pair of you still sound like a pair of bickering old hens, clucking away, fluffing your feathers, he said, she said. Anyone listening in would be tossing a coin between thinking you're related, or trying to decide which one of you the actual fool is."

"We ARE related Jools."

"Only through a blood transfusion Lezzers, not DNA, and I'm sure that doesn't count as a bona fide reason to call us related, however, there's plenty of time to address that."

"Keep your hands off my family Angy, please."

"No promises, everything's a lair in love and war, Lezzers. Not sure that the same blood alone is a legal binding sibling document if you ask me. Hm? Doesn't sound very plausible, now does it. Hmm??"

"Maybe it is, but Shirley that would make me not only your YOUNGER sister, but your next of kin. Am I your next of kin? If you were to die, then I'd inherit your henhouse in upper manhattan or wherever you live, your low booties and ALL your lovers."

"All my lovers? Careful what you wish for, could make for a low gene pool Lezzers. Look I'm pulling your stump, besides you can have my Louboutins, I believe that's what you meant, and mark my words you DON'T want my amours, not your type, too close to the boner, not sure you'd be able to get your blonde, fluffy head around that one."

"Not my type? I'm much more open these days, you know. When I was younger I was much more selective. Even though I've only ever been with Mikey, I think if he was dead or something then I'd be more open to you know…"

"I will bet you a pair of Louboutins that you would not want what I have right now Lezzers."

"You'd be surprised Angy, I am so much more open these days."

"If you say so Lezzers."

"We can't be too far from our first pit stop, but if this Dick behind me gets any closer he's going to penetrate Gertie's rear exhaust pipe."

"If I'm not mistaken,you can't say dick these days Jools, it's not poetically correct to say dick these days. How do you know it's a male anyway? I can't see beyond the furry dice bouncing from his rear view mirror."

"Definitely a dick Lesley as after penetrating Gertie from the rear, he'll be up your arse first, then mine ...but he's got to keep up with me and Gertie if he wants to play with us."

"What the hell are you doing Jools? Slow dowwwwn."

"A side wheel wheelie, I can still pull them you know, he'll never catch me. Check the burning rubber tyre smoke. When you got it, you got it. Look at the steering wheel, it's like a gawd darn fairground ride. How cool is that? Eat my dust sucker. OOOF what was that? Must have been another speed bump?"

"I felt it on the side of my passenger door Jules, so it must have been one of those flying speed bumps you don't get. You've surely lost him in that skree storm, like hamster shite flying from a very fast wheel spin. What is wrong with you Jules? I could have spilled my drink."

"Bet you're glad you're strapped in Ange or you could have nose dived into my lap of opulence."

"Coincidently, the words "opulent" and "repulsive" have the same letters Jules, however, and for what it's worth, and before you can say labia minora, in America, it's illegal to drive a four wheel van on two fucking wheels, especially in the middle of roadworks, the fines double."

"Where's Lesley? Lesley?"

"Here, I'm here, behind your seat Jools. That wheelie took me by surprise. I was eating my Chicksmix and wasn't quite buckled in. No harm though, I'll get it tidied up, every last crumb, I promise. A few things have tipped out of some of the bags and cupboards: chocolate, lighter, salt, lemons, letter from Pradip, a costume, and Batman mask with mouth zip."

"A Batman mask with a zip Lezzers, give it here. Let me try it on. Look fits perfectly."

"Especially if you close the zip Ange."

"Thanks for that vote of confidence Jules."

"You're whale cum Ange, gives you that lovely metal ring of confidence. You okay back there Lesley? You haven't surfaced in my rear view mirror yet."

"Still here, still here, thanks for asking Jools, every time I get traction, and find some form of balance, it seems you hit another speed bump that's all. I've managed to prise my cheek from the mat with only a slight acrylic carpet burn. I think my body took a flight higher than any mile high club you've ever been on Angy."

"We can relax Lezzers, she has finally managed to control this rusty beast and we are now back on four wheeled terre track."

"My life flashed before me,so it did. I could see the light between the door sill, floor, speeding tarmac, and my face. Images of a male silhouette opening up a brolly zoomed by me. I could only think that if the door opens, then I'm a goner for sure. Funny thing is I knew Mikey had closed this door, so I felt calm and safe given the danger. I didn't even know my body could contort into those positions."

"Lucky, lucky My key, it's never too late to teach an old dog new tricks, or is it old pricks, new cogs, and the day is not even close to being over. And you were in the front passenger seat when he shut the door, not the back."

"Glad I didn't remember that at the time Jools, sorry, everything has emptied back here, tell me, whose chewing gum coloured pair of old, baggy, yet surprisingly comfy looking, how shall I put it without making them sound sexy, or glamorous, granny pants are these?"

"More like a grungy sheet, no, a t- shirt or a pair of .....underpants. Passion killers for sure. Are they yours Lezzers?"

"Indeed they are not Ange, they're mine, I am the very proud owner of my Sunday to Friday Grinny pants."

"These are crimes of passion Jules, and crimes of logic, those knickers defy both."

"Are they really yours, Jools? Like you wear them yours? or are they a torn up cleaning rag? Or? Angy? No judgement here you understand."

"Rest assured those howlers Lezzers do NOT, and never will in any shape or form, belong to me, I'd never let my standards, or age slip that much, you understand? Comprendez?"

"I occasionally prefer no cover, going commando, get a bit of an airing and all that. No undies is safer, as it's easier to hook your thumbs under one trouser elastic waistband than 2, and have them whisked down before there's even the slightest inkling that the water park is about to open for business. This is when I'm in a toilet, and not when I'm in aisle 7 of the grocery store beside the cans of pees, or in a 'pishing wagon'."

"Speaking of canapes, I notice your exotic cocktail pantalons are very similar to the pair I'm wearing, Angy, same floaty, shimmering chiffon."

"Eh, hardly Lezzers, these pants of mine are shimmering silk, not slimey nylon."

"Allow me to translate for her Lesley, "pants" in Amerkin means trousers to us and everywhere else in the world."

"So, if pants are trousers, then..."

"Cut to the chase will you Lezzers, spit it out."

"Is it only me here, but what do they call knickers if pants are trousers."

"Panties, we call them panties Lezzers."

"Panties? There's something terribly sexy about being our age and wearing "panties", only not in the case of my granny "panties"…that doesn't sound in the slightest bit sexy."

"Sexy Jools? I was thinking quite the opposite, in my mind only little 3 year old girls wear panties."

"I'd like to add that there's nothing, not one dayum thing sexy about ANY of your panties Jules, anyway, as I was saying until I was rudely interrupted, my "pants", are designer, 100% silk, one of a kind, a piece of art, not your usual bog standard, off the rack, acrylic rags you see in the high street these days. Not saying yours are from the high street, Lezzers, but mine are categorically NOT the same as yours."

That's so unkind! Is it unkind? Am I thinking too much into all this? After all, mine aren't the same, not by a mile, which is the exact difference in our leg length- one mile practically. It does sound like another putdown to me though. It's so childish! If she wants to play like a child, then that's exactly how I'm going to treat her, like the spoiled, petulant child she is.

"Was that meant as a putdown Angy?"

"What? No, I didn't really mean anything by it, just an observation that's all. Don't take anything I say to heart Lezzers, it's just me being my usual bitter heliacal self without the gin and tonic."

"I know, thank you Angy, from the heart of my bottom, I do know you're not really that bitter, an acquired taste maybe, but not totally bitter."

"Good. Tell me, how are your little leggies Lezzers? Enough room in the back behind me?"

"He he, yes, plenty, plenty, thank you for asking Angy, more than enough for these "wee stumps" of mine"

"Good, you won't mind me putting my seat back and having a recline for a bit then will you."

"We're coasting merrily along here on a wine and a prayer, not much juice left in the old rust bucket, and I refer to myself here as well as Gertie. If we don't fill her up soon, someone will have to run/walk and get petrol."

"As Angy has already established, I have stumpy legs, so it may take a fortnight for me to get to a garage"

"And I don't walk anywhere Jules, that's why I have chauffeurs, walking is for 'others'. Howzabout the damsel in distress approach, shaking our highly desired pins at the side of the road, and hollering, "huyulp, huyulp", some hunks of burning love are bound to stop and help fill us up, all the way up to the 'pussy's bow', and beyond. Before you get ahead of yourself Lezzers, I'm talking about the hair accessory Marie wears on her head in the Aristocats."

"The only exercise I choose these days is to chase those darn, suspicious, taco 2Go trucks down, and get me a double stuffed Verde with seasoned and grilled courgette, yellow squash, red onion, mushrooms, & carrots over vegetarian black beans, topped with chipotle crema, but if it's an emergency, and I can't wait that long, I call 9 Juan - Juan. You know Ange, back in the day, men may well have stopped for us, when we were naturally lubed up, bristle free, tanned, muscular, young hitchhiking legs flexing from the side of the road, causing a traffic jam, however these days, there is more likely going to be a considerable pile up when drivers tried to avoid the rotten, knobbly, dried tree stumps, flapping their cellulitic/loose fleshy lower limbs from the side of the road."

"Speak for yourself Jules, my legs are still in pretty great shape, and I'm sure they could still stop traffic."

"Maybe so, Ange, maybe not, peoples senses and thoughts can be distracted and hijacked by so many things, which in turn impact their immediate choices. Shock horror, they may have been looking in a different direction, and didn't notice you at all. We're all addicted to our thoughts. Is it a mere coincidence that the word 'addict' is contained in the word 'distracted'?"

"And she's off, give her an inch and she takes a fucking mile, another drink please Lezzers, Dirty is not the only one running on empty and I am very much in need of something that I'm addicted to that's going to numb and distract me from all this bullshit."

"You can avoid whatever it is you're avoiding Ange, but it's a fact, people only notice and get distracted by something that is from their own personal past, a desire, an aversion, which is directly linked to a happening long since gone, a feeling they'd like to repeat, or, more often than not, ignore. At the end of the day, it all depends which direction we're looking in, and which of our senses is vying for the lion's share of our attention, each one seeking their personal preference or resistance as to how their reality should unfold for them. Not everyone sees us or the world through a clear unobstructed lens, often lost and caught on the train of thoughts, speeding on a return journey from the past, directly on the express train to the future, missing the opportunity for the thought train to remain idle and be still at the station of Here & Now, each carriage carrying the extra baggage of anger, sadness, fear, missing the three old bags completely shaking an empty can of petrol from the 'platform'/side of the road."

"Challenge accepted Jules, I bet they'll see us as windswept, interesting, and come immediately…. to our rescue that is. From where I stand on your bullshit station, see it as me sharing a random act of kindness to the world, in your case, more as an act for charity."

"Pity more like Ange, what are they really getting from helping us? Is it an act of unconditional kindness or a selfish act, what do they get from it? You know what, I'm not going to wait to see who or who doesn't come to our aid, I'm going to make a decision right now, hang on to yer hats Laddies……uggghhh. My bad, sorry about that. You okay? Ange? Lesley? I keep forgetting I had the brakes repaired and it only needs a light stroke on the pedal for Gertie to react. I had intended to stop closer to that group of kids coming over the hill and ask them the way to the nearest garage, but we stopped quite a bit short."

"No shit Sherlock, perhaps I should hail a taxi to get us closer to them."

"Thanks for the kind offer of a taxi Ange, but I'm quite sure they'll walk to us quicker than it would be to call a taxi to take one of us to them. Let's 'idle' here until they get to us. Tum te tum te tum ti tum. It would scare the beejuice out of them now by driving a Volkswagen kombi van slowly towards them, like Ted Bundy did. We'll wait till they get here, to us, then you can casually ask them for a petrol station with an atm machine. You have enough time to take the gimp mask off Ange, that would scare them even more than any serial killer."

"I don't think it is a chimp mask Jools, I think it's Batman, or one of those action hero masks they wear, I should know, I've had 4 boys."

"I can't get it off anyway, even if I wanted to, the zip is stuck at my neck, however the mouth zip works perfectly. Here, hold the map, then we won't look too suspicious, they'll think we're lost, that's all."

"Angy, you can't ask them with that monkey mask on, they'll think you're going to either kidnap or murder them at the very least. Are they little dwarves, definitely not kids? Can I even use that word these days?"

"I think you can still say "kids" Lesley."

"No Jools, dwarves. Even if you think a banned word, and not actually say it, does that still make it poetically correct?"

"Politically Incorrect Lezzers."

"Whatever Angy, does it count? I mean, I'm not trying to be insulting or bring them down in any way by saying, or thinking it for that matter, but how do you stop the words that involuntarily pop into your head."

"You mean bring them further down than they already are Lezzers?"

"Now that's totally uncalled for Angy. Is this better, there's a group of Little people, is that okay, midgets? No, they're bigger than that, it's not p.o.r. g. either, I think that's impolite too. Definitely grown ups, well, almost, I can make out two men/boys, same age as my Vinny, so 19 ish, and looks like they have a carry out from the offie."

"Really? That's what you see Lesley? I can now see 2 blokes, can I say that? Walking a dog? Is that okay? dog?"

"You're both wrong, it's 2 women pushing a stroller. Look? Besides, no one should be questioning me, I identify as a threat, I use pronouns try and me."

"It's rude to point Angy, you're right Jools, it's definitely two blokes and they've got a carry out."

"Ahhh, you found my binoculars Lesley, I thought I'd lost them. Isn't that funny though, not everything we see at first glance turns out to be exactly what it actually is. Depends on our own unique perceptions. Here they come, wind your window down Ange."

"They're not grown ups, they're mere children who illegally underage drink. Has the legal drinking in Australia gone down to 11?"

"They're older than that, Angy, my.."

"Quiet in the cheap backseat, I can hardly hear myself think. Excuse me chaps, ignore these two, a little bit of rohypnol and it goes straight to their heads. Do you know the way to communique? I've been away so long, I may go wrong and lose my way, do you know the way to get some gas today? One with an atm machine. I need to get money first before they fill up with gas, more than they have going on intestinally at the moment that is. I'm like the queen you see, and these are my servants, not the one in the back, she's a prisoner. I personally don't carry cash, and I don't think either of you would appreciate the American dough lars I have, and neither of my minions have cash either. Do you know where the nearest one is? Down there? far? No? I'm so glad I brushed up on my silent charades for dummies before landing. Great. Thank you. So helpful…NOT, thank you, bye now, see you around…"

"I'll take it from here boys, she doesn't bite, it just looks that way through her mouth spaver, unless of course you're hiding something long, oblong shaped, and very delicious in your trouser pocket that is, then I'd run if I was you. I hope it's a snicker bar you have in there. They've gone. That was fast, not even a cheery bye. I think I managed to get the gist of where they're sending us anyway. Very strange wouldn't you say though, they either didn't speak english or didn't understand your Amerkin accent Ange."

"Or the chimp mask scared them like I knew it would. They looked putrified if you ask me."

"It's not a chimp mask Lesley, and Ange wearing it is less scarier than the alternative, bizarre that all they did was stutter, point and gesticulate."

"You're right Jools, it's so rude to do that, I have always taught my boys that manners marketh the man."

"I still can't unzip it, maybe you can try to fix it when we stop Lezzers. No rush, I'm enjoying the up close and personal smell of its leather interior. There's something very sexy about the smell of leather wouldn't you say? Maybe on a tight pair of biker leather pants."

"There are people out there that believe, especially children, who already think I'm wearing a leather mask, even when I'm not."

"No wonder those poor wee lads look scared, both you wearing leather masks of some description, besides you scare the life out of me Angy, and that's not only because you're wearing a balaclava mask or whatever it is. Jools, your red lipstick has bled, giving you a Vampire vibe, and the flapping joint stuck to your bottom lip is terribly distracting in any event. Anyhoo, that aside, I know exactly what they were trying to ejaculate as I have experience with children pre speech, and it looks like you're heading in the right direction. I'm a professional in no speech, monosyllabic male grunting and waving of arms, my Deano still doesn't use his words much, preferring to not engage with anyone older than 17. The petrol station should be up ahead and round that corner on the right is my best guess."

"Nawwww, you're wrong Lezzers, surely they saw 3 sexy, older, windswept and decidedly experienced women and not something scary."

"Did you not notice them stepping back from DGT? I did. One of them even took his phone out and held it up to his chest. He was either trying to film us or dial a number, but his fingers were trembling and he almost dropped it. It was about then that you took off like a bat out of hell Jools, leaving them in your smoggy, backfiring wake and me back in the all too familiar foot well."

"I didn't actually mean to take off that fast, I took my foot off the brake that's all and gently slid it over to the accelerator, thinking I'd let Gertie tick over for a while, but I was distracted by an itch on the ball of my foot so I scratched it with the accelerator pedal accidentally taking off, quicker than a little blue pill sale at the erectile dysfunction store I might add. My Bad, that's on me. Sorry Lesley."

"Their final impressions of me as I waved goodbye, is of my loose underarm skin battering the inside side of the window, flapping and slapping like an unfurling canopy. No matter how many arm curls I do, nothing seems to work. You'd think lifting all those boys, for what seems like years, an added bonus would be toned arms, but no, and they throw a fat arse in for good measure."

"If Jules had been driving any slower Lezzers, your flaps would have slapped both their chops instead."

"Like an under arm skin pillow fight. I could not only play you at that game Lesley, but very likely beat you for sure. You'd be shite Ange."

"That's a shame, that means I won't get to play in that childish game with you Jules. Thankfully."

"Put your head out the back window Lesley, and I'll do the same with the driver window, and tell me if you feel assaulted when my jowls catch the wind at 80 mph, my chins can straddle different time zones, tell me if your facey gets slapped. Perhaps I was too quick off the mark, I didn't even know Gertie could do a back wheel wheelie. Besides I did the street cleaners a favour by doing their job of clearing the gutters of road stew. Those lads should be thanking me that they stepped back in time before being unceremoniously showered by a wave of watery gutter, and road debris. Yaaay, look there's the petrol station, we made it. On a swig and a flare."

"In America we're not allowed to drive across the central reservation like you've just done Jules, we're encouraged to stay in our own lane, as..., let me think as to why...ah yes, it's FUCKING safer for starters."

"We're here now and all in one piece Ange, no harm done. Gosh what have you been doing in the back there Lesley? Everything is strewn everywhere. Are you looking for something? I thought you said you were tidying up?"

"Tidying up by wearing a pair of rubber gloves and a family sized bag of crisps as a horse's nose bag? Interesting combination you have going on there Lezzers."

"I didn't know I was going to be involuntarily spinning about in the back like the Tasmanian Devil on speed, along with the vortex of contents from the open cupboards and rubbish to be perfectly honest with you Angy."

"It won't take you too long to put it all back together I'm sure. Here, take this credit card Lezzers, fill Dirty up to the gunnels while Jules and I get a few bits and pieces from the store."

"Hold your horses Angy, I might need something from the store, and I need a pee."

"We all do Lezzers. Use the loos over there, or hold it till we get back, your choice, don't make this harder than it is."

"I've given birth vaginally to four strapping lads Angy and that particular door down there has a mind all of its own and opens and closes at the drop of a hat. There's no way I can hold it while I'm fueling either, that would start me off for sure."

"Here's an idea Lesley, click and lock the hose in the tank, leave it running while you go to the loo. We'll go to the ATM machine, then go get some knick knacks from the shoppy. What do you want?"

"Great idea Jools, aside from one small detail, I don't think you can leave a vehicle unattended."

"It's not unattended. We'll be watching the CCTV from right inside there, see? Why do you have bright orange cheesy crumbs stuck to your face Lesley?"

"I was thrown head first into a bag of cheerios when we received your accidental emergency brake back there Jools."

"Sorry about that again Lesley, my bad, I don't know my own strength sometimes, pretty impressive though, you have to admit. Did you catch the look on those two lads' faces? It was priceless, mouths agape, eyes bulging, one of them looked more worried than the other one, who didn't look quite 'right' now that I come to think of it, there's a word that sums it up, but I'm sure it's on one of those on the barred lists, run by the intense politically correct brigade, who make it their life's mission to correct others on the should and shouldn'ts, according to their personal attachments, and then they go off and have a sneaky check at their texts when they're driving, just after tutting another driver for doing the same. Hypocrites, every single morally righteous one of them. We all know people like that, anyway, thankfully we've made it to the petrol pump at Truckies by the skin of a hymen."

"Being met face to face with me in a bondage hood isn't exactly what they had in mind when they took off for a stroll to get a carry out for an afternoon's entertainment? But more importantly Jules,why do you have this sex accessory mask in the first place. Explain yourself young lady."

"It belongs to Drew Peacock. He's the president of the commune's amateur dram society. He gave it to me to fix the zip at the back, but I hadn't got round to it."

"I don't think it's a sex accessory, Angy, more like something to do with primates. Am I right, Jools?"

"It's a prop Lesley."

"Oh, is the local amateur dramatic club putting on Fifty slaves for the gay? For the bold and firm Jules?"

"Ha ha, not quite Ange, would you believe, it's for our end of year performance of the Cocky Horror Show."

"Horror being the operative word here, it's your story, you tell it any way you care to Jules, who am I to add, remove or have an opinion about your perverse choices. Changing the subject to far more pressing issues, remind me to top up our booze supply when we're in the gas station."

"Ange? Reminder to top up our booze supply when we're in the garage."

"You pair of silly billies, you can't buy booze here. It's a garage, and it certainly won't sell the expensive stuff you drink Angy, and if they did it would be lukewarm pishy beer and even pishier watery wine. They don't actively want to encourage drunk driving here like they do in the States."

"What do you mean Lezzers? "Can't" isn't even a word in my vocabulary? You watch. Do you honestly think that not selling alcohol in gas stations prevents people from driving drunk? What exactly have we been doing since Sydney? Hmmm?? Where I'm from you can buy anything, even machine guns."

"Machine guns? Oh my word, I'm not surprised it's a prozac nation."

"Cheese buns", Lezzers, that's what I said, "cheese buns", not machine guns."

"I knew that, I was winding you up, I knew what you said. I meant, buns, not guns. Makes more sense also, why would selling cheese buns be illegal? Come on, I'm bursting now go the pair of you, I'll stay here and fill DGT up. I'm trained to retain liquid like a camel, so I don't need to go to the loo just yet, but to save time, you could get me some toothpaste please, and while you're in there, can you please get me a bag of crisps, a mars bar, some antihistamine cream, maybe a wee ice cream cone, or something like that...ooo, oooo, and a bottle of water...BIG.....SPARKLING..... LEMON flavoured. Did you catch all that? Jools? Angy? Hello? Do you hear me? Forget it Lesley, they can't hear me from inside. I'll do it here, to save time. I'll use Jules shewee, she won't mind. I did learn something from all my camping and family driving trips. I can pour out the stale contents from this silver metal water flask in the leather hamper. I'll put it back in my handbag and dispose of it at my earliest convenience."

Do You Prefer That You Be Right Or Happy? - A Course In Miracles

A tree that is unbending, is easily broken. - Lao Tzu

All you really need are good friends and a full tank of gas

"Do you remember that time you used your toothpaste as face cream Jules?"

"I think it was the other way round, Ange, they both come in similar tubes with similar looking contents. I can still taste the emollient between my molars, but that ring of confidence around my smile has slipped for sure and is very likely going to choke me, an easy mistake at any age."

"I can only speak for myself here, but my "ring of confidence" has never been so overworked, especially if I end up having to wear this mask for the rest of my life."

"I still can't get over the look on those poor boy's faces. What did we come in here for again Ange?"

"Hmmm, I'd say it was a mixture of curiosity, pleasure and desire. And, no clue."

"Sure as hell wasn't what I saw Ange, they looked, well one of them for sure, like, you know, not quite all there, there's a word I'm thinking of that sums it up, but can't quite mentally grasp it yet. I'm sure it's one of those words that's on the "you can't say that", naughty Santa's list. We'll all be mute like those two blokes back there if we carry on like this, second guessing what we can or can't say without offending someone and their sensibilities. I'm so tired trying to get it 'right', it amazes me what I say sometimes, and what my mind does and doesn't think, let alone say out loud. Why can't we go back to the good old days when we could offend anyone and everyone. Those were the days."

"I miss those days. People need to lighten up and not take themselves quite so seriously. I wish Lezzers had a control volume button, my head's dirling."

"The less we say to ourselves either with an internal voice or an external voice, then the less likely we are to be misinterpreted Ange. The minute we lock in to one of our senses, then our judgy mind automatically jumps in, and begins to type: I am too this, they're to that. It's much easier to experience others as if they were flowers and/or weeds, rather than people. We learn absolutely nothing by hearing ourselves speak. There are occasions when silence is a blessing in disguise, speaking of disguise, can you not just rip the mask off."

"I've tried, it's stuck, besides I thought it would be fun wearing it in here, more fun than listening to Lezzers bleating on or painfully watching her trying to insert a thin, long, black, pulsing hose into Dirty's ring of confidence. Remind me to pick up some vaseline or butter for the zip or alternatively a pair of scissors to cut me out of this contraption."

"I have vaseline in the van Ange."

"Of course you do Jules, ask no questions, tell no lies, besides, I always carry a travel sized pot of petroleum jelly."

"We're not as young, juicy and moist as we once were eh Ange?"

"Speak for yourself, besides it's for my lips."

"Mine too, but I do use it for cooking also. Check these tshirts out Ange. I like these beautifully coloured shirts with Chinese writing."

"If it's Chinese, how do you know what it says, unless you've got the book, Chinese for Crumblies?"

"I don't know what it says, but it can't be too bad, they're selling them here in a service station in the middle of bum feck nowhere, the edge of the Bush, NSW, Australia. And if I'm ordering a tofu stir fry from the menu, then what a lovely surprise that would be. I like the orange one with the black writing. Looks comfy. I'm going to get us all matching ones, I'll get Lesley the white with purple writing. What colour do you want? Don't look at me like that, it can be our slumber wear. Come on. What colour?"

"We'll be mistaken for old bag ladies if we wear them in public, I'll have the green with orange writing, but only if you promise you won't wear them out in public. Check those two old broads over there staring at us Jules? At least the one in the rouge shirt looks friendly, the other one looks like my grandmother."

"Good news, bad news here Ange, the good news is that it's spookily similar to the red shirt I'm wearing and the bad news is, that's a mirror, and you're your gran. Explains the cracks."

"We can see your crack when you bend over like that Jules, you could easily be mistaken for a slip road."

"I dropped this, check it out? A tequila flavoured, scented air freshener."

"Give it here, suck it Jules, let me know if it works."

"No, you suck it Ange, I'm sure you've had worse in that zip of yours."

"Yuck, tastes like foosty papier mache Jules."

"Sorry, did I say flavoured, I need my readers, it says scented, not flavoured, smell it Ange, don't suck."

"Bit late for that, but I am getting wafts of agave …and salt."

"Give it here, let me try it. Lick, sip, suck. You're right, still more like cardboard than tequila."

"Not the best I've sucked, and believe me, when I say this, not the worst either. I have sucked objects boner dry."

"If there is any hint of alcohol in its rigid kangaroo shape Ange, I'm sure you'll suck it within an inch of its air freshener life."

"Try the other one Jules. Margherita? Rum Punch?"

"I'll grab 3 that haven't been in our gobs/"

"Super Jules, leave the pale gray chewing gum colored, mushy ones we tested dangling from their string for someone else."

"What else do we need Ange?"

"Skins."

"I know mine is loose, flabby and has seen better days, but it's mine and I'll stick with it. Thanks for the offer though, Ange."

"Not your skin Numptie, the ones for rolling. Paper cigarette skins."

"Rolling?"

"You know. Spliffs? Reefers? Oh fffff sake Jules."

"I know what you meant, now wheesht, let me think here, what else do we need? That zip comes in handy, glad it still opens and closes, let's keep it closed for a while I have a think as to what else we need."

"Mmm……ghhhhmm..nn."

"Excuse me? Is your friend okay? I think maybe she's having a seizure under that balaclava."

"Seriously she's fine, thank you for your concern, we'll check out now anyway, she enjoys the attention if I'm honest."

"Mmmghh…mnnn."

"Sssh Ange, you're disturbing this lovely cashier. It's not easy being her support worker I can tell you, and at times, if I'm honest with you, I lose the will to live trying to make sense of the jumbled, muffled string of words trying to escape from her pleather pleasurable mouth. Now I have completely lost my train of thought and have no idea now what I should or shouldn't be saying here. Help me out,what does your name badge read?"

"Sheila."

"Of course it does, only in Australia, that's us Sheila, I think we've forgotten everything we came in for, and more, what's the damage for this lot? Thank you. We stopped these two blokes Sheila, still not sure if I can use that word, back there, these two guys, can I say that? We stopped two people of the male variety carrying bags and they directed us here."

"You can say whatever you like in front of me Sheila, I'm a big girl, been there, done that, bought the Tshirt, so go ahead, say what you like."

"Thank gawd for that Sheila, everyone is getting so uptight over the smallest things these days, the overly principled, liberally imposing and imparting their self-righteous, morally superior ways from the dizzying heights of their own heavy egos, without due cause, permanently branding anyone in their wake with their prejudices that they own and believe. When everyone relaxes a bit and realises it's an inside job, then we'd get along a whole lot better, it's only our limiting beliefs that divide us, address them and we'll find we're all in the same global flower patch. Regardless. It is always the story we tell yourself that creates division."

"Hallelujah, saved by the zip Sheila, believe me, that 'convo' was heading somewhere neither of us have the will or the strength to go on. She frequently travels Australia with her portable soap box, and steps on it for the occasional preachy rant. Take no notice of her, she soon runs out of steam, and in the blink of a beady eye, she'll be hairy dust, and we need a pack of cigarette papers too, thank you. See Sheila? Her mental train has already left the station without her. Her thoughts have slipped further into an invisible grateful void, or is it a grateful invisible void?"

"What was I saying? Honestly, I've completely lost my train of thoughts again. Is that everything? Have we got it all? Ange? Anything else?"

"According to you Jules, forgetting the past moment is a good thing."

"I can't stop thinking of those two boys though Ange, and that word I'm thinking of, I know I almost have it. So frustrating."

"My word right now is "patience" Jules, and Sheila here, behind the counter, is "disbelief". "

"It's here, right here on the tip of my tequila pulp, grass coated tongue. Come on help me out here, think of the word I'm trying to remember, one word that sums up those two boys back there. They didn't quite look the full shilling."

"Dunderheads from Downunder?"

"Good one Ange, but no cigar. I'm sure it's only one word."

"How about Jerk, bone-head, dork, dingbat, jackass, Jules?"

"I'm sure it begins with an 'r', or maybe 'f'. A foreign word, maybe French, maybe Doric."

"Do you remember when this sweetie used to be called a "marathon", not "snickers" Jules?"

"Yes, they changed it because everyone was snickering watching people who had eaten a tonne of them trying to run a marathon. It's now called a marathon to inspire people. We should have some kind of sweet/savoury magical treat called "Menopause" readily available for women of a certain age. Its miracle ingredients can accompany us throughout our hormonal highs and lows, softening our perspiration surges as they rise, express themselves and move on. It can also be used as an aide-memoire to anyone within firing range, that if they value their lives, they need to cultivate awareness around the unpredictability and fragility of menopausal hormones, they need space, stillness, patience and absolutely, on no occasion, for any reason, eye contact. I'd buy one and use it as a threat/warning/ get out of jail/and or speeding ticket/ empathy/ camaraderie gift. They'd fly off the shelves, they'd fly off the shelves, but what's that got to do with my lost word Ange?"

"Nothing whatsoever Jules, but I remember back in the day, they used to be the weight of a decent sized brick, a block of pure chocolate goodness, not a miniscule, fun /1/2 sized mouthful. $15 for a snicker that's been shrunk is a ridiculous price. Someone out there making all the money is snickering for shuwa."

"You're not helping Ange, this is so infuriating, it's within my reach, teasing me, tantalising and tormenting me, I know I almost have it, it's dangling right here on the tip of my mache coated tongue. I'm sure the tutting self righteous smugs are already building up their saliva for a proper tut. It's not a French word, it's a Scottish word. When we listen and converse with only ourselves, we often say wholly inappropriate things. Those mental conversations rarely end well. Does it matter if we don't say it out loud? I think not. The impact of the negative energy of a thought alone can be immense mentally and physically. It's still being formed and given potential weight in some way or other though. Doesn't always need to be said out loud to make an impact somehow."

"FEEL. FEEL. They both looked "feel". That's your word isn't it Jules? BUYA. Feel. Ya Beauty, I thought you were losing your hareballs for a New York minute Jules."

"Yes. FEEL yes, well done Ange, that's the very word I was thinking of, well done you. You did just scare the bee juice out of Sheila here though, pointing and waving that very dangerous stick of Spearmint wrigley gum whilst shouting "FEEL" at the top of your more than ample lungs will do that too a cashier. You can settle back down now Trigger, holster that packet of gum."

"Apologies Sheila, I didn't mean to lunge over the counter at you like that, but I got over excited when I remembered her word. You know the one that Jules here couldn't remember, "feel". Scottish for, well you know, I think we've already established that, a right pair of Numpties they were. And one can 'cop a feel', that's another use for the word, but that's not what she meant in this situation. Was it Jules? Sorry if she offended you."

"Offended me? It takes a whole lot more than a couple of old, screaming dags to frighten me Sheila. I wasn't scared, I haven't laughed out loud like that for ages. Don't get too many of those belly laughs in here these days, everyone is in such a rush, no time for a chat, it's so refreshing to be with people who don't take themselves seriously. I haven't heard that word used for decades, and I think it probably is on one of the banned word lists somewhere, for a split second though, before it clicked into place, I

thought you were calling me "feel", or better yet, trying to 'cop a feel'."

"We left that one filling Dirty up, didn't we Jules."

"Oh for heaven sake Ange, thanks Sheila, glad I remembered that word, it would have done my head in trying to remember it. Like a dog with a bone.".

"Look, up there Jules, Lezzers is on candid camera. Check her out on the monitor up there, live entertainment from the comfort of your friendly, neighbourhood gas station. S'cuse me, that's my cell phone going, let me take it quickly. Give me a moment Jules, I'll come back to take care of all this. And for what it's worth, it was my word Jules, I actually remembered it first. I deserve the credit. Look, I have to take this. Scuse me. I'll be back."

"But I thought about it first, Ange, before you actually said it. Does it not count if you've been thinking about it? I'd better go check our friend Lesley's okay and don't need some more Depends, or something. If she does, I'll be back. Batman will be back to settle the bill. Thanks Sheila."

"Wait for me Jules, reception is horrible here and I can't hear a bloody thing over the fly zapper. You'd think these days, even in this remote place, you would be able to hear New York. I have a really important meeting coming up, and my team is flying in on Sunday, so they need to be prepared, and I can't hear them properly."

"What took the pair of you so long? I have sensitive skin and even the fumes have me coming out in hives. Did you buy the place out?"

"Here, have some of my special cream for sensitive, hivey skin, Lesley and a matching slumber t-shirt, here you go. Ange is dealing with some very important work stuff, or some trite like that."

"Thank you Jules. Is it Chinese writing? I don't speak Chinese. What does it say?"

"No. 34. Chicken fried rice Lezzers. Now let's go…please. I need to find better reception for my phone. Hop to it Jules, no dilly dallying time is of the essence here, I need reception."

"I thought you needed the loo Lesley?"

"I'm fine, thank you for asking Jools. You know how resourceful us mummies are."

"Depends Lesley."

"Yes, indeed it does Jools."

"A woman is not a camel you know Lesley."

"If you're lucky though Lezzers, you'll have regular humps, not just on hive days and holidays."

"Or Wednesdays Ange. We were having some lovely chats with the cashier lady, Sheila from Down under, Lesley. Can you bloody believe her name's Sheila?"

"Oh, that feels so much better on my skin Jools, it really does seem to calm the irritation down a bit. GEM? That's a great name for an antihistamine cream."

"Antihistamine cream Lesley? That's the toothpaste you asked for Casper. The antihistamine cream is in the drawer to the right of the sink."

"I'm afraid Drew Peacock is going to have to get a new zipper for his debut and potential standing evasion. He won't mind if I've had to tear it will he."

"He might Angy."

"That was rhetorical, not even a question Jules. Does feel so much better to have it off."

"How am I going to get all this white stuff off my face before it begins to burn?"

"Said the actors to the Bishop. Don't sweat the small stuff Lezzers, I've been wearing a bondage hood for the past hour or so, and I wore it in public, not once, but twice. And look? it hasn't done me any harm."

"Speaking of small stuff Laddies, Sheila's come out to the forecourt to wave us goodbye. How nice is that? Like I say, sometimes, it's the connection that you make with the locals that makes all the difference to an experience. Say BYEEEE. BYYYYE. AURa VOIR S'long. S'later. Right, where now? In the words of Peter Pan, let's head towards the second star to our right and head straight on till morning. Keeping a beady eye out for the guidance of our north star."

"Never mind our north star Jules, how about the second bar on the right and drink straight through till dawn?"

"Now, we're talking Ange, a few sundowners won't go amiss. There's a lovely wee town about an hour north of here just on the edge of The Bush, we can stop there."

"Tim's my uncle, Jan's my aunt."

"It's Bob's your uncle, and Fanny's your aunt Lezzers."

"I'm very aware that Bob and Fanny may well be your uncle and aunt Angy, as you speak of them often enough, but they're no relation to me. Tim and Jan are mine. What does it even mean?"

"Apparently it means to easily get exactly what you need when you know someone in a position to give it to you Lesley, it's called nepotism, every family has one potential opportunity."

"Have you ever considered getting in one of those dividers Jules, like they have in London black cabs, and hearses which prevent noises coming from the back?"

"I wouldn't hear you now would I Angy if there was a divider between us, now would I?"

"How would you get to all your luggage and caravan of pharmaceuticals Ange, as My key says, a hearse doesn't come with a roof rack you know."

"Life is too short, I'd give all my belongings away Jules and more than likely, the pharmaceuticals put me in said hearse."

"Deep down, you're all heart Ange. Deep, deep down. 6 ft deep down perhaps."

"I'm ravished, can we please stop somewhere soon to eat, Jools."

The one who has a good friend doesn't need a mirror - Rumi

If you see someone without a smile, give them yours - Dolly Parton

On The Road Again

Laughter is a smile having an orgasm

Lesley

She doesn't fool me, she's definitely up to something, I can't quite put my finger on it, but she's definitely plotting something, maybe it's to do with that meeting she mentioned or maybe she's involved with some 'unavailable' man, regardless, 6 feet does sound very shallow to me, but I'm no digger, gold or otherwise. I know deep down she does love me, but oof, she can be brutal. Imagine living with that. No, thank you. I'm trying, but it's tiring always trying to second guess everything I say to her. Maybe I just won't bother saying anything in the future, or maybe I'll give her back as good as I get or maybe I should just let it go. After all, I know deep in the heart of my bottom it's actually not about me, it's more about her and all the heavy designer emotional bags she models so well. You only have to look at the majority of her past relationships to see she pushes people away from her before they get too close to whatever has made her disgruntled. The sooner she sees that she's emotionally unavailable to everyone including herself, the better off, the more open she'll be to longer-lasting relationships before it's too late, it may already be too late. No more, I have bigger fish to fry than worry about whether she likes me or not. Deflection I think it's called, easier to reject or make others reject you rather than exposing your suffering. Mikey calls her a "rabid chook", maybe it's "ravaged cheek?" "Ragged chick?" No mind. Well missy, not on my watch! I'm going to get to know what she's really been up to in the past 30 years, like it or lump it, show her that I value and am interested in our friendship.

"Remind me what is it that you do in NYC again Angy?"
"I'm a Hedge Fund Manager, Lezzers."

"Really? That's so funny, I was just thinking about chickens. What happened to them all? Bird flu most likely, it can completely wipe out an entire flock I hear. Good for you, someone has to find them, and make sure we get fresh eggs."

"Try "HEDGE FUND" manager for size, roll it round, see how that fits Lezzers. Have one of those Miracle bars on you Jules?"

"I didn't think you did the menopause Ange."

"I don't, but right now, in this very moment, it might distract me from ungracious, yet serious thoughts of murder."

"Oh sorry Angy, my bad, I really did mishear you that time. But seriously, who in their right mind would eat fudge made from hens, not I. But I guess there must be a market for it if you're this successful. Each to their own is what I say, live and let live, or as the French say, lazy fur."

"Not quite sure I know where to start with this one, but let's go with, laissez faire first shall we? It's laissez faire Lezzers."

"Now, you're the one being a silly billy again, I know that's exactly what I said, I'm not as stupid as I look. Like loosey goosey, you know loosey fur."

"Speaking of being a goose, leads me directly to fat and liver, and I know when my liver needs to be fatted. Do the honors Lezzers, this would be my last supper, pate de foie gras with slices of crusty peasant - style bread."

"I love geese, especially wrapped in a pancake with plum sauce, so I'm certainly not going to get angry and/or upset at being called a stuffed one, or getting stuffed, eh Ange?"

"We'll be friends forever won't we Pooh" asked Piglet

"Even longer" answered Pooh - AA Milne

People …Not A Big Fan

Ange

She makes me smile and recoil in equal measure. She really is a goose, a dame, a female gander, she's always so…together, poised, perfect, not a hair out of place, immaculate, that's it, no chipped polish, 24-hour lippy, not a wrinkle or crinkle on her clothes let alone her skin. In the same breath that I know I love her, she is still one of the only people in this world who can get my goat. Her name alone can drag me back to the past and to some very difficult emotions that were part of the 'motherly' package deal. She kinda looks like her too, she's about the same age as my mum was when she died. She looks great for her age, her skin doesn't have a single wrinkle, hardly any. If I didn't have support workers who cost an arm and a leg literally to keep any loose, potentially flabby, wrinkled skin at bay, then I'd be like an old Sharpie bitch. I HATE the loose flesh on me, and if I didn't attend to it, I'd be sailing the world alongside Jules, on a single, flappy jowl sail alone.

"All this chat about geese is making me more hangrier than I usually am, hurry up with the stuffed olives at the very least Lezzers."

"Do you know that foie grass has been banned in over a dozen countries? They force feed those defenceless, beautiful birds, which is excruciatingly painful, I might add, damages their liver, and people then pay through the nose for the privilege. Where did you say it was Angy?"

"Decades of liquid consumption can also be excruciatingly painful and can damage the liver also Lezzers, especially the effervescent type produced from French grapes. You'll find some in the platinum wine flask in the leather hamper basket."

"Hand the wine goon over to me instead, and one of those cardboard recycled straws on the floor there, Lesley. Three girlfriends and the best x rated beverage adult juice box on the planet."

"You do realise the "straw" is actually a tampax tube Jools? No judgement you understand, although somewhat surprised you still have your periods. Aunt Flo hasn't visited me for years."

"Hell no Lesley, that bloody mess all ended years ago, thankfully, traded for far worse hormones instead, all champing at the bit for control of our minds and bodies."

"I haven't menstruated since I was 14."

"That doesn't sound right Ange, are you sure you're not mixing your digits up? I use tampons as wine stoppers, and I recycle or chuck the cardboard packing out, but it works perfectly as a straw until it turns to mush, I see it as my bit for the environment. I'm still hungry, this adult capri sun doesn't quite cut the mustard."

"We all know that a liquid lunch without some kind of physical consumption, is neither funny or clever. I was a nurse, and I know that the stomach lining needs something to prevent the full onslaught of alcohol before potential bursting. You need to eat something. Most of the food in these cupboards Jools is circa 1975."

"Can we please stop and eat soon Jules, before I take my sarcasm out on some poor unsuspecting, innocent victim, ain't that right Lezzers?"

"That really surprises me, Ange."

"What would that be, Jules? That this cool, calm, confident, in control being gets sarcastic?"

"No, that you eat Ange, I always assumed you had a liquid diet, I include juices, cocktails and smoothies in that mix."

"Being a hedge fudge manager must be so exciting Angy, it certainly sounds like there must be loads of soirees and socialising. Being wined and dined must be fabulous."

"It's hedge fund Lezzers."

"That's what I said, didn't I?"

"Noo Lezzers, you said hedge fudge."

"I'm sure I said hedge. Sorry Angy, you must think I'm really, really stupid..duh!! My heid's like mince sometimes, and I still don't know whether you're a butcher, a baker, or a farmer. I'm not the wise one."

"Don't forget the handledick mater Lesley."

"Oh please don't add any more to the mix, Jools. My short term memory and powers of patience are slowly being shot to pieces, I can remember stuff that happened decades ago, but minutes ago? Forget it. Either of you remember that time you fell through the private hedge Jools, and it closed up behind you and we took forever to find you."

"I do Lesley. I don't know what took you so long to find me, as if Patrick, the large giant starfish compressed shape in the hedge wasn't a dead giveaway."

"Not that simple Jules, cos the entire PRIVET hedge sprung and closed up around you. It took us ages to find you, possibly days. Here one minute, gone the next."

"Like life then Ange. There are hedges all around the world that I have made an impression on. Believe me, but, call it an age thing, it never even crossed my mind as I pushed or as I was pushed, that the hedge may well be hiding long, rusty metal fence spikes, already waiting to impale, or prick us at the very least, claiming us as its latest unsuspecting hedge victim. There could even be a horror movie made about it. "If hedge's had eyes", "Hedgesuvseen", "A nightmare on Hedge Street ", "Hedgexist" ."

"Saved in the prick of time then eh Jules. My recollection is that we've all had plenty of pricks in our time anyway, with or without the involvement of hedges."

"Speak for yourself Angy, not me, Mikey was and still is my one and only. Now, I'm not saying that I don't imagine the taste and qualities of what's out there, like a sweetie store, or my Chicksmix jars, but I've never really cared for prick n mix personally, I prefer to know what I'm getting."

"Before you put it in your mouth you mean Lezzers?"

"I'm not saying you girls were promiscuous or anything, but you both used to have "NEXT" labels on your knickers. No judgement here you understand, we all need someone next in line to lean in on, to share your experiences, especially if you're single and lonely and all that. If I had all those support workers that you have on hand Angy, I'd be less exhausted all the time. However, I'm already knackered thinking how many support workers I'd need. I can only imagine the very, very, long list you must have to keep up with your demands, and expectations. Doesn't matter how much money you have at the end of the day does it? If you're lonely, you're lonely. How many support workers would you say you have Angy?"

"Let me see now, there's my yoga teacher, my barre, spin, rebounding teachers, my masseuse, chef, pool 'boy', cleaner, manicurist, and a nutritionist to optimise my metabolism, and everyone else between. My actual therapist handles all the extra invisible baggage. I find it helps my energy levels stay high having someone else take care of the small stuff. ”

"You must have them all on a retainer, or speed dial at the very least Ange. I personally have a very slow metabolism, so reading suits me, I'll stick to that."

"I've taken my retainer out in preparation and anticipation of some real food, can we please stop soon Jools."

"We can stop in this cute little place coming up, it has a lovely Japanese restaurant that gets great ratings. Blimey, there's hardly any parking spaces, Lesley, be a dear, and jump out, see when the next table is free. We'll circle the block."

We've been friends so long, I can't remember who the bad influence is - Unknown

Only that in you which is me can hear what I'm saying - Ram Dass

The Happy Tofu - Dumb Duck Nowhere

Lesley

"It's madness in there, not surprisingly, there's a wait list."

"I'll tell you what's more surprising than a waitlist Lesley, that as "I'm driving in my car", Madness are still alive and kicking and eating Japanese food in this "house of fun", in the middle of bum fuck nowhere, outback, bush, Australia."

""My Girl", that's "one step beyond". I wouldn't even wait that long to get into Dongers in New York… actually I would, but this isn't Dongers, and this shit hole place sure isn't New York. Jules, get yer "baggy trousers" out of Dirty. Out of my way Lezzers, I'll sort this out. S'cuse me, pardon me. scuse' me pardon me. Make way, I'm coming through, one step beyond. It's not always what you know, it's who you know. All eyes on me, step aside. Watch and Weep you two, this is not our house, this is "My House" "

"You say it with such authority and confidence Angy, that I am in no doubt that watch and weep is one of their songs, even though I don't remember it, I believe you, there's no messing with you, sometimes I wish I could be more like that Jules."

"Brash Lesley?"

"No confident Jools."

"You are confident Lesley."

"Not really, I'd never bull my way through a crowd of strangers like that."

"I've seen you do exactly that, remember when were were watching Sam and Vinnie play rugby and there was a scrap under the huddle, and you marched straight on to the pitch, forging a rajin path through the crowd, scattering parents and children alike, like a cat amongst pigeons, next thing you're knee deep in a sweaty, testosterone fueled scuffle, and you roared at the top of your voice "ENOUGH" and they all just fell to the ground like the naughty, quivering, petrified, school boys they were."

"That's different Jules, and well you know it."

"Lives were at steak Lesley, unlike this vegetarian place. We all have the ability to bring that confidence with us to any situation Lesley, it's what we tell ourselves about the scenario that robs the trust. That's all. We just forget it sometimes. The world is coming for us, it's not against us. The weight of our own doubts sabotage the portal of every moment, that next sceptical place which can be like a deep, dark cave full of uncertainty, ready and more than equipped to reflect back all that we lug into it. Best to put it down, leaving it at the entrance, carefully choosing our unseen colour palette. Armed and ready to paint the next Monet, oops I mean moment on the blank canvas of our known 3-D realm unfolding before us."

"Not a "grey day" after all. We have a private Horigotatsu room at our disposal, biatches get things done. After you, Jules, Lezzers."

"Tell me what you did Angy, how did you pull that off? Maybe I don't want to know, it's very kind of you non the less, but I'll be honest, not sure I like tofu girls, it always tastes like memory foam insoles to me no matter how much marinade it's soaked in, doesn't disguise the unmistakable sponge texture. Not sure about the name of this palace either, can anyone actually be truly happy eating tofu? I'll ask them to leave it out of my dish."

"I wonder if they serve deep fried cannabis leaves here, like an onion rose, we could share an order of that Ange."

"No credible restaurant would have tofu, either on it's menu or in its name, who in their right mind would be happy with that when they could have a juicy steak tartare with pomme frites, fried in animal fat from "Rob's roos ribeyes" down the road, answer me that Ms vegan flip flop?"

"I could say something cheesy Ange, but I'm only an inspiring vegan, so queso is not off the cards for me yet."

"Being vegan is a big missed steak Jules."

"Everyone's a little bit vegan anyway Ange, aside from the cheese, wine, makeup, ice cream, animal carcass shoes, and social 'meat' ups that is. Take a look at my feet though Ms C. Anibal, these are dehydrated mango skins, besides I have no beef with you here Ange, so no need for the pissy tempeh."

"I hadn't noticed you were even wearing shoes, Jules."

"Did you know that the word "vegetarian" is derived from the hindu word for "bad hunter"? I only found that out fairly recently when Robbie was doing a project on Asian cuisine."

"I think someone is pulling your perfect short pin Lezzers, whoever runs this place better be a Wagyu cattle farmer as far as I'm concerned, and not some dehydrated, green fingered, fruit peel crofter."

"Who needs to hunt these days when we have perfectly decent butchers at our fingertips, that's what I say. We have a fabulous local butcher in our suburb, a baker, a grocer that we can walk to when needed, I love that it's safe for my boys to walk to the shops for me."

"Sorry Lesley, but the thought of any fingertips, a butcher or any other carnivore, probing and poking dead flesh gives me the 'ick'. Butchers are the ones that should be called Grossers, and fruit and veg sellers should be BUTCHers. Watch out for people who pull your leg instead of your hands. Why did the tofu cross the road?"

"Because it knew it was time to get To Fu?

"Nope Ange. To prove it wasn't chicken."

"Not funny seitan, perfectly foul, pure offal, besides I'm not vegan because I love animals, I just really hate plants."

"Don't want to sound ignorant, but what food does this Japanese serve? I've been used to Mikey and childrens palates for a couple of decades now, but even with 4 boys, I'm not sure I've ever had Japanese food."

"You've never had sushi Lezzers? Which planet do you and your boys live on."

"I've had plenty of sushi Angy for your information, just not Japanese sushi, or not that I can think of anyways."

"I like the way you roll Lesley, however, the down side to sushi is that almost immediately after swallowing an entire paddy field of California, pinwheel, sticky thingymajigs, accompanied by a vat of dairy-free, avocado-based cado ice cream, than you're hungry again."

"Cadeau Jules, what a gift."

"The only gift that I ever get from avocados Ange, is the same bloody wooden balls in the centre, every time. People can become too lazy, and unimaginative to even change it out for another toy. Creativity takes courage, but is often lost in fear."

"That dessert sounds quite revolting Jules, like mushy, inedible baby food. I'm hoping for the usual ice cream made from melted gelatin, found in horses hooves with castoreum sprinkles."

"Excuse my ignorance Angy, did you say castrated horses? Please tell me they don't."

"I hate to be the bearer of sad, bad news here, Lezzers, but you've likely been feeding your husband and children the contents of a squeezed beaver anal gland, and possibly the shreds of some recycled foreskin previously worn by Black Beauty."

"How do I tell Sam, that he's been licking mint chocolate chip beaver anal glands wrapped in a burrito all his life."

"I wouldn't mind being licked till ice cream either, not by Sam, Jules, let's be clear here. On that note, hopefully the beef here isn't as dead as the atmosphere in this place is, and don't you pho get it."

"I'll try and control my tempura Ange."

It is the same life whether we spend it laughing or crying, same life - Japanese proverb

Never Let Your Besties Be Smug, Keep Annoying Them

Lesley

Jules's wink sums Angy up perfectly, whatever she did, she did, and here we are going to some private "hairy goats soup" room, sounds revolving if you ask me, but I'm sure she knows her soups, let alone her goats. Credit where credit's due, when I asked for a table not 10 minutes ago, they told me that not only was there a queue outside every night, it would take weeks just to put my name down for a reservation. It doesn't really surprise me that she managed to get us a private dining area though, very few people want to experience her wrath. I wonder what she said?

"Who in their right mind wants to sit in a room with hairy goats while eating their dinner is one step beyond even me. Is that how you got the table Angy, no one else wanted it? Is it like goat yoga? Doing a down dog with a goat rather than a down you go on a fork, much more my thing, and wine yoga, I enjoy that. Do they serve wine in Japanese places or is it all that sucky tea stuff? My word, the place is full of little people, what did we decide was the right terminology again? Wait no, they're all sitting…on the floor! Now I remember from Robbie's school project that Japanese people typically eat at low dining tables and sit on a cushion placed on a reed-like mat. In formal situations both men and women kneel, while in casual situations the men sit cross-legged and women sit with both legs to one side."

"Reminds me of page 35 in the Karma sutra Lesley, or the dance "Oops upside your head", everyone sat on the floor as if in a canoe, straddling each other from behind, then pretended to row along to the dulcet tones of The Gap Band."

" "I want all you gappers, and finger snappers, you toe tappers and you love rappers", such fun, and I think it's page 37 Jules. I'm sure I was almost penetrated from behind by some true, kilt cladded Scotsman on a number of occasions to that very song."

"Angy! Stop snapping your fingers, the waiter thinks you want him to come, and I'm not ready to order."

"It's the lyrics Lezzers, however the ability to come at the snap of the fingers could come in handy."

"Unless you're at a Flamenco dance convention Ange, that would just be downright embarrassing."

"For what it's worth Jules, I have never faked a sarcasm in my life."

"Andreas at your service, allow me to show you to your seats. Walk this way."

"He's keen, and I don't know what kind of establishment this is, but I for one am not taking off my clothes, that better not have been part of the deal you made to get a table Angy."

"I wouldn't mind him at my cervix."

"His name is Andreas, Lezzers, not undress, he's not asking you to be naked, thankfully. It's not an Nyotaimori experience."

"I knew it was a simple misunderstanding, Angy, and for everyone's constitution, it's not an experience with a naked goat either."

"Undress here is very impressed that chef Dobber, the head chef at Dongers, is a great friend of mine, and let me tell you, I have frequented my fair share of Japanese restaurants and have consumed raw flesh, Nyotaimori style, wrapped in skin canoes, and this exquisite bijou place is already going to make my top 10 favorite restaurants in the world. Let's hope the cuffs match the collar. We'd be able to tell if we did strip, eh Lezzers?"

"I feel like such an idiot, it's a combination of my hearing and the pronunciation of his name that has me bamboozled Angy, it isn't my fault. His name is Andreas, but it's pronounced "UNDRESS", an easy mistake. Besides, it's not a very Japanese name is it? John would be so much easier don't you think. I can't tell if you're pulling my leg or not Angy or am I completely missing something."

"All the clues you need are in the pointy, raised, tattooed, unflinching, perfectly peaked, shaped, shadowed eyebrows, accompanied by a sneer."

"That's my unnatural besting rich face Jules, not much wiggle room for anything else. Yes, I'm teasing you Lezzers, we're all delighted to hear you can keep your clothes on."

"Phew, and I'm glad there's not a hairy goat in sight…oh no, is it on the menu? I'm not eating that Jools, no matter how good it is. Is that our table? Down there? In that hole? How in god's name do we get down there? Abseil?"

"Engage your core Lesley, take a giant leap for mankind, a leap of faith, and freefall into those giant silk cushions, trusting that your weight will lower you delicately to the correct level. Have Ange's confidence and you'll float down like a delicate, baby feather."

"With my weight I'm likely going to go through to the core of this earth and end up physically in Japan. What if I hurt myself? Who is going to be able to take care of Mikey and The Boys? I can't do it, Jools."

"The moment you doubt whether you can fly, you cease forever to be able to do it. So come with me, where dreams are born, and time is never planned. Just think of happy things, and your heart will fly on wings, forever, in Never Never Land."

"Take all that gobbledygook Peter Pan soup stuff in with a teaspoon and a pinch of salt Lezzers."

"What if we fly, soaring further and higher than ever before, or worse, we never take the risks, telling ourselves we can't, then we'll be right, and we'll nose dive straight into the bowl of boiled rice already waiting for us. A whale has this incredible power surge followed by complete surrender and trust that they'll land perfectly."

"It's illegal to eat whale meat in Australia even though commercial whaling in Japan has been resumed apparently. There's another one for my G Spot diary. I'm not the complete imbecile you both think I am, and I'll tell you something for nothing, you're going to need a crane to lower this whale calf into that pit. I'm sweating on the mere notion of getting down there safely. Is it hot in here? Or am I having a combined day and night sweat…again?"

"It does feel a tad warm Lesley, I swear there's swell gel in the air, look at the size of my feet?"

"Hejzus Jules, check your toes, or are they fucking claws? I'll ask Undress to bring an additional bar to suspend across the dugout, so that you can invert yourself like a bat, only using the grip of your curled toes. You'll feel more comfortable suspended than being down there, touching all the non vegan, stuffed, silk, duck feather cushions. Take the weight off your feet after all that driving, perhaps settle in and roost for the night, however on closer inspection of those gnarled dried mango plates of yours, it might put me off my food."

"They're not that bad Ange. It's probably because I hardly ever wear shoes, preferring the earth, soil connection."

"I feel your strong soul connection Jools, not that I fancy you, it's the vibe you give off."

"Grovelling is almost as unattractive, as Jules's grisly snakeskin Dr Martens soles. Have you ever considered a pedicure, perhaps a landscape gardener?"

"Seems like in your line of business you'd be able to help her find one of those Angy."

"Blessed are we who can laugh at ourselves, for we shall never cease to be amused. I'm going to the little gorilla's room to moisturise my reptilian digits. I usually call the toilet "jim", it sounds better when I say I'm going to the "jim" at 1 am…3: 30, 4 am, 4: 30, 5."

"Alright, alright, alright, we sadly get the picture, only pulling your dry, flaky leg Jules, now go moisturise those piglets, an intervention of sorts, or a public service. Careful not to rub them together sparking a batik fabric fire. Help me down there Undress, thank you kindly, beautifully executed Sir. Now, speaking of execution, your turn Lezzers."

"Och I'll be fine up here Angy, I don't need to join you down there in the glory hole, I am more than happy to stay at floor level."

"Awa n shite, Lezzers, now get yer fanny down here."

"No need to swear Angy, Andreas…. don't be silly, what are you doing?…seriously…oooo…put me down…Ooooo you are deceptively very strong though aren't you, don't be…oooo, and you have very thick muscular arms under your kimono, and …hairy. Hairy?? Put me down, I promise I'll do it myself, now put me down immediately."

"You're wasting your breasts there Lesley, not sure he speaks inglese."

"You're back Jules.That was quick. Get yourself down here, Lezzers is full on resisting any help from Undress."

"I can usually pee like a racehorse, my record is a constant stream for 2 minutes, but I decided that I didn't want to miss watching Andrest escorting you two down to your seat, so I didn't really go. Besides, the toilet is blocked, so I wouldn't recommend going in there if you don't have to."

"Come on biatches, I'm getting lonely down here. Undress, would you kindly continue with the honor of transporting our fair maidens down here to join me in this chasm of pure sumptuousness."

"I'm far too heavy for you John, OOoo, put me down. Okay, if you insist...oooo… ooo, in for a penny in for 140lbs, slooooow mind, I have a dodgy back, ooo and I get dizzy easily and my knees have probably locked. Aggh, that's better, thank you Andreas."

"There you go, very graceful Lesley, very elegantly done, now since you're already down there Andrest, would you mind catching me? A hop, skip and jump should do it. From this angle you do remind me a bit of Patrick Swayze. You're young, fit and more than capable of handling this body aloft.Teach me how to jump on the wind's back, and then away we go. Look, look, I'm flying Peter. Thank the lard for soft landings."

"Not that I'm complaining Jules, but that soft landing happens to be attached to my crotch."

"And such a luverly, inviting, welcoming pouch of Douglas it is Ange."

"Who's Douglas Jools? I thought his name was John, or undies or something like that, or is it a kangaroo pouch? For his tips? My tip would be to have seating above floor level, not in dugouts, saves plenty of blood sweat and tears in my humble opinion. Sometimes though I think you two have your own language."

"We do Lezzers, it's called Igpai atlinai."

"Who are you calling a pig Ange?"

"Pig? Who's a pig? You're not calling me a pig are you Angy? And I still have no clue who Douglas is and what his pouch has to do with anything."

"I bet that these eiderdown cushions have a story plucked straight from their forefathers."

"You quack me up Ange, let's wing it and pluck dishes randomly from the menu."

"I'm not hungry anymore, I'll only have water, or I know, some sucky tea, I'll have that instead. Nothing to eat, well, maybe a wee lettuce wrap or two, nothing with duckling, or hairy goat in it, not many calories in that, maybe a crispy pancake roll or two? Mmm, a few of those won't break the tank bank will they?"

"Mikey's a lucky man to have such a...delight.....every night, every single night to come home to. I'm sure he's missing you immensely Lezzers, the mere mention of the pouch of Douglas makes me think of velvet tacos, finger licking good. I'm starving. Let's order."

"Mmmm, velvet tacos Angy? Now that does sound tasty. I might even try that, nothing adventured nothing blamed. Have either of you had them before?"

"It's one of my favourite kinds of taco, stick with me, I can guarantee you'll get a taste for them Lezzers, if you lick."

"Awww, how kind, yes, please Angy, that would be lovely, I'll try one, maybe two."

"Not here though Lezzers, dessert. Later."

"Oh velvet tacos are for afters? Maybe I can have them with poached pears. Love pears, my gran used to bake a lovely…"

"A stranger listening in wouldn't know which one of you is the youngest child."

"Technically I am Jools, chronologically that is, her blood is older but only because of the transfusion, not the DNA, which I do believe would be the legal definition."

"It was only a teaspoon of blood, and the rest of it was narcotics, barbiturates mixed with alcohol. Might explain some things. Could be a perfect explanation and example as to the side effect of drugs and transfusions on the human body, what do you think Lezzers?"

"You mean like second hand smoke Angy? Wards are full of adults who do not smoke, but have been exposed to secondhand smoke and are now battling coronary heart complications, lung cancer, and other diseases."

"Where did Undress go? I need to drink more."

"Och forget it Angy, I'm teasing you, the past is behind us and it doesn't help to keep looking back as if you're behind in the past. There's more than enough tea here to share."

"Some of our behinds are still behind us, Lesley. Far behind us, different time zones in my case."

"I'll play the familiar role of mum, shall I, and pour. Bottom's up."

"Shake your tail feathers Laddies."

"Stop it Jools, those poor birds. If I'm being totally honest here, I'm still surprised they serve any kind of tacos in a Japanese restaurant, duck, hairy goat, or velvet ones for that matter."

"May the best ye've ever seen, be the worst ye'll ever see, may a moose ne'er leave yer girnal wi' a tear drap in his e'e, may ye aye keep hale and he'rty, till ye're auld eneuch tae dee, may ye aye be jist as happy as we wish ye aye tae be." Cheers Ange, Lesley. And as Rabbie said "Here's to us, who's like us?"

"Damn few, and they're all dead" As Mikey says, "false friends are worse than bitter enemies"."

"Or as Oor Wullie said; "Haud yer wheesht an get oan wae it." Ooo, what was that noise? Like a suckling pig being detached from its mother teats."

"I hear it, and it's not me this time, it sounds more like a cork popping off the sucky bottles, music to my ears. Were you referring to someone as being or sounding like a pig Jools? Me?"

"Lesley, you were put down here gracefully and gently by Andrest, no need to add to the weight by putting yourself down any further."

"Jules?"
"Yes Ange?'

"SHUT THE FUCK UP. Are my eyes not rolling loud enough for you?"

"Let's drink to that. Chin-chins up. Andrest having you over his shoulder like that Lesley reminded me of the game we used to play as kids that I continue to play, only with my groceries, coalie backs. Remember that game?"

"I haven't lost my penchant for playing with cool mens bags Jules, we called them "piggy backies" "

"We called them "coalie baggies"…or was it "cool backies". No mind. I know what you meant Jools. The origin must have been either from someone who carried coal or pigs on their backs."

"Sounds more like a 'trapping' night out at a good old Scottish ceilidh Lezzers. The lucky man or men of the night are selected, scrubbed, cleaned, and carried over lassies shoulders to the nearest outdoor boudoir, left hanging out to dry at a later date. I'm the Captain of my ship. The landlady of the apartment block. The QueenBee."

"The jobby in the toilet?.... Don't look at me like that Angy, I'm only giving you another analogy. Am I being completely stupid here, I don't really understand what you mean."

"It means that I'm The Boss Lezzers, I control the narrative of my own mentally typed story, I'm in charge, the head honcho. I have no other responsibilities, commitments or accountabilities for anyone other than myself."

"Does that make you a pig or coal....or cool? It doesn't take much I know, but I'm still confused here. Help me out, Jools."

"I can tell by the faint twitch on the otherwise frozen, frosty, unbudgeable face before us, that Ange here has never contemplated BEING the one carried, she is the strong support, the boss, the full enchilada, bigwig, in charge.. her own jobby."

"Ahh, clear as mud...I think, thank you Jools."

"Here you are, Undress, couldn't have timed your arrival better...actually 5 minutes earlier would have been a bonus, but you're here now. This place is truly exquisite, there's a refined beauty in the colors and fabrics that hasn't been affected by time or social changes. Kudos to you and the team, and another teapot or four of your delicious sake, the last lot seems to have disappeared, evaporated into thin air. And bring plates of nibbles for us to share while you're at it."

"I'll pass on the pig nipples, Andreas."

"I'd like to piggyback with Lesley on that one Andrest. As I sit here swaddled in all this luxurious orange and gold silk, spun from the abused bodies of innocent worms, I'm reminded of Ange's "pants" and the impermanence of being alive to our bodies' sensations. Hair one minty, gone the next."

"And she's off. Put a much needed cork in your bouche will you Jules. Ignore her Undress, she does eventually run out of psychobabble steam, and those sensations are most likely effervescent bubbles leftover from the shed load of fizz you've guzzled over the past flirty decades, escaping from your pores."

"I'm not putting a cork in my own bush or anyone else's Angy, and I can personally vouch for both your fifty decades of debauchery."

"That sounds exhausting Lesley, even five decades would be too much for the average human bean."

"You know, I've never actually tried sucky tea before, someone once told me it tasted like fermented Cumboocha, which I know is meant to be good for the gut."

"And unwanted pregnancies I'm reliably informed Lezzers."

"Is that so? Shows what I know. Must be something new they've come up with, I would remember if they taught that in nursing school. I'm so glad I don't have to go through all that learning again. Been there, done that, dusted, bought and got 4 boys t-shirts to display for it."

"What's all that racket? Are they actually bloody vacuuming while we're still here and eating."

"It's called hoovering Angy, not vacuuming Sue - Ellen."

"I'm trying to eat and drink up as fast as I can, must be closing time and Andrest has disappeared. I think he's gone home. We must have drunk about 20 pots of the sicky tea, washed down by gallons of swine, now we're stuck in a hole without any way of getting out. I think it's time to go, don't you? We're pished and I need to get out of this hole we're in. Le weed to neave. Now."

"That was easy for you to sway, Drools, now give me a leggy up. Since I'm the only one that has only had tea, I'm going to go get and get DGT, time is moving on and so must I. What do they put in their tea in Japan? I feel light headed with an involuntary urge to dance."

"Allez oop la Lesley."

"Wheeee, I can fly, Peter. You don't know your own stwength Ghouls."

"She was the shot putt captain at school Lezzers."

"Really?"

"Eh no Lezzers, I was joking. Is it even a joke if you have to explain yourself?"

"Is it even a joke if it's not funny Angy?"

"Anything said out loud is open for misinterpretation, every darn thing Laddies. We all know that, that's probably why Amerkins talk with a soft, elongated droll, cos we don't want to take the risk of being misunderstood and shot in the process."

"You okey up there on terre ferme Lezzers, you kinda took a nosedive, and I can only see your very lovely peachy ass in the air, so can't tell where or how you face planted."

"Thanks for caring Angy, s'nothing to worry about, I'm fine, but boy that tea sure has a kick to it. I can hardly woll my woyds. It might be easier if I stand up. I'll go get DGT, Duels."

"You're not really walking in a straight line up there Lesley. Pretend to dance little pony, dance, that way no one will notice you swaying and stumbling about. Do you think she knows that sake is alcoholic Ange?"

"Not a Scooby Doo Jules, but she'll know tomorrow when she's reaching for the advil."

"You okay? Lesley? Lesley?? LESLEY?"

"I'm fine, thank you for asking Drools, nothing like a wee bit of carpet burn on your chin, oops I mean, shin. My tongue is snumb. I'll get Bathsheba, and meet you out front. Thatch t ish velly, velly stwong. I had no idea Japanese tea leaves had this effect, I feel almost a bit boozy would you believe."

"I'm a beeleber / bee blubber, a Beleiber Lesley."

"I can't be steemin though, tea, Chaponknees or otherwise doesn't have any alcohol percentage poof..poof.. Pwoof. pPROOF! Who's looking at me anyway, and if they are, they pwobably think I'm dancing, slow, shuffle, cha cha cha, quick involuntary circle of the pit, cha cha cha. I'm going to pay for this, I'm sure of it, cha cha cha. Definitely going to pay for this."

"What is she doing up there? Weaving between the tables like a deranged rabid dog, salivating, sweating, circling. THE DOOR IS TO YOUR LEFT Ginger. And Who the fuck is Bathsheba when she's at home Jules, and why is Lezzers paying for all this, I was going to take care of the check. Remind me to settle up with her later."

"I thought she meant something else, but no mind. Bathsheba was a woman who endured much suffering and overcame many obstacles with strength and courage."

" ……and she's here? In this restaurant? Where? I can't see anyone, Jules."

"Not in here ya big galoot, that's what Lesley called DGT, Bathsheba…"

"That's interesting, why do you think she did that?"

"No clue. It's only ever a guess as to what anyone else is thinking. The only thing I'm sure of right now, is that she can't handle her tea and we're stuck in a hole. How are we going to get out of here Ange?"

"Climb up on my shoulders and when you reach the floor, you'll be able to pull me out like they do in the navy seal workouts. Where's Undress when you need him? I need to pay him for all the sake, unless Lezzers is paying for everything, that's probably why she was hovering at the cash register. Allez-oop Jules. I'll square her up later, now pull and slide me gracefully out of this hell hole. PULL >>>>PULL, PULL dayum you, put some back bone into it, for the love of a dog."

"You're stuck Ange, don't just do nothing, relax, you're tighter than my jeans were in my 20's, now surrender, let go, not my hands you buffon, the controlled grip that's preventing me from extricating you, trust that I got this Ange. I'll pull your wrists, you kick off from the bottom will you. After 3. 3. PUSH."

"Where have 1 and 2 gone? PULL Gawd dayum you Jules. PULL. I'll push."

"Heave ho, heave ho, no wucking furries Ange, I'll pull you out of there like one of my reluctant, resilient, white chin hairs. Look what the cat drugged ouy."

"Wheeeeeeee, plucked from oblivion. FREEDOM. I don't think I can stand Jules, my legs are like a pair of well toned, stoned, Japanese, jelly eels."

"How about I drag you gracefully behind me, like a sled gliding over ice, how does that sound Ange? This is an absolute breeze, you're sliding beautifully along the carpet, like a greased suckling pig, and you're as light as a feather. I think I can even run."

"Wooohoooo, Jools? Angy? I'm over here…whoooo, you two, here's me, now hurry up and get in DGT. The sooner we're back on the road, the sooner we're at our lodgings."

"You can't drive Lesley, let me take over."

"I've only had tea Drools, so I'll be fine. Can't be too much further."

"There's a lovely wee pub on the way, calling to us and it's only a few miles down the road from where we're staying. What do you say to that Lesley, since you're the driver."

"I'm happy with whatever, we must have missed some kind of celebration at the Japanese place though as all I can see in my rear view mirror is flashing blue lights on the horizon behind us. The jet black night sky looks spectacular with all the blue beams circling the stars don't you think?"

"When we look at the night sky, we see a vast empty space interspersed with stars: likewise when we look inside, we experience a vast stillness peppered with thoughts, feelings and sensations, and those beams are blue lights Lesley, blue lights? Any bells? The cops are flashing at us to pull over, remember that I'm deaf, you're blind and Ange doesn't speak english, then we should be just fine."

"Makes more sense if I'm the driver, that I'm deaf, you're blind, and Angy doesn't speak, full stop."

"This should be fun, loves me a flashing copper I do."

"Wheesht Angy, you're the mutt remember. Good evening Occifer, how can I help? Was I going over the speed limit?"

"Your speed was fine."

"I've never peed on a fire in my life, it could be flammable."

"Ssssh, quiet in the cheap seats back there, put your gas down to a peep, let me handle this Angy. I apologise in advance for these pair of twats, but I'm their support worker and it's care in the community day. My advice would be to ignore them, give them half a chance, and they take the mile. They like to play to a crowd, or even a single, solitary police person like yourself. The one in the back makes faces behind my back all the time... well, it looks like she's making faces, but with all that bull seamen injected in her cheeks, who knows which grimace is intended. She does it all the time. How can I be of help?"

"Your backlight is out."

"Fine her $100 for that and add an additional $3,000 for misleading the public Officer."

"And why exactly am I misleading the public Angy?"

"When the light is fixed Lezzers, this lovely police officer will be able to see Dirty's private number plate reads "1M 5EX1". "

"Very funny, you just made my otherwise monotonous night entertaining. Get it fixed at your earliest convenience and be off with you before I change my mind and give you more than a warning."

"I'd like more than a warning from you Officer Dribble. Perhaps you'd like to give me your no?"

"Oh please stop Angy, see what I have to put up with occifer, I'm telling you, they don't pay me enough. Pay no heed, you really don't want to go there with that cougar, trust me."

"I prefer cub whisperer Lezzers."

"I wouldn't say that Ange, more like a life coach with a very hands on approach."

"Have you been drinking back there, Mayam?"

"They have, lucky for them I only had tea, making me the dicared driver."

"I am more than capable and happy to blow whatever you have close to hand. What does your name badge say "Hood", Officer Hood."

"Angela!"

"No need to "Angela" me, Lezzers, that's what breathalysers are for after all, you blow into them. What on earth were you thinking?"

"Is that so Angy? Show's what I know, now can we go now, before she says or does something that's only going to cause me more mental and physical torture."

"In our defence, we are all peri/full blown menopausal women officer, and as we don't have any miracle menopause bars on hand, might I suggest backing away slowly, not making anymore eye contact with any of us, turn and run the feck away."

"Heard loud and clear. I have a mother and an aunt around your age, so I'm going to let you all off with a warning tonight, but please drive carefully, and get that light fixed."

"Thank you. Byyyye. That was close, you're welcome, no thanks to you Angy, all I'm saying is be thankful I was here to drive and get you off a potential ticket. Now let's consecrate on celebrating my oldest and by far the widest friends I have, all turning, or turned in some cases, 50 this year."

"How very dare you Lezzers, first off, I for one am 39, so was not the one he was referring to as mother or aunt."

"Plus shipping and handling Ange."

"You know I almost had to ask Chips back there out on a date only to save your life. …again Lezzers. He was about to breathalyse YOU."

"I'd have passed that test with flying collars Angy."

"It's colors Lezzers, and I think not."

"Is that so? Well, shows what I know eh? Look Angy, you should be thankful, I'm the one behind the wheel, driving us."

"Oh thank gawd you cleared that up for me Lesley, for a minute I thought I was driving."

"You can relax Jools, you've done a great job driving so far, I got this. Where are we going anyway? I have no idea, someone direct me, not you Angy."

"Keep straight. A couple of miles further and you'll see The Wobbly Bottom Sip on the left. It's a small town, only one way in and one way out. We can stop there for a snifter or three, our abode isn't too far from the pub, that way you can continue to drink Lesley."

"Sounds like a plan Stan, but I think I'll push the boat out and have more than tea this time Drools."

Every time you judge someone you reveal a part of yourself that needs healing - Unknown

Friends cheer you up with comforting words. Best friends cheer you up with sarcasm. - Unknown

Best Friends Ask For Advice Then Do The Complete Opposite

Lesley

When is this "old enough to know better" supposed to kick in? It's futile trying to suggest whether we should go straight to our accommodation, drop the bags, have a quick freshen up, and then go back to the pub, or not. I can tell they're on a mission, and it would take a very brave person to try and stop them, especially Angy who is still snarling at me, more than her usual growl, something is definitely eating her up and she's taking it out on me. I get it, she may be jet lagged, more likely something else, it's challenging trying not to get entangled in her sarcastic snares. She can be like a rabid dog, she just wants to keep going and going. My mum used to always say, "Don't keep returning to the dog that bit you". My bet is that she's trying to avoid something, that's what people do sometimes, they react to someone or something because of a piece that's in them that keeps popping up, showing its true colours. That's what I keep telling myself anyway. No one can keep that kind of anger going for that length of time without fuel or breaking, and I will not be that spark or straw that ignites that particular fire. It must be such a cross to bear, or is it such a bear to cross, or never cross a bear or such… no mind, life makes her cross, almost everything, including me, has her raging at the injustices of the world. If she took the time to slow down, instead of speeding physically, literally, and medicinally through life, numbing every experience with drugs, alcohol, and a smattering of suffering. No judgement here you understand, a mere observation that's all. We all have our own not coping mechanisms, mine's sausage rolls, buuut, it's a whole different ball gown when you haven't been drinking or taking drugs and have to witness the immodesty. You have to go through the ups and downs of life, avoiding, or pretending things did or didn't happen, only causes more psychological and physical damage. I tell the Boys this all the time, life lessons keep coming back to kick you in the backside until you learn what you need to learn or accept your life the way it is, warts and all, despite its presence. What are you missing learning from continually returning to the ass that kicked you?

"There's a parking space Lezzers, quick…..on the left, pull in, quick, quick… fuck you dosey cow, you missed it."

"No matter where I pull in, I can still forget where I park the van."

"Oh everyone does Jools, unless you have a driver that is, I guess part of their job would be to remember where they are parked."

"Yeah, but I shop online Lesley."

"Will you stop already, Lezzers, and park for fucksake. Doesn't seem too hard a task to ask."

"Put a muzzle on back there, ignore her, no harm or rush Lesley, slow down and disregard the peanut gallery behind you. Go round the block if you need to, there are plenty of spaces. Look, there's the pub's fire exit door on the left, pull in there. Loads of room for Gertie and we can walk round the corner from here."

"Whhhoooa, the brakes really do work Lezzers, last time I was thrust forward and back again like that was in the back of the original Dirty, with some nubile, young surfie."

"Blimey Ange, that feels like a 100 years ago, when we couldn't, or didn't care whether we threw our backs out or not, the moans and groans were from pure deid pleasure and ecstasy, not to be mistaken with the aches and pains penetrating the joints, muscles and bones, from Lesley's emergency brake. Nothing WD 40 can't fix."

"Let's face it, the only joints you two have ever really cared about are green and rolled."

"The only rolling I do more of these days tends to be over my ankles, filling saline fluid in them sucked directly from my vagina, which is dryer than a mouthful of Jacob cream crackers on a good day, so a stroll round the pub would benefit the head, ankles, liver and libido. Welcome to the menopause Laddies. Hashtag Me too. It SUCKS. BIG TIME."

"Yet Hejzus sandals, car bar shoes like my Jimmy Choos are a choice."

"I'd choose comfort over your Chimney Shoes any day Angy, at our age, our choices must be carefully selected, although I wouldn't mind wearing yours at one of your mile high club get-togethers."

"Spend a minute in my head, Lezzers, that should convince you enough that you don't want to be in my shoes. The thoughts alone would freak you out, and have you signing up for a frontal lobotomy."

"I'd take the bottle in front of me every time Ange, that wee B Itch menopause furry, hairy, scarey, fairy has stolen my figure, my sleep, mood, patience, eyesight, brain cells and has replaced me with a Freddie Mercury moustache, muffin top, muffin biceps, triceps, jowls, thighs, bum and ankles, and do you know what? I'm fine with that, in fact I'd go so far as to say, I don't give a flying feck, not one flying feck do I give. It's still a smoking hot body, only heavily disguised in the form of menopause. No men…or even pause. Turns out the chest pains I've been having is only me stepping on my nipples."

"Me too, Jools. I know it can look ugly, but these puppies are easily hidden beneath my vest which is concealed under my pop button denim shirt."

"That's quite the look, not your vest day ever Lezzers."

"It's for my anxiety, Angy. I wear a weighted vest when I think I'm going to be stressed."

"Oh for fuck sake, don't you start Lezzers. Stressed is just desserts backwards, there's enough of this claptrap nonsense from her dis grace here. How on earth does a weighted vest being worn under a denim shirt help anxiety. And before you answer, it's not a question, I personally don't care to hear the answer."

"Does it help Lesley?"

"It really does Jools, thanks for asking, it helps me when I'm beginning to feel anxious or stressed out about something coming up."

"What on earth do you have to be stressed about Lezzers? You have a husband who even to this day is completely besotted with you, 4 amazing boys who are a total credit to you, and you still have a head full of beautiful, bountiful, lush, glossy hair."

"Are you feeling okay Angy? That was almost a compliment. I'll take it though, thank you, and you are more than welcome to use my natural bristle brush anytime you like. It's in my bag, help yourself anytime. I'd be more than happy to do it for you if you'd like."

"If you're Happy Lesley, then which of the 7 dwarves does that make me?"

"I'll take you up on the offer of the brush Lezzers, but I can do it myself thank you very much. Hey wait, speaking of Happy, has someone been helping themselves to my antidepressants and temazepam? The lids off the container, and they're all over the bottom footwell."

"You sound like Grumpy Ange, then I must be Sleepy."

"I told you they'd all spilled out Angy, I wasn't rifling, if that's what you're implying? If Jools hadn't gone round the wrong way round the roundabout, then this wouldn't have happened, every choice has a consequence, might take its sweet time to show up, and it may not be pleasant, so choose well that's all I'm saying. Seriously though, Angy, they don't work, you seem more like Grumpy when you've been consuming them, like night and day, almost making you Dopey."

"Lesley wears a weighted vest and you take happy pills, sounds like the beginning of a great story. We all have our own ways to numb our discomforts."

"You're going to feel your discomfort for shuwa if any of my stuff gets stolen, Jules. That bag lady sitting on the sidewalk could be on a look out for a lucrative opportunity."

"I'll ask her to mind Gertie for us, I don't have anything of any value in Gertie, or anywhere else, if it gets k nicked, it gets k nicked. Nothing is permanent, it can all be taken in a spit of a second. There's enough pain and suffering out there with people resisting and not accepting the impermanence of everything and everyone. We live, then we die, not a spoiler alert, it's how we choose to live between those two points, despite the challenges that determine the level of one's happiness. We get to show up on our very own invisible red reality carpet as it unravels and unrolls before us. Careful how we write our script, cemeteries are full of unfinished manuscripts, ideas that never saw the light of day, relationships destroyed, resentment, anger, shame, all carried away on the wings of the final breath. Unhappiness can be seen as a good thing, it can show us where our work is, taking us back to that place at birth, the pure, unadulterated void of happiness."

"Jules?"

"Yes Ange."

"My eyes have had enough spin classes to last a lifetime, now, SHUT THE FUCKETY FUCK UP. Stop with the gobbledygook nonsense, the only unravelling and unrolling I'm planning on doing is if Officer Robin Hood back there, shows up at the Wobbly Bottom Strip."

"Robin Hood, rubbing the bitch, giving in to amour?"

"Not bad Jules, besides IF I were on my very own red carpet, I'd be wearing some of my terribly expensive sparkly designer jewellery which I happen to have with me. Do you expect me to take it into this red neck joint? On second thoughts, looking at the place, it might well be safer left in Dirty"

"Hide it under something Ange, my clothes, the seats, anything really. Who in their right mind is going to rifle through all this dirty laundry and plastic landfill tatt to get to a blood diamond? Noone. That's who. Maybe take a few more of your happy, clappy, slappy, crappy pills Ange."

"I'm not that bad Jules! Here Granny Clampett, take this $100 bill, you're very welcome, and there's plenty more where that came from if you manage to keep your beady, wrinkled, old eye on this VW for us while we have a sherry or two in The Wobbly Bottom Strip."

"And here's a little something from me, a jar of Lesley's homemade Chicksmix to keep you company. What a beautiful bag you have there, looks familiar. Go easy on the gummies, nod, nod, wink, wink, they were the druggies choice for the Chicksmix. Enjoy. We'll be in the pub if you need us."

If you haven't learned the meaning of true friendship, then you've not learned very much - Muhammad Ali

There are things known and things unknown and in between are The Doors - Jim Morrison

The Wobbly Bottom Sip

Jules

The best friendships are built on a solid cemented foundation, constructed using lashes of laughter, strands of sarcasm, acceptance, and love, all beautifully encapsulated in a net of mischief and nonsense- the perfect safety blanket.

"Do you know where you're going, Jools, we seem to be going in circles. If we keep going, we'll end up back where we started."

"Come on biatches, let's get cracking, let's rock n roll, help yourself to these happy, clappy pills, heavenly disguised narcotic tic tacs"

"Are you sure they're tic tacs Angy, there's a barcode on them. You'd better be careful, you don't know what you're taking, might be tic tacs, might be antidepressants, might be birth control pills, so the question I should really be asking you is do you know what they're actually for? There's a big difference between birth control, hunger suppressants, prozac and tic tacs."

"Why on earth would I have birth control pills at my age, Lezzers?They might be my antidepressants, diet pills or valium, my own personal pharma Chicksmix."

"You can tell she's more Grumpy than Happy about that Lesley, but maybe in about 30 minutes the roles will reverse..hopefully."

"I don't think they're my antidepressants, I put them in another pouch, and not my pouch of Douglas either, and they'd better not be my laxatives I've just consumed."

"I thought you didn't give a shit what you put in your mouth Ange."

"It's worse than that, Angy. Sorry, I think those are my pills. All the pills got mixed up, and well, these might be mine."

"Don't tell me they're Vitamin fucking C Lezzers?"

"No."

"Moringa."

"No."

"I think they might be Viagra Angy."

"That's why you look like you could key someone's car with your nipples Ange, I can hardly wait for this one Lesley, do go on, don't let me stop you."

"For your information, they're not for me, but I suppose indirectly they really are for me. Call me shellfish, but I grind them down and add them to the homemade breakfast muffins I make specially for Mikey, but only when The Boys are staying with their grandfather you understand."

"What you're saying is before he actually gets up in the morning, he's about to anyway after his breakfast. You remember Lesley's father in law, Richard, don't you Ange? No viagra needed there if memory serves me right."

"Let me get this straight Lezzers, you have Viagra pills for reasons we now know about, and aside from trying to erase that terribly disturbing image from my mind of Mikey eating your muffins, I have been swallowing them like they were going out of fashion."

"I thought they were tic tacs Angy, seriously. I'm sorry. How many do you think you've taken?"

"I'd say she's gobbled about 12 inches worth.... shouldn't be too hard to crack a smile Ange, you've had a whole lot worse in your body, so relax Darlene, things are looking up for sure. It's one experience out of a gazillion others you could be having right now, so, come on now, stiff upper lip and all that, lean in and enjoy ... .and if you don't, I don't know though, it's HARD to please you sometimes Ange. Take some with your prozac, that way if something were to come up, you won't care. Perfectly normal to feel aroused around me."

"Being around you Jules,makes me wish I'd taken the diet pills."

"Where there's a pill there's a way, here we are Laddies, The Wobbly Bottom."

"Says "The Cloak and Stagger", Jools."

"That's the dirty bar Lesley, nothing but the best lounge bar for u.s."

"Both are equally appealing to me. My kinda pubs."

"Let's face it Ange, most pubs are your kind of place."

"I told you, we've walked completely round the block, exactly back to where we started, not surprising my feet hurt. If I peek round that corner, we're going to see DGT and the old woman. Look? Told you, we have literally been walkjogging for the past 10 minutes to come back to almost the same place we started at."

"Stop your pinging and get in here Lezzers, I started off walking wearing high heels, and now they've been ground down to designer plimsolls after all that, am I complaining? No. These are car bar shoes, and not car, trudge, stagger stilettos, but I managed to put a positive spin on what is likely turning out to be the hardest day of my life. Follow me, my little monkeys, watch and learn."

"On the plus side Laddies, we got our 100,000 steps in. Don't know about you two, but that walk has left me positively parched, chicksmix isn't enough, I need a 'snake or roo' or two. Speaking of "stagger". Let's grab a table that's not too close to the karaoke/disco/band, yet close enough to the toilets, but not too close so as to make it too obvious that we're old and our pelvic floors leak, and not too far away from the powder your nostril room, to make it a dangerous flood zone. A couple of cocktails wouldn't be stiffed at, what do you say Ange, you're always up for a stiff one."

"If you eat much more snackery Jules, you'll be the size of your van."

"I've been given extra airbags because I'm precious, have you eaten in the past 30 years Ange or do you still manage to function on liquids and slices of the occasional substance, verbal abuse."

"I'm at that point in my life Jules, where everything calls for a drink. There's some tasty looking bait in this place, be still my beating vagina."

"Glad yours still beats Ange. The only time I get a pulse down there is when they roll out the dessert trolley. Any other requests, Laddies? Lesley? Come on my little partners in wine, how about over there beside the fire exit, close to the toilets, facing the dance floor and the bar. Ange?"

"Excellent choice Jules, perfect vantage, preying, bordering on stalking booth. Full vantage point. And it's happy hour, win, win."

"Like Goldilocks Syndrome, not too near the DJ, not too far, just right. At my age , happy hour is considered a nap."

"Don't worry about me, but a bit too loud in here for me Jools."

"Great Lesley, glad it works for all of us. Quaint dance floor where sweat meets pheromones, yeast meets yeast, meats mingle and dance under the strobe of disco lights, highlighting one sweaty gyrating body at a time, snapshotting and freeze framing the entire experience, a pdf memory flash file of our life in our very own hands."

"I'm thankfully way too old for some paedophile Jools, more like a recycled teenager."

"Good to know Lesley, I'll make sure someone else gets the memory pdf file. I remember navigating very similar floors like this in our heyday, crossing it without getting pissed, stoned, or pregnant in the process was a miracle. I regularly contribute bodily fluids to floors, not solely confined to disco ones, my entire body cracking like a glowstick whenever I move across one, yet refusing to actually glow, terribly disappointing. Slut drops have had to be removed from my repertoire, replaced with dirty slops, slip and drips. Do you hear that Laddies?"

"All I hear is the screechy nasally melody, of a group of redneck Australian hillbillies at the bar, sharing their limited knowledge with one another."

"We sound like a doomed threesome on Australia's Missing Talent, groaning and moaning as we try to keep our balance on the wet, sticky dance floor."

"Funny Jules, slip n slide, meets snap, crackle and pop."

"I despise it when people say something is funny without actually following it up with a sound or look that reflects what they're saying, in my humble opinion that is Angy, no offence, but Shirley if something is funny, then it should be paired with the matching image and sound."

"It can be hard to tell what someone else is experiencing due to the unnatural frozen state of their tampered fine facial muscles. Nuances are drowned in fillers/botox, truths concealed behind masks and labels. They could literally and figuratively be pissing themselves with laughter, let's face it, easily done at our age, a dance floor covered in beer is a perfect cover for a loose bladder. Every crowd has a slaver lining. There's so much spillage on this dance floor that adding our own personal source can be an advantage if we run out of time, and don't make it to the loos. Can't stop a speeding express tinkle train once its left the station."

"No matter what they say Jules, two stepping into someone else's golden shower has never really appealed to me funnily enough."

"I've always been partial to a bit of water sports myself, especially the surfing ones. Not actually me, but I love watching Mikey and the boys surfing at Bondi beach."

"What do you call someone stuck on a desert island, Lezzers?"

"Don't tell me Angy, I LOVE these guessing games. Someone stuck on a desert island?"

"Correct."

"Castaway?"

"Nope."

"Outcast?"

"Naw."

"LEPER?"

"No."

"Outlaw?"

"Try again. Louder."

"Give me a clue."

"DESERT ISLAND."

"Shipwrecked?"

" Close…very, very close… a color, make it loud Lezzers."

"MAROONED. MAROONED. MAROONED."

"YAAAAYYYYYYY."

"Why is everyone suddenly cheering and clapping, scared the holy ghoulie out of me."

"You bought everyone a drink Lezzers."

"I did not Angy."

"Yes, you did, you shouted Ma ROONED, and mine's a large gin and tonic, and I don't want that pish they serve from a hose gun, proper bottled tonic. And don't fuck it up Lezzers?"

"Yes Angy, I got this, a double gin and bottled tonic. What would you like, Jools?"

"Hmmmmm, I'll have the house porn cocktail without the tail. Put some marching china cherries on top please Lesley."

"I fancy the sound of that as well Jules, perhaps a slice or two of pineapple, sounds very refreshing, and healthy, at least one, if not two of my five a day. Lezzers, what's 6 inches long, 2 inches wide and drives women wild?"

"I'm not playing your childish games Angy."

"Spoilsport, the answer is a $100 bill, take it to pay for the round."

"Need a hand Lesley?"

"No thank you Jools, but thanks for asking."

"Hey Lezzers."

"Somebody hold me back, are you offering to help me Angy?"

"Kinda, I'm paying for it. Bring back a menu."

"Thank you Angy, very kind and generous, and much appreciated."

"Now, get on with you, before I change my mind. WAIT. Lezzers, sit back down, it's table service."

"Sorry about the wait, I'm Ty, I'll be your server tonight."

"Hi, I'm Lesley, Scottish originally, and I've been to Bangkok, and Phuket, a beautiful country you have. A half pint please, and don't worry about the weight, it happens to the best of us doesn't it Jools. The older we get the tougher the battle. I seem to be on the losing side most of the time. The not winning side, you know what I mean."

"Allow me to push your stool in."

"Oh you naughty, naughty boy Tie, we've only just met."

"Ignore the Uhmerikan. I'll have a half pint of light beer, and please make sure it's light, I'm a bit of a lightweight these days, I can't handle much more than 2 %, besides I might be the impregnated driver, again."

"Righty o, one half pint, and? You?"

"I can't fully hear Thai, what did he/she they/them/ it say, the music is too loud."

"He asked what you'd like to do to him, Jules?"

"Can you ask Thai to speak louder Ange, I still can't hear him, get him to shout."

"She's hard of hearing Tie, you'll need to SHOUT."

"Tell him to shout louder, Ange."

"SHOUT…...**SHOUT.**"

"YYYAAY."

"You've just bought everyone a round Ange, you've been tricked the same way you tricked Lesley."

"I knew exactly what I was doing Jules, merely indulging your childish humour."

"Is that so Angy, show's what we know."

"She's a cunning linguist, Lesley."

"Go and ask him for sex on a beach, Lezzers."

"I know your game Angy, you can't pull the sheet over my eyes. If you want sex on a beach, ask him yourself."

"The music is too loud for him to hear me properly, Lezzers, charades it is."

"I can't tell if you're winking Ange, or your false eyelash is stuck to your cheek, you look like a downright terrifying, scarier version of Columbo, on a good day. Maybe we can stay till closing time and you can use that particular parody to help clear the bar with that brass neck of yours."

"One of Lezzer's pills has lodged itself in the back of my throat and now I have a stiff neck, not at all brass."
"We might get a lock in if we play our cards right, every crowd and all that, every crowd. Come on Laddies, time is money, I'll have a pint of your best, lukewarm, wine pish please and three bags of your nuts, thank you Thai."

"I'll still have a pot of beer. In case you've forgotten Angy, they call a half pint of draft beer, a pot of beer, which can be very confusing to you. I know, you want to make sure you're getting what you order."

"Actually I fly here regularly, Lezzers."

"I didn't know you came here for work, you've never mentioned it before, Angy."

"I'm mentioning it now, don't fret Lezzers, it's rarely NSW, mainly Queensland, but there are opportunities in Sydney."

"I didn't know you worked up in Queensland, close to Hamilton Island, eh Angy. Agggh, DJ's getting louder, I can hardly hear myself think over this music."

"Sometimes that can be a blessing in disguise Lesley. It is LOUD though, where's the volume control?"

"Okay Sheilas, what we got here, we've got a pot of beer, a pint of... something. You?"

"The porn cocktail, with an umbrella please Tie."

"I can tell by the stunned expression on Thai Juan Hahn's face, Ange, that this establishment is not known for its seafood, too far from the ocean for prawns is my best guess. Lest we forget, it's a true blue, real, deal, Aussie pub in the outback."

"You know what Tie, bring a round of tequila shots instead. Three each please and three pots of draft beer chasers."

"I don't think they're free Angy, but it's worth the try."

"Free is her lucky number Lesley, and yes, 3 each please Thai. My lucky number is 5."

"Okay then Jules, 5 shots of tequila, each."

"Changed my mind Ange, it's not actually 5, it's 7."

"Coming up Sheilas."

"I'm sure it is Tie, I have that effect on men, it's a gift and a curse, believe me, and don't forget to bring me a menu, I'd like to see what's on offer Down under."

"We may look mildly absent Thai, but we're not, well I am marginally, but for the most part we all fire on all cylinders. Although they often backfire on us, besides age is merely the number of years that everyone has had to enjoy us."

"Speak for yourself Jules, absinthe makes the heart grow fonder, they say. Now off you pop Tie, and don't dilly dally on the way. Speaking of draft, I need one. It's stifling in here, anyone mind if I wedge the fire door open, get a gulp of fresh air."

"At my age Ange, I appreciate a draft, a gulp, a gust of fresh air wedged in my nether regions. It's music to my loins."

"Okey then, I'll just jam it open a bit then."

"It's a fire exit, Angy, not sure it's meant to be open, promise me someone will close it when you feel cooler. Have my menopause hand held fan instead."

"Eh, no, I don't want people to know I'm having hot flashes. I'll leave it a crack, a smidgen Lezzers, so we can at the very least get the faintest breeze of relief from the DJ's smoke machine."

"Be it on your own head if you get yourself into trouble, Angy, there are always consequences to actions, and leaving a fire exit door open is not a good sign."

"I tell myself it's my inner child playing with matches, sounds more fun than hot flushes. I promise to make sure it's closed when we leave, and I'll have the menopause hand held fan Lesley, I don't care what others think, besides I'm no mind reader."

"I'm going to hold you to that promise, Jools. You can both share my tequila shots, I'm not really in the mood for one, even if they are free. Have mine."

"Don't mind if I do, bum's up Lesley. Cheers ma dears, here's to a fun eventful time, where conviviality is combined with cocktails without the tails, comestibles, familiar melodies, reminders of timeless occasions where dear friends intertwine to create the narrative. Slàinte. Chin-chins, Old deers."

"To my partners in wine, the only 2 people on this planet who have ever really put up with me and stuck by me."

"That's not quite true now is it Ange?"

"You must have others in your life, Angy?"

"Perhaps Lezzers….but it's complicated."

"How complicated can it be? Do you love him/her/them/they?"

"Bizarrely enough Lezzers, I believe I do."

"Then what's stopping you? Life is far too short Angy, mark my words, take the chance while you can, take the risk, what's the worst that can happen? Please tell me not that his wife finds out..again."

"I eat risk analysis for breakfast Lezzers."

"Look Angy, I know we have our differences, but as a friend I accept all facets of you, even your many shortcomings. Regerts are only a reflection of what you didn't do, so for what it's worth, I say take the risk, you have nothing to lose, and from where I'm standing, everything to gain."

"How terribly generous of you Lezzers. Anyway, as I say, it's complicated."

"How complicated can it really be? I tell Mikey and The Boys all the time that there's a solution to practically everything in this crazy life, the challenge is digging deep enough, peeking beneath the layers of our own judgments, opinions, and criticisms which cloud, and obstruct the way. Whether you spend the rest of your life laughing and loving or angry and bitter, it's the same life either way."

"Terribly profound, even for you Lezzers, I'll try to keep those wise words in mind."

"I think you should go for it, take the horny bull by its testicles and all that. Life's too short, and it gives you plenty of chances to see what you need. "You've got to search for the hero inside yourself, search for the secrets you hide, search for the hero inside yourself, until you find the key to your life." Being scared of what hasn't happened yet, only makes us more of a flight risk."

"Wow Jools, that was incredible, well said."

"I'm faking it Lesley, it's M People circa..1990's."

"Speaking of fake, you have the most fabulous voluminous breasts, Lezzers. Are they real?"

"All mine I'm pleased to say Angy. Steady girls, it's not a race, you want to get to the finish line in one piece, not completely bladdered, speaking of bladdered, it takes me ages to decide whether I'm finished widdling or not, I think I am, leave the toilet and bam...bladder feels full again. 4 natural childbirths will do that to you."

"Have you not had any breast work Lezzers? They're seriously fabulous."

"Absolutely NOT Angy, these boobs have fed four hungry bairns, and although large and somewhat droopy, they did exactly what it says on the tin. Are yours fake?"
"Every last shiny silicon ounce of them Lezzers. They've been bought and paid for cock, shock and toking feral. My nipples are pert, alert to the many different erogenous time zones. They could garrot the most pathetic of mortals."

"My nipples save me from buying flip flops. Your cleavage is amazing Lesley, the last time I saw that amount of bulging was when Ange took out her wallet."

"My denim shirt is from the 90's, same as your "empty people" Jools, positively vintage, and I bought it brand new. It's …well, old I guess….. like us."

"How very dare you Lezzers, you're only as young as the men you sleep with. How old do you think Tie Boy is?"

"Late 20's, looks a few years older than Jonno, my oldest…."

"Oh goody, goody, another Goldilocks scenario, not too old, not too young, just right. You shouldn't hide those Bad Boys Lezzers, at least undo another popper or two, and show off those natural, ample assets. Stand up, let me do it. Just you wait to see the reaction when we release these cheeky, chubby chest cha chas."

"BOMB!!!!"

"Who said that? WHERE? RUN RUN FOR YOUR LIVES GIRLS, there's a bomb somewhere."

"Blimey, Thai's been shot in the eye, everyone's panicking, we need to take a breath and stay calm."

"Can I remind you Jules, that this is very likely, the worst fucking time to stay calm when there's a fucking maniac in our midst shooting at everybody."

"Don't panic, I got this girls, part of my anxiety check is I'm always on the lookout for any exit to escape from, in fact, anxiety and any exit contain the same letters. Thankfully it's behind us, and thankfully, you opened it earlier Angy, hold hands, follow me."

"Lead on McFluff, our leader, our leader."

"Everyone is stampeding the other way, Lezzers, shouldn't we follow them?"

"My mum always said, "When things aren't right, go left." Trust me, I got this. Relax and trust ME Angy, YOU wedged the fire exit door open earlier. Remember?"

"I can hardly breathe Lezzers."

"Lean on me Angy, look, see, we're out. Well done, you did great, you're safe. Here, take these, these are my anti-anxiety meds."

"Give me a couple too please Lesley."

"I don't think you need them, Jules."

"I don't, but it's very unfair that Ange gets all the thrill pills, I should have some fun with all the medications you have stashed in your leathery crevices Lesley, besides just because you see a swan gliding across the surface of the water doesn't mean it's not paddling the feck below the surface."

"Those words "Leathery" and "crevices" have the power to make me feel rather ill. Please tell me, I haven't just swallowed something crammed from deep inside one of your crevices Lezzers?"

"Look Angy, never mind my crevices, I've just saved our lives. In case you'd forgotten again, I was a nurse, and that's what I do best, I save lives, and ... .well, I do owe you that at the very least, you saved mine back in the day. Just returning the favour. I have your blood coursing through my veins, that must count for something."

"I'd be double checking that if I were Lesley, her blood contains 94% proof alc. Tequila. She sucked the poison out of your derriere, which as far as I'm aware of, was the first and last time she didn't swallow."

"I feel I still owe you Angy and well, you may not have noticed, but I've been trying to return the favour all these years by kissing your derriere all this time."

"What? You don't owe me anything Lezzers, seriously, that's not the way I see it...at ... all in any peachy shape or form, anyone would have done it in my position, not everyone is able to maintain the down doggy balanced posture in the back of a speeding van whilst sucking spider venom from a rather lovely ass, I might add."

"Can we have this come to BeeJuice love fest moment another time, the sirens are coming and quite frankly I personally didn't see or hear anything of any value, so I suggest, we make like sheep and get the flock out of here."

"Ahh men to that Jules, and low and behold, there's Dirty, she's still here. The old hag did look after her after all."

"Who knew the fire exit was beside where we were sitting, and opened right beside Gertie, sliding doors or what. Everything that happens is so perfectly designed. I love it."

"You're not designed to drive Jools, you've been drinking and consuming medications all day. I'm driving. Get in the back Angy, Jools can navigate."

"What else do you have in that Mary Poppins Medicine bag of yours Lesley, aside from viagra and anti anxiety drugs, what other fixers, elixirs, tonics and hydroponics, skills and pills, lotions and potions are you hiding from us, you dark horse you."

"We can discuss all that when we're back on the road, right now, at this very moment, I think we should frappe la rue, and make like trees, and leaf. Hurry up, get in, I'll drive, do as you're told, and get in the back Angy, so Jools can try and give me the directions to The Four Reasons."

"Don't Go Inn Lesley."

"I'm not planning on going back, let alone in Jools."

"That's where we're staying, Lesley, it's called the "Don't go Inn. Ange ? What are you doing? I just put you in Gertie, get back in the van."

"There was a metal road sign underneath her, and a real live scorpion, but don't worry, there was a glove stuck in the door handle, so I used that to get rid of them. You're welcome."

True friendship is based on mutual respect and understanding, and is characterised by a deep and genuine affection between individuals - Ralph Waldo Emerson

Friendship is not only for companionship and comfort, but a reflection of all that you are, and are not - Sadghuru

The Outback

Friends are for life, and not just for Christmas

Jules

"Here we are in the middle of nowhere, woop-woop.com, look up, not you Lesley, eyes on the road. Have you ever seen anything quite so spectacular, and to think here we are, little old us, on this spinning ball of earth hurtling through space at a gazillion million miles an hour, skimming this jet black canvas, twinkling with non blood diamonds, each one squeezing their celestial bodies through the gaps in the colander sky, joining with the other numerous, stunning star clusters. Each one of those orbs produce energy which they generously, and unconditionally share with space and us. Who needs drugs to have that blow your mind wide open, and when we're ready, we'll all connect in that invisible, still void in space. Star light, star bright, the first star I see tonight; I wish I may, I wish I might, have the wish I wish tonight."

"I wish we weren't being followed Jools."

"Leshley? Shooo, those wotating bluw lights and whining, piercing noise ithn't the bush noises then? Watch wong wish ma woyds?"

"Might have something to do with the alcohol mixed with recreational and prescription drugs, Jools. I've seen it before in hospital emergency waiting rooms. When I pull over, which I have to do, give me your id and I'll show them that. I dropped mine in the back earlier and it could take years to find. Fanny's her aunt and all that."

"Heya go Leshley, my Australian dwriving lyshens."

"I can't use this Jools, you look more like Miriam Margolyes than she does in this photo, Shirley you have something better than that."

"I have a cowpy of my UK whone, I losht the copied whone, but thankfully I kept a cowpy of owiginal, but I have nevva evva had to youse it…until now, I knew I kept it for a reason."

"You look 12 in this photo Jools, and a female version of Billy Connolly without the beard."

"Windswept and interesting, I'm now more like him with the beard."

"More like windy and sweaty Jules."

"This isn't helping us get anywhere, I have an idea, I'll pull in, show them your licence Jools, it's dark, they'll never really know it's not you, but we need to pull over NOW, it'll only make matters worse if we don't. There's now a full spectrum of flashing blue lights radiating across the night's chasmic sky behind us. It's a cunning plan, and if they breathalyse me, that's a big IF, I'll pass, so let me be you Jools. What's the worst that can happen?"

"Very smart Lezzers, you be her, she'll be you, prevents her Majesty here blowing into anyone's, breathalyzer or otherwise, flashing her titties at the officers. One of them will no doubt make a date with me, and we'll drive off into certain oblivion. The good news is your driving Lezzers, he'll run it through the database, there'll be nothing on it…they'll be nothing on it right Jules? You know what Lezzers, I've changed my mind, life's too short, I say, FUCK IT… buckle in, plant your foot down and drive like you have wind."

"That, in my humble opinion, is an awful idea, Angy."

"PULL OVER>>>>NOW LESLEY < NOW!!!!!"

"This is it, it's down to the crunch? Who are you going to listen to Lezzers? Me ? or… Phyllis Diller beside you? Who do you pick? Crunch time. Hold onto your hairypieces, this might get bumpy."

"7 billion people on this planet and you're the weirdos I chose as best friends."

"Are you both okay? Jools? Angy? Even I need a stiff drink after that emergency brake."

"Girlfriend, you need more than a stiff drink, you need to reward your personal trainer, that was some leg flex Lezzers. What do we think, if we all flash some flesh, then maybe we can pull it off'

"And if that doesn't work, then Ange can always step in, and pull it off for you Lesley. Gosh, I'm feeling very shhleeppppy. I need a mmmmm bar."

"Me too Jules…."

"Oh nooo…what did you take? I warned you both. Jools? Angy?……. What a pleasant, yet somewhat surprise to see you again so soon, Occifer Hood."

"I cannot begin to express my delight that we get the chance to meet again Ladies."

"We may look it Officers, but we're certainly not ladies."

"Ignore her back there, remember, care in the community and all that, now, how can I be of help?"

"Can I see your Id Ma'am? Do you know why we stopped you?"

"You saw the number plate again and wanted to show it to your colleagues? Sorry, I couldn't help myself, it worked last time. In our defence Occifer Hood, we all have the highly sought after, much coveted menopause, not. So I may well have been driving erotically. As my Mikey says, I don't just have hot flashes, I have pirate holidays to the tropic."

"Step out of the van please……..all of you. Empty your pockets, then spread your legs, hands against the van."

"Been awhiley since I've been invited to spread 'em against Gertie. I'm vewy shleepy offf…sher..I'mm emptee ma pochets, hey u gw, cryshtals, Source Vital, Millenium oil, a white feathersh, a sage stick, for smudging, not for shmoking, I think that's it, I'm empty, please frisk me if you don't believe me, look there's more, these pockets are like Aladdins cave."

"That's why her eyeliner looks like that, I think she used her palo santo stick instead of her kohl liner. Immm tyad o off ..a shud..my legs, my legs…"

"Ah, there's more in my bra, you're right MAnge, Palo thanto, rothe water facial spwitz, pepper spray."

"Rose water Jools? Does that help with the menopause symptoms?"

"Not weally Lessss Ley, I'm not just sweating over here, I'm also having a power surge, so I need to shpway myself with the rose water, fweshen up some of this sweat. It also works with tequila over ice. AAgggh, that's my peppa spay. My eyes, my eyes. I'm blind."

"May I be bold enough to suggest that you two are blind drunk. As Officers of the law we're trained to look out for psychological signs of guilt and sweating is one of them. We're waiting to run your licence through our database system...... PUT YOUR HANDS AGAINST THE SIDE OF THE VEHICLE...NOW!!"

"Shirley drawing your weapons is totally unnecessary occifers. I am cold, stoned sober, and these two…. Three? I'm seeing double… triple even. Who's she? Where did she come from? Nice bag though, very familiar."

"We've run your driver's licence ma'am, and it appears we have captured one of the Australia most wanted criminals."

"I'm happy to be wanted anywhere, let alone Oshtralia."

"Jools, be serious, don't slip on me now, wake up, this is major. What do you even mean, Australia's most wanted? Explain yourself young man? There's a simple explanation to this. Jools, Angy, get up off the ground and help me out here."

"FUGITIVE FUGITIVE ARMED AND DANGEROUS...stop struggling or we'll shoot. Get on the ground with your pals and spread em."

"I'm spreaded...zzzzzz."

"ANGY!! ANGY!! Get up. Get your hands off me sir, I'll have you know I'm a suburban housewife, mother of 4 boys, and the most dangerous thing about me is my menopause, Shirely no need for cuffs, give them to the red head she's used to them, and I'm not who you think I am. JOOLS! You're making a big mistake here, but I'll come quietly, there's a simple answer to all this."

"PLEASE PLEASE do ma'am. Put those two sleeping beauties in the paddy wagon with the grandma, you, you're coming with me. You're in serious trouble."

"JOOLS. ANGY. WAKE UP."

There's a morning inside you waiting to burst open into light - Rumi

We all take different paths, but no matter where we go, we take a little of each other everywhere -Tim McGraw

Friendship isn't a big thing-its a million little things -Paulo Coelho

Back In The Clink

BRRRING.. BRING ..BRING…BRING ..

Jules

Heavy plods trudge their way down the hallway towards me, increasing its weary volume the closer they get. Hopefully someone coming to free us.

"OY SHEILA?"

Is this my tinder date? Is it a he? she? I can't really tell as he/she/it/they/them is behind the wrought iron bars, and shaking my mobile phone at me.

…BRRRING…

"OY Sheila? I'm not your private secretary, I shouldn't be doing this at all you know, but your pal's phone won't stop ringing, so, please come and take the call."

BRIING….. BRRRING, BRING…..

"Hurry up, someone keeps calling your friend, Jules's phone."

Interesting. I am Jules. Maybe another piece to this puzzle. The thot plickens.

"Jules's phone you say? How do you know who's phone it is?"

"Cos it says on the back of the case, "It may be tempting to take me, but I belong to Jules, give me back please", now stop trying to be a smart arse and take the phone."

BRRRING..

"It's from someone called "Knobber." "

"Knobber?? Oh my gawd, why didn't you say that in the first place, give it here will you."

BRING… BRING…

"No, you come over here to me, I'm not coming in there. Your mate Jules isn't here, so you might as well answer her phone, no skin off my nose if you don't want to take it."

"What do you mean Jules isn't here?"

Briiing

"She's not going to be able to answer any calls for a very, very long time I'm afraid, I hate to be the one to tell you, but your mate Jules is in BIG trouble, the only cell she'll be getting is a jail cell. You and your pals here will get to protest your innocence when you appear in front of Judge Crooks later. Now take the bloody phone before I change my mind. "Knobber" is very persistent and determined to chat to someone, and you'll do Lesley."

"Lesley? You called me Lesley?"

Wait what?

Briiing

"That's the name they booked you in under last night, not that you'd remember, now hurry up will you before I change my mind, and hang up on them."

"No…don't do that. Give it here."

Brrring, briiing

"Hello?"

"Hey Jools, at last, I've been trying to call you for ages."

There's no mistaking his voice, there's only one person I have in my contacts under that nom de plume, he's not even a real knobber, not now at least, not ever really, but Ange got hold of my phone one day and I've never got round to changing it back to Mikey, Lesley's lovely husband, Mikey, or My key as I call him. Lard only knows what my name is in certain address books. Sam has me down as "Birth Giver" for instance, but not to be mistaken for hostility or even resentment, there's a beautiful ebb and flow of pure unadulterated love between me and my only child. I have him down as "favourite sun", it makes us both smile. "Knobber" is the nickname Ange gave him many years ago when he came out of the surf at Bondage Beach wearing a pair of pale blue lolly bags, clutching a limp, sodden box of milk tray chocolates to give to Lesley, pretending to be, you know who, what's his name? 007 dude, not Sean, not Pierce, one of the other ones. No mind, it'll come back if it's meant to. Should have been a romantic moment between them both, and everyone else there watching the proposal unfold, it would have been perfect had it not been spoiled by Ange whispering in my ear;

"Knobber."

"No Jools, it's me, Mikey."

Darn, I must have used my outside voice.

"Is this a good time to chat Jools? Lesley's usually up with the birds, the feathered kind, not you and Angy, phnar phnar. I'm hoping she might be out walking."

"Jailbirds?"

"All birds, you know Lesley, she loves the dawn chorus, you must have heard her morning trill, if you haven't already, you will. She calls it her morning "thrill", always makes me smile, Jools. Sunrise is her favourite time of day, so I thought she'd be her usual up and at em, bouncy self."

"Lesley?"

If they think I'm Lesley, which I'm not, then maybe that's not her over there in the corner, but if it is her, then who am I? Apparently, Jules is elsewhere. Very confusing.

"No, it's me, Jools."

"S'mee who?"

"Not Smee...ME."

"Me who?"

"This is beginning to sound like a bad knock-knock joke. Me, Mikey."

"Mikey who?"

"My key doesn't work, help me out here will you? Phnar, phnar, you fall for it everytime Jools."

"Ahhh, Mikey????........ As in Mikey???.... MY KEY?? Sorry, there's a whole lot to take in right about now. I'm not quite with it yet."

"The one and only, tall, dark and handsome... ha ha ha...not so dark these days, more like a well seasoned badger."

Breathe

"Okay, not so handsome, and just you wait, wrinkles will make a return some day, but still tall, slightly stoopid these days, but tall..ish, and I'll confess to being a wee bit of a "knobber" some of the time."

He heard

"Is this a bad time Jools? Is Lesley there?"

"As it turns out My key, she's still sleeping, so we'll have to whisper."

"Ha, ha, good, it was really you I wanted to chat with anyway, to make sure she still doesn't know anything about the surprise party. Does she?"

"I cannot for the life of me think of a bigger, more surprising shocker right now My key, remind me again, what party?"
"You tease you, it's all coming together beautifully at my end, all you have to do is have her on Bondi Beach at sunset, tonight."

"TONIGHT? Blimey, that's come round quickly, where have the past few days gone?"

"Everything okay Jools? You still know the plan of A?"

"Yes, yes, I'm fine, what do you take me for My key, some middle aged, inept, ageing old hippie who smokes too much weed, loves psychobabble shite more than cannibals love having friends for dinner?"

"Now that you mention it, Jools."

"Look My key, no offence and as much as I'd like to continue chewing the fat with you, now is not the best time, I have to go and work on a few cryptic puzzles we set for each other. Besides, I'm still half asleep, having been rudely woken from my reveries to the jailbirds exercising their daily dawn drill. Not a spoiler alert, but I still need more beauty sleep."

"Ha Ha, you haven't told her, have you Jools? Does she suspect anything?"

"Suspect possibly, no, no, not a suspect, but maybe, she is totally absent, absent of any cunning party plans that you have come up with, she has no clue, well, not that I'm aware of anyway, but you know me, more than one glass of wine and it's a free world."

"I have absolutely no clue what you just said, does that mean you've told her?"

"No, I'd forgotten it already, so how could I tell her if I don't even remember myself."

"How will you remember to get her to the party tonight if you can't even remember it's on? This is why she calls you Dora."

"The Spanish quine with the monkey on her back? Maybe so, I have skills, they're multiplying and I'm losing my .... my.... What were we talking about? Seriously, what were we talking about?"

"Your memory Jools."

"Oh yeah, that's right. Look, I got this My key, trust me, I am Adam Ant that we will have her delivered safely to Bondage Beach tonight at sunset. Is that it in a seashell? Any other orders El Capitaino?"

"No worries, I trust you Jools. You and Angy are two of Lesley's oldest.."

"Look My key, I have to go, but I'll see you in 1 sleep."

"No, tonight..Jools..not 1.."

"Did you say1 sleep? Tonight? My key, My key? One ? Two ? It's a bad line."

He's gone. Think. THINK Jules.

"Bloody amnesia."

"Pardon Jools, what's that?"
Bollocks, I thought I'd hung up on him.
"Sorry My key, I sneezed. One's a wish."
"You sound funny Jools, everything okay?"
"Sure, it's my 'cell' phone playing up that's all."
"Remember I want this to be a surprise."
"Guaranteed My key, life is full of surprises."
"Is she there with you?"
"She's so 'with us' My key, and I meant to say she's at the Monet Coffeehouse…. getting her Monet caffeine fix."
Shut up Jules.
"She doesn't drink coffee."
Told you!
"Getting it for Ange, you know how kind Lesley is My key…. and she'll be out walking off our very large dinner from last night."
Did we eat? Doesn't feel like it.

"I don't know about you, but I'm hungry enough to eat an entire kale, falafel, and cauliflower burger in a gluten free pumpkin seed bun with dairy free, coconut, cashew mayonnaise."

"Good to know Jools."

"Sorry, did I say that out loud, didn't mean to."

I can feel the bile and temperature rising.

"Let's round this up so you can escape off somewhere nice and enjoy your time together."

"Spooky My key, you literally took the words out of my mouth."

"Go do whatever you've all planned for the day, and if I know Lesley, and I do, then your day has already been micro-managed to the last second. I'm only calling to remind you of her 50th birthday surprise party, the emphasis on SURPRISE Jools. You really haven't told her have you?"

"Surprise? Every moment is a surprise My key, especially this one and as far as I'm aware, I'm still an unflinching, reinforced cell wall of courtesy and discretion."

"You've told her, haven't you Dora?"

It's Dory, but I do not have the strength or the will to take that particular malaprop of Lesley's up with him.

"Relax My key, by hook or Judge Crooks, we'll have her delivered safely."

"I trust you Jools…Angy not so much. You and Angy are two of Lesley's oldest and best, well you are, her Bezzie"

"Oldest you say? I'll have you know that I'm actually the youngest, and Ange, as she keeps telling us, is only 39 with 11 extra years of pure, contaminated experience, is the eldest."

I have to go and make sense of all this. If I'm not Jules then who the feck am I?

"Look My key, I have to go, feeling a bit cooped up, and ready to get the hell out of here. I'll see you later, it's a bad line, and I think I can hear her melodious humming having a twosome with rattling chains of all things. And the bars are definitely calling us. Better go before she catches us. I'll mark it in my diary. BYE."

Feck sake, that's all I need!

Don't mistake my silence for ignorance, my calmness for acceptance or my kindness for weakness. Compassion and tolerance are not a sign of weakness, but a sign of strength - Dalai Lama

A good friend calls you in jail. A great friend bails you out, and your best friend sits beside you and says: I guess we screwed up, let's hope it was fun at least - Groucho Marx

Prison Inmate 138

Jules

"I can handle this. Relax and release. I can handle this. Relax and release..I can handle this. Relax and release......Blimey Ange, we need to get out of here. Lesley might be in some real trouble, possibly danger and it might be our fault."

"Eh yeah, no shit Sherlock. Wait what? What do you mean "our fault?"

"It might not be all our fault necessarily, but it is our responsibility as friends to go to her rescue before it's too late Ange. I have an idea. GUARD. GUARD. Ange, work with me here, I think Lesley may be in real danger, we need to get out of here now. GUARD GUARD. Get on the ground Ange, trust me, GUARD GUARD we have a medical emergency here, my friend needs her medication. I have an idea, Ange, roll with it..GUARD. PLEASE."

"Every thought, every emotion, every feeling, are all only life's gatecrashers. Let them come visit and kick them out when, before they get too much" - Mooji

"My sex life is so bad, my G-spot has been declared a historical landmark." - Joan Rivers

Trust The Processing...Out Of Jail

Jules

"Boss? Oy Boss. Guard. Here. Come here. Sir, please."

"Can I help you Sheila?"

"Sir/mam, my friend here has a chemical imbalance and we all need her to have her medication which is in her makeup bag."

"It's Officer Hogg to you and you'll be getting all your belongings back as soon as you've been processed out of here, you have to appear in front of the judge Crooks first, and I'll need that phone back before someone finds out. I could lose my job, but I feel sorry for you all. It was so pitiful trying to book you 48 hours ago. Funny, but pitiful. Hand the mobile back over."

"Here. We've been here for 48 hours? Where does the time go when you're having a black out. I apologise profusely for anything we said or did in our stupor, but it's not who we are right now."

"Bring my medicine bag and a couple bottles of tequila Officer Hogg, come back in 30 minutes, and take it up with us then. I wasn't there, I have no memory of it whatsoever, it's my brain's way of clearing my memory's browser history. You'll need to revisit with me when I'm back in a stupor, and take it up with her."

"I doubt tequila is the answer, Ange, but it's worth the shot. Do you know where our friend is, the other girl that was with us, Officer Hogg?"

"You mean the one they're referring to as the second most wanted dangerous felon that Tasmania has ever seen, evading the police for decades. That friend?"

"Eh? I don't think so, she's absolutely not who you think she is, Officer Hogg, our friend is a dumpy little peroxide blonde housewife married to a very basic man, no hidden extras, well not that I know of, unless extra inches are hereditary if you know what I mean, and I'm not talking height here, very different from his charismatic father, wouldn't you say Jules, and she has what? 3 ? 4? 5? boys aged from 10-20…yada yada yada. The most dangerous thing about her is that she knows the words karate, judo, jujitsu and kung fu. On the other hand I am mentally unstable and not medicated. I'd be afraid if I were anyone other than me."

"That does sound like the description of the driver we arrested last night."

"Arrested? She can't be arrested, she has her surprise 50th party to go to on Friday, Buddha here promised her husband."

"It's Friday, you pair have been practically comatose for 2 full days. The only surprise waiting for your friend is going to be when she faces a judge in Tasmania."

"Tasmania Officer Hogg?"

"She's in a whole lot of trouble, I shouldn't really tell you this, but it's the most exciting thing that's happened in this small, rural community since our mayor had his testicle torn off in a kangaroo meet and greet. Your friend is none other than the notorious Tasmanian kidnapper, who has evaded the authorities for decades. Between you and me though, it does seem like a bit of a witch hunt from the arresting policeman, one Officer Cox, who's now Chief constable Cox. I think he took her evasion personally, this being the only blemish on his otherwise exemplary career. The one that got away and all that, until last night that is."

"I wasn't even aware she'd ever been to Tasmania, she never mentioned it to me which is odd. Have you ever heard that she's been to Tasmania Ange? What happened exactly?"

"The judge knows more than I do, but I'm told that after a police chase and kidnapping, she failed to appear at the courthouse. Officer Cox took it upon himself to take out an all-points bulletin, a broadcast alert from one police station to all others in an area, state, etc., with instructions to arrest this particular suspect. This was decades ago. They believe she's part of a much bigger trafficking racket."

"Naaa, you're gladly mistaken, you have it all wrong officer Hogg, it doesn't sound like her does it Ange?"

"The database says it was originally an innocent traffic stop, but it turns out that your friend had kidnapped a girl from England."

"That's categorically not what happened, Ange, help me out here."

"To be honest, I haven't got a clue what's going on, not until this very kind officer gets me my medi-fuck-ation."

"Look Sheila, if you girls have the money, you can post bail. After I process you, you'll have to briefly appear before the judge, you'll likely get a fine, nothing on your record."

"The only record we need right now is please release us, let us go. A piece of unadulterated advice here Officer Hogg, try not to make eye contact with us, especially with this wired one on my right as her levels of sarcasm have now reached a dangerous boiler point level, she doesn't know whether she's kidding or not. Is our friend going to be in court at the same time as Ange and I?"

"I wouldn't bet on your pal seeing the light of day before the end of this century, let alone xmas. Like I said, the Tasmanian Chief of Police, Chief Cox has taken a very special interest in this case as he was the motorbike cop who stopped her in the first place."

"That can't happen I'm afraid, she has to be at her surprise 50th, in Sydney in…What day is it? Friday? TODAY, we have to have her there tonight for sundowners, I promised her husband, My key, she'd be there. I'm confused. Can you please explain again why we're here, keep in mind, I'm peri menopausal here, so go slowly."

"The other night, at approximately 11pm, the four of you were arrested whilst driving at breakneck speed along an unsealed, dirt track, deep in the bush, in a clapped out rust bucket."

"Four of us? We are a threesome, not a foursome Officer Hogg."

"It was initially thought the fugitive may have kidnapped yet another victim, but during booking, the kidnapee claimed she was taken voluntarily, says she's one of your "gang""

"No need to yell at us, we're menopausal, not deaf."

"She is, I'm not old enough. If I'm not the woman of your dreams, Officer Hagg, then please allow my friend here to step in and lower your expectations. There's clearly been a case of mistaken identity, the woman you are holding against her will somewhere else, but not with us, is absolutely NOT who you think she is, and I need my drugs."

"According to this rap sheet, she's been off the radar for decades, but just in the last few days alone, she's accumulated more serious crimes than you can shake a stick at."

"This is ridiculous, furthermore, I don't think this is the time or the place for you to be shaking your snake, or anyone else's. Games over, where are the hidden cameras? Someone is having a laugh with us. Australia's funniest. Ange? Help me out here."

"It's no joke. Please meet your fellow sleeping cellmate, Nina, that's all she'd give us, Nina."

" Nina, Nina, her name is Nina nina?"

"At least someone knows who they are. Nina is Nina, that's a relief, we can now forget about that complete fucking stranger in the corner."

"I do think that's really cool by the way, don't you Ange? I mean how many times in your life have you ever met anyone named after an ambulance? It's unusual."

"Officer Hagg, you seem like a 'normal' red hot blooded Aussie bloke of the male variety, I think, and I can see with your very own eyes, what a pair of glamour pusses you have before you. Listen, the personage that you are holding against her will is a retired nurse, runs her family like a well oiled machine, a housewife with four boys, an adoring husband. Like an antique teapot."

"Delicate and precious Ange?"

"No, shorter and stouter. There's a fine line between a fitted sheet and a sausage casing, and she frequently crosses that line."

"Come on Ange, that's a tad rough, even after 4 boys, she has a somewhat flat stomach, unlike my jelly wobble after only one."

"The l is silent in the word flat, and if memory serves me, she has a penchant for biscuits and sausage rolls."

"These days the only sausages she likes the best are her dogs Toulouse And Lautrec."

"Too Loose and Low trick?"

"Her hairy daxies Ange, do you even know her?"

"Is that a euphemism for something?"

"My late departed dog was called Fatty, it amused me no end calling for her in the dogging park, people with body image dysmorphia give themselves whiplash, accidentally looking for the person that they believed had shouted at them. Would you turn Ange?"

"Only if the dog was called "Queen", "Drinxonme", or "Pearl"."

"Our pal also likes sex daily, that might be important for you to know, sorry I meant she has dyslexia, so she may not know what she's signing."

"Call me pedantic Officer Hagg, but let's get a few things straight, you're saying our friend is being held somewhere, captive, against her will? I believe in the good ole system we have in the Us of A, we call that kidnapping."

"She's been arrested, which kinda supersedes your kidnapping claim. She's a wanted felon, a fugitive of the worst order, top 10 FBI most wanted."

"Hear that Ange. Most wanted eh? How nice would that be."

"Look, she's bad, but surely not that bad, she might be feral, but not a felon. Look, why don't we just check out, I'll take care of any charges incurred Officer Hagg. Give me back my belongings, my platinum American express card, my drugs and I'll take care of whatever damages have occurred. You do take cards don't you?"

"You'll need to use your card to pay for the accommodation, the hire of the orange jumpsuits, which you refused to wear, the ankle monitors, even the untouched bowl of gruel, all courtesy of Her/His/Them/ Their majesty's service. You Sheilas, and Nina are appearing in court in 30 minutes and counting."

"Remind me how Nina is involved in any of this, actually forget that, forget that, I don't actually care, I'll pay for her accommodation also, please tell me you have showers we can use, someone is honking like they've taken a golden one very recently."

"You pair were in a right state when we booked you, we couldn't wake you up for love or money. We even threw cups of water at you."

"Is that why I'm wet? Thank the lard, I thought I was the one took the golden shower, or had one of those, you know, those dreams."

"More likely it's because you spray spittle when you talk, can I say that orange is categorically NOT the new black, unless the teletubbies and Mr Blobby are making a come back which I highly doubt, glad we refused to wear them, but I'll pay for them nonetheless."

"Teletubbies? Mr Blobby? I've never heard of either Sheila, they must be before my time."

"Whaaaaaat? How old are you if you don't mind me asking? In Fact, don't answer that… la la la….I don't want to hear, and again, I don't actually care."

"Let's begin processing shall we, necklace off first please."

"Look, I get why some blokes, and or dames get their kicks out of being with a cougar, but I'm not taking my knickers off for you or anyone else I'll have you know, not until you promise to give me back my medication. It would make me sound too promiscuous otherwise."

"Ange? This may be hard for you to hear, but Officer Hogg asked you to take your necklace off, not your knickers."

"I knew that, having a laugh that's all, what do you take me for, an older person who is hard of hearing? I think not, I was merely informing him, her, they, them that I was keeping my knickers on to protect my honeypot from any potential chafing and rubbing from the boiler suit's ruff, coarse, rough orange fabric, against my smooth, milky, sensitive inner, augmented thighs. On second thoughts, wrap one to go with Officer Hagg please. Let me just finish my 'sweetie' necklace before handing it over."

"Life's so unfair Ange, my legs are bloated, transparent, mottled, hairy and thick."

"Mine are a tad, shall we say processed, so don't waste your breath comparing what you have to me or anyone else, not worth the suffering. Okey Quick Draw McGraw, put me out of my pain, how much for the three jumpsuits we didn't use, criminal fitbits, accommodation, cuisine and company?"

"Strip towards me please Sheila."

"Naughty, naughty, not wasting a minute with even a tiny smattering of foreplay. Not sure you're ready for these bad boys to be let loose, Officer Hagg."

"I'm sure Officer Hogg is positively dying to wrestle your bad boys Ange, but I don't believe you're meant to strip, as in take your clothes off strip, although you'd benefit from shedding a few of those invisible damaging layers, he means the strip on the card you're using to pay for all this, strip towards the machine. Perception realises it is part of a wave within a much bigger picture. We are all waves, ripples, sways in life's bigger body of water, the goal is to create stillness on the surface, not turmoil. Life changing magic happens when we slow down and open up our heavy drapes of awareness. Tagging a belief to our thoughts and senses only prevents and distracts us from our genuine reality, worth asking how much valid evidence our senses bring to the table at this moment, possibly even altering the authentic truth."

"Changed my mind, you can keep this one locked up, she can bail herself out. I was only having a laugh anyway, can't you tell I'm teasing Officer Hagg?"

"Teasing and abuse contain the same letters Ange."

"No they don't."

"Teasing, no need to get angry, Ange. For everyone concerned Officer Hogg, I suggest we address the chemical imbalance in the room. How do you think I got all these bruises? I'm not sure I'm going to keep this one piece orange boiling suite/sweet either, I don't think it would suit me. I'd look like the Big tent at a circus convention."

"They're not bruises, they're your makeup, and I'll have you know, I didn't even realise I was an angry person until you started me meditating."

"I think you mean medicating Ange."

"I know what I meant, I still feel slightly twitchy, and nothing is kicking in to take the edge off yet. Officer Hagg, would you kindly deliver my drugs back to their rightful owner, which also happens to be me."

"Would a pizza help Ange? I quite fancy a pizza. Officer Hogg, do you think they deliver?"

"Unlikely Sheila, they don't do liver in these parts...unless they've struck roadkill gold that is. This is a one horse town with one sheriff, Sheriff Bushe, one officer, me, one pub, The Wobbly Bottom Sip, A dodgy motel, that I can give you more than 4 reasons not to go in, and a pizza parlour called BOP WKTD (buy our pizza, we knead the dough) and they won't even cross the red grit, unsealed road to bring one to me, and to make matters worse, it's my mum who owns it."

"Enthusiasm is the yeast that raises the dough, look, our hanger is going to have to wait, you at least have enough juice, disguised as lard, in your tank to sustain you until we get out of here. Aside from finding our very dear friend of course, my utmost paramount concern other than getting my makeup bag that is, as I'm getting jumpy, itchy, bordering on bitchy and positively tetchy, and I don't have to be wearing the jumpsuit to smell the previous sweaty, dripping, alcohol fueled mass of illegal human being seeping through the seams. You'll soon find out, Officer Hagg, that without my medical "support workers", I can become a hormonally challenged homicidal, facts wielding psycho."

"Or a normal menopausal middle aged woman like the rest of us Ange, she really does need her pal's Pharma Sue Ti and Cal though, she's like a bear with a sore head under all that murky film of anger, it would be so much easier for all concerned if she gets what she needs before meeting the judge, and pray let's pray that her medicine and my meditation kick in before then. We are all a mere bag of bones in drag carting our hand picked, heavy, toxic, emotional baggage filled with the weight of all the stories of our past, visions and dreams of our future, luring us towards our inevitable, unavoidable final destination, which I'm not in a hurry to get to. We carefully scribe the narrative for ourselves, often forgetting that we're on a spinning ball of dirt hurtling 1, 000 mph through outer bloody space, focussing on being bothered by the small stuff, which, let's face it, is only a fragment of our life's bigger picture. Finding ourselves lost and caught in the story that we carefully cultivate and glean with our much loved, carefully selected, valued opinions, and self beliefs. If we did wear these orange costumes Ange, we have no control over what everyone else may or may not be thinking, that is if they're even looking at us, they may think we're extras in the Charlie and the Chocolate factory remake for all we know."

"Where is the firing squad, Officer Hagg? I need to execute my "support worker" here, look, this whole thing's a misunderstanding, let me pay for everything, including these 3 costumes, and we'll be off."

"What if we are paying for it by being here Ange, thought about that? What if it's not a misunderstanding either, what if 'she' really is a wanted woman? Have you considered that? We were in Tasmania once, she wasn't there…and we were stopped by a motorbike cop."

"Yes, but I was the one driving, not her, she wasn't with us. I wouldn't be in the slightest bit surprised if I'm the wanted one they're after."

"I do hope not Ange, I'm so ready to be wanted for the first time in my life, and I mean really, really wanted. Someone who wants ME. Let's face it, someone out there does want you, Ange, all you have to do is believe he's worthy of you and not the other way round."

"GUARD ? GUARD? Officer Hagg, come back, forget the firing squad, bring me a pistol instead, I'll do it myself."

"Look on the bright side, who would want to kidnap three orange, foosty lumps. Speaking of foosty lumps, do you smell cheese Ange?"

"I do smell cheese, why Officer Hagg, you brought pizza for me to line my pharma empty blood stream with."

"Are those garlicky, cheesy puff balls you have there Officer Hogg? I'm starving, are you allowed to share them with us? I am partial to the oddball now and again, take a good look at Ange here, if you're not convinced."

"Here's your prescription medicine, I can tell you need them urgently almost as much as we need you to have them. Are you meant to be taking that many in one go?"

"Don't worry about her, she's a well seasoned narcotic guzzler. She believes leftovers are for quitters. Would you like your pizza cut into 8 or 12 slices, Ange?"

"Ehhhh, 8 please. What kind of piggy do you take me for? Oink oink? Surely only a pig could eat 12 slices, isn't that right Officer Hagg? Did you hear that, did anyone hear that, like a duck being stepped on, did you just trump?"

"In this neck of the bush I believe they call it, duck-billed flatulence, and it happens to us all at some stage Ange. I don't know how you heard it anyway, it leaked out like an invisible silent wisp, but possibly turned out more deadly than anticipated."

"Hear it? Hear it? The entire world was rocked by it. It sounded like said duck-billed platypus was being systematically rolled over by a large freight train. Can I add here, that it wasn't only the herbal emission that assaulted my auditory function, all my other senses involuntarily joined in on this not so joyous occasion also."

"Better an empty jail over a rowdy cellmate, that's what I say Ange. Ain't that the truth, Officer Hogg?"

"Let's go ladies, this is a serious sombre affair."

"You need a sample Officer Hogg?"

"What did he say, he needs to take a sample?"

"Who's ass is ample Ange."

"I said sample, I wonder if they test for drugs, alcohol, blood, urine, and pregnancy."

"What did you say, Ange."

"They need your underwear Jules."

"That depends if they give me paper pants in return."

"Thankfully we don't need your underwear."

"Phew, I was beginning to think whose needs are being met here. Where were we, you know, my thoughts often take a stroll out through my mouth without due authority, and it's not always a good thing, even I can be surprised by the colourful parade of words. We're ready, motivated, she's medicated, and raring to go, let me just find a hat, and we'll be ready to meet the judge."

There is nothing in the world so irresistibly contagious as laughter and good humour - Charles Dickens

There is so much good in the worst of us, and so much bad in the best of us, that it ill behove any of us to find fault with the rest of us - James Truslow Adams

COURTROOM No. 2 - The Honourable Judge Crooks Presiding

Jules

"Let's grab our hats and be off, let's face it Ange, the worst thing Lesley has ever done is spotted an albino dalmatian, so my guess nothing can top that."

"Grab Nee nor Nee nor Jules, I'd rather be boiled alive in Campbell's chunky chicken soup, and be fed to a mob of hungry Tartan Army fans than stay one more minute in this cell. Come on Jules, we don't want to hold up the judge!"

"HOLD UP Ange? I wasn't there, it wasn't me, I didn't do it, the gun was a mistake, it was someone else. I'm an innocent bystander."

"Back in yer buckie Jules, save your innocent protests for the judge before you have a heart attack and we really have to call you an ambulance. We're in prism that's all, but don't worry it'll be a light sentence."

"I was thinking something before we were rudely interrupted somehow. Oh, yes, we need hats, where are our hats Ange?"

"What are you bleating on about now Jules? What hats?"

"I want to start this court appearance off the way I intend Ange, by being respectful of the court's wishes and honouring, shall I say they're rather obscure but uplifting requests."

"And somewhere in all this I assume you feel the need to wear a hat of all things. We're not heading to the Mad Hatter's fucking tea party Jules? Are we? Is this all a big joke?"

"Officer Hogg was the one who told us to wear hats, as it was a serious, sombrero affair."

"He did not say that Jules."

"Yes, she did, she said, quite clearly, this is a serious and sombrero affair."

"HE said the judge is not going to see the funny side as it's a SOMBRE affair, you absolute fanny Jules."

"Same difference, and an easy mistake Ange, Mz Imso Perfect, which also has a certain ring to it."

"Enough talking Sheilas, let's get you through to the judge without any more drama, walk this way please."

"Pretty sure I can get the knock kneed pace, clenched buttocks shuffle, but you got me on the gait Officer Hogg. Nina, Nina, Nina. Come on, keep up, let's go. Hahahaha, sorry, so funny."

"Honestly Jules, you're so childish, we do have more pressing concerns at hand other than your 12 year old boy's sense of humor, remember gorging yourself on Officer Hagg's garlic cheese dough balls?"

"I do Ange, and very tasty they were too."

"Turns out those highly colored balls of puffed rice coated in enriched cornmeal, ferrous sulphate, niacin, thiamin mononitrate, riboflavin, folic acid, vegetable oil, milk, cheese cultures, salt, enzymes, canola oil, maltodextrin, natural and artificial flavours, salt, whey, neon hesperidium cheese seasoning, have left their mark Jules."

"Neon he sperm Ange, is there any other kind?"

"Neon hesperidium Jules, however, it looks you've had fellatio with at least one of The Oompa Loompas."

"Away with you, it's the cheese balls, I promise you, no sperm, neon or otherwise have touched these lips in decades. Let's make like the jailbirds we are Ange and fly this coop."

"Sit down and wait here until the judge arrives, then you'll be instructed to stand and face the bench for the duration of the proceedings, and when Judge Crooks enters the courtroom, I shout….. "ALL RISE". You stand up, and wait for further instructions."

"If we're not going to be here for that long Office Hogg, I don't mind standing, but any longer and we'll need snacks and a shewee…oh, sorry, they're entering…..should I salute? Ange, should we salute, or clap, or something? "Good morning Judge, how are you today? we're in trouble, please put us away, so happy she doesn't wanna be free, so here's the deal judge, keep her, and let me be free. Yeah?" A bit of 10cc lightens the mood."

"ORDER Order in my courtroom, please sit, aside from you two in front of me, you pair remain standing."

"Don't ... .Jules? I'm warning you, take this as the threat it's intended to be."

"But it really lends itself Ange …"

"Nooooo, please not now Jules, I'm losing the will to live, let's get this debacle over and done with shall we. I'd rather be stranded in Simpson Desert and groomed to death by a koala's sharp claws, than prolong this suffering any longer than necessary. Please excuse us, continue judgey, the floor's all yours."

"Before we start your Holiness, I'd like to state something for the record, so listen up, drunk me, stoned me and sober me are not the same person. So, if I drank, I might have said or did something that got me arrested, my suggestion now would be, to bring me champagne and wait until I'm drunk and take it up with her, don't come at sober me, all holier than thou because I wasn't even there. I have no clue what happened."

"Hope you're not in a hurry to get out of here soon, as a mere glance at this rap sheet in front of me is enough to keep you from the light of day for a few years. Now order, ORDER. Court is in Session. ORDER."
"Here goes Ange, nothing to lose.."

"Other than our freedom Jules."

"In for a penny in for a pound burger, and all that Ange. At our age we have to get our kicks where we can."

"ORDER. I say "ORDER NOW."

"Here goes, if this is going to be my vast supper, then I'd like to order a Brewdog IPA with a side of cheeseballs..no wait, I finished them, a bag of Walkers cheese and onion crisps, even though I haven't had a bag of those in almost 30 years I still miss them…oh, and a can of irn bru, perhaps a white pudding supper, and..?"

"Oh please excuse me for interrupting your order, but perhaps you need a more formal introduction, I'm the judge, the one who reads the charges against you, then, hallelujah, I get to decide what to do with you. So, I suggest you keep your order until later."

"If you're sure Your Holiness, I don't mind waiting till a little later to place it, but not too long mind, I get faint if I don't eat often."

"Ms Wellard I presume?"

"Wellard? That's Lesley's married name Jules? They're all Wellhards? Mikey? The Rugrats? Richard?"

"How could it have escaped you that Richard's surname is Well Hard? Surprised you forgot that nugget Ange."

"Well, well, well you live and learn. Life is full of surprises Jules."

"Stop whispering you two, I can't hear you when you do that. If I have to shout "ORDER" one more time to either of you again, I swear I will hold everyone in MY courtroom in contempt. Are you or are you not Ms Wellard?"

"Yeah, but no but, Your Holiness, it's not quite as simple as that, you see there's been a case of mistaken identity here we believe, hasn't there Ange?"

"You can refer to me as Your Honour or M'lord, Ms Wellard. Suffice to say that this case goes back over 25 years, when a panel van with NSW plates was being pursued by one of our police bike patrol officers, one Officer Cox, on the outskirts of Hobart, now the Tasmanian Chief of Police."

"I've never had anyone want me for more than 2 days, let alone over 25 years M'Lard, let me get this clear, are we talking about Tasmania, Australia?"

"Is there another Tasmania that we don't know about Ms Wellard?"

"There's The Tasmanian devil, and my good friend to my right here is very similar to said devil, aren't you Ange?"

"I'm not sure I'm ready for this, but please go ahead Ms Wellard, pray tell us how your accomplice here is similar to the Tassie devil."

"I can't wait to hear this myself, your judginess, the floor is all yours Ms not so Well Lard. Go for it, I for one eagerly await this one with hated breath."

"For one, they're both insane bundles of narcotic energy and forces to be reckoned with, especially when they want something or someone, ESPECIALLY when that something, or someone is laced with cocaine. Secondly, they can be impatient, short tempered and angry, but in their defence Your Lardship, that's part of their unique, wild charm."

"Uncanny the similarities we have Jules."

"You know this is all bringing back memories M'Lard, truth is, we don't remember how we got here before your learned, wise eyes, let alone what took place 30 years ago. Having said that, somewhere in my mind mallow, there's a distant scrap of a memory trying to gatecrash in from the selective, dim and distant past. Ange? You? Anything?"

"No. Nada. Nothing. We were in Tasmania, but our fiend Lezzers wasn't. If mammary serves me, Jules was looking for her more so than me. I do recall being indifferent and reluctant as to whether we found her or not, but that was then, and this is now, and we really do need to be moving this along so we can find her. This is beginning to feel like some trippy, deja vu shit. Back then, we had to find her and get her back to Sydney by a particular day and time. Bloody hell, this is terribly spooky, this is almost exactly the same scenario we're having now, but not. She was lost somewhere in The Bush....although this time she's been taken hostage by HMS, now this is spine chilling, eerie even ....That was some good shit in my makeup bag and round my neck Jules."

"Enough, enough of this nonsense, please, time is of the essence. And par for the course, I have a tee time this arvo."

"Comforting to know M'lard that I'm not the only hangry one here, sorry for interrupting you, carry on regardless, you're the judge as you keep reminding us, don't mind our musings. I can't remember what I had for brekkie, let alone what happened a squillion years ago."

"So you've already said."

"Really? Repetition is like diarrhoea, it runs in the family."

"A police biker judgey? Am I the only one getting memory flurry's of leather? Mmm leather, takes me back, 9/10 times, on my back."

"Look, the only leather I'm interested in, better be holding my clubs, please, let's get on with the proceedings. Officer Cox made the traffic stop on the outskirts of Hobart, and arrested your friend."

"Did he? Did he Ange? I have completely forgotten that."

"Gives me thrills just thinking about the smell, the texture, the look ...mmm of leather.....the only chills I get from leather are from the smell of the passenger's seat in my chauffeur driven limousine. I'm sure you feel the same sensations with your golf bag Yer Hornor."

"Moving along, in his statement, Officer Cox, now The Chief of Police, states that the van was driving in a chaotic and dangerous fashion. The officer initiated a stop, and it appears the back doors must have sprung open, and the kidnapped victim escaped screaming something in a pitch and accent he didn't quite understand, but now believes she told him she had been hijacked. The driver approached Officer Cox, straddled his bike, only getting off when he agreed to meet her later at the …..police station… She, the driver returned to the van's passenger side, and the passenger took the driver's seat. Very vague description of her/him, Officer Cox couldn't be certain."

"I object to M'Lard, I may have been slightly chilly, but never vague, and I believe she shouted, "hitchhiker", which she was, and not a hijacked kidnapped victim, as is claimed she was."

"May I continue? Before you add anything else here, that was categorically not a question. They then drove off, leaving the victim to hitch a ride elsewhere, driving off with her belongings, never to be seen again…until last night that is. They never showed up at the police station later, however, in a bizarre twist, the driver had dropped their UK licence, which the officer planned to return to her later, but never got the chance."

"Wait. What? This is pathetic, are you telling me that for 25 years… Officer Cock's precious, sensitive ego was slighted because he was stood him up? And he's continued this petty vengeance to this day, keeping the warrant alive and kicking for 25 fucking years."

"That's where my Uk driving licence copy went, Ange. Remember? I lost it and thought a seagull had carried it away in a crisp packet I sometimes hide my belongings in."

"I'm more surprised to hear you hide important items in a crisp bag than I am to hear you lost it? Do you seriously think Officer Cocks felt a bit peckish, and… gosh… look… by a happy coincidence there's a bag of, let's say, for argument's sake, Walker's cheese and onion crisps. "Oh, what fun it looks like a lucky bag and look, look what 'treasure' I've found…the driving licence of a 21 year old Scottish female. I must keep this as a trophy of the time I was stood up." Get real Jules."

"For your information, Ange, I always use the family sized prawn cocktail flavoured crisps to hide things in, seagulls don't seem to like them."

"LADIES, you need to speak louder so everyone in the court can hear your ramblings."

"Apologies M'lard, did you say 25 YEARS ago?"

"25 years, that's what it says here. It does seem that the officer may have taken it upon himself to keep this investigation going all these years for some reason."

"For 25 years Judgey? Let me get this straight, so that I'm not missing anything. Lardy the HITCHHIKER, not the kidnap victim, and if you saw the size of her you'd know that it would have been hard for one of us, let alone two of us, to kidnap her. For the record, and secondly, she voluntarily decided she no longer wanted to share a ride to the ferry in Launceston, leaves of her own accord by whatever means she chooses, in this particular case through the back door of the original Dirty Gertie, our trustworthy steed disguised as a panel van. She inadvertently forgets to take her snacks, which we eat, and if memory serves, we did her a favor, and not the other way round. There was categorically no kidnapping involved other than taking her snackery that is, and like I say, we did that as a favor, believe me."

"You have no knowledge of anyone being kidnapped?"
"Look, Judgey, she was only 35 lbs off being named by google as a roundabout. We categorically have no knowledge, desire or inclination to kidnap some French quine, not today, or ever."

"She was a Brummie lass Ange, probably still is, she was definitely from Birmingham. I ate her mars bars, crisps, and other fine snacks she left behind. I thought they were a donation of sorts, not a potential reward for her safety. Come to think of it, I don't think we gave her a refund for her share of the petrol Ange."

"Rest assured Jules she had more pressing issues to address before any refunds were given."

"We're getting nowhere with this, I'm beginning to feel I'm on a hamster wheel. Let's move on, we can circle back to this at a later date. There are additional, relevant and more recent serious charges to be addressed first. Let's follow the paper trail beginning three days ago, and work our way back, if I still have the will to live

that is.... Please hand me over the next charge sheet Ms Terry. Let me see, oh yes, seems to be a theme developing here, you were pulled over by the police last night in a VW kombi van."

"Dirty Gertie Too M'Lard, that's what the van's called, Dirty Gertie Too."

"I'll come back to that Ms Wellard if there are still any signs of life in me, that is, the van was driving erratically and failed to stop even when officers of the law had their lights and sirens on."

"I appreciate you recognising that we were driving in an erotic fashion your lardship, but you've got to understand the scene, we were pleased to be leaving The Wobbly Bottom Sip, as it turned out to be much more dangerous than we could ever have imagined, and we were well, excited to be on the way to our next adventure, which as it turns out, is so much more exciting than we could ever have anticipated possible. We happened to be enjoying the night's light show that's all."

"The light show you speak of happened to be the police."

"Definitely not The Police M'Lard, I'd never play them, yon wee gadgie Stung gets on my tits, so he does. If anything, we were playing Wham. That's another funny coincidence, we would have been playing Wham when Officer Cox stopped us in Tasmania as well, I thought it was all part of the illusion, me, George, Ange and Andrew."

"I had George Jules."

"You did until you found out he batted for the other team Ange, so you took the only straight guy left, giving me George, we even offered Pepsi and or Shirley to the Brummie lass."

"She's mistaken Judgey, the girl wasn't from Birmingham, she was French, because all she said was "Je m'appel, je m'appel" and that's all she ever repeated over and over again, she never did finish her sentence and tell us her name. Looking back now, I think she likely had tourettes, I am fluid in French and asked her over and over again, more out of politeness, what her name was, but she never did tell us, which is why I ended up turning the music of "Club Tropicana" to full blast. I'm not proud of my actions, no one likes to have their conversations drowned out."

"You don't remember blankety blank half the time Ange, but you remember that! I'm sure she was from Birmingham anyway, we even discussed it later. She did tell us her name I'm sure of it, but she was so instantly forgettable that I forgot, her name was…I forget. What was her name, M'lard?"

"Her name is Gemma Peel, and she was indeed from Birmingham if that makes any difference whatsoever."

"Remember Ange, wake me up before you go-go, an innocent Brummie lass who got lost and caught in Close encounters of the Thin Crowd."

"I'm blown away, the French lass, who's actually English, seriously, all these years I would have bet my designer thong she was French. Just shows you. Maybe I'm not the credible witness that you need today Judgey, please release me, let me go."

"Me too, I'm far from credible, doesn't matter at the end of the day, she was never kidnapped, she willingly paid to carpool, and her choice to leave before we'd even reached our final destination. Besides, if anyone was holding her captive it was the motorbike cop who almost rear ended Dirty Gertie, penetrating the red hot tip of his large, flashing pulsating police bike into her backdoor flaps, pinning Gemma temporarily inside until she threw her weight against them, opening them up wide, knocking Officer Cox sideways. Ange wasn't stealing his bike, she was helping them both up…so to speak. Officer Cox, and his bike."

"Officer Cocks never wrote a speeding ticket, so no crime was actually committed. I'm no lawyer, but I know enough to know that there is no evidence of any crime being committed, so the best thing to do all round is dismiss the charges, so that we can get on with the more pressing job of trying to find our fiend, who is currently being held somewhere against her will, innocent of almost everything, believe me, she never does anything wrong. A real goodie two shoes who is being held captive somewhere in the bush, probably worrying herself sick as to what has happened to US. So if you could just bang your hammer, wave a magic wand, or swing a club, then we'll be moving swiftly on. We absolutely have to be in Sydney, she absolutely has to be there, to hear it herself, it's imperative she be there. It wouldn't be the same. I want her to hear it from me."

"Hold your horses ladies, not quite so quick, I'm only just starting, she is still a wanted felon, so, try, and I do mean TRY to make the following brief…please. Explain to me the following charges which are longer than a kiddo telling a short story, and

have only been filed in the past few days alone, not to mention she's been here illegally almost 30 years, but I'll get back to that later."

"This isn't right, what a conundrum we have here. I for one never saw this coming, did you Jules? You're saying our fiend has been living ILLEGALLY downunder for 30 years. Well, blow me."

"Funnily enough Ange, I too have lived here for almost all that time, oblivious of the fact that someone I call one of my symbiotic best friends is an illegal alien."

"Ahem?"

"Okay… good friend? Friend? Surely I can say that Ange? Let me get this straight, which I am by the way, and don't let my taste in clothes, or Ange convince you otherwise. You're saying that a very, very close friend of ours, genuinely, one could almost say we're conjoined, we're that close, we could almost be one in the same person, we're that alike, is an illegal alien?"

"Like shit and shovel I'd say Jules."

"Your vote of confidence has been noted Ange. She's been a notorious, illegal, wanted criminal for over 2 decades, M'lard?"

"For decades now, there has been an all-points bulletin, an alert broadcast sent to all police officers within the area, and beyond, instructing the immediate arrest of the suspect, one Julia Kelly. Which is precisely what our officers managed to do last night."

"Agggh, the penny has dropped. You're looking for Julia Kelly for something she didn't even know about or actually do? From where I stand, I reckon she'd be chuffed that you all believe she's been on the run for 25 years, obliviously evading everyone that she didn't know were looking for her, only to finally be apprehended, and now it appears, involved in hold ups. Between you and me, can I tell you that the only hold ups that this fugitive is capable of, is putting both her legs through one trouser leg, hopping about because she has two legs in one hole, falling and repeating over and over again."

"Judgey? Does it say that Julia Kelly is a middle aged, patchouli soaked single mother hippy with questionable dress sense and even more questionable morals, her looks alone are single handedly responsible for the invention of the doggy style?"

"I haven't got that far, there's, let me see, an additional, 1, 2, 3, 4, 5, 6, 7, 8 additional charges on this rap sheet… but first I need a break before we continue."

Silence is the most perfect expression of scorn - George Bernard Shaw

Between what is said and not meant, and what is meant and not said, most love is lost. - Kahlil Gibran

Recess

MS TERRY - Court stenographer

"All rise. The Court of the Second Judicial Circuit, Criminal Division, is now back in session, the Honourable Judge Crooks presiding. All stand."

"I wish we were back having a session somewhere, an all day drinking session. Age before beauty, you first Ange."

"Pearls before swine Jules."

"You're whale cum."

"Order in my courtroom, and please, please ladies, only speak when spoken to. Let's take a look at the most recent charges and continue to work our way back 25 years.

It's claimed that someone in a VW kombi van, coincidentally similar to the one you describe as Dirty Gertie Two, assaulted a luggage handler, Mr Bruce Darcey, at Sydney Kingsford Smith airport, driving off off whilst he was still on the roof fixing down the suitcases, almost breaking his neck in the process. He managed to grab the van's handle as he fell, but eventually let go only after he was almost dragged under the wheels, losing his leather glove instead of his hand."

"Wait? What? You say the luggage handler at the hairyport Your Lardship? That must have been the noise we heard, which we thought was a speed bump. I hope he's okay. Aside from a bruised arse that is. I don't recall seeing a leather glove, you Ange?"

"I did use a leather glove to throw a dead scorpion out the van, and as it was a man's glove, it may have slipped off my delicate hand and followed the arachnid out the door."

"It was dead Ange, wouldn't have hurt a fly, besides it was the jewellery piece you gave me years ago."

"I think I know the difference between a skeleton and a platinum scorpion. Don't test me Jules, my sting is much worse than my bite, and if you can't tell, let me introduce you to my expression of scorn. Back to business, there was a significant amount of shrieking and excitement, Judgey, as we hadn't seen each other properly, in person, all of us together, for years. There was a cacophony of squawks, shrills, hugs, kisses and dancing. I'm sick so I asked Lezzers if she'd sit in the back, she has wee T rex arms and doesn't have the strength or the length, and we all need a bit of length now and again, to slam the side door shut: it's a slide jobby door, not a pull jobby. I have a very personal trainer as you can no doubt tell by my honed, toned Bi tricepterous arms, and helped her out by shutting the door for her. I sometimes don't know my own strength, I was totally unaware that the baggage handler was even on the roof, let alone off it, so I gave the onwards and upwards, tally ho, let's go to Jules, our chaufloosey, and she did."

"This is so funny Ange, I don't actually remember the full door/glove/ gate fiasco. I mean any of it really. I do remember the shrieks and dancing, but that could be any day of the week with friends. How long ago did you say this was anyway? Wait. I do remember, Ange, you tipped the chapette with the bags, I can no longer tell or assume a gender these days and Lesley was about to shut the door when I noticed your Dolce & Banana jewellery case on the pavement, you jumped out, grabbed it in the nick of time, slammed the back door, hopped into the front passenger seat beside me, and off we went. I do remember shouting "watch the fingers", but I didn't for one minute mean the luggage handlers. Is that why they call them handles? After handlers, or the other way round? If it almost took his/her/they/them fingers off, then I apologise immensely. It was never my intention to knock him off the roof, or to sever his fingers or knick his glove, it might have been my kangaroo driving that dislodged him from his lofty perch above. Dirty Gertie was backfiring quite a bit, baring that his fingers are his livelihood then he's perhaps looking for compensation? Or another pair of gloves at the very least?"

"If he's looking for financial compensation other than his glove back, I'll make sure he's handsomely tipped for any inconvenience. Michael Jackson made it a thing with one glove, but if he'd prefer two, then two it shall be, and I'll throw in a brand new state of the art back brace for good measure."

"It may have escaped your mind, but I'm still the judge, and I control the narrative, not you. Let's move on to the NEXT…charge. The claim is that you went round a roundabout the wrong way, causing distress to the on coming traffic, loose road chuckies were sprayed in all directions from the reckless, erratic driving, pelting a number of vehicles with divots of road chips, cracking car

windscreens, chipping paint in your gravel storm wake, and I believe a workman almost drowned when you enveloped him in a cascade of dirty, murky watery scum from a large puddle he was working on at the side of the road, and to add insult to injury you stole their men at work triangle."

"What is this you speak of? It was an innocent mistake yer Holiness, I simply went right around the roundabout, not left, then missed our exit, that's all, so I had to go round again. If anyone is at fault here, it's the local council who hadn't sealed the roads in the first place, or filled in the potholes properly, and my human GPS beside me here, telling me to go right didn't help. I do remember being really impressed by the magnificent rainbow tsunami wave that erupted from a pothole that we ploughed through. How was I to know there was anyone on the pavement surfing UNDER it? Surely I can't be blamed or responsible for something that wasn't my fault, if there's anyone to blame here, it's the Men at Work, can I say that these days? And here's me, "Travelling in a fried-out Kombi. On a hippie trail, head full of zombies."

"I'll pay for any damage to the cars involved Judgey, even a new set of clothes for the workers, but the council can pay for the crater sized potholes. Be thankful our driver is not filing for damages done to her van, I found a metal triangle men at work sign under our van, which I left outside the Wobbly Bottom Sip, along with a leather glove, and apparently a very expensive, one of a kind platinum encased scorpion. Nothing stolen, where I'm standing, you could be sued for accusing us of much less."

"Can I actually do that Ange, can I counter sue for damages done to my undercarriage?"

"NO!!! You ACTUALLY can't, this is Australia, not the good old ununited states."

"Look Judgey, this is dragging on a bit now, so is there anything else, or are we done? Time is pressing on, our fiend needs to be rescued, and I can see by my other friend's puce face that she's hot, then cold, and always sweaty. She's standing in enough sweat to be able to start her very own personal ice rink below her."

"That does sound lovely right now Ange. Cold therapy is the new black."

"May I remind you both, that I'm the one in charge, not you, I call the shots."

"Did he say shorts? Who's Short? Lesley? How does he know she's short Ange?"

"QUIET. Court is still in progress lest you forget."

"As far as I can tell Your Holiness, there's been nothing valid so far to hold us any further, unless of course, there's more."

"More?? More? It feels like I've only just started? You tried to abduct two young men when they realised you were bank robbers."

"WHAAAAAAT did you didgeridoo Ange? I feel like I've come straight from a home for the utterly bewildered. There must be a really simple solution to all this. I think it's best if you tell us your version first, M'Lard, then we'll fill you in with our truth as it happened, if nothing else it may prompt a memory. We're not trying to be evasive, it's an age thing, I know you in particular must get that."

My life has been filled with terrible misfortune, most of which never happened - Michel Eyquem De Montaigne

Judge Crooks

"Back to business, according to these records, quote, unquote, "Dodgy looking, bashed up old banger". "

"OBJECTION your Holiness, I'd like to put in a formal complaint here. I am no more a dodgy old banger than Ange here is 40, but we are guilty of behaving terribly inappropriate for our age. We've never been this age before, so not sure how we should behave."

"I resemble that remark Jules, please strike that last comment from the record Mys Tery."

"Enough the pair of you, I decide what the court stenographer can strike, and not strike, not you. Now, your VAN, Dirty Gertie Two, t w. o."

"Too. T, double oo."

"Pardon?"

"It's too, Dirty Gertie TOO."

"That's what I said TWO..two.."

"Yeah, but it's not..easy mistake, you heard "two", t.w.o., and assumed it was two, but it's not, it's too, t.o.o. T double oo."

"If it's okey with you Judgey, I'd like to be sentenced now. You can deal with her on your own."

"It changes everything Ange, for one she's NOT Dirty Gertie TWO, she's actually, Dirty Gertie 4, but, Too has a je n'ais ce quoi ring to it."

"SILENCE!!!! You approached TWO young men in what will now be known in the future as THE VAN to save any more confusion, and you do so at an "intimidating, snail's pace"."

"Quote, unquote, "YOUNG MEN"? They were pushing 30 Judgey."

"It doesn't really matter whether they are 30 OR 13, they were in fear of their lives."

"As reluctant as I am to say Ange is right, on this occasion she is right, your Holiness, there's a huge difference. There really would be a problem if three gorgeous women, of a certain age tried to coerce 13 year olds and not the 30 year olds they are, and they must have meant, "illuminating snail's face". Snail serum makes my face so naturally shiny and tight, only $13. Bargain, slows down the whole ageing process."

"$13? For snail sperm? Ive been ripped off, well parts of me have been, let's face it. I pay almost a thousand doughlars for a scalpel and a tiny vial filled with over 3,000 ingredients."

"Before you even start trying to list them. Don't. LET ME FINISH. THE VAN pulled up alongside ...two ...PEOPLE, and the passenger who was wearing a black, bank robber's balaclava, stopped them, and asked for the nearest bank. Sounds like a slam dunk, in the bag threat in my books."

"They took one look at Ange's mask, put two and two together and came back with an assumption she was going to rob a bank. We didn't ask for a bank, that's how they must have interpreted the scene. We asked for an ATM machine, to withdraw cash, legally, and Ange wasn't wearing a bank robber's mask either. Again.... facts can get lost in the details. I won't elaborate any more on, given the sombrero of the situation."

"In my defence Judgey, I have never ever worn such a garment before."

"This isn't the game Truth or Dare Ange."

"Oh, right, in that case, I have worn one on several occasions, but this particular scenario was entirely different. Although I was being mischievous in both situations, the zip was broken and I couldn't get it off, so had no choice but to ask where the nearest gas station and ATM were. Gawdam, innocent enough request."

Let me remind the three of you..."

"She's not with us judgey, and it's still somewhat unclear as to how she got in Dirty, in the first place."

"Ange? It's not Gemma Peel is it?"

"Don't be ridiculous Jules, she was the same age as us, remember? So unless this old skinny bird had a few paper rounds and a gastric band when she was younger, then we too have aged. Fuck, are you Gemma Peel?"

"SILENCE< LADIES< May I remind you again. THIS IS A COURT OF LAW, we get mostly uncomplicated, relatively straightforward tasks out here. We glean all the information, decide

what really happened and what should be done about it, we then get to decide whether a person or PERSONS committed a crime and what the punishment should be. Is this beginning to make any sense to either of you?"

"I can provide any financial rewards, and compensation as a peaceful way to resolve all these rather trite disputes, this entire debacle has been about he/she/it/they them said/ said, she/it they/them said. Where's the E V I D E N C E? Haven't seen much of that, have we?"

"My patience is taking on stretch marks. What I now hold up carefully, very carefully, before you is the mask we retrieved from the van's glove compartment, which on closer inspection, does look more like an accessory in a sex act rather than a bank robber's mask, not that I would know first hand, don't print that in the local Gassnette Jenny, or you'll be next on the firing squad. Jenny? Ms Terry, stop typing. Immediately."

"An easy mistake Judgey, I too was a tad confused as to what had been found, so I tried it on to look in the mirror to see for myself which it might be, sex, or crime, or balaclava, or baclava, then we had to stop and ask for directions, I did try to unzip it, but it broke."

"This mask is about whatever the voyeur wants it to be about depending on their own personal data, this is Ange's story, your Holiness and she's clearly sticking to it. Seriously though, to put you all out of your misery, it's a prop I had for our local, amateur dram group, "The Dram Queens". It's a prop for our xmas panto," The Gimp who stole Xmas?" Yet another example of misperception, it's not actually a real gimp mask anyway, as a real one was out of our budget, but is an extreme cold weather army mask left over from our summer show, "Rob in a HOOD, meets the babes in the wood."

"Sounds fabulous, where can I buy tickets?"

"Oh don't worry about buying a ticket your Holiness I'll take you in the back door."

"I was joking. There was no intention to hold up a bank, garage or anywhere else for that matter?"

"None whatsoever yer Holiness, the only hold ups we have any part of, are the spandex ones, which give promises of confining our loose, wobbly, cellulitic legs in a pair of sausage casings."

"Speak for yourself Jules, I pay a monthly subscription to "A stitch in time, look Divine". This, this divine body to die for, comes at a price."

"Mine too Ange, I just look more like Divine, I attribute this 'misdemeanour 'to jello shots, drugs and alcohol, with a smattering of abhorrent, hedonistic behaviour. Nowadays, a hip joint involves creaking, and shooting pains, not the original hip joint out on a Friday night it used to be. Takes on a whole different meaning altogether."

"I needed Australian dough lars judgey, so I was asking the vulnerable, vacant looking men/boys for the nearest money machine, so I could get cash out, not as in Johnny, but a bone fide atm, hole in the wall machine. I don't carry cash on me, but thought it may come in handy being that we were in the middle of bum fuck nowhere, somewhere in The Bush, where my platinum American card may not be instantly accepted."

"You were looking for an automatic teller machine?"

"No need to add full words when initials suffice judgey, wasted energy best spent in other areas. I'm splitting hairs here, I am not responsible for what they heard, or what they saw that wasn't factual. Carry on regardless, don't let me stop you."

"Speaking of splitting hairs your Holiness, I have a five o'clock shadow sprouting from my upper lip, jowls, and under my chins. That isn't usually a problem, but left unchecked for, say 12 hours and counting, these coarse pesky fibres dig their pointy, sharp barbs further into the hair bed, cementing and embedding their thick roots into the pit of my facial fascia, those galling hairs then miraculously and liberally transform into the most rampant of hares, breeding like feckin rabbits, and before you know, there's a five o'clock shadow spreading across my entire neck, face, and torso. I'm sure you can appreciate that this can be a very traumatic occurrence for the majority of women, especially if left unchecked."

"You're not alone in the trauma department it seems, the two kidnap victims were also left traumatised and in fear of their lives."

"That's what they were telling themselves, Your Holiness, a belief is only a thought repeated over and over again. They were only ever as scared as the story that matched what they were telling themselves, and couldn't see, or hear beyond that. If we can't think of anything nice, then don't think of anything at all."

"I'll take over from her here judgey, that is categorically not the way it went down. I took their rather wishy-washy demeanour for one of curiosity, as one would naturally expect, being witness to three, sorry, I stand corrected, two and a half attractive birds in a clapped out rusty van. I was giving them an educational public service of sorts, a gift to expand their sexual apparatus knowledge, they should be thanking me."

"The only thing criminal about it is that you refer to it as a piece of sexual apparatus, it's an extreme cold weather mask, not the rubber, latex, BDSM sexual role-play gimp mask, you thought you were teaching them. Do you remember that rubber, latex condom game we used to play, Ange?"

"The one where you prise a condom over your head and eyes, leaving only the mouth to inhale, and the nostrils to exhale. BLOWING through the nostrils like a raging bull, inflating a rubber latex rocket above your head. That game? We need a prophylactic to show y'all."

"Ange, let's face it, at our age, we need and carry pro probiotics around with us, much more than we need condoms. It was a very funny game, blimey, that brings back so many memories. How we larfed. We need to do it again sometime don't you think? I still do it on occasion, you know? My party piece, nothing else to do with leftover unused condoms, other than use them as bin bags, and balloons under the xmas tree. I showed Lesley's kids how to play that game years ago, they were pros at it. Great for breathing exercises. There should be an actual exercise class offered called "Blowing off steam", or "Blow me", I'd sign up. My record is blowing a condom up to 5 ft. like a vertical zeppelin, all the way from my crown chakra havenward."

"Hah, we need a blow off when we're out of this shambles Jules. Perhaps a demonstration might get us a get out of jail free card, perhaps a 3 ft stiff head balloon will convince you it's worth a case dismissal. Would you care for a demonstration Judgey?"

"What a terribly kind, generous, somewhat enticing, bordering on revolting offer you suggest before this court of law. Sadly for the rest of us, I still feel as if I've only just begun. I'm not sure how you can explain away the next charge, but I must say, there is a part of me very much looking forward to hearing the explanation. How do you talk your way out of the petrol station hoist you committed?"

"HOIST? The only hoist I now recall is the one needed to get you know who beside me into an eating dugout in a Japanese establishment.

We need to see some decent evidence other than he/she /they / them said Judgey."

"I'm so glad you brought that up, I'll get to the restaurant shortly, but in the meantime let's watch the CCTV video footage of the entire garage "hoist". No sound unfortunately, but I get how that can be a blessing. Let's take a look, we see the van pulling up alongside pump 5. There are 6 pumps in total and you park at the furthest, closest to the exit, conveniently located for a quick getaway."

"Or unselfishly parked your Holiness so that when other empty tank travellers drive into the forecourt on a song and a prayer, we are not blocking any pumps."

"It's a bit grainy, but if you squint, you can see three people alight from the van, one stays behind and begins to fill the tank, and the other two, the tall, rail thin one is wearing the, now established cold weather mask, and the other one, are seen entering the petrol station."

"Thank you Judgey, your kind words are noted and very much appreciated. Make sure you got that Mys Tery, "rail thin". "

"Haud yer wheesht would you...gosh, you've even got me slipping back to my original dialect. Back to the case, we now cut to the footage from inside the garage, and as you can see, it looks like a scene from supermarket sweep as the chimp is seen here, dragging her hand along the shelves knocking the contents into a trolley they're now pushing."

"I did tell her we had enough Chicksmix in the car, your Holiness, but she was on a roll, no stopping her when she's in that frame of mind."

"What's Chicksmix?"

"It's a homemade concoction, a combination of individually chosen ingredients from best friends, and/or family members, for birthday parties, hennies, girls weekends etc. There were batches of Chicksmix for our Reunion back in the van, each jar containing one single ingredient carefully selected specially and independently by the three of us. You can have as many ingredients to players/ ratio as you like. I chose double cheese, baked shark bites, Lesley chose milk chocolate, peanut butter pretzels, and Ange chose gummies, she was only upset with herself here in the video because she was scared her Chicksmix would have more of Lesley's pick, and she professes to being allergic to nuts. She's helping herself to everything on the shelves to cover all her tastes. That's why we left the trolley in the middle of the aisle, it was getting out of hand, she was a woman possessed. Very needy. That was a bit naughty, we did leave it there for someone else to empty, but when I told her I had 10 'laced' friendship Chicksmix jars leftover from a drugs anonymous group get together, back in Gertie that she could have, she seemed satisfied, and calmed down."

"I filled a basket with some goodies as we didn't need all the things I had in the cart anyway. Now that I remember, you did promise me that at least one of the jars contained psilocybin edibles Jules."

"Ssssh, do you want to get us into trouble here Ange?"

"You both seem to be managing that quite well yourselves, now back to the video evidence, we see you in your apparently cold weather."

"Extreme, it's an extreme cold weather mask M'Lard."

"We can see you lunge aggressively across the counter towards the cashier, waving a weapon in her face. From this angle, please do correct me if I'm wrong, but the way I see it is, you're holding her up at gunpoint, demanding money. There is a brief pause, then we don't pick up anymore footage until the forecourt camera kicks back in and we see the blurry image of the van, which I can only assume you are now all in, and you take off like a bat out of hell, burning rubber in your wake. To add insult to injury, three hands appear from the van's windows and gesticulate at the distraught cashier who runs out to the forecourt trying to prevent you from leaving as you hadn't paid for the full tank of petrol and the other products you had in your basket."

"You didn't pay her Ange? I thought you paid her."

"I thought you did Jules."

"I didn't, I thought you did. You said you'd pay her after you took the phone call? Who paid for the petrol then?"

"No one according to this statement."

"As I stand here before you in this dock, I can see plainly that this is all a simple misunderstanding Judgey. We all thought each other was paying. It's not a problem because as soon as you free us, I can get my cards and take care of any cost and trauma caused. More importantly though, we didn't hold her or any gas station up. If your video footage had continued you'd have been able to see that in actual fact, the cashier was laughing WITH us over the counter, not in fear of her life."

"I'm not sure if you realise just how serious all this stuff written down in black and white on plain paper is, it's as clear as day to me. You are guilty...of something...or should be"

"I don't take life very seriously in any case M'Lard, let alone this one, and certainly not the truth that others have deemed to be fact, written down on pieces of paper, regaling a story from their point of view, peppered with their limiting perceptions, depending on their prejudices and discriminations. The only thing I take seriously in any paper, is a fish and chip supper wrapped in newspaper, and even that I take that with a pinch of salt. I'm not even sure whether my friend Ange is saying "dick"? "duck"? Or "dock". Changes the context of everything when you mishear. Ange, you've lived in Amerkin too long for me to differentiate between your vowels, I can't tell the difference between your i/e e/i. o...ei, ei, o."

"Not the time for nursery rhymes Jules, you keep Old Macdonald and his farm to yourself."

"Another example of how words can be misinterpreted yer Holiness, how they are said/pronounced and how they are heard can change the narrative completely, because is the honourable Judge Crooks now looking AT us in the dock or looking at us with his dick? See, completely different. Would you rather be seen or heard or heard over-seen Ange?"

"No question, I'd much rather be seen than heard. For example every male present gets to see me in my whole gorgeous glory with their ample sized dicks. I only get to see me when I have the good fortune of admiring myself in a reflection, y'all get the full visual enchilada all to your unbridled selves. I have to be prepared at any moment to be seen."

"I prefer to be heard over seen."

"Clearly, or you may have taken a bit more care applying the eyeliner and lipstick."

"Harsh, but fair, we all have to be prepared for whatever is coming our way from experiences in our outer life with no personal preferences as to how it should be for us. Unhappiness is a great opportunity for us to see that events have not met our personal expectations. Make sure those senses are taking a nap, and not interfering with a very neutral reality unfolding. That's the problem, many people cling to their likes and resist their dislikes like they have a magic feckin wand."

"And as the presiding Judge I prefer to speed this process up so I don't get to see or hear from either of you again, ever. Let's carry on, shall we...now don't get me wrong, this is not an interactive, audience participation, although I do feel like I'm at a pantomime, so believe me when I say, this is not an opportunity to interrupt, deflect or answer anything till asked. I prefer to be the speaker. The video still appears like you're holding the cashier up at gunpoint."

"Gunpoint? As in with a gun? Gunpoint? I may be Scottish-American and that many people believe most of us are packing, well the only thing packed here, is in fact a packet of Wrigley's spearmint gum. Are there laws against being held up at gumpoint?"

"Chewing gum? You held the cashier up with a stick of gum? It still appears that you're being rather aggressive non the less, you're halfway across the counter, screaming in her face, waving...."

"Carry on Judgey..don't let us stop you. Waving?? What is in her face exactly? Waving gum in her face, a stick of gum in her face."

"Who checks the evidence before it's presented to me Ms Terry?"

"Ooooo, how shocking, let's chew over that. At the very least, controversial your Holiness, a real live stick up in action, not sure we're ever going to be able to Wrigleys out of this one Ange."

"It's Extra for sure Jules."

"I know, I hear that all the time, everyone says I'm extra extra."

"I meant the gum, it was EXTRA, extra spearmint gum."

"Then why wasn't it included in the bill then, why was it extra? Surely we were paying enough with the petrol and goodies we were buying?"

"Which you didn't pay for I might like to remind you."

"Were we paying Double ... .Mint Ange? My life is now complete, we can't wrigley's out of this one, but we didn't mean to not pay, we thought each other was paying, an innocent misunderstanding yer lardship."

"Let's pause the video here where you're threatening the cashier, and examine it all a bit closer shall we."

"I admit, it does look that way, but it wasn't. There is an easy explanation for all this. We were trying to remember a word, a word to describe the two men/boys who'd used basic sign language to direct us to the petrol station, but neither of us could remember the word, it suddenly came back to Ange, and she involuntarily allowed her outer voice to takeover rather than leaving the outlawed word firmly in her very mental playground. We weren't trying to offend, only retrieving some long forgotten vocabulary, these days more and more words, names etc disappear into the invisible menopausal void. You wouldn't understand, but it's a real struggle at times to remember the basic things. What was the word again Ange? I'm telling you if I had a penny for everytime I forget something, I'd be...it began with an "A" maybe."

"That's amnesia Jules."

"This menopause is pure dead madness, age related for sure. What was the word again Ange? Remind me of the word you used to threaten the poor cashier with a stick of chuddy? How many syllables? Meaning? Rhymes with? Any clue will do. Words can be so powerful you know, they can be like a sword, penetrating, thrusting, landing and slicing directly to the core of the heart centre, which is waiting patiently, ready to heal or harm the individual. I can see all the misinterpretations going on in this shit show, and all you have to do is see it with your own eyes, minus preconditioned perceptions and use your own words to liberate us."

"Or I could use them by continuing to read all the charges against you in the hope of shaming your soul."

"She doesn't have a soul yer holiness."

"Sole? That's the whole porpoise here is it not?"

"I'm close..F...f.....what was the word again Ange? The one we were trying to remember to describe the looks on those lads' faces? Something about being vacant, you know, not quite there, still gaun about. I would never normally condone using words or phrases that are considered outlawed, but it was a word used, that is no longer, meaning slow, holding back in terms of progress, it's on the tip of my tongue.

I'm sure it means slow, delayed, still on their developmental path. "Feel", that's it. Phew, I was beginning to think I was forgetting all my vocabulary, that's what Ange shouted TO the cashier, not AT her. "FEEL". A perfect example of only seeing what you want to see. Put it all in context, and it changes EVERYTHING. We were using our words, not to create defences, as you seem to think, but to melt them…speaking of melt, can we stop for a break? I'm very hot and sweaty and an ice cream would go down a treat."

"I'm going to use a few words of my own here to shatter your dreams of an ice cream …NO, this is not an amusement park you're in, no matter how it looks and feels!"

"I beg to differ. I'm finding the entire show energising AND amusing, how about you Jules?"

"If you think it, you still think it, whether you say it out loud or not. It's like all this Be Kind movement, it's great if it doesn't come with the additional, extra weight of mental dictated prejudice or opinions, revealing where the carrier needs to be healed. Opinions hold the peripheral tears of onions, if your actions and internal dialogue don't match, then they cancel each other out, just saying. We couldn't have been that bad, as we thought Sheila came out to wave us off, which we thought was lovely. I really thought we'd made a super connection."

"Balancing precariously on a knife edge between inviting connection or aggressively obstructing it. It says in the evidence written down in black and white before me that she was trying to flag you down, as you'd driven without paying, for anything, and not wishing you Bon Voyage as you seem to think."

"We did forget to pay, our bad, that's on us, but at our age, forgetting is the new black, am I right or am I wrang Ange?"

"You're a meringue Jules, and I don't mind a nut or two. I shall take care of any expenses and trauma caused to Big Red for the non hold up at gumpoint. Look, I hate to race you, but time is marching on, and we need do need to get out of here to find our friend, get her back to Sydney for her surprise 50th and the big reveal."

"You've decided then have you Ange? Now that is exciting."

"Not quite Jules, 50/50, but getting there slowly, a few more pieces to slot in first."

"She's not wrong M'Lard, this is well past its sell by date. I mean your decision Ange, not you. Now, if there's nothing else that we need to resolve, then we can be off. There does seem to be a simple, and I use that term very loosely, explanation for all this, wouldn't you agree? Am I allowed to say "simple" ?"

"I think that just about rounds it all up, so can we go now? Get her Queenship here an ice cream."

"I think I'd actually prefer an ice pole Ange."

"A nice pole? As in dancing? She's full of surprises this one, you'll have to show me your skills sometime Jules."

"Hold your horses Ladies, let's rein it in. You're getting ahead of yourselves again. Perhaps we're in the wrong places, maybe you should be here calling the shots instead of me."

"Really Your Holiness? Well I personally wouldn't mind."

"SILENCE. Please, I'm pleading with you now.. Ssshhhh, ssssh, I feel I've aged 10 years and it's only been an hour."

"Now you know how we feel Judgey."

"NEXT CHARGE. Setting fire to a Japanese restaurant, defecating...sorry, easy mistake, defacing, and trashing a bathroom, and, what a surprise, leaving yet another unpaid bill to be paid."

"WHAT?? C'est non possible, we didn't do that, did we Ange?"

Distance doesn't separate people, misunderstanding does.-
Jeff Hood

I like a good story well told. That is the reason I am
sometimes forced to tell them myself. Mark Twain

Come from a space of peace and you'll find that you can
deal with anything- Michael Singer

Don't judge each day by the harvest you reap but by the seeds that you plant -Robert Louis Stevenson

The Happy Tofu - Dumb Duck Nowhere

SHOKUDO - Japanese cafe

"According to my notes, you arrived at a Japanese restaurant."

"A Shokudo Judgey."

"Bless you Ange, one's a wish and all that."

"Thank you, I wish to get the fuck out of here, but in the meantime, the term SHOKUDO is a Japanese term given to a traditional cafe. The one we frequented is in the middle of its rhyming namesake is called "Dumb Duck Beware.""

"Nowhere Ange. It's called Dumb Duck Nowhere."

"Does it matter whether it's "nowhere" or "beware?"."

"To the duck it does M'Lard, it has to be aware, or it'll be sliced diced, added to a wok and served in a crispy pancake roll with plum sauce. If it's nowhere, then it's a vegetarian/vegan restaurant, as in this case. Might have been simpler if they'd just called it "Tofu". She believed she had eaten meat, sushi did. Now that I think about it, is it Japanese? I'm sure there are plenty of Asian countries that eat tofu sushi, and crispy pancake rolls, not just the Japanese."

"Should be "Get Tofu", pedantics I know Jules, but I think crispy pancake rolls are Chinese, not Japanese, you'd be more likely to get Yakitori-style pan roasted pound duck breasts rolled in dashi powder, sprinkled with toasted sesame seeds and deep fried in peanut oil. Mmmmm, that does sound delicious."

"Let's get back to the task at hand, and not let ourselves get carried away by the dietary requirements of an entire population. Apparently, you pushed your way past the hostess and marched directly through to the VIP suite, tore open the shoji blinds? Let me stop you right there, before you try to correct me on the pronunciation. Don't. Pyromania, and yet again, leaving before the bill was paid. How do you plead?"

"I believe it best to be guilty until proven innocent, howeva, that's not quite how it went down your Hiragana, or how she went down to be more precise. Jules was in front of me and tripped over the hem of her rather unflattering, ageing MooMoo, or kaftan, harem pants, difficult to tell where one bit ends and the other starts. I've seen salads better dressed. I'd like to try to make the entire scenario sound sexier and trendier than it actually was, but am failing miserably. I very nimbly darted to her side as she went down and swept the blinds apart to allow her to fall easily and gently through them without tearing them, but mostly I did it so she wouldn't hurt herself against the bamboo trims. She flew through the air like a not so graceful cart horse, landing head first on the rim of the floor level dining dugout, some blinds may have got torn in the process."

"I'm not quite sure how prepared I am to hear the following explanation as to how the sink was wrenched off the wall and the toilet was blocked with... a Duoshido? A Japanese cushion apparently."

"I may be able to shed some light on that Your Holiness, you see, after I tripped over my hem or Ange's foot, fine line, my elasticated waistband was pulled down slightly and I belly flopped, accidentally on purpose ended up doing some form of the worm breakdance, across the tatami floor. I've taken to elastic waisted trousers for 2 reasons. 1. Waistbands with buttons and zippers actually leave a permanent zigzag impression from my belly button to my mound of venus, and I still have a levi logo, imprinted from decades ago, permanently stamped above my root chakra. I'm sure it'll still be there if you want to look, I haven't seen that particular part of my body since before the plague 2. Because it makes ablutions easier, let's leave it there shall we."

"Excuse me Yer Judgeyness, but I'd like to interject and correct our learned friend here that it's the wrong season for a tsunami."

"Not tsunami Ange, tatami, a style of flooring ubiquitous throughout Japan.Traditionally, rush grass is woven around a rice straw core to keep the mat firm, nowadays the rice straw core is often replaced with more modern materials, such as wood chips, polystyrene foam, tofu, so it makes for the perfect exfoliation chemical peel or dermabrasion for my jelly belly and thighs, all rolled into one giant tatami mat. A human sushi roll, or highly flammable hazard."

"And how exactly is this all connected to the blocked toilet and cushion?"

"That's easy Yer Lardship, after inadvertently falling and bouncing off my bladder, be thankful there wasn't a tsunami right there and then. I knew I needed to go directly to the loo, but couldn't see properly because my eyes were impregnated with crud from the unhoovered mat on which I had face planted."

"Sorry, you were impregnated?"

"Impregnated by a foostie tempura tiger roll, smooshed into the folds and creases of my crepey eyelids."

"Don't be so hard on yourself Jules, they're not that bad, perhaps a tad baggy, but nowhere near crappy, strike that from her record Mys Tery."

"I said crepe, Ange, as in crepey, not crappy."

"That's what I said, Jules. Spooky really, it's as if Lezzers has been reincarnated in your body"

"Anyway, I digest, there were decades old panko crumbs imbedded like stalactites gripping my eyelashes."

"Mites, stalagmites Jules."

"It's tites Ange. Tites are like tights, they pull up, well mine do, perhaps you spend more time taking yours down, which is precisely why she you should wear "NEXT" clothing line and not those ageing, provocateur thong stringy things that make your arse look more like two low hanging, well squeezed, wrinkled scrotum sacks, and not quite what you imagine."

"You can strike that from the record Mys Tery, I'd like it documented that I never wear tights, I'm a stockings, usually, commando girl. Good for shocking the troops especially for all the hit-and-fun raids into inner territories."

"I however, on the other hand, yer Holiness, prefer to wear comfy, large, high waisted knickers as I need to get those thumbs hooked in the waistband as quickly as I can. A mere thought of a toilet seat can have those flood gates open. I stopped wearing tights for an entirely different reason, getting back to my story, I managed to get my floppy-arsed carcass off the floor, but in doing so, I must have accidentally, inadvertently, scooped one of their zabutons up and into the folds of my MooMoo dress with legs, a loose, flowy dress worn by Hawaiian women. Am I allowed to wear that these days without being jumped by the self proclaimed, non Hawaiian, righteous brigade? Is it culturally inappropriate to be wearing another culture's traditional dress? Should I wear my Scottish heritage attire or my adopted Australian one? Should only Scots wear tartan? Oh Pandora, you should have stayed in your box, look at the global confusion that's been caused. You'd have to wear "pants" of varying lengths, or Daisy Dukes, a polo shirt, trainers with long socks, topped off with a baseball cap, and a mouthful of gum, and a non concealed handgun Ange."

"Noone in their right mind would go out of their way to deliberately copy that look Jules, other than an American that is."

"Is it copying though Ange, it's easy to mistake inspiration for jealousy, everyone should check out their own choices before being the judge and jury on mine or anyone else's. Thoughts on life are an unconscious reaction to what's going on around us. Aside from you, your Holiness, you can judge away, I'm here for it, as we all are. Anyway, where was, I don't want to lose my train of thought when I'm on a roll, getting carried away by the verdict given by others, on my choices, again, other than yours that is M'Lard. Where was I, yes, on this occasion the Japanese cushion was enveloped in my fabric folds, I couldn't see well with my porn cracker eyelids, and ended up with my trousers slipping further down, next thing I know, I'm hopping around like a vertical deep fried caterpillar. I was always good at the sack race, so was able to bounce my way towards the toilets. I managed to pull them up slightly after a battle of wills, to mid thigh, but the elastic was constricting, cutting off the blood supply from my knees to my toes. Not dissimilar in appearance to when a boa constrictor tries to swallow a Geisha girl whole. I'll leave that one with you for a while. When I had finished my business, and stood up, the cushion must have fallen out of my gusset and blocked the toilet, which I then flushed, tots unaware that the cushion was stuck in the u bend. A shrimple mistake. I was at the sink, washing my hands when I noticed the floor was wet and slidey, which on reflection may have had something to do with the blocked toilet. It was bloody slippery, and I almost broke my feckin neck on the slick, toilet treadmill floor. I felt like those skating champions without the Bovril, or the Bean. I had to horizontally sprint just to keep myself from falling flat on my face…AGAIN. Excuse my language your Holiness, but it was well dangerous, and I had to hold the sides of the vanity and run almost as fast as Ange's mouth on a disgruntled campaign. I remember feeling chuffed that my core kept me going for a short period of time, before succumbing to gravity, like a whale breaching just before surrendering to the non resistant, inevitable 'drop'. I gave up and slithered across the cold wet tiles, using the puddles to clean my eyes out, and without standing, I crawled out of there. The door closed behind me and I swear I have no idea what happened next in toiletgate, because I was long gone. When I got back to the girls, all I could see were Ange's two flailing alligator gloves waving at me from the bowels of the cavernous pit hole. The funny thing is, she wasn't wearing gloves. Arms were flailing from the ground, not so patiently waiting for mine and Lesley's entry from above."

"Speaking of patience, you're both trying mine for one, it may only be one, but it's a big one. Can we move this along ….quickly. I mistakenly assumed we'd be done with these proceedings in less than an hour. How wrong was I?"

"I tots get it Your Lardship, I'm exhausted, even long words tire me out these days, I'm also totally famished, can't even remember the last time I ate anything other than Officer Hogg's foostie cheese, garlicky ball like, thingymajigs, but that shouldn't count as it is full of fake cheese, preservatives, additives and leaves permanent orange mouth stains. These alleged incidents all took place very differently from the way you describe them, other than containing an arrayed and varied view of perceptions from questionable genuine witnesses. And their point of views are clearly not as credible as you are led to believe, because all these incidents have been grossly exaggerated. I could go on. You only have before you a small piece of the entire picture as it played out. The fool incident has not been taken into account, you've missed the fuller picture completely. We tend to focus our attention on only one or two pieces of a puzzle, ignoring the bits that complete the fuller picture. You describe it as if it were a scene from the movie "Honey, we wrecked an entire state", or "Honey, we're wrecked", look at us your Holiness, do we look like the villains of this story you tell before this court? The only thing we're capable of is ingesting fermented tofu, not investing in pyromania. I'd also like to reiterate and have it noted that Ange is ready, willing and more than able to totally pay for any damages, or wrecks notcured, oops incurred."

"ORDER."

"Oh thank goodness for that, about time, I've been waiting for you to say it again for ages. Is it possible I could get a farrah, quinoa bowl, with avocado? And a stick of celery for my friend Ange here."

"Great idea Jules, bring the celery with some vodka, tomato juice, worcesterooster sauce and we're talking."

"Hear hear, or is it here here, Ange, I can never remember, they sound the same to me, I think it should be here, hear if it's not. From the eucalyptus growing in the neighbourhood, to the flickers of dark and light dancing through the kitchen window, a curtain blowing in the breeze, a random human doing something amusing, or a surprising pop of colour when you least expect it, there is always something nudging its way into our field of perception, working its magic, quieting the mind, enlivening the senses, lifting the spirit. Like a radio, all we have to do is tune in to receive it. Can you hear me now? I'll have one of those drinks Ange wants also your Holiness."

"STOP. Ladies, PLEASE JUST STOP. Can we please put a stop to all this HERE and now, and hear me out. This has to be resolved soon before anyone dies of old age."

"At least it won't be from boredom your Lardhip, I've personally found this to be surprisingly fun and entertaining, stories are how we make sense and maybe come to all our senses, in a senseless, crazy, neutral world after all. I can't remember jack shit, and there's always an interruption and distraction taking me further away from the point, especially when I'm on a roll and something or someone sidetracks the flow. I can lose my train of thought…and…well, … .where were we? What were we even talking about? Food? Food. Rugs, sink Was it food? Drink? A drink ..sink? I'm not sure anyone present is able to keep up with the thread of this conversation, let alone me. FIRE! FIRE!"

"EVERYBODY OUT, clear the courtroom, there's a fire. FIRE? Wait what? where? Don't panic. Everyone stay calm. Where's the fire?"

"Sorry to cause confusion M'Lard, there's no physical fire, you said we were pyromaniacs, so I concluded there must have been a fire in the restaurant, but it must have happened after we'd left, we never saw a fire, did we Ange? Maybe that's how you got those burn marks on your thighs? I had to haul her skinny 35lb arse out of there, but needed some assistance from a liquid sustenance source which came from a flaming sambuca on a tray near the kitchen, I took the biggest breath known to mankind, pushing my breasts out, stretching my side torso like wings and as I expelled the energy, the flame temporally rose to the occasion almost setting my face on fire, before succumbing to being snuffed….ahhhh, now we're getting somewhere Ange, removing my fringe in the process, singeing its swan song finale, in a farewell spiteful act. I wrenched and grabbed Ange by her scrawny, reptilia, boney gnarled wrists, and yanked her, she shot out like grease lightning from the bowels of the dugout. Her acrylic trouser legs enabled me to glide her across the flammable seagrass floor easily and gracefully."

"Silk Judgey, they're silk, not acrylic, and she knows it. Strike that from the record Mys Tery, but to be fair that extra liquid courage did give you the slide and glide that was needed to take us all the way to the front door, Lezzers was already waiting in the driver's seat of Dirty Gertie outside, but how on earth can Godzilla pulling me out of the cesspit, dragging me across the rough floor have anything to do with a fire, how can that happen?"

"It's not rocket science Ange, when two sticks, your legs in this case, are rubbed together, the action creates friction, which causes heat. Heat coaxes the acrylic…"

"SILK Jules, silk. Please, carry on, the floors all yours, sorry it's not actually, it belongs to the Japanese restaurant we are accused of trashing, and setting fire to."

"The spark created by your silky legs it seems Ange."

"When I die, I want to be cremated and my ashes added to a lemon tree."

"That's nice Ange, so we can make a lemon drop in your honour?"

"No, to remind y'all how bitter and twisted I was."

"I want to be added to an hourglass, that way I can always be a part of game night. Only time I'd have a real hourglass figure, more chances of winning also. Have you thought about having your ashes blended with tattoo ink Ange, that way you can continue to get under people's skin. I think at least a gram or two of each of us should be put in a firework so we can sprinkle our love, or in your case, salt over the world."

"Why thank you Jules, I'll take that as the compliment it wasn't intended to be."

"You're whale cum Ange, the fabric of your "Pants" must have sparked into a substance not dissimilar to smouldering plastic, then it was painted across the full length of the flammable floor by your leg brush strokes. Any child knows that a spark can lie dormant for a little bit before igniting, which might be the cause behind the horizontal charred stairway to heaven scorches that we see in your evidential photos M'Lard. The combination of speed, friction, dexterity, skill, grace and effort playing their roles beautifully, synchronising, synergically, working together with the raw grass flooring to become a fully-fledged fire which, incidentally, we were oblivious to, our attention somewhere else completely, which is why we left, we didn't know anything had happened behind us. The past is a place to learn from, not to revisit and move there. Experience casts an unseen net over us, leaving its shadow to drag behind in our wake. Who doesn't want to go back in time and punch themselves in the face. When I was a kid, I wanted to be older, this shit is not what I expected. I really try to contain my crazy, but the lid keeps popping off."

"Being a cold hearted motherfucker wasn't really what I expected either, but here we are. I'm like 10 people in one body, spin the wheel, and, come take me on if you think you're brave enough, be it on your own head though. Take it as the warning it's intended as."

"I need a speed bump between my brain and my mouth, yet I hate it when the voices in my thought station go silent, I never know what the wee feckers are planning next."

"Noted. You apparently left without paying…again."

"We all assumed each other had taken care of the bill, you know what they say about assumption? It makes an ass out of you and me, not YOU, or ME, but..someone your Holiness."

"My eyes are rolling so hard, I'm checking out my own ass, look this face you see before you saves me from so many conversations I don't want to be part of, including this one, so I'll make it quick, all I recall Judgey is my wrists being grabbed, and flying from the comfort of a silk cocoon, like a graceful Greek goddess being pulled. I felt like a passenger on an Olympic bobsleigh, spontaneously hurtling from the Japanese silk grubby folds, torpedoing through space and time, straight across the floor directly to the front door, then straight into Dirty Gertie's inner sanctuary. I had no idea as to whether the check was paid or not, but it's not a problem, I can take care of all this right now, and we can be on our merry way. More than happy to pay for whatever needs to be paid for, and slam dunk, job done. And we can get off, find our pal, who at this very moment could be head-down, strapped on a sloping board, nose covered, water pouring over her face in a steady, continuous, copious stream."

"I don't mind a bit of waterboarding myself, without the water though, maybe some white wine instead, like Cloudy Bay or something like that."

"Now that you mention it Jules, that does sound like fun. If we could check out Judgey, settle up, then we can be free to go join in all the fun and exciting drinking games that she's currently not having at her/his majesty's secret cervix without us."

"Check out? Cheque? You are aware ladies, and I use that word loosely, that this is not a hotel, or any other hospitality establishment, even one mildly representing one. You are being held at HMS until we have sorted out through all this chaos and destruction that you seem to be central to. A coincidence? I think not, AND you can't for one minute think that waving a platinum credit card is going to make any of these charges go away. I'd love to add a charge of my own for audacity, the fact that you feel entitled enough to assume all this can be written off with one swipe, and it will all disappear, but it won't, not on my watch. I can't just leave it at that, and set you free whether you pay or not. I want to establish whether you are GUILTY or not. That's my job. Have I made myself clear? If there are no charges to be had at the very end of all this, then I will gladly take your card to pay for the outstanding damages and trauma compensation, and swipe it through the machine myself. Until then we have to address the FURTHER charges on this ever growing rap sheet that is unravelling before my very eyes."

"Here's the way I see it Holiness, there are no real, credible witnesses in most or any of this really. Everyone seems to be so caught up in their own conditioning, limiting beliefs, programming, and are putting their spin on the same story, at the exact same time others are spinning their personal data on the same scene. Different writers, different camera operators, that's all, it's all about perception, who was standing where, and which one of their senses grabbed the lion's share of their zoomed in, focussed attention. Most of what we're accused of never actually happened the way you believe, what we see is only from a viewpoint, literally, everyone is only ever a sum total of their own personal life experiences. Branded by their own past circumstances, adding to the heaviness of their already firmly established opinions, and judgments, their interpretation of an event, it can then become part of their belief system, and that's only ever a thought on spin cycle. Noone can ever share a very neutral outer world experience and have it the same as someone else's, they just can't, they're the only one that's looking at it from where they're standing, looking, smelling, tasting, touching, hearing, from their own unique, individual point of view. It all depends on where their focus/attention lands. Noone can have the same exposure to the bits in any event as it's happening, quite often provoking a physical reaction, revealing a part of the bearer which needs to be addressed. It really does require paying."

"I am offering to pay Jules, or have you forgotten?"

"I was about to say, attention, Ange, one has to pay attention to the invisible weight and choices of the dish handed to us the day we were born, that we bring to life's banquet table, a smorgasbord of every moment, laden with the religious/political/societal judgmental, criticisms, expectations, prejudices, views, carried on the plates brought by others, meeting here and now in an instant jiffy on a giant global, revolving, evolving table. No personal preference, desires or resistance to anyone else's chosen dish…even the ones that have liver on them, accepting each chef's selected, personal, unique palate."

"Please, please Judgey, I'll take the sentence if it means I don't have to listen to any more of this."

"Here's how to see it, your Holiness, if everyone slowed down a todger, pressed their pause button and realised that life isn't a race to the finish line, it's coming, like it or not, the final destination where we disembark, whether we're ready or not. If everyone paid a bit more attention, gave a wide angle lens to every moment with every breath they take and return, indulging and savouring in a threesome, a reuniting of their mind and body using a full breath as the body's global positioning system, providing navigation, and timing services for every attentive customer. A perfect threesome of space segment, control segment, and user segment. There would be less problems in the world, less divisiveness and more credible witnesses if people learned how to have threesomes. Am I right or am I wrang Ange?"

"The amount of debt and damages incurred by all these events could easily be mistaken as celebrities trashing hotels, restaurants, and lives belonging to others. In a relatively short time, as far as we're aware of, you have left an accumulated trail of destruction even the likes of Keith Moon would be appalled at."

"You were warned Judgey, when she goes off on one, there's no stopping her. Like a speeding train, each carriage full of psychobabble bullshit."

"Boozers can't be choosers your Holiness, anyhow, I had no knowledge as to what was happening until I was back in Gertie, and even then, again, I had no knowledge of any wrongdoings. You know, knowledge is like knickers, most people, present company excluded, have them, but not everyone shows them. When you know, you know. You know? And when you don't know you don't know. You know?

"The only thing I know at this very moment is that I'm confused, weary, drained, hungry, frustrated, perplexed…somewhat amused, I won't lie, but exhausted trying to unravel all the bullshit, sorry highly complex misdeeds."

"I know I'm extremely exhaustipated with all this, and quite frankly my dear, I don't give a dayam, I'm far too tired to even give a shit. Life is being sucked from me one slooow, graceful cellular whisp at a time, even the crumbs of self doubt and sarcasm are flaking off my lips."

"Lovely segway, speaking of "Boozers", let's take a look at the following charges shall we? PLEASE, if I can muster enough energy which is being slowly squeezed from every parched, drained cell in my body."

The Strongest people are not those who show strength in front of us but those who win battles we know nothing about
Jonathan Harnisch

The Wobbly Bottom Sip

Jules

It's downright knotty, challenging, and frustrating juggling the constricting energy, surfing the squalls of malaise as they rise, as they express themselves, then move on, and not be consumed by them. Facilitate their growth as they build, crest, and evolve into waves, turbulence, and storms. Relax and move with the natural rhythm and motion of the ocean, not fight it. Too much effort is required for that. Without rain nothing grows, so learning how to embrace the storms in one's life can make the adventure so much smoother. We grip, or give free rein to our energetic emotional controls, allowing the raging currents to course their flow through our inner pathways, like unnoticed golden liquid transporting us across the waters of each moment. If our river is blocked with the residues of anger, uncertainty, and grief, then every minute reflects exactly back what we set sail. What are we holding on to, and what are we willing to let go? True freedom carries no luggage or preferences. The best place to cross a river is at its source folks, and most folk use thinking as the wingman to awareness, but the secret to peace is that it's actually the other way round, thinking should be the wingman to awareness. Awareness beyond, yet inclusive of loose thoughts, not too tight, not too loose, just right, The Goldilocks approach to all of life's dualities.

"The Goldilocks effect stems from our inclination towards finding an optimal point that satisfies our needs or preferences. Whether it's temperature, taste, size, or complexity, humans have a tendency to seek out options that are neither too much nor too little, but rather fall within an ideal range. What I'm trying to say is that life is all about balance, the good the bad, the highs, the lows, the gins and tonics, so the Wobbly Bottom Sip was the perfect place to be in the full spectrum of polarities, until it wasn't."

"There's a recurring destructive theme going on here, culminating in a human stampede, and a plausible, sorry, possible act of terrorism. One of your party was wearing a suicide vest at The Wobbly Bottom Sip."

"You have that totally out of context ..again, it was a weighted emotional support vest for anxiety, not a suicide vest, and it was only mistakenly exposed when Ange ripped open the denim shirt she was wearing to cover it. But what that has got to do with someone called Hugh, stamping on anyone's heid is beyond me."

"Innocent bystanders said there was a bomb, a sniper and a spray of bullets, hence the stampede!"

"I don't even know who Stan is, and his toilet habits have nothing to do with me, and they weren't bullets, your Lardship, they were buttons, Levi metal stud like buttons to be precise. Ange tore open the denim shirt, thinking they were poppers, the easily pulled apart sort, but the buttons flew off in every conceivable direction possible. All I remember, yes, was a resounding shout of "SHOTS", yes that was it, "shots". "

"Witnesses claim a half naked woman and her friend were gyrating near the dance floor, in some kind of apparent, scarring, horrific sex display."

"Now that you mention it, there were shouts for "shots" from the patrons, maybe required to support their journey watching the rest of the disturbing floor show you mention."

"Always trust Tequila goggles Jules."

"I stopped trusting tequila in general when it lied to me at Lesley and My key's wedding, telling me I could dance. Video says, noooo, besides we were too busy seeing through our own tequila lenses, when someone shouted "BOMB", and then panic set in, there was screaming, people running around like headless chooks, so we took off for the exit which had been wedged open to give our gussets a much needed gust of fresh air. You have to understand something here your Holiness, we are all women of a certain age, and needed the cool, scraps of air carried in from the cool, fresh outback outside to the stifling, muggy, heavy, dank, smoky air on the inside, so I admit, it was opened, albeit, marginally, opened. BUT, I made sure it was firmly closed when we left."

"With everyone left inside?"

"Now that was a funny thing, everyone else seemed to be running towards the front door, no one came with us, they all seemed to be running in the opposite direction. That is strange come to think of it. Ange? Don't you think that's strange? What do you remember?"

"All I remember is pulling the rather cheap, supposedly vintage, denim shirt apart to sexpose a more than ample, highly sought after natural cleavage, to the world, and not to hide it from the rabid dogs, the shirt was way too tight anyway and would hypothetically have caused Madonna in her leather caged corset to have an anxiety attack. Next I hear someone is getting a round in at the bar, so I swipe the bottle of tequila left on an unoccupied table beside me and take a shot ..or two…, anyway, that's right, I ended up keeping the whole bottle because someone screamed that there was a fire."

"Let me clarify, you heard someone shout "FIRE"?

"It might not have been the actual word "fire", maybe something close enough to it though, hmm, it was burn, yes, BURN, that was it, same difference right? Burn? Fire? Burn? Then everyone started screaming, so I joined in. I'm working with my therapist on my fomo. Next thing I remember is being outside on the sidewalk, Dirty was there, Lezzers was already behind the wheel, so I opened the back passenger door, that's when I noticed the metal men at work triangle under the chassis so bent down to remove it and propped it against the wall, when I returned somebody had closed the door again, so I opened it, got in, and slammed it shut, there was a dehydrated scorpion skeleton in the floor well, and not a priceless, irreplaceable, disregarded, discarded gift, so I put on the leather glove that had been stuck in the handle and chucked it out, the glove accidentally slipped off in the process. Lezzers was driving, because she hadn't been drinking, and we had been…LOTS, I may even have polished off the bottle of tequila downed with some vitamin chasers that were still lying in wait, left over from when she spilled them in the footwell earlier. I remember that because Lezzers specifically said to take the ones on the right, the other ones were sleeping tablets. I went for the ones on the right when Jules screamed " LEFT"."

"I screamed "left" Ange because we had to take the turn on the left you dozy cow, that's why I screamed "LEFT", not for you to take the pills on the left you eejit. That explains our blackout yer Holiness, and why everything went horribly visually pear shaped for everyone concerned, us included. Ange believed she was taking Vit C tablets, which were on the right, not the left. Our malleable memory is hazy, patchy in places, lacking credibility and not just because we're old, menopausal, forgetful, outrageous, incredible, strong human beans, we are innocent. I get that it's not our fault, but it is our responsibility for being voluntarily drugged. I remember sharing what I believed to be the Vit C tablets liberally with Ange to prevent any impending hangovers, and the tequila was on hand, so was consumed for medicinal purposes only. Noone was actually driving with drink and/ or illegal drugs in their system. At our age, we're already considered chemically, and physically imbalanced, in any case, drugs, alcohol, mischief and us not giving a toss as to what others think, certainly helps all the medicine go down. This entire incident, where others honestly believed we were terrorists, was nothing of the kind, only a story that grew in community fear, changing the entire script of the actual play. A complete misperception jumbled up in their own preconditioned data of limiting beliefs. When limiting beliefs are accepted, it doesn't take long for them to become our truth. The only terrorising thing about this is that the anxiety support denim vest was unattractive, sexually repelling, and organ constricting apparently. When anxiety is experienced in the body, it is usually triggered by something we have told ourselves about something or someone, and the physical body isn't able to keep up and metabolise the extreme feels of discomfort and all that the body wants in that moment, is to get as far away from 'it' as possible, and in most cases, "any exit" out of that particular experience will do, even if it involves reactivity. We didn't for one moment suspect that we or an anxiety vest of all things would be the cause of all this chaos, pain and suffering. Blows my mind."

We communicate in ways that muddy the very meaning of what we're trying to convey with our words. We sometimes complicate the simplest conversations until those involved are left feeling confused around the intent behind the chat. Usually, the last thing that we intend. We are often unaware that our words or tone may have an entirely different implication for the folk we are addressing. Vocabulary, inflection, and accent can mean different things to other cultures. Innocent conversations may have unintended meaning for someone whose life experience differs from ours. So, if we are aware that the perception of the person receiving the message may be different from our original intent, how do we avoid hurt feelings and misunderstandings? Seriously people, how hard is it to convey meaning in a way that is relatively fool proof?

"It says here, that as the pandemonium unravelled, the regular revellers stampeded in the opposite direction to the three of you who were last seen to be hot footing it out the fire exit. Now, call me pedantic, but somehow after hearing all this and being an actual first hand witness to you both as you tell your tales, the only part of this particular piece of evidence I'd dispute here is the part that

says "hot-footed", so for the record Jenny, shall we change that to, maybe "Goofy Gaited?" "

"I'd prefer graceful gazelles. But you're the Holiness, so fill your high heeled boots."

"By closing the fire exit, by your own admission, barricading everyone inside."

"All I know is we left everyone inside a very lovely safe bar with disco music, alcohol and pub grub, didn't we Ange."

"Luckily for you, there were no casualties, and other than an unpaid bar bill, the "terrorists" made their escape and disappeared into the night without causing any damage other than a stolen bottle of tequila, now call me an old fashioned pedantic, but it still smacks of guilt, even I'm captivated as to how you're going to wriggle out of that one."

"You're an old fashioned pedantic, after you Ange, I need to regroup my train of thought here as it seems to have departed the station without me again."

"Where shall I begin? Yes, you old fashioned pedantic, in the beginning there was a door inside the Wobbly Bottom Lip, which Jules wanted wedged open due to her very unattractive hormonal flashes, which were in full flow, more like a flash flood warning if I'm perfectly honest, terribly unattractive, and she wanted the door open to relieve her of some of the night, day, morning and afternoon sweats she was experiencing, the cool breeze from outside and the constant fanning of her hand held fan, did the job somewhat, penetrating and displacing the stagnant air of the pub. Lezzers was also raging hormonally and had brought her soap box with her, waxing lyrical that opening a fire exit, which in her opinion was meant to remain closed unless of an emergency, was wrong. It was then unanimously decided without her permission that the door should be opened a smidgen, welcoming the refreshing, light air in, diluting the muggy fermented bar air, marginally. Jules promised, she promised that when we left the bar, she would make doubly sure to close it, which she did. I was totally oblivious to the fact that when I tore the cheap denim fabric apart, the metal studs flew in every direction at 90mph leaving contrails in their dusty, musty atmospheric wake. Those metal orbs must have been the "shots" your bystanders refer to and not the tequila kind of shots that I believed them to be, taking the bottle, as directed, in my stride. I for one Judgey am a lover, if you can't already tell, and a great one at that if I may be so bold, but not a fighter, well, by that I mean, not a physical fighter, I'll fight anyone verbally with my sarcasm, intelligence, wit and repartee, but I didn't get the chance as I was whisked by my ride or die pals who took me under their wings and escorted me from what they believed to be a volatile situation. I'm sure it was a fun night at The Wobbly Bottom Lip, sorry to have missed the final chapter, but we were well on our way by then."

"It's not "lip" Ange, it's not "Lip"."

"I am not giving him any "lip" Jules, I'm merely sharing my side of the story for further clarification as to the events that took place from MY perception, and not yours, as you keep bleating on about."

"It's The Wobbly Bottom SIP, that's what it's called Ange, The Wobbly Bottom Sip, not the wobbly bottom lip although that's exactly what you're showing us right now."

"Ha ha, got ya, sorry, yes, sip, easy mistake. That was pretty much it, we escaped the harrowing and traumatic ordeal believing we were the innocent parties in it all, and still do BELIEVE. I tell you what's goofy about all this though Judgey, is that you think we had something to do with it. We had doodly squat to do with it, we were out of there like a lesbian eating out with her girls, lickety split."

"If I was a drag queen that would be my name Ange, Lickety Split."

"What do you mean IF Jules, you already dress like one."

"Harsh but fair Ange, harsh but fair."

"As a consultant hedge fund analyst, I do my quantitative research in order to identify the assets to trade with the fund's money as it adheres to its trading strategy and mandate. So, I do my homework on current trends, for instance do y'all know that it's illegal to be drunk in a public place, including pubs, in Australia? Not many people know this, but Aussies drink 1.7 billion litres of beer per year, that's about 680 bottles of beer for each adult. Now, I may be going out on a limb here, but by my somewhat over qualified highly skilled calculations, that would mean that almost 3/4 of the population of this wondrous land would be incarcerated. Am I right, or am I wrang?"

"You're a do nought, without any filling Ange, I'm the meringue remember? I reckon that ¾ of the population would be quite content spending time incarcerated in The Wobbly Bottom Sip, seems like the perfect fit for the average human bear."

"I can identify with that Jules."

"I identify with being a female, mother, friend, but according to Marks & Spencer's luxury sticky toffee pudding, or frozen cheese, olive and pineapple pizza, I am a family of 6."

Between what is said and not meant, and what is meant and not said, most of love is lost - Kahil Gibran

Without rain, nothing grows, learn to embrace the storms in your life - Unknown

Standoff At The Not So Ok Corral

Jules

This is like some farcical, realistic, unscripted reality show.

"Your van, took off from the Wobbly Bottom Sip, dislodging the unsealed skree from the road, spraying departing, final shots at the innocent onlookers."

"Onlookers? In America, we call them Ambulance chasers."

"With due respect yer Holiness, on the advice of my own personal counsel, I invoke my fifth amendment privilege against self-incrimination and respectfully decline to answer any further questions."

There is very little to learn from hearing our external voice. I'm going to take all that indoors to hear what's really going on. We should make room to answer three questions before we react. 1. Is it the truth? 2. Can it be fixed? 3. Can I live with it and accept it despite its presence?

"It was at that point that the ONLOOKERS witnessed an older lady, being dragged and bundled into the back of said van, in what appeared to be the kidnapping of an innocent bystander, who when later rescued by the police claimed she was one of your friends..hence..anyway, I'll get to that. A police chase ensued, out into the outback. The vehicle being pursued did not stop, in fact it appears that they increased their speed. How can you plead the fifth to that?"

"Having not seen, let alone been in the outback for many, many decades, living in the good ole USof A for, shall we say, some time, I was captivated by the wonders of the vast heartland of Australia that unfolded with immense speed before me, faster than Usain Bolt's100 metre dash."

We are so lucky to live here, truly awe-inspiring to be present in such a place of exquisite, unique beauty and wildness. It's an area of extremes, alternately lush and bountiful, harsh and inhospitable. This particular night, the blackness enveloped the sky as it took its place as the background scene to life's events as they unfolded. The people and land of the Outback embody much that is most distinctive and characteristic of Australia. I love it here.

"It sure was a speedy drive yer Holiness, all I remember was everything became slightly hazy, my lights of experience began to fade, slipping quickly into a state of surrealness and oblivion. I now believe that I was having a chemical reaction which then caused an imbalance in Brian, my brain, more than usual admittedly, but we had accidentally consumed large quantities of pharmaceuticals, which I believed to be vit C, or tic tacs at the very least, admittedly we had also consumed a few alcoholic beverages in the hours leading up to our capture."

"The reluctant kidnap victim and the driver were the only ones that passed the involuntary breathalyser, the latter whom we've already established has evaded authorities for decades, avoiding persecution….. PROSECUTION. You've got me at it now. I digress, she is now thankfully where she needs to be, in custody, courtesy of HMS and behind bars at St NotsoOkade, and not creating havoc in them anymore."

"It is our unanimous decision, M'lard, that there has been a wrongful incarceration here. You seem to be almost at the end of the rap sheet, so shall we call it a day and put all these ludicrous, far-fetched perceptions to bed once and for all. The presumption of innocence is based on the prosecution's burden of proof. In other words, the prosecutor must prove beyond reasonable doubt that the charges before the defendants are true. Known as a "due process" requirement, the principle is reflected in many judicial opinions and legal statutes." How can you be so certain that we kidnapped an innocent person, at the Wobbly Bottom Sip or anywhere else, because as it turns out, we, Ange here and myself were actually, physically there, in person, in Tasmania at the time you say our friend, the fugitive was there, but wasn't. Officer Cox has carried a vendetta against the wrong person, the person you have detained was 1000's of miles away working as a hard working, happily underpaid, nurse in a reserve in the middle of the outback. She needs a medal, not metal."

"She has to be an illegal alien at the very least. No?"

"No. She may well be an alien M'lard, but definitely not illegal as I was at her wedding almost 30 years ago. If she can legally wed, have a driver's licence, vocally vote and have a KFC loyalty card, then she can legally be here wouldn't you say? I would donate my liver on the fact that she is not an illegal."

"She doesn't have the wit, desire or drive to be able to muster that amount of deceit energetically, and for the record no one would benefit from this one's liver other than a goose that is."

"Harsh, and let me add, that her energy comes from a totally harmless, almost non judgmental place of kindness, and nurturing, would you agree Ange?"

"Well, yes, you have a point Jules, albeit her altruistic behaviour is usually without due authority, and more than a tad annoying. Either way, she wasn't with us. This is all balderdash, and doesn't make any sense at all."

We are, after all, the total of our unique, one-of-a-kind past depending on where, and to whom we are born into. We continue to resist and block the emotions that we don't like, preventing them from naturally rising, expressing themselves, and moving on, choosing to pick and mix the ones we believe are going to make us happier. We spend our entire lives storing incomplete, unfinished emotions in our bodies, turning the natural energetic spring that courses through our inner realm opaque. Those pesky stored sensations related to anger, fear, and sadness keep coming back in the form of something, somewhere, somehow, sometime, and more often than not, are triggered by a special unsuspecting person, and the body keeps the score. Emotions that try to get our attention, showing us their journey has not been completed. The special someone is also more often than not, exactly the teacher and/or student that we need to learn our individual lessons. Whilst in the throes of discomfort, anxiety, stress, etc, they can offer us the key to our self-imposed invisible straight jackets, squeezing the living bee juice out of us. There is always a learning lesson in our adventures which we all need in order to untether ourselves from any tension stockpiling in our body's physiology, gathered in the form of memories, judgement, negativity, and viewpoints, creating the emotional narrative, restricting and damming all the effervescent, babbling, flowing pathways in our inner realm. Red flags waving somewhere in our bodies, each and every one training chances. The incessant, comforting, reliable, spacious, yet unnoticed constant throb of aliveness pulsating its course through our innermost sanctums, often ignored and disregarded in preference to the toxic opinionated, prejudice of our critical inner voice. The voice of our own making, keeping us hostage in our own thought train, speeding its dulcet tones on our own mental racetrack. The real kicker here is that it might not even be our own personal shite we're damming the flow with, we build our own dams, we place the hurdles, we slam the inner doors, dimming the lights, which may well be inherited, not our fault, but our responsibility to release ourselves from our own personally chosen shackles, tightening the chains with our cravings and aversions, reacting rather than responding to life.

"We all carry some dregs from the past M'lard, some of it ours, some of it inherited, who knows, we may even be carrying some of Ned Kelly's unfinished karmic, leftover crap."

"Can I interrupt her here Judgey, I'd gladly accept a plea deal of 20 years if it stops her on her tracks right now."

"Tempting as that sounds, not only would it not resolve the proceedings at hand, she does have a point. Might I also remind you again, that you're appearing in front of me,The Judge to be judged on the crimes that have been committed in a 48 hour crime spree. I'm The Judge, the boss, the head honcho, the one who gives out the sentences, me and me alone, and Jenny is my stenographer, so let's round this up shall we and hopefully we'll be out of here shortly. Read the charges back to the court please Ms Terry, beginning from the most recent and working backwards. This is going to surely give us clarity and shed some light on all the accusations."

"1. On the night of the 28th, alleged perpetrators evaded police at The Wobbly Bottom Sip after firing shots and threatening to set off a bomb worn by one of the party."

"How do you plead?"

"Not guilty M'lard, I speak for both of us here, I can't speak for the sleeping beauty to my left as she's not really here with us, even though for some reason beyond all comprehension she has claimed to the authorities that she's neither a kidnap victim, but a friend, that we've not formally met. The only shots fired were down our necks, and the vest was the unattractive weighted anxiety singlet type contraption worn by the person you have detained elsewhere."

"This is going to take too long if we go through them AGAIN individually so can you please read them all, one after the other, then we'll see how the pleas lie. Hold your plea until we get to the end of the long list. Carry on Ms Terry, no stopping for anything, including a breath if you can. Channel your inner Hoff."

"2. Arson, graffiti, destruction, malicious damage, 'armed' robbery, theft, intimidation, kidnap, reckless driving, careless driving, driving whilst under the influence, grievous bodily harm, undocumented immigrant, driving without a licence and felony."

"How do you plead?"

"NOT guilty on ALL counts, M'Lard. We have to be deliberate and accommodating with our assumptions about other people and we'll find calmer seas and fairer weather ahead. The choices we make in every second, may not yield results for years, for instance, anger like the other restricting, constricting emotions are an unconscious reaction to whatever happens around us. I lost a driving licence years ago, and Ange doesn't even drive, let alone hold a licence, other than leading others to distraction that is. If we're going to be honest, upfront and totally transparent here, you need to hear the whole truth, and nothing but the truth. Settle in, make yourselves comfortable, take a full breath in, here we go. I lost the copy of my UK driving licence …..years ago, not too long after we'd arrived in Australia, but I had the original one which I never ended up never using, as I had an Australian licence by then. When we were stopped in Tasmania, I was going to give Ange the copy of my driver's licence as she was the driver, but didn't have a licence, provisional or otherwise, so I was doing the only obvious thing at the time which was to give her mine so that she could pretend …to be me. Wait. ME!! Who exactly are you about to extradite to Tasmania again? What did you say her name was?"

"I thought we already went over this. The felon apprehended is Kelly, first name Julia. Julia Kelly. She's currently being held in a local facility until we can have her flown back to Hobart to face possible deportation. All I can say is that Ms Julia Kelly is exactly where she belongs, in the custody care of HMS."

"STOP RIGHT there M'Lard, I gotta know right now, before we go any further, I apologise that the beginning of my sentence interrupted the middle of yours, but you have it all wrong. For the record, pay attention Jenny, you don't want to miss any of this. The person you are holding isn't Julia Kelly. She isn't who you think or say she is? She's not in the slightest bit dangerous, in fact the only thing I'd say about her that's dangerous is the way she yields her hairbrush at any random stray head that happens to have stood in her way. She is emfatically not Julia Kelly. You have Lesley Wellard incarcerated and I'm here, standing in all my glory before you. Julia Kelly."

"Wow, how can you top that showstopper? They're holding Lezzers, believing her to be Julia Kelly aka Jules. Who'd have thunk it y'all. In Lezzer's defence, it's still a miracle brush she has, ever since I started using it without her unwanted input, my hair has never looked more lush. You have to admit that you have very likely noticed how shiny my hair is? It's her brush I've been using, she's not at all dangerous if you keep her obsessive hair sweeping bristles at bay."

"You're not using her brush Ange, you're using Fatty's brush, but that's another story. The fact of the matter is that you have the wrong person in custody. FACT. You have in your possession, one LESLEY WELLARD."

"I can vouch for every word, Lezzers is a short, stout, middle aged suburban housewife with a somewhat dull husband with a surprisingly charismatic father. Jules, as you can all see with your own eyes, is an ageing, patchouli pickled hippy, who sprouts psychobabble shite for a loving. Fatty's brush? Now look at who's name calling."

"Wait. Let me get this straight, if you are who you say you are, the fugitive Julia Kelly, then we have one Lesley Wellard, an innocent, middle aged, vanilla housewife from the burbs of Sydney in custody instead?"

Friendship isn't a big thing- its a million little things- Paulo Coehlo

Clear as Mud

Jules

"Let's take a minty for the mud to settle and for the water to become less murky, unmoving till the right action naturally arises by itself. Righty O, I'm ready. Our friend Lesley, is probably already organising a xmas party, social event, fundraiser, and a raffle for the inmates, families and staff of the detention centre, and you are holding her in against her wishes. Even her husband doesn't know where she is, so it is my suggestion to the court that you set us free immediately, so that we can go get her and reunite her back in the loving embrace and safety of her family nest."

"Jules Kelly you say? Julia Kelly who has evaded police for over 25 years, Kelly? Larceny, evasion, theft, robbery, assault, illegal immigrant?"

"Maybe so, M'Lard. As for larceny, evasion, theft, robbery, assault, and being an illegal immigrant… plausible, all very plausible, but at this stage, I'm neither confirming or denying any of the allegations, it certainly explains a fair bit of the misunderstandings though, from where I'm standing that is. However, I'd appreciate it if you would tell me how you caught me, I mean her, the mistaken criminal, Lesley Wellard. Anyone else confused here, I still don't get how you actually found me, Julia Kelly aka Lesley Wellard? And I still don't really get why you wanted to either."

"The officer at the scene in Tasmania noticed only after you'd driven off that the driver must have dropped their driver's licence, now identified as a copy of your UK licence, which keep in mind, didn't have a photo back in those days, so I guess he assumed the driver was you, Julia Kelly, and not your accomplice standing in the dock beside you today. The plan was to give it back later at the station, but when you didn't show up at the jail, he must have put out an apb, all points bulletin for you."

"We were never meant to meet at the jailhouse judgey, we were meeting at a local public house in Hobart, for a date I assumed, not to be locked up, which I shall admit I had hoped would happen later after a few cocktails, IF I'd been there, which I wasn't. I was on a ferry with Jules here, heading back to Melbourne."

"Awareness is everything, literally, awareness is everything. Officer Cox must be so resentful in his pursuit of revenge. Revenge is like returning to the dog that bit you, so toxic for him and those around him receiving those angry ricochets bouncing off his delicate egotistical heart centre."

"When you stood him up, he took it upon himself to put out an APB for one Julia Kelly, which was still active until you were stopped by the police last night, and a driving licence for one Julia Kelly was used as personal identification. The only coherent one other than the alleged kidnapped victim confessed to being the driver and confirmed that her name was indeed Julia Kelly. The ephemeral Lesley Wellard, mother of 4 strapping boys, wife to Mikey, chair of the PTO, SRU, MAG, and FAT clubs, is no more an illegal, dangerous felon than I am, but YOU madam are Julia Kelly, the very much wanted and dangerous illegal delinquent."

"MAG?? Make America Great?? She is part of THAT group Jules?"

"No Ange, it stands for Merkins Are Great, I bought it for her 40th birthday, and if I'm honest here, after all these barren years, it does feel good to know I'm wanted in some capacity by someone or other, the entire law enforcement community or not. But, the established truth here is that no crimes have actually been committed, intentionally or unintentionally by Julia Kelly, Lesley Wellard or Angela Badden, and as for illegal, well, can I just say Ned Kelly lives and breathes as I speak. Such is life."

"Unfortunately, and as much as I'd love to see you both locked away for good, and the key thrown away, I can't seem to make it work. Who is the third person here with you today, the non kidnap friend, non accomplice who has slept through most of the proceedings? Let's hope she holds some insight?"

"I believe I may hold the answer to that Yer Holiness, but why not wake her up and ask her yourself. Oi, Nina nina, welcome back to the land of the almost living, would you be kind enough to state your full name for the courts, and perhaps help clarify a few minor details before this whole performance is declared null and void. Can you please shed some light to the court as to why you're actually here?"

"I'm not sleeping, I'm not using my sense of sight, that's all. I prefer to use my other senses instead, because seeing, in particular, can cause an onslaught of personal bias, and can cause an unconscious reaction

to whatever is happening around us. I've been listening very carefully. When your world is noisy, best to be silent and listen, which coincidentally contain the same letters, cultivating as much spacious witnessing to the sounds around me. For the courts, my full name is Regina Minehard, but most people call me Nina. I was having a much needed, well earned break after spending most of the day doing some philanthropy work, and was sitting outside on the pavement of the Wobbly Bottom Sip waiting for my driver. I also had in my possession a bag of my late husband's unfinished, left over pharmaceuticals which I was planning on disposing of at the chemist on the way home, but I'll circle back to that later. I was minding my own business watching the world unfold in front of me, enjoying a much needed coffee when an old rusty, clapped out, state of the art, one of a kind, original VW kombi van pulled up alongside me and parked somewhat. The van began to spill out its human contents, beginning from the back passenger side, an instantly recognisable, sophisticated, yet dishevelled, slender character in shredded designer clothes, she put a $100 bill straight into my half full, iced ristretto, 10 shot, venti, 5 pump vanilla, 7 pump caramel, 4 Splenda, poured, not shaken, cup of coffee without so much as a second glance. She was followed by a chirping small person, who alighted from the driver's side, she glimpsed at me briefly, but didn't really see me, then the person, I now know as Julia, appeared from the front passenger's side, made eye contact with me, smiled, something that isn't done too often these days let me tell you, came up to me, and handed me a jar of Chicksmix. She asked me kindly to keep an eye on her van, I can only assume they thought I was panhandling."

"I did Nina nina, and I'm terribly sorry about that and apologise profusely, I didn't notice the designer bag, the 5 carat diamond ring you have, until fairly recently as my attention was lost and caught elsewhere ie, I was more focussed on what Ange and Lesley were saying and doing. We all only see/hear/feel where our awareness is mainly focussed on."

"No apologies necessary Julia, it's all good. They walked around the corner, Your Honour, and I didn't see them again until they came tumbling out of the fire exit door beside me. There was chaos and commotion all around me, the next thing I know is I'm being stuffed in the back of their van alongside an extraordinary amount of black bags. An American gets back in, having left to place a metal sign against the wall, but doesn't notice me behind her, slamming the door behind. She then picks something up, and throws it and a leather glove out the

window for some reason. The blonde was driving and the American broad started popping, what she believed were tic tacs or vit c tablets, but were in actual fact my late husband, Frank's drugs, which had fallen out of my bag when I was mistakenly lobbed in the back. Each prescription drug contains information about the product's origin, batch number and validity date which you can double check, if there's any left. Noone even noticed me amongst all the junk. You were lucky I was there to tell everyone that you'd taken more than you sensibly should have, you consumed enough to knock Mike Tyson out...each."

"The evidence? All the pills? They're YOURS, not theirs, that changes everything legally."

"That's what I'm trying to say Your Honour, all the drugs found in the van are all mine, perfectly legal, even the illegal ones, next thing I know I'm here, but let me tell you something at my age, there's not too much adventure going on in my life, so I decided to lean into the experience and go along for the ride. They looked like they were having fun, so I decided, nothing ventured, nothing gained, didn't resist the bundling, and stayed in the back like a shadow, and went along for the ride. I had a mix of valium, sleeping pills/viagra in a ziplock bag which are all perfectly legit, and legally prescribed. You can check if you don't believe me."

"It was a sizable amount, madam."

"It would have been even more, but between the two of them, they consumed ⅓ of the bag. I was taking them to have them destroyed as I was clearing out my beloved, not long dead husband's medicine cabinet which he obviously no longer needed. Again, check the serial numbers if you don't believe me."

"You're saying you haven't been kidnapped, and that all the drugs confiscated were your late husband's prescription medicine."

"Kidnapped? Hell, no. I'm almost 80, and at my age, we need to get our jollies while we still have a breath, and what a lovely, totally unexpected surprise it has been. I haven't been this amused or this entertained for years, it's such a privilege to have such an exciting adventure, especially in our twilight years."

"If I may Judgey, I'd like to contest if I can, not the slender bit, but she can have Jules all to herself, they can dance, skip, and sing happily hand in wrinkled hand together in their "twilight years", but leave me out of any age thing. I'm ageless, totally natural."

"If I may M'Lard, I can verify that there are parts of her that are very natural, however, other parts are plumped up and out with melted down whale blubber, her lips are permanently stained with ground up beetles, squeezed into plastic tubes made from pig tendons, then tattooed on."

"All perfectly natural like I said Jules, these are not how the cosmetic procedures are described on the labels in the glossy brochures, they call it squalene, which makes it sound yummy and a necessity, and not the byproduct from pained animal suffering."

"I'd like to add my tuppence worth here if I may M'Lard, squalene is often used in skincare products due to its anti-aging properties, but it's harvested from the livers of sharks: carmine, guanine, honey, lanolin, shellac, glycerine, collagen are only some of the names that avoid using the words "animal byproducts." One of the most visible uses of animal byproducts is in our clothes and shoes. ... cosmetics and beauty products. Animals play a big role in many of our daily beauty regimens, sports equipment, plastic, jelly, gummy sweeties, medicine, and adhesives. Who doesn't use toothpaste and shampoo? Coincidentally, the wig you're wearing M' Lard is cheap looking, unclean, unkempt, poor quality, expired lanolin giving it the appearance of wool grease from a dead sheep."

"We are not here to discuss the ethical rights and wrongs of the beauty industry, and secondly, but more importantly this is not a wig, so no animals have suffered in the process of nesting on my head."

"It's not a crime to use any of these products or procedures I might add Jules, so before any of you go judging me with self righteous thoughts and words, check what you do? Clean your teeth? Wear clothes? Shoes? Have furniture? Clean your teeth? I've already said that, haven't I? Walk in your own grilled, dried eggplant shoes before trying someone else's Louboutins on."

"Your Honour, if you're going to jail this pair, then let me tell you, you're going to have to incarcerate me as well, I haven't had this much fun since my high school reunion. Jailing an innocent old lady, labelling her as a criminal never looks good for anyone, least of all for the judge. We all struggle with our own labels, which ones fit, I mean, really fit. We all try different types of labels on for size, size being one of the more

*damaging ones, it can make everyone paranoid. I digress, we all
identify with one label or another, we've all got them, and they're all
true at the time, we can learn from the heavier, darker, more limiting
ones untangling ourselves from the bind of their weight. Which ones do
we truly identify with, which ones take the majority of our attention,
which ones no longer serve our blooming and blossoming in this life,
some stick and become heavier, our crosses to bear, some open us up.
Some have us revolving, some evolving. Which ones really suit? Which
ones make us feel open, light, alive? Which ones are like coming home
to a place of belonging, settling in and taking off a very tight pair of
shoes, that place, that's a good place to be. Prepared, ready and armed
with each hopeful breath, carrying the deadwood sticky labels we've
attached and identified with. Ultimately, we're all the storytellers of our
own lives, so pick the best seat in the live theatre, front and centre, grab
your popcorn, and take in the entire panoramic vista; the actors, the
backdrops, the wings, the unseen scenes, the unscripted acts, all waiting
backstage, note all the details without preference as to how the show
unwinds, allowing and accepting every moment as it reveals itself
before every one of your senses. Lights, camera, action. What gives you
that place of expansion and what offers you that place of contraction,
only the bearer can be aware of what opens them, and what shuts the
spaces down."*

"No offence, but I don't buy any of this same baloney you and Jules
share."

*"None taken, and that's okay, I'm detached from losing people that
don't want to be in my life anymore. I've lost people that meant the
world to me, and I'm still here and doing just fine."*

"Seriously M'Lard, look back at all the claims, and see them for what
they are, claims, not truths, take the luggage handler at the airport for
instance? Who noticed him? And I mean really noticed him? His story,
his personal, circumstantial timeline that led him to appear in our reality
shite show? Then the two guys on the road? When the teacher is ready,
the student appears, and when the teacher is ready, the student appears.
They thought one thing, and we thought something totally different.
We're all coming to this instant's Vast Supper with the plate we were
handed the moment we were born, no one dish is better than the other,
or right, or wrong, tastier, or more revolting over the other, lighter or
heavier, it's our personal preferences that we've been conditioned and
programmed to believe which makes all the difference as to how we

appear in the world. Like the hold up at the petrol station that wasn't even a hold up at all, we did forget to pay, but that was an honest mistake from some very menopausal women, which I believe needs to be taken into consideration. This can all be rectified as soon as Ange gets back her platinum American Express Centurion card, the same goes for the Japanese restaurant M'Lard, she'll futon the bill so that they will be suited, booted, handy and japandi and the duck of the town."

"I am also happy to pay the bar bill, and any other costs incurred and have an open bar for three hours?"

"Three hours? You do know we're in Australia Ange?"

"I can afford it, Jules."

"I don't mean money, it's still illegal Down under to be drunk in a pub, other than BBQ's, and picnics. The majority of Aussie's have been drunk at some stage of their lives, perhaps turning one of these local establishments into a jail cell, may well address that archaic law. Not a lot of people know this, but it is also illegal to roam the streets wearing black clothes, felt shoes, and black shoe polish on your face as these items are the tools of a cat burglar. Wait. Does that mean if you dress like a prostitute, look like one potentially, does that make you one? A hooker? Asking for a friend, not about a friend standing close to me. You could be arrested on that assumption alone Ange, never mind the rest of the stuff they have on us. By my reckoning that means we're off the hooker, everything seems to have been addressed, and all there is to do now is for you to find us not guilty, pardon us, give the old bird a fresh latte on the jailhouse and free Lesley before she's sent to Tasmania to face charges she's oblivious to. No matter what she's done since, she's not done anything bad enough to warrant that, and if you get on it like white on rice, then you can still make your tea time, the scones will still be warm and the sandwiches fresh."

"Not quite so fast, you're still an illegal alien Miss Julia Kelly."

"Ah well, I suppose it has come to this, and the truth must come out, no matter how shameful it is, but my great- great, great grandfather is none other than the notorious Australian bushranger, Ned kelly, which makes me a bone fide citizen of this fair land."

"This is music to my ears, I can feel my body waking up from this nightmare. I can see nothing else for it, and against my better judgement, I have to free you and let you go, but, please know that

with every ounce of my being, that if I ever have the misfortune of having you in front of me again, I shall not be quite so lenient. Ms Terry, please hand me the payment terminal so that I can swipe Ms Badden's card. Court is thankfully adjourned forever, and my tee time is still on the cards. I need a game of golf to destress. CASE DISMISSED."

Labels are for wine bottles, and products, not people - K.G Cooper or Unknown (I stand corrected if 'someone' else said it first)

Thoughts become perception, perception becomes reality. Alter your thoughts, alter your reality - William James

Personal perception is not everyone's reality

Jules

"Not the first or the last time we'll be hammered, Ange. I apologise for all the misunderstandings M'Lard, but the absolute truth of it all, is I'm not really sorry, as I'm not sure acting my age would actually bore me to tears. Every chakra in this battered old piece of recycled drag is on high alert, spinning in anticipation of a big laughter explosion. As our Lesley says "I have absolutely no regerts, not one single letter." If and when I ever have cause to act my age, please stop me in my tracks, and remind me that when I do, it's as dull as the unnatural, grey coloured, underwear I have on."

"Let's leave while the going's good Jules, and before she finds something very indecent in the image of you in your large elasticated off white, baggy knickers."

"She?? Well, blow me Ange, I could have sworn she was a bloke with a wig. I didn't mean to offend her/him/they/them."

"That's an added bonus Jules, let's face it."

"I honestly can't tell these days Ange. I think of one thing and it turns out to be nothing like what I initially thought. Look, I'm fat, but identify as skinny. I am trans slender. Why can't we move on with our own lives? It must be exhausting being offended by everything around us, highlighting the fact that we can't control our emotions, so everyone else should do it for us. Can you imagine if they heard the stuff I hold back. Being offended is like choosing to step on dog poop instead of walking around it."

People jump to conclusions based primarily on permitting their sense of sight to take charge over what they interpret at first glance, over personalising their reality. It takes knowledge, experience, and a heightened skillset of awareness to take in all that there is beyond in-depth things. Beware or more likely, be aware when we judge a person or situation too fast, slow down to an idle, and give the considered response a chance to kick in over impetuous reactivity. We have just proved in this very courtroom how easy it is to experience a series of genuine events that have been completely misinterpreted from fact. We all carry restricting beliefs of regrets, anger, frustration, jealousy, and fear and use these imprints to interpret our outer and inner worlds, lugging the weight of our personally collected, individual burdens. We'd better be bloody sure of the additional unnoticed bulk we're transporting around, and I don't mean in the form of fat, I mean in the form of negative thoughts carefully selected, stored, and tethered down somewhere in the bowels of our inner pathways. Every step we take, every breath we make, reverberates in and around us. The mind interprets every bloody thing through our eager senses, filling the carriages of our thought train with more judgments, opinions, and viewpoints, too busy speeding to the lure of the future, or reversing back to the past, missing the chance for the thought train to slow down, and gently tick over. Noticing any pain and negative self-talk constricting the flow of energy the body is holding helps us untether whatever we're holding on to, and what we're willing to let go. The best way to release the tension in a game of tug of war is to let go of the rope, not too tight, not too loose, just right. We may believe ourselves to be one of life's credible spectators, but really? Who can actually claim to be credible? We all take in and assimilate everything differently depending on our past experiences, cultures, religion, politics, and every other opinion that we hold dear, again at the end of the day, we are all a product of that.

"Boy, didn't see that coming Ange. Sure?"

"I'm as sure of the judgey's gender as I am that Vagina is a bag lady."

"What makes you think she's a bag lady Ange?"

"For one she was begging on the streets. I put some money in her hand, and secondly she has a bag. A knock off Hermes to be more precise."

"What makes you think it's a knock off Ange?"

"Why else would a homeless person carry a designer bag Jules? Hmm? Answer me that."

"Didn't you hear any of her evidence, Ange? Did you listen to her testimony?"

"Not really, it kind of all disappeared into a blah, blah void, but tell me this Ms kissy kissy missy missy, know it all Kelly, why else was she on the streets at that time of night? I confess to her not being your typical, street walker hooker."

"She was waiting for her driver Ange?"

"That's nice to hear that these shelters provide transport to come get you, take you back to the hostel, keep you safe from all the elements, wouldn't you say Jules."

"I think you're missing the bigger picture here, Ange. She's not homeless, are you Nina nina?"

"Nope."

"That IS a designer bag isn't it?"

"Yup."

"You weren't pan handling were you?"

"Nope, just innocently waiting for my chauffeur to take me to the airport, enjoying my coffee, when you pulled up alongside me, I tried to say that I liked your ride, but I assume you believed me to be shaking an empty cup looking for some change. You then dropped a $100 note straight into the dregs of my coffee, and Jules handed me a jar of Chicksmix."

"$100.. and a jar of the highly sought after Chicksmix, your lucky night Nina nina. I am sorry, you must have missed your flight. Hope you can reschedule whatever it was you were heading to. Lovely to have met you by the way, but we have to go find our friend now, that's if she hasn't been extradited to Tasmania already to face the overturned charges against me. What on earth are we going to tell My key Ange? "You know that surprise 50th birthday party you've spent months organising? Good, can we have it in Hobart instead cos that's where your wife is." No, that's not happening, she's our friend and we need to go rescue her."

"I didn't miss anything Julia, I can get a helicopter anytime."

"Superb, how about you conjure one up right now and fly us to the facility where they are holding Lezzers against her will, call it even Steven's for almost killing us with Frank's highly effective narcotics?"

"I happen to own a few Ms Badden, and they weren't Frank's pills, they must have been yours, I thought I was helping out by giving them a legally binding, plausible story."

"Wow, thank you Nina nina, how can we ever repay you?"

"Ignore her Jules, she's delusional, who owns a few helicopters? I don't even own one."

"My name is Regina Minehard, as in China without the CH."

"Got it like Va GINA without the VA? What would you prefer we call you Nina nina, or Vag?…Gina? "

"Nina or Gina will do, pleased to meet you formally, even though we've shared a van, a cell and a guilty box for quite a few hours now. And I'm more than aware who you are, Ms. Badden."

"Nooooooooooo. What are the odds? Surely not."

"You're Gina Minehard, the one and only, Gina Minehard from the richest mining family in the entire of Australia, if not the woooorld. I am Angela Badden, and we have a meeting next week with your company to discuss a merger with ours. I can't believe after all the emails, texts, phone calls between our staff, this is how you and I finally get to meet. Let's go find a place to drink and chew the chat. What a small world."

"Ange, can I stop you right there? See how I did that with my hand Nina nina, you're not the only one who can mime around here."

"Pay no attention to her Ms Minehard, back to us. Where would you like to go so we can get better acquainted and all that."

"Ange? Stop. It doesn't matter whether she's related to Charlie Chaplin or Marcel Marceau, we have more pressing matters to contend with right now."

"Other than getting to know my new friend and potential business partner, with a freshly squeezed lemon over crushed ice in a looong glass, topped to the brim with gin, fresh mint and a slice of tonic? Don't tell me that doesn't appeal to you Jules? Come on. Where's your sense of adventure?"

"I know you're disappointed Ange, but we're going to have to hold off for the time being, we may be scot free, but we're not quite squeaky clean…yet, we have to redeem ourselves by getting Lesley out of incarceration, frocked up, suited and booted and delivered unharmed into the loving bosom of her family, before she's shackled and whisked off to not so sunnier climes."

"A trip to the wombat state may be exactly what she needs Jules, all expenses included, a retreat of sorts, who wouldn't want that?"

"Nooo Ange."

"Come ooon Jules, don't be such a spoilt sport."

"Ladies, if you'll permit me, I believe I can help out here."

"Great, let's go. I assume you mean you've got a bottle of gin stashed in your… WHOA…. that's not…whoa …it is…..FUCK…of course it is. Can I touch it?"

"What is it Ange. Hendricks?"

"Better. It's, and it really is an original Hermes Plume 28 Gris Cendre handbag."

"28 % alc proof? Not bad for starters Ange, I'll have a wee drop of that if I may Nina nina."

"I pride myself in knowing my bags Jules, coincidently, I actually bid for this very bag last year at Sotheby's, there's only two in existence …. Wait! Were you?…. Did you bid for this bag Ms Minhard?"

"Ha ha, I did Ms Badden, and, well, here it is, and if I may be so bold, you were a worthy opponent"

"Ha, I certainly gave you a run for your money, did I not."

"Excuse me? What am I, chopped liver, can someone fill me in please? Ange? Nina nina?"

"Gladly Jules.The natural gray crocodile skin used to make this particular Hermes bag came from a rare breed of Nile crocodile, what makes it even more rare is that there were only 2 made in this particular style and natural gray color. It came up for auction, with a starting bid of $15,000."

"For that price Ange, I hope it came with a couple of litres of Hendricks bottles."

"It didn't take long for the bidding war to begin, Jules, it started off as a bit of a frenzy. Bid cards were held up, calls coming in through mobiles $15,000 ... .15,500…..17,000, we lost a few of the stragglers around the $20,000 price mark… there was palpable tension in the room, everyone was lost and caught in the bidding battle. It was quick… almost as fast as a game of Pickleball played by octogenarians. The auctioneer was incredible, she played us both like a finely tuned fiddle, catching us in her unique rhythm, luring us here…$45,000……….dragging us there, $47,000, delivering her chant, slowly, gently, gracefully, then quick spitfire, lifting us up and down with the variable melody. It was breathtaking and quite hypnotic, I was transported to another realm, suddenly snapping out of it when I heard… going once…. The mallet pointed… to me … … … ..going twice, at $125,000………. .and then from the other side of the room I heard the silent auction over the mobile shout…$125,500…. I almost threw up over my alligator shoes."

"They're nice Ange, I'm glad you didn't, they really suit you."

"Thanks Jules, but I'm not wearing them right now. I was so relieved and so grateful to the winning bidder. I'd gotten totally lost and caught in the bidding drama that I lost sight of the bigger picture."

"That you could buy a gin distillery in the Scottish Highlands for that amount of money, and invite me to be Chief gin taster?"

"No, well, yes, there is that, but my color me beautiful chart says to avoid gray and dark colors, choose lighter tones."

"What about the black ostrich Merkin bag you have Ange?"

"It's not a merkin purse, it's Birkin ... .agggh, I broke, I couldn't control it. You almost had me there Jules."

"Real friendship is annoying each other and thoroughly enjoying it is the added bonus, you should know that better than anyone Ange, but I don't get why anyone would want a black ostrich merkin or firkin birkin bag is beyond me. Nothing surprises me these days, aside from leakages from my nether regions, they come from nowhere, even when I've just been to the toilet or otherwise. Each to their own Ange. It's very moving to see you putting your Heimlich skills to the test in the hope you'll bring life back to the extinct, dead beast you're clutching."

"Only hugging, caressing and kissing it I'll have you know Jules. It's given me a wake up call for shuwa."

"The camouflage is quite magnificent. I'll give it that Ange. I can't really tell where your hands end and the bag starts, or is it where the bag ends and the hands start? No offence Ange, it's a compliment, the bag is sooo …shiny..not at all gnarled and ridged..anyhow..I digress…. What was your wake up call?"

"That I can run faster than Ms Minehard, so would be miles away before she could say..tick tock tick tock..see y'all later Wally Gator. It's a joke, but a potential deal cincher."

"We're wasting time here, all this can wait till we have LESLEY safely back in Sydney."

"Ladies if you'll permit me to be the Dame to the rescue, I might be able to help you out."

"You're The Boss now Gina, anyone who owns this bag deserves reverence, adulation and admiration. Tells me you must be ruthless, bold, and have balls the size of a Nepalese mountain goat to wear it out in public, so kudos to you My Queen, we'll follow you to the ends of the earth. Let's make this snappy, lead on Mcfluff, what do you have in mind?"

"You're not contemplating stealing that bag are you Ange?"

"Caught. I am the real crookodile authorities have been searching for all these years."

"I'm a flyer Ladies."

"We call them "swingers" stateside, not flyers Gina."

"I have my own chopper."

"Boy, I didn't see that coming either Nina nina, I think that's very brave of you to come out like that, and tell us a piece of trans information that's so personal, it takes all sorts to be part of the circle of life. We should all be evolving, not revolving, going round and round in circles. Staying stuck in the spin cycle for an entire life."

"I'm a pilot."

"Even better. I see what you mean Ange. Strong, powerful woman... Can I say woman? Not offending you or anything am I...you having a chopper and all that."

"Changing the subject, do your helicopters have clitpits Ms Minehard?"

"I think you mean cockpit Ange."

"No Jules, a clitpit, because if we ever have to escape from sex traffickers in helicopters with a clitpit, we'll be safe knowing that no man will ever find us."

"I have the perfect one for us, let's go get your friend Lesley."

"Really, how fabulous, absolutely, totally Your Mimeness, lead the way. Coming Ange? Or going to the pub?"

"It shouldn't matter to me in this moment if you're a part of The Blue man group or a fierce business woman, we've been incarcerated and on trial together, I haven't had a shower for hours, my veins are coursing through my body void of any alcohol, my nasal passages are throbbing in anticipation of their regular pampering, but it does matter, doesn't it? It's a close call as to whether I come with you, get Lezzers, have a bit more time holding Hermes here or get legless at The Spread Eagle pub across the road, but the sliding door moment of you being here with us Ms Minehard trumps any cocktail, so lead on Steve Irwin."

"Take us to our leader Nina nina."

Rough diamonds may sometimes be mistaken for worthless pebbles - Thomas Browne

To The Rescue

Jules

"It's like one of Lesley's Chicksmix jats, but for helicopters, is it not Ange, a real pick and mix. I'll have that one, not that one, that one. It's a real treat to have friends with benefits. These days my friends with benefits are someone who can drive at night, and the elusive G spot is life's Gratitude spot, almost as hard to find, equally liberating when we do."

"We'll take this one ladies, it's smaller, and easier to fly, it'll allow me to hover and drop directly into the middle of the prison courtyard. You can hop out, grab your friend, climb back aboard, and we take off. Sounds like a plan?"

"Second star on the right and straight on till mourning. We owe you a massive apology Nina nina, and I hope you can forgive us for trampling all over your life with an intensity that vibrates through the body like a Van de Graff generator."

"Speak for yourself Jules, I'm not sure I can actually physically do that, it's against my nature to be a snivelling apologetic weak crater, no matter who it is. My personality is who I am but please don't confuse that with my attitude, that depends on who you are, so you're safe Ms Minehard, Jules, you're on a knife edge. I'm so used to giving orders, not accustomed to asking nicely or politely for anything. These adventures have certainly challenged my perspective on things, being nice to anyone isn't easy for me either, but I am learning, keep in mind we only have four hours tops to rescue Lezzers and deliver safely into the boozewam of her family, friends and loved ones. And counting. Let's make like sheep, and get the flock out of here Amelia, you take the front seat, I'll lead from the back."

"Help Ange, I'm stuck. These useless, cheap flip flops are melting into the tarmac, and I need your assistance to extricate me. Free me one waffer-thin mango sole at a time, peeling their sticky, sinewy, chewing gum bind, all the way from my cracked, dry heels to my clawed, clutching toes, one blackened foot at a time. Or I risk stumbling, landing in the seething, unforgiving, scorching asphalt face first. I'm glad your stilettos are managing to germinate the runway with those pointy, sharp heels though."

"Looks like you're caught in a game of stick in the chud Jules, and as much as it would make me laugh to see you imprinted in the tarmac, I shall choose to free you using grit, determination and laughter. Here grab my hand, we'll pull through this together, that's what friends are for after all"

"Double checking Ange, it's not everyone who's willing to get down and dirty when friends are stuck." "Friends come and go, Jules, like the waves of the ocean, but the ones of value stay like an octopus stuck to our face, besides I'm a sucker for you really."

"You're not squidding, crazy, beautiful friends, doing crazy shit, pulling the magic out of each other, not the mire, now let's get our sorry, sticky arses in that helichopper, and go find Lesley."

The bulbous, black bird glides upwards, the tarmac's melting entrails clinging on to the last remnants of the ground for dare life, resisting gravity, eventually yielding to the lure and enticement of the heavens above. The gravity fairy can be such a cow, not only has my skin slipped to the ground, but I'm hormonally challenged by hot flashes and insomnia. One hot flush should count as one hour at the jim, and sleep is so overrated, that one hour a night is more than adequate. Reframing is having a positive outlook on life without a negative mind.

The helicopter's grasping blade slowly sweeps a rotation, one full cycle after another, swinging us this way, that way, riding the wings of air currents with ease and grace. Dipping sharp right, heading directly towards the spectacular gleam of the sun's glow. 95 million miles away, and we can still feel its power, how cool is that? The dark-bellied chopper enveloped in the brilliant gaze, reflecting and casting our shadowy silhouette over the red palate of the lush Bush below, reducing it in size as the mighty beast rises higher and further away from red, arid Earth. The inside of the giant rotund whirling Magnum, not to be mistaken with Magnum, the actor with the enhanced spaver, blocking his giant chopper- not the worst image in the world. It's not nearly as melodious or as spacious inside here as it is in Gertie, and that's okay, cos very soon one of these seats will be pressed firmly down by Lesley's peachy buttocks. What do we have here? 5 pairs of matching ear defenders. Ange has hers on, our pilot, aka the ambulance chaser, Nina nina, has hers on, eat your heart out Princess Leia, all safely buckled in. These muffs actually work so they do, I can see Ange's lips moving, but hear nothing coming out…. Mmmmmmmmmm. Bliss. Maybe I'll ask Nina nina if I can keep them, they'd certainly come in handy. My inner voice sounds so much more appealing these days. Let's face it, we only have ourselves to blame if we get worked up by our own thoughts, those are our privileges to keep. Giving someone else control over how we feel is the utmost slavery, and although I occasionally like to be shackled, I don't in this context. That power is ours and ours alone, nobody gets to take that from us, I've learned it's easier to keep that private. The ultimate prison would be to have someone else the master/mistress controlling how we should feel. I can hear my inner narrative, as clear as the sky around us. If we can't think of anything nice, then we shouldn't think of anything at all. Can you imagine having all our thoughts written out across the sky's blank canvas by a skywriting plane for everyone to read? How awkward could that be? A blended threesome of inner chatter, feelings, and thoughts for the world to experience with us. I feel somewhat relaxed and at peace with all this, who would consciously want to add emotions into that melee, they can easily escalate, and change everything the wee feckers. Aside from the odd interruption and potential disruption from sensitive egos dumping and burdening the very neutral world out there, life is good, most people should get one.

The throbbing machine comes to an ease, supported and balanced on the wind's wings, back to Tom Seelick again...I wonder if they called the Magnum ice cream after his manhood? I'll ponder that next time I pick, lick, and suck on one.

As a child, we would ride in cars with no booster seats, reluctant seat belts, no airbags, bald tires, sometimes no brakes, always secondhand smoke, and an intoxicated family member at the wheel. Reluctant containment, so being harnessed in a line of identical electrope chairs to Ange, a glamorous, ambulance driver and entrepreneur at the controls, seems perfectly safe and completely normal. Projecting skywards at what seems like 3,000mph, the speed showcasing my loose, flapping skin to the world at large. Reaching full peak, what a climax, then just as quickly, dropping 1/4 of the way back down, briefly reacquainting the empty contents of my stomach before bouncing even higher up into the heavens. Then as if in slow motion, everything stills and settles, hair falls back in motionless place. I should have told Ange that she's been using my dead dog, Fatty's brush instead of Lesley's much coveted one, which she believes she's been using. However, when we really know something, we tend to attach a judgement, and everything changes. Her hair does look extra glossy with Fatty's golden retriever locks entwined with her dyed tresses.

When we have a thought around say, a fear of spiders, and we are asked to go explore a deep, dark grotto, then I'd bet my bottom, that with every uncertain step we take into the bowels of the cave, our mind begins to tell us that we can see, hear, feel spiders all around us, by belief alone. Imagine that? By thought and belief alone we can conjure up mind movies, imaginary uncensored scripts, sensations, magic. Through words and/or imagery, and thoughts alone, blows my mind. Think about that, choosing to explore each scenario without the weight of intensity, opting to bring a sprinkling of joy, happiness, laughter, and mischief instead, then that's what we'll see, hear, feel, maybe smell, and hopefully taste with every delightful, optimistic step taken deeper into the unknown/uncertainty of this moment's cave. Life can be likened to jumping out of this machine without a parachute, only hitting the ground towards the end of our own personal flight. Many of us resist, grasp, flail against life, and are scared shitless throughout the entire free fall. It's the same life whether we spend it laughing or in angst, same life. We never quite know when the ground will rise to meet us, but it does, no one gets out of this adventure alive. We even attract a few battle scars along the way, so the suggestion is: relax, there's no rush. Take the time to enjoy the thrill, the wonder, the humour. Be amused by the childlike awe of it all. From the second you find the slippery thought that has shifted your natural inherent state of happiness to the polar opposite, then it's checkmate, we're back here, here and now, nowhere else to be other than here every single time. When we catch ourselves hook line and sinker being lost and caught in the future or the past, then we can learn to catch and release by asking ourselves these 3 questions. 1. Is this true? 2. Is there something I can do about it to resolve it? 3. Can we accept it and make our lives, and those that share it with us, better despite its presence? Choosing where to position our seat for optimum balance on life's seesaw of all life's dualities.

From this seat, I can see the incredible panoramic landscape of the Australian bush directly below me as it reveals itself, inching its way into the wings of awareness. I'm in it for pure fun, death is going to catch up with me one day or another, until then I prefer to be an impartial voyeur of life's dramas narrated by the dharma. Quivering in the wings of everyone's awareness is the final delivery of an in-breath and out-breath, it's going to happen one day, we can only avoid it so long, so we may as well choose to embrace the performance, flip it on its head, and turn it into the best, uplifting, funny, sad, enraging, awesome live Broadway stage show. Enjoying, embracing, and accepting our very own reality show, act after act, treading those boards beneath our feet, like we own the feckin joint, radiating the gawd damn given power we were born with, with every rippling full breath. A big secret to happiness is not to allow the shite behaviours of others to get under our skin. I literally sweat the small, big, ureic, alcohol stuff. Life can be messy, but we can all get back to that clear, still, calm centre we came to this world with, no point getting buckled out of shape or we will find ourselves tighter than Jim Morrison's leather trousers.

"BUCKLE IN PROPERLY PLEASE JULIA."

This tells me one of three things: 1. I have delivered my entire silent inner dialogue, directly through the built-in microphone in my head muff, and she heard "buckled", or 2, Nina nina is psychic. Saying things out loud is not always a good thing, it can get you into a whole lot of trouble, and 3. Is there a 3?

"JULES. On this occasion, trust Gina, you need to be buckled in, as when she dips the helicopter to her left, you will arrive in the centre of the prison camp 10 mins before we do, remember the telly ad CLUNK CLICK EVERY TRIP. REMEMBER?"

Sometimes, Ange makes absolutely no sense, but I'll harness myself in just to be on the safe side. I never quite know where to put my boobs with these straps, Ange looks sexy with her perfect mammaries bulging and pressing happily against her restraints, meanwhile, my breasts are like a fluffle of bunnies; Foppy, Floppy Droopy, Flappy, Pappy, Crappy, and Snappy, which have long since departed their burrow, leaving empty sacks running in parallel lines, like a useless pair of braces.

"Happy Ange? I can't tell."

"I don't have the energy to pretend I like you today Jules."

"That's okay Ange, not everyone has good taste, now silence is golden."

"And the duct tape is silver Jules."

"I'm preoccupied with my thoughts right now Ange, so me pretending to listen to you will have to do for now."

The sun casts a spotlight directly above us, casting shade over us before leapfrogging onto the red sandy earth beneath, the scene unfolding naturally as we drift and sway gently, closing in closer to the bullseye of the rigid, square, steel barracks beneath, gliding effortlessly, lowering with each warm gust, taking us gracefully towards the enclosed loose gravel pit below, a cross between rusty panko crumbs and sand, engulfing and shrouding us within the inverted red vortex of mixed earth, tears, dreams and hopes. Swallowed whole in its spiralling spacious pattern, sucking us in the direction of the whirlwind's chasmic core, the puckered, red glory hole of the open prison's centre. Dark shadows loom up, forming individual human beans of different shapes and sizes, and that's the way it should be, a real Heinz 57 variety. The intruding Magnum belly flops, greeting the dry gravelly ground, entering in on its terms. The residents have no choice other than to surrender to the stamp of the flying monster. The earth releases its tempestuous grip on the billowing rusty dust, surrendering to the powerful intruder, reluctantly rolling out its red, rippling carpet for us. I feel like I'm arriving at the Ozcars. The gritty swell waves its thunderous ruffles away from Magnum's penetration, the earthling herd of onlookers circling the confines, shoulder to shoulder in the cagelike sanctum. The shadowed drapes ripped apart, displaced by the trespasser's landing platform, creating the sandy fluster, exposing long-buried secrets clutched beneath the cooler earth below. The entire live show reveals Act 1 under our steady gaze, luring us to uncertainty, spreading its suffocating thick, heavy dirt formations under the flimsy doors that line the encampment. Settling down like an over-excited stallion, the displaced sun-baked grit, scorched gravel, and grizzly grime come to a place of impermanent rest. The sun's beam spotlights a variety of well travelled, ingrained footprints carried on the soles of the visible and invisible, remnants of the global souls from every continent, trapped here forever. Their weary, dusty, impressions layering their blistering soles of suffering, tears, and pain with the unseen ones carried by others who stood in the exact same place in a different past. The sun gracefully begins to elegantly take a bow behind us, casting its stupendous light around the rusty barbed wire-clad fortress, spraying beams of yellow, orange, red, and gold brilliance, reflecting the copper earth tones perfectly. Drawing the depths of her magnificent laser beam to our attention, zooming in on the silhouette of a minuscule, cherubic angel clad in red sprinkles wobbling toward us. Mesmerising. From this height, the blue Chinese characters against the white T-shirt clearly say "FUCK YOU". We've found Lesley.

*Of all the roads you travel, make sure some of them are dirt
- TravelOutbackAustrlia.com*

To live will be an awfully big adventure - Peter Pan.

Don't grow up, it's a trap - Peter Pan

Mile High Flyer - Has its ups and downs

Ange

Move over Gina! Make room for a new Queen in the hive; the more queens the merrier, working together with the lesser drones to create a powerful, invincible female-led world. You can't be a Queen if you continue to believe you're a drone. When you got it, you got it and it's about time the tide shifted from a male-dominant, toxic environment. I can't believe it, of all the sin joints, in all the world, Gina Minehard was banged up in mine of all the places. I can see for myself the great lengths and risks she is taking in the hopeful search for great returns. It sends thrills up and down my spine, they're electrifying. I hope she sees beyond my stern appearance, revealing an even sterner persona. That, I don't mess or fuck about persona, same face whether I'm copulating or clarifying a point, same face. Not afraid to take on anyone or anything that tries to block my way, but further disclaimer here, I'm not for the hate-hearted. Only take me on if you think you're hard enough, or stupid. I think this could be the perfect pairing, especially if she throws Wally Gator into the negotiations. We might be onto a Winner Winner Crocodile Dinner here. Bring it on. Badden and Minehard. B and M without the domination and submission.

I can use these sliding doors set of circumstances, this chance meeting with Gina, as an omen and a golden business opportunity. A McDonnell Douglas helicopter, very nice, I like her style, essentially a $2,000,000 flying bug. The earphones are perfect for me to strategise what thought processes and ideas behind my best investments are going to impress me the most. What a dag Jules can be at times, not only did she look ridiculous gimping her way across the tarmac back there, she now can't work out how to put the seat belt on. A 3-year-old having a full-blown toddler tantrum, physically crumpling from a normal acceptable state, into a collapsed, spasmodic, writhing, flailing lump of jelly, could still fasten and be restrained quicker than Jules can do it herself. My own rampaging, emotional gatecrashers make me so angry, I can lose my shit just because the concierge succumbs to the requests of the other occupants of the heaving elevator, selfishly demanding their floor buttons be pressed before the more important office at the top of One World Observatory. He clearly knows who I am, and how important that makes me, if he pushes my buttons one more time, I swear he's out on his scrawny, pimply, prepubescent ass. I can absolutely lose the plot if the design on the top of my daily, hand-delivered latte comes smeared, and don't even get me started on manners, that can also have me losing the rag, what do they teach in schools these days, that was rhetorical, clearly not manners. Who should be responsible for teaching those life skills? There's a complete disregard for each other these days, everyone bulldozing their way through their insular selfish lives, taking no prisoners, clutching, grasping, greedily collecting their likes, dislikes, wants, and desires, ignoring and resisting their lessons, oblivious to the suffering they are causing themselves. In all the many, many mumbo jumbo mindful workshops they offer employees, they tell you it's an inside job, maybe to anyone in the slightest bit interested and willing to pay attention. Constant reminders bombard the reluctant, confused listener, usually not me though. Most everyone is woke or whatever the daily fucking buzzword is, and they consider themselves among the privileged woke tribe. They really get on my silicone tits they do. In any case, what the fuck does woke mean? All this, "I've had my third eye opened with a hot poker" bullshit, and "my higher self says this is my journey", I swear I want to wake every fucking one of their spinning chakras with a boot to their Muladhara and skim them like a plastic frisbee across the still, calm pond of their now unsettled mind. The sooner they go back to fucking sleep the better for everyone concerned. It brings me out in a hot sweat, and my hormones are chomping at the bit, to be released. Fine line between reigning them in and giving them free rein to play out their chaotic fantasies. Where are my pills? Where are my fucking meds? Fair chuffed I still have some Xanax, Valium, and Prozac around my neck, they can all take the edge off my raw nerves, as Jules would say, "upstairs for thinking, downstairs for dancing, and in the middle for a cheeky fiddle" I've tried all sorts of pills, surgery, concoctions, ayahuasca, kambo, even actual physical food in pill and powder forms, but still feel Itchy, bitchy, fatty, batty, cranky, dry, wanky, including psycho making a surprise guest appearance now and again, making an unwelcome but more frequent grand entrance whenever they fucking feel like it. The little fuckers can sneak by the wings at either end of my virtual peripheral 3-D stage and can create involuntary, unwanted havoc, giving me the homicidal, word-wielding, intimidating maniac look. The toxic blighters make it look easier and easier to catch me unawares these days. I'd like to blame it on age, but I'm not getting any older. Besides, they've been my accomplices for as long as I can remember. They seem to be winning, unaware of the devastation that they have created in my life, leaving ruins in their wake. Dumping their waste like piles of dog shit on my professional and personal path. Now where's the Chicksmix, a handful of them washed down with some… aghh, only water…still should do the trick. I'd better not end up with even one of Lezzer's nutty pretzels, heads will roll. I still have time to mentally recall the Minhard proposal and portfolio, including the sketches, plans, drafts, and projections before formally meeting Ms Minehard next week. I need to be respectful, and this advanced preparation should reflect and clarify the work our company provides. Bloody hell, we're coming down already, unlike the stock exchange share prices I'm currently working on. I'm going to make lots and lots of luverly doughlars. The full-blown coarse, sandy exfoliator on the outside had better settle before I take one high-heeled Choo step onto its grainy terrain. In fact, better yet, I'm going to stay inside here. Let some other pit pony go get Lezzers. Litter is caught up in the sanguine dust cloud, an interesting spectacle of torn pleading, begging, pathetic, 'love' letters, a chewed postcard, and discarded vacant condom packets for hopefully used condoms - the world is overpopulated as it is, shredded pieces of passports, what looks like a Lancome face cream label, a sausage roll wrapper, and a cuddly toy. Looks like we've found Lezzers, they all sound like her belongings. This place looks completely barbaric if you ask me, no one should be allowed to live in this remote, hell hole, involuntarily or voluntarily. It's inhumane, not one coffee shop in sight. What is the world coming to? Can you imagine 1,000 women, many with menopause, held in a small, confined space without a coffee, let alone alcohol and drugs? It's barbaric, something needs to be done, if I'm thinking of helping out, then it must be pretty fucking awful. There's barbed wire, electric fences, and towers with armed Aussie blokes dressed as guards, eager and ready to flex and whisper their call of duty to their like-minded peers "Take the shot. Take the bloody shot". Trigger-happy galloots, armed and dangerous, loaded with the bullets of their own self-imposed sensitive ego, ready to fire on the unsuspecting, innocent contained masses. Lack of awareness is never a good sign. I wouldn't put my most detested acquaintances, let alone friends in here, not even Lezzers deserves this. I'm going to have a word with someone the minute I'm back in civilization after I strategise the accounts, perhaps involving the potential collaboration of Minehards in the quest. I'd still like to be wined and dined with her clients, before getting down and dirty with the authorities that run this place, maybe a sneaky botox appointment down under and I do mean down under, and not here in Australia, Downunder. Vaginal augmentation is the thing these days, nothing worse than having an old, dry, hideous camel's hoof as a vagina, no matter how old you are. I can secure the funds from my work transactions into my personal bank account, adding further to my financial gains, do a yoga class, then I'll speak to someone…if I remember, that is. Anyway, it'll get done by hooker or by crooker, I don't care, truly, I really don't care what they say about me, but I'm a doer…if nothing else, someone will be paid to do it on my behalf, I bet Lezzers is already on the cause.

A good rule to remember for life is that when it comes to plastic surgery and sushi, never be attracted by a bargain-
Graham Norton

Some Dodgy Holding Facility In The Middle Of The Australian Bush

Lesley

Shooter? Who, what, why has me being in this god foreskin place got anything to do with a shooter? It beggar's belief, and to add insult to injury, apparently I'm an illegal alien who was not only at a shoot-out at the Wobbly Bottom Tip but has been wanted by authorities for decades. Everyone who is anyone always wants something from someone, and Muggins here is always the first to willingly oblige to see and meet everyone else's needs. I wouldn't want them to think that I don't want to, or can't. I'm only trying to help, but my deeds go unnoticed, and unappreciated. I've never heard so much mambo jambo nonsense in my puff, well not since Angy told me she'd never had plastic surgery. They should recycle the vast amounts of environmentally unfriendly plastic tat, by reusing landfill rubbish to plump up cheeks, boobs, butts, and lips. I'd take her word for it if it wasn't for her taut, non-twitch face. It would be a complete and utter waste not to use it, someone could make money I bet. That would make sense if they did that, rather than having it dumped in our oceans, have them injected into aspiring shiny, expressionless faces. Anyhoo, in all my 5 decades on this planet, it's beyond absurd and prosperous to think that there was an active shooter in the middle of nowhere, at exactly the same time we were there, and we didn't notice a thing. Excuse my French, but it really, really is so far-fetched it's almost funny, all I noticed was some of those sparsely clad cowgirls who sell tequila 'shots' from their gun bottle belts, not the type of girls you want your sons to bring home, not that I'm judging, just saying that's all. They can almost draw those tequila guns from their holsters faster than a caustic, acerbic put down from Angy. Only now am I told that we may have been present when an actual shooting with real guns and bullets was taking place, can you believe that? Wait till I tell the girls at yoga, they'll never believe it. I had already begun to hustle the girls out of The Wobbly Bottom Tip before this particular occurrence even happened. We were in a bar chock-a-block, full to the brim with a bunch of lairy, hairy clientele ready and more than capable of consuming the planet's entire stock of tequila shots, I mean seriously, it's like taking an alcoholic to a distillery, a sex addict to a brothel, a fox to a henhouse, me to a sausage roll bakery, Angy to the slagging bee contest, Jules to a crystal store. Things were already getting messy and out of hand, the signs were beginning to split at the seams, a recipe for disaster, so I got us out of there faster than a speeding ticket. I didn't want any of us to be crushed in the alcoholic-fueled frenzied commotion, maybe it was the $1 tequila night that started it all, hence all the giddy inebriated excitement, but I wanted no part of it, and was so ready for a nice cup of good ole English Breakfast tea and some of the homemade shortbread I'd brought for us to share. We'd had quite the day already, and to be completely honest, I was bushwhacked, ready for my jammies and my fine piece, or is it peace? Before trying to corral the girls out of there quicker than me untagging myself in an unflattering PTA photo, Angy, for some bizarre reason, only making sense to herself, decided to tear open my shirt, I think in the hope of showing my cleavage but exposing my weighted singlet instead.

I can't even begin to phantom out why I'm in this open-air enclosed facility armed with burly, menacing, hairy, testosterone-filled guards, and that's just the women. I crack myself up. It has to be a case of mistaken identity, I'm completely innocent of whatever they believe I've done, and completely trust the abilities of Jules and Angy, wherever they might be, to get me out of here alive and in one piece. The last thing I really remember is being pursued by the guys, and dolls I guess, in blue, flashing lights, sirens, and a thing, the fool police enchilada. I'm surprised that there are that many coppers in this neck of the woods to be quite honest with you, I wouldn't have thought there was that much crime around here to warrant such a cavalcade of navy. They didn't even listen to me when I tried to reason with them. In the end, I put my hands behind my back, let them cuff me, and take me away in their squad cars. Jules and Angy were practically comatose playing 'dead' on the unsealed, natural dry, red, dusty road on which they lay, fell. They remained incoherent, the occasional burp and, or fart, hard to tell what was what and from where, or whom, having consumed too much to drink too quickly, which is precisely why I needed them out of the Wobbly Bottom Tip and tucked up in bed, safe and sound. It's neither funny nor clever to get to that state at our age, or any age for that matter, one wine, one water, that's my motto, but did they listen to me? No. You just had to look over at the two crumpled, slavering, snoring wrecks to see and hear they clearly didn't and don't pay any attention to any of my suggestions. I thought that telling them to take some vitamin C might help raise their sugar levels, give them more energy, and wake them up slightly, but apparently not. The birls in blue, the unofficial label for a blend of boys and girls, best to be on the safe side of someone else's gender choices, didn't even give me the time of day. The youth of today, no respect for their elders, and those two idiots I call my friends did not help matters in the slightest. I had to take proceedings into my own hands and take control of the situation, as usual. Here we go again, I thought. Little did I know then that I was the one identified as the guilty party, unceremoniously cuffed, transported, and separated from my pals without so much as an aura voi, do not pass go, do not pick up $200, go directly to this detention centre in the middle of goodness where Bush. Mikey would be so worried if he knew where I was, he warned me that things may go awry if it involved those two, but in their defence I told him they were grown women, and didn't still behave as they had done in their 20s. WRONG. One of the younger cuntstables was particularly kind, even though I was itching to brush his unruly hair back into its rightful, manicured place. All of a sudden I remember feeling itchy, and had these tickling, prickling needles running amok all over my body, I felt like a menopausal pin cushion and began to involuntary, embarrassingly, humiliatingly squirm, spasm and unspiral in front of their horrified young eyes, it happens more regularly these days I have to shamefully admit. Me No Pause sucks, plain and simple, it just does, it sucks big time. It's REAL, and women of a certain age should be allowed to carry special exemption cards when they do hit it, with at least one get-out-of-jail-free card. We shouldn't be held accountable or responsible for the hormonal fat hairy, fairies rampaging through our bodies, a free-for-all, causing unprovoked psychopathic rage in their wake, and everyone needs to know and hear that these menopausal fairies are fluffed in the head, excuse my language, but they are, they kidnap our bodies and mind, bending our thoughts to their will. I think I've finally figured out why they call them hot fleshes. Because "The Raging Inferno of our youth going down in flames" is way too much of a mouthful and instantly forgettable.

The entire group of police officers watched on in hypnotic, alarmed disbelief as my body began to move like a contortionist. You can't ignore those uncomfortable hormonal rhythms jigging their hot, cold, clammy, rough, dry, sharp sensations, like shock waves rippling from the top of the head, crashing all the way down, the full 5ft, almost 2" 'drop', in my case, that is, all the way to the tip of your corns, and bunions. They all examined me with shocked skepticism, stumped as to how to deal with this onslaught, should they resuscitate or throw some water over me, or maybe put me out of my misery by shooting me? It's shameful and humiliating that they A) have never been taught to identify full-blown menopausal signs that take up residence in women's bodies and minds and B)? If there even was a B, I've lost the thread. Shirley at least one of them has a mother, grandmother, aunt, cousin, sister, who has not escaped this internally challenging imbalance! It shocks me that they don't teach these life-changing, threatening circumstances to the bright-eyed, bushy-tailed, ready-to-make-the-world a better place, youths at, not only the police academy, but schools as well. Educate the messes, that's what I say, life would be so much easier if the world understood the damage that can come with the no-instructions-Menopause-Madness-Manual. It is and has always been a natural female occurrence in my humble opinion, and as females, we shouldn't feel ashamed, apologetic, or guilty when we break down uncontrollably, inconsolably, cry, sweat, leak, totally lose the rag, fall asleep. Do they even understand the suffering that comes with the urge and desire to punch the stuffing out of something or someone, to be free and comfortable to swear like Angy on a regular fucking basis, and go on a disgruntled marching rant for the slightest infringement, even a toilet seat left up can cause me to have a momentary meltdown, where I want to rip the testicles off every bastard on the planet, excuse my language, but on occasion it's necessary and acceptable. I've threatened the boys numerous times that I'll wash their mouths out with soap if I hear that kind of foul language under my roof, but they haven't, and will never personally experience Me no pause themselves, only vicariously through me, and at some stage, if they haven't already been affected by me, will be affected by any menopausal female within a 10-mile radius of them. It should get me a free "get out of jail" card, but clearly, this is not one of those games. Like the time I burst into tears when stopped after accidentally going through a red traffic light, I didn't even notice I was the driver until I was stopped by the polis, held captive in my own train of thought, almost derailing myself completely in the process. Thankfully they were very understanding, and even went back to the patrol car for some clean tissues for me. My guess is that they might have had a mother around the same age, anyhoo, they let me off, so maybe I used my freebie already. I wonder if there's been research on menopausal women and global warming, if not there should be.

They took the other two comatose, thankfully incoherent, there is a Lord, floppy, drunken floozies somewhere else, possibly to sleep off the alcohol. Good luck with that, I distinctly remember telling the occifers that they'll be waiting weeks for that pair to pass an alcohol and drug test, if indeed ever. They laughed, mark my words, that was just my warm-up act, somebody try to stop me when I'm on a roll, that's what I say. I'm quite sure I heard a wee giggle leaking out from the dark, black, bush night, could also have been Jools farting again, now that I think of it, she honestly thinks we can't hear her, even when she turns the music up, or coughs to hide it, we cannot avoid but hear her, it's louder than the brass section at my Deano's school concert, she could cause a pulse to flatline with all those legumes she consumes. I know for sure it was her bottom puffs in DGT, she can't fool me. I shouted through the police car's metal grill that they'd made a HUGE mistake, the female occifer nodded her head in fellowship, or had a slight tick, can't tell for sure. It's fairly typical to have someone at a PTA meeting who appears to concur with the proposals, yet after the meeting has concluded, found to be freely sharing her criticisms behind everyone's back, well, let me tell you, that is the best vantage place to kiss my behind. I gave her my most often used, secret empathetic, eye wink, a peace, piece offering of sorts. She totally got it. Men share their own insecurities, inferiorities, knowledge, and misogyny through various thumb rolling, palm tickling, tongue gymnastics, sports, and other useless shenanigans, like shaking hands and golf, and we have eye winking. It's a real thing you know, almost everyone with a full-blown uterus, vagina, and Marks and Spencer's loyalty card knows this, other than men that is. A problem halved is a problem shared and all that. Us women need to stick together when it comes to things that men have absolutely no scooby doo about, what to do about, or what to do-be-do-be-do, as Sinatra sang. All women, regardless of ethnicity, colour, sexuality, religion, politics, culture, and beliefs, have to unite and handle life's challenges, including endocrine secretions that come hand-in-hand with menopause madness. Or go live in a silent retreat, that way if you get disturbed in any way, you only have yourselves to blame. My boys don't think I listen to them, and that I'm impolitely correct most of the time, but I do listen, and I try, I really try not to upset or offend intentionally. Those pesky menopausal molecule monsters send subliminal undercurrents, creating internal and external damage as they course and carve their merry way through the dark, invisible inner tunnels, trashing everything in its course, leaving a sticky residue in their slipstream, depositing the heavy whispers of limiting beliefs, angst, doubt, worry, in the sealed vaults at your core, the real heart of the matter, the treasure in your chest, your very own treasure chest, your hearts. Keeping the leftover unfulfilled emotional scum of ego under lock and key, often misplaced, misguided by the lure of preferential desires, or resisting unwanted occurrences attached to your neutral outer reality. The cause of all your own personal suffering and pain, collected from historic traumas, events long since departed, leaving a scarred mark. Being tethered to the past or a preference to a future not even determined. Ego is an emotion that has its own colour on the palette wheel, and you get to paint how your picture looks. Call me shellfish, but you should keep that prerogative to yourselves, nobody or nothing should determine your own personal colour scheme. That's why I love Zumba. My absolute favourite class is, "Shake That Shit Off" by Sailor Tift. I personally don't consider "shit" to be a swear word, but that doesn't mean the boys can use it, no, sirree, not on my watch, that wouldn't be right or respectful in my humble opinion, you have to draw the line somewhere between parent and child, laying the parameters of acceptable behaviour down. Swearing is on my banned list. " Shake that Shit off" is an exception and is on a Tuesday night at 7.00 pm, the perfect tonic without the gin, to begin with, that is. Anyhoo, I like to be tucked up in bed by midnight on a school night, not that I get or need much sleep these days, my days of Beauty coming to visit me, have long since sailed, only Beast frequents I'm afraid. The class regularly lasts longer than it says on the schedule, as we often go out afterward to decompress. There's a lovely wee joint that also sells wine, not for the drivers you understand, called "The Wee Glass Gin" or is it "The Glass Wee Gin", anyhoo, not really important, we live round the corner, so I can walk it off later, a couple of hours there and we're all brand new, buckled, but brand new, lighter now that we've put the world to rights, then off to bed, tucked under the weight of my silk eye mask, sheets, and cashmere duvet for at least 5 hours before I have to get up to prepare for the day ahead, making sure Mikey and The Boys are catered for first. The way I see it, if I'm going to be in bed for such a short time, I may as well make it the most incredible, luxurious experience ever, putting the spa in spaciousness, I've even trained Mikey and The Boys to always, always take the extra time, regardless how late they're running, or how daunting the day ahead of them might look, to slow down, put in the extra time to make their beds, and I do mean properly, wrinkle-free, smooth, making it inviting and enticing to come back to, coming back to a worthy, completed task at the end of the day can be so rewarding, especially if the day's been bad, just seeing a beautifully made bed can settle inner doubts, sense of lack, insomnia, and those not good enough feelings. When you see that you've already achieved something good and admirable before you even set foot outside the front door, then it can change everything. Everything. Perception is so important. I think so. Even here, in this jail, I've already made my bed and encouraged my other 5 roomies to do the same, an asylum seeker, an immigrant, an illegal immigrant, and an alleged criminal awaiting trial for something she apparently didn't do. She felt safe enough to tell me that she's an undercover reporter. Come to think of it, I must ask her what she's reporting on.

I showed a very appreciative cleaner how to mop a floor properly and efficiently, it took me ages as she didn't catch on as quickly as I had initially anticipated, but was full of thanks after the fact at least. Every potential criminal is innocently awaiting trial over something they did or didn't do, aren't they? I'd make a great detective, or investigative journalist at the very least, I might help the undercover reporter uncover some of the inhuman, inhumane conditions here, such a worthy cause I think. Truly fascinating to deeply get down to the nitty-gritty of a single topic of interest such as serious crimes, political corruption, and wrongdoing in places like this, hidden from the eyes of ignorant city do-gooders, who might be willing and able to reform laws, but don't. Seems karma has missed a few people on their rounds. Apparently, there's been a fair amount of unrest around the camp recently, so much so that some big city fat cats and others are coming to a meeting being held here later today. I personally can't wait to hear what everyone has to say and share my thoughts on how this place should be run. Some of the other residents have been here for years. My roomies have filled me in and dished the full dirt on this place, getting it off their chests, although I've only been here a very short time, I feel much better prepared and ready for the meeting later.

From my camp bed, I can see natural light squeezing its way through the carved slits on the arid adobe moulding, silent tears of unfulfilled dreams, visions, and goals lodged alongside the graffiti held in the bricks and mortar. The rays reluctantly settle their distorted twinkling beam on the faded whitewashed walls, highlighting and featuring the scribbled artwork of the previous in-house artists in residence. I've been informed that I'll only be here a short time though, as my case is being extradited for some reason, and I should think so too, no point keeping an innocent person locked up against their will longer than necessary. When they eventually come to their senses and realise they've incarcerated The President of the cricket, macrame, bunko, bingo, book club, boys class representative, voluntary blood donor, volunteer at the local care home, animal shelter, farmer's market, only once a month, so not sure whether to include that in this particular list, then they'll know that I need to be darn well extradited pretty ensuite, before there's a complete horror story even the likes of Stephen King couldn't have imagined returning to. That's if there isn't one being written as I live and breathe. I've never had so much as a speeding ticket, not one, and the shoplifting charges were never proven, it's easy to forget what you have and haven't paid for, I've found myself in the car park with my paid-for shopping, and a blouse still on its hangar, tucked under my arm, who hasn't done that during the perimenopause, menopause years? Hmm? I thought not. I can vaguely hear the whoop, whoop of a helicopter's blade slapping the stagnant, stifling air outside, let's go girls, the offals have arrived, scrambling to our feet to formally greet the officials landing in the dirt exercise yard outside, lining the inner perimeter with our bodies, they are here HOURS earlier than expected, only the translators look marginally relieved, the rest of the staff are running around like headless chooks, far from ready. I've chaired many meetings and can easily step up to the plate if needed, I've seen and heard enough here to have and voice an opinion. Eyes shielded from the bleezing sun, the billowing red sand, grit, tears, and the occasional dog turd, dislodged from its temporary resting place as the helicopter lands centre stage, meeting the unsettled ground, rotors sending an explosion of rippling waves carrying dirt, sand, and chuckies in all directions. The big black beast comes to a hypnotic hover. Must be someone important though, as most everyone else is apparently usually bussed here, took me hours, I tell you, hours to get here, makes sense to fly, but how much does that cost the taxpayer, not to mention the carbon monoxide impression it must take to get here. Thankfully I drive everywhere, we all have to do our bit.

We were all meant to be locked up in our cells until after the official meeting was over, so I'm surprised our doors are unlocked and open, must be their early arrival, arriving unexpectedly to see what's really going on behind the unprepared scenes, very clever, caught off guard. I'd never have met Connie, a lovely lady from England, the one who's been mistakenly arrested for a crime she vehemently claims she didn't commit. She was initially reluctant to share further details, not my rodeo, not my clowns, and all that, I didn't pry or press her too much in front of the other roomies, I know when to butt in and when to butt out, but with gentle persuasion, she eventually told me she's an undercover reporter. Mum's the word Connie. I can keep a secret, unless there's alcohol involved that is, then it's fair game. Joke! Apparently, I was saved the humiliation of being strip-searched and photographed, I don't know about you, but I don't even strip for myself, let alone anyone else, thankfully I don't have to face the lens and stares that reflect back the ravishings of time, I feel so incredibly thankful to my Gspot and safe in the knowledge that if any photographs, which thankfully don't exist, but if they did, and were slipped into nefarious hands, my images would be the first to be discarded. "Burn them, lads, no money to be made here" unless ugly, cellulitic fat turns you on, that is. My lack of hearing prevents me from the stifled laughing and giggling of those judgmental arseholes at least. I've tried and tried over the decades to lose it, and I have, but it keeps finding me again. I must have lost over 1,000 lbs in total over the years, but it always finds its way back. I don't actually care, being a nurse, I've seen my fair share of arse holes, and I'm more than delighted not to be showing mine here today or any other day for that matter. There is nothing that can shock me, other than Angy that is, who constantly does and says things to shock and irritate me, however, I'm learning how to muddle along and accept her many shortcomings as well as her well-hidden better traits, and I'm so much better than I used to be. Mikey and The Boys gave me those lessons on patience. Somewhat. I do try not to rise to her bait, but she can still hook me in. That's the nature of how our friendship is I guess, like a pair of bickering, almost siblings, she's harmless really, her bite's much worse than her bark, and I know better not to take her bitter and twisted behaviour personally. She can be so aggressive, stress pulsating from every constricted cell in her warped body. Hopefully, I'll get the chance to chat and say something that I've been wanting to say to her for ages, not the stress/anxiety stuff, but something else. She needs a 'filler' intervention if you get my drift, hopefully, that'll help break down her barriers, showing her that friends, true, ride-or-die friends, love, accept, support, and lift each other up, not put them down. You don't only focus and pick on the flaws as you see them, the bits you don't like, all because it doesn't suit your likes and dislikes, you take your friends exactly as they are, or not. You'll lose countless friends along the way, but you won't care about the ones who don't want to be in your life anymore, you'll lose others along the way who mean the world to you, and you'll be just fine. You watch.

The staff here are so polite, no complaints there. It would be hard to fault them actually, but Connie says there's more to it than meets the eye that never sleeps, I disagree, not my experience here so far. I think manners maketh the man... or woman, and I'm really good at being fully inclusive. Good manners, kindness, and civility cost nothing and are essential to humanity, mark my words, or the world will unravel into anarchy, chaos only exposing the weight of the sensitive egotistical invisible cloaks you're wearing to life's global pity parties. Now, don't get me wrong, I love parties, especially those themed ones. Me, Mikey, and The Boys have been to many, many fancy dress parties over the years, there's so much fun to be had dressing up, playing a role, and being free to be silly for no apparent reason, I do love them and, if I'm honest, am secretly hoping Mikey has planned one for my 50th birthday which is coming up quicker than one of my prized, most coveted cheese souffles.

      I can see how poorly organised it is run here though, and the impact it's having on the weary-looking staff, there's hardly any communication it seems, no one really knows what their left hand is doing. You can't cheer and clap for each other with one hand. I know from experience on the wards that this added stress can lead to uncertainty and that can lead to anxiety and other mental and physical health issues, so easily rectified in my humble opinion, which I'll openly and willingly share with the board members when they disembark. I'm somewhat glad this is civilian clothes month, but when I retell this story, I can always add the striped jumpsuit, maybe say the food was more like gruel. No that's mean and unnecessary, you should only report the truth, but it should keep my yogi friends entertained, a captivated audience for a wee whiley at the very least. We all like to share a good life story, which can be difficult to read especially when the place is pretty dire, when the majority of the inmates seem mostly innocent, or so they tell me, how would one really know? We tend to accept false ideas and beliefs from ourselves and others, taking it all in like soup, we should take it all in with a slotted spoon that's what I say, there's no such thing as a genuine credible witness, only someone who appears to be competent and worthy of belief in the eye and auditory perception of the Beliebers, there are too many permutations as to who or what is reliable. These days everything we see, hear, feel, taste, and touch can be manipulated by factors we're not even aware of. I've noticed a few eye contacts going around amongst some groups which have lasted more than the 6-second rule, without looking away or blinking, which can reveal a desire for sex and, or murder in my humble opinion, at least that's the case in Miss Marple. It's so frustrating knowing how terrible a fake person actually is, but everyone loves them because they put on a good puppet show, shady people expose themselves when you sit back and really pay attention to them. My mother used to always say, "When someone shows their true colours, believe them."

This place is so much more than it seems, not at all the singing and dancing in the garden of Eton, that the authorities would have the unwitting public believe. They call this dilapidated palace a detention centre which in my book means that it's meant to be a brief and cursory holding facility before the questioning of someone. Some of the involuntary residents have been here for years it seems, the meaning of brief and mine are poles apart, it's going to take some Big girl panties to work with the powers that be on this one, but I'm not going to let it go, it's not right, fair or just, I've always been literally and physically part of the big girl pants brigade anyway. I cannot for the life of me see any comfort or joy in those flimsy, unflattering ones, on me anyway, dental thongs, mainly the youngsters wear. Most women I know grow out of them thankfully, literally in most cases, arriving on the slippery transition slope, the conveyor belt from young to old, one day you're young and wearing sexy knickers, and I use that term loosely, and in the blink of a wrinkled eye, it's M & S big punts, promising the comfort of soft cotton, a liberal give and other indulgences in its folds and creases. I do wish they came with a bell to alert me to an involuntary, imminent tinkle though. What is that about? Okay, 4 babies don't help, but I feel more like a colander these days, I can't tell what's coming out of where, when, or how. I actually don't remember the last time I had a trip away without Mikey and The Boys, let alone a girls' trip with my oldest, ride-or-die chums. It's not that money's tight, and Mikey would never say "no", but there is always someone or somebody else that needs it before me, I don't feel like I'm going without either really, I like to give back in some small way. I'm not doing it to make me feel better either, maybe in a small way I probably am, but nothing brings me more delight than being part of someone else's joy and laughter, that's how I get my positive strokes. There's no such thing as a selfless act though. Anyhoo, I digress, where was I? Doesn't matter, probably a lie anyway as Angy always says, are they really lies though, little white ones? If they're intended to make yourself or others feel better? We all wear masks, thankfully the chimp mask Angy was wearing is in the minority. We all take on various roles in life, showing only those particular vulnerable bit parts to a select, safe few. Life's difficult and uncomfortable enough to go through on your tod, but with the right teacher, showing you a way back to the neutrality of your senses, before you collected your personal beliefs to hold in your, now not so impartial

Little Red Riding Hood picnic basket, helping you realise that deep down, behind the masked adhesive labels which you carefully, diligently attach to yourself over the years, in the hope to protect yourselves from being hurt. You're all the same at the core, only choices separate us. My yoga teacher says that you get to an age and stage in your lives where you need to become Strippers of sorts, removing the excess layers of restricting notions, including prejudice, in order to expose your birthright of pure awareness and creativity. I know of at least 3 occasions where Jools and Angy have removed all their clothes in gay abandon, in public as well. Looking back now, I wish I'd done it, but I was not only far too self-conscious and ashamed of my body, what if I was caught and got into trouble, or worse…seen naked? Ah, but regerts are all about the opportunities you didn't take, life offers us all the answers you need, but more often than not they go unnoticed, and unheard, besides, anyone ever meet my parents? God rest their soles, or is it souls? Is it even their or is it they're? Doesn't really matter, it only matters when you write it in black and white and not conjured up by some imaginary thought in your mental playgrounds. Or does it? Agggh, can you imagine if all your thoughts were seen, and I mean your deepest, darkest, most secret personal stuff, the passengers on your own carbon footprint-free thought carriage, etched on invisible tracks? Playing for your mind movies, speeding to the future, coming from the past, missing the opportunity to wait here. Your heads are jam-packed with your own subconscious internal, infuriated diatribe, interpreted only by the thoughts of others. If you see someone's thoughts without seeing the person, you'd have no clue…about anything really, we'd all be a tad more cautious with how much fodder you give those pesky thoughts, when to settle them down, softening them to a relaxed state. Believe me, it passes all too quickly. Relaxing the mind works wonders for the mind, body, and breath- almost as good as a lavender Epsom salt bath, although I do prefer oat milk. It calms my psoriasis. Works wonders. Speaking of settling, the helicopter has come to a steady rest.

Noooo, are you kidding me…. It can't be …..it IS!!!! My second get-out-of-jail card has arrived…I knew My Girls wouldn't let me down.

As I grow older, I pay less attention to what men say. I just watch what they do - Andrew Carnegie

Touchdown

Jules

We drift towards the parched earth, the whirring mesmerising blade, circling one large slow circle after another. Round .... and round…like a slow-moving horizontal hamster wheel, the shiny blades scoring the stale, late afternoon air, slashing through the sweet aroma wafting from the bush. Complex floral combinations of fresh green grass, sensual floral, leafy notes, a mix of citrus, herbal woody quavers, pine, eucalyptus, vegemite, wafts of overworked barbies, sunscreen, and kangaroo scat. The sun's slow descent whitewashes the vast blue sky with a gentle hue of orange, not dissimilar to a cheap artificial face tanner, almost spent, preparing herself to slip as gracefully as a hot knife through butter behind the backdrop of this day, only to appear stage left in all her brilliance to the delight of her next quivering audience patiently/ impatiently, waiting for her beyond the dark cloak of night, biding her time, no rush, no hurry to deliver the spectacle that is her daily swan song/ finale for this day. She and I are feminine, not at all masculine like they say, this is my narrative and she can be whatever gender I want for her. SHE glows because she can, having spent the past few hours delighting her mostly unaware, global spectators, belting out her full power and energy to the somewhat preoccupied masses, inhaling her unconditional energy with every forgetful breath in, and breath out. Feel the earth move under your feet, and I'm tempted to burst full belter into my rendition of the Circle of Life, that moves you all, no need to sing it out loud, preferring to listen to the whisper of the solo singer in my mental thought station. As we get closer to the ground, shapes and silhouettes expand and begin to take shape, a halo aura around a straw hairstack, almost looks angelic, a bit rounder than your average cherub, the wings are in actual fact.... outstretched arms. Little Bo Peep and her sheep.

"LESLEY. LESLEY, up here. WoooHoo, up here, we're here to bail you out, a real Thelma, Louise adventure, come on, come with us, we've taken care of everything, come on, QUICK GET IN HURRY. Who's she?"

"This is Connie, you can trust her."

"We can't take another prisoner with us Lezzers, aside from anything else it's against the law, and quite frankly, I for one am not prepared for any more incarceration whether it be mine, yours or anyone else's, now quick, jump to it, climb aboard matey, we've wasted enough time already, we have to get you out of here as soon as."

"She's not a prisoner, she's an undercover reporter, hence the Maria Von Trapp attire, here to investigate the running conditions and state of this place, if she comes with us now she can get the full gorey details on the front page of the Sydney Gazette before the midnight deadline. I've told her to be careful with her words, as once they are written down in black and white, then they can only be forgiven, not forgotten. Come on, what do you say? Jools?"

"Sometimes we need to walk in a different direction from some people from our past, because they no longer belong in our future, but if you're sure, then who am I to decide. What the hell are you waiting for climb aboard cellmateys."

There are many answers you have received, but have not heard - Course in Miracles

The Earth Revolves Around The Sun, Not You

Ange

The sooner we're airborne and away from this cesspit, then the sooner I can properly look at the proposal from my staff, Genevieve, and the rest of the team from the Badden & Minehard potential collaboration. As we leave the confines of the compound, an approaching motorcycle cop is almost knocked off their bike by the billowing red earth grime created by the helicopter's blades. We don't wait to see whether they emerge from the grimy dust devil.

Lezzers doesn't look any worse off from her ordeal y'all, she's been bleating about needing a break from Mikey and her beloved boys foreva, so she has nothing to complain about, creating her own personal prison when she does. I have spent 90% of my life consuming drugs and alcohol, seducing men, and taking risks with no prisoners, the other 10% I have wasted on anger. Wasted. I'm quite sure Mikey and The Rugrats have been relishing the peace and quiet that they've had from her constant need to involuntarily 'help' without due consent, drives me fucking insane, I don't need or want her opinions imposed on my experience thank you very much, her incessant, twittering, brushing, combing, smoothing, repeating could be used as an interrogation torture tool, even the hardest of nuts would crack under the dull diatribe that supports every verbal wavelength. I know she's harmless and only wants a positive stroke for her kindness, but I can't be assed with it, her good deeds don't go unnoticed by her own muttered validations, good, bad, and, or indifferent, but her bag, not mine, and I know, I know she'll have a judgement either way. I haven't had an opportunity to tell her anything as of yet, because whatever I do say, I need to be prepared for her point of view, her eye rolling and tutting, that's why I don't bother telling her anything, my therapist says that my emotional reaction to her is the gift waiting to be unwrapped and explored. Absolute bullshit I say; dullness, stupidity, patience, kindness, and texting whilst driving are NOT gifts, the only gift I personally see in any one of these is to play pass the parcel with them, keep handing them onto someone else, recycle that bullshit. Lezzers can verbally share her knowledge and experiences to her voluntary, muted audience, always ready with a reply, a retort, a one-up, only skirting any intent to understand. The one thing that most successful people have in common is that they listen more than talk. I'm going to treat her to some Botox to fill those two deep, very deep troughs of worry, the track lines etched between her sparse, historically over-plucked, manicured brows. What a difference it would make to her relatively smooth, wrinkle-free skin. I once made the mistake of asking for her secret, and three decades later she continues to share her secrets without due consent. The journalist she brought along with her is well shifty looking and keeps giving me the side eye, most people are uncomfortable if I nail them down with my best 6-second intimidation glare, but Ms, bound to be a MZzzz, seems completely unfazed, maybe that's her natural resting bitch face, she'd make an excellent bodyguard, I might hire her. I can easily keep her locked in an eyeball standoff and mentally prepare to make loads of money at the same time. By the time we land, I'll have my proposal couriered to NYC, where it can be endorsed by the board of which I am ChairWOMAN. I'll have it drafted, drawn up, and delivered directly to the offices of Gina Minehard before the stocks open first thing on Monday morning. I'm going to make her millions, more money than either of us has ever dreamt of, but these days, I'm beginning to think there might be more to all this accumulated vulgar amount of money I make. Then reality nips and tucks, checking back in, and says, get a grip, there's always more room for one more luxury yacht.

I'm so accustomed to being flown everywhere, that the slight dipping, turbulence, air ducking and diving of the helicopter goes almost unnoticed by me, Jules looks like she's praying, as she hasn't taken her eyes off the ground since we took off, her lips chanting faster than a vegan's hand going up when asked for dietary considerations. Where's divine intervention when you need it? Lezzers is still talking, thankfully the microphone button in my headphones is now off which gives me some peace. I'll tap Jules's leg, get her attention.

"Is that 'the' trash bag under your seat Jules?"

"Not too bad thanks Angy, I'd say palatable. Had worse, had better, it's all about perception…take Connie here, she'll agree with me, in fact, most of the time, we chatted about how we could make this place much more like a community, a place of temporary belonging, and not like a human zoo."

I don't know why Lezzer answered Jules's question. Blah, blah, blah, yada yada yada, the incessant, invisible verbal drone flatlining the current of now even more stagnant vibrations, drifting further away, dissolving into the vast open, unseen void of infinity and beyond. Bye, please stay there. Cunnie's pained expression imprinted with hours of continuous chirping, I totally get it, believe me, Cunnie, I know. I need to speak to Jules who's still bewitching the flora and fauna with some mumbo jumbo incantation or other to the scene below us. What I'd give right now to be decanting something, preferably a Dom Perignon Rose 1959. Jules is propped against the backdrop of the sundown behind her, swaddling her in its kaleidoscope embrace, she is completely captivated by something out there, I can't even begin to imagine what has her so enraptured, bewitched. What has attracted and kept her attention? All I can see is a vast reddish, undeveloped, semiarid open land with mulga and eucalyptus trees, spiny spinifex grass, and termite mounds that point towards the belly of the chopper, dry creeks, and rivers lined with shady river red gums, the entire vista punctuated and popping with hop, skip and jumping kangaroos. Beats me.

  The strap across my lap and chest is thankfully taut, holding me firmly in my place as we undulate through the dusky landscape. I'm a well-seasoned contributor to air travel so I do know the effect of how these acrylic chest bondage straps look to fellow travelling spectators. They frame my firm breasts beautifully, speaking of which, I need to book my next appointment at "Globes". Do not judge me, keep your self-righteous discernment to your own schoolyard antics, and keep them out of mine. Those of you who suffer from vertigo caused by the dizzying heights of your own self-imposed moral high ground, whispering your unbelievable beliefs directly onto the experiences of others. Fuckers. One day I might even understand, let alone believe what it all means by an inside job, I looked it up in the dictionary one time to see what the actual fuck it was and it said "Inside job - a crime committed by or with the assistance of a person living or working on the premises where it occurred." What does that even mean? All very well to say that people incriminate their experiences with their own judgement, but I'd bet money that if anyone got the chance to fly in a helicopter or a private jet with hand-picked passengers, they'd take it, screw their principles, they would change their beliefs faster than the sinking Titanic, kidding themselves they wouldn't, without a shadow of a doubt they would, and I fucking know it. Unless the excuse is some pathetic horseshit like," I'm scared of flying", then a motor-powered, luxury yacht instead? Yes? Scared of water as well? How about a luxury resort with everything your greedy heartbeat personally desires, putting the 'spa' back in spaciousness? Think about it. Judged, plain and simple, you judge MY choices, unless of course you are a judge, then you can, but even then I might take it like my margarita, with a pinch of salt, and not accept it. Fuck, you know what I mean. This altitude isn't helping me think straight. Jules is still offering muted lip service to the microscopic landscape below, jumping out of her baggy skin as I tap her knee, waking her from her spiritual dwam, trance, reverie. The shiny, black bag between her Batik-clad thighs flutters faster than an aged set of jowls in a Force 10 hurricane, begging for attention.

"Is that THE trash bag beneath your seat? I'm talking to Jules, not you Lezzers."

Gina had her assistant grab them from Gertie's trunk, and pack them in here for us. Mikey gave Jules some black trash bags sometime before she even picked Lezzers up. Initially, I didn't get the whole bag thing, the cunning, conniving, covert operation they seemed to both be relishing in behind Lezzer's back. I wasn't part of all this as I had my own covert operations going on, but pretty sure all of these shenanigans weren't part of the initial plan however. I'm told the trash bags have a change of clothes for the three of us which we need to be wearing for our grand entrance to her big, surprise Gatsby-themed 50th fancy dress, birthday party. Initially, I thought, what a stupid fucking idea, who wouldn't open a plastic bag to see what's in it, that was until I saw the state of Dirty, opening her back door is like I'd lifted the lid off one of those industrial garbage containers, there were more bags crammed in there, than you can shake Lezzer's follicly challenged hairbrush at, speaking of which, she must have captured a gingerhead boy with her beaver's bristles, she hasn't even noticed her brush missing. I've managed to squirrel it away, some would use the term steal, but I see it as my necessary contribution to my beauty regime. I had to move things, bags around the van in order to have my Louis Vuitton matching trunk, suitcases, hat box, cruiser bag, and jewelry case fit in the minute space, not enough room to swing the chat in. No one is going to miss a few missed trash bags, which I left on the sidewalk at the airport. Lezzers did look slightly disgruntled when extracted from the front passenger seat but seemed pleased enough with herself when I said it was because she was petite and pocket-sized in a hue of sickly powder blue, like a knock-off Tiffany's box, but not. Besides, I'm shit hot at reading maps, so shotgun for me all the way, the co-pilot, the wingman, the bestie. Yoda.

I refuse to join any club that would have me as a member"-
Groucho Marx

Curiosity thrilled the chat - K. G. Cooper

Frogs Are Happy Because They eat whatever Bugs Them

Jules

Only 100 miles west, that should get us there in time, we dip slightly to the right heading directly towards the eye of the slinking sun, responding to us by enveloping us in her welcoming gaze, unconditional, caressing her magnificent white light gently over Magnum's shiny, toned, sleek, belly. The power behind the sun's glare courses its way to my heavy eyelids, massaging, fondling, and warming them in their caress, 93 million miles away and she still has the strength to radiate her energy into the world. A lotus flower has the ability to rise out of the mud, blooming and blossoming out of the darkness to radiate her beauty for our eyes only. Our hearts too have the ability to expand, to break free of the voluntary emotional shackles that keep us tethered to the lure of future fantasies or the drag of the past, caught in anger, fear, sadness, and uncertainty, eventually finding the sweet spot in every moment on the spinning circle of life, straddling our sea legs between all of life's polarities, balancing perfectly in the peace, stillness, and calm. Placing ourselves front and centre of our very own live reality show, without expectation or preference, comfortable in the knowledge that the show is going to attract our thoughts, ready to be part of an impartial audience. Bring it on, I say. Where's the popcorn?

Wow, wow check that out, the perfect, panoramic vista unfolding all around me, only for my perceptive eyes, everyone else lost and caught in their own perceptive performance. The disappearing time-forged red rock formations etched deeply into the landscape's fabric, the shapes, silhouettes, and shadows shifting away from the chasing beams, stunning colours of red, yellow, and orange, tinged with spun gold, mingle and merge with the bush's gravelly jim. The sun's softening intense, protective glare greeting us in her warm embrace. Feck sake, Ange, that was my arthritic knee. Ahh, My key's black bin bags with our costumes, well remembered.

If you are patient in one moment of anger, you will escape a hundred days of sorrow - Chinese Proverb

Wine Flies When You're Having Fun

Lesley

I am beyond excited to see them, I knew they'd show up and not let me down. I can't wait to tell them all about Camp Life and find out what they've been up to, but they're not engaging with me, even Jools is looking away and out the window, she usually always still sees and hears me, maybe she still does. Angy still looks, I was going to say grumpy, but to be perfectly honest I can't tell how she feels just by looking at her. All that work. For what? It doesn't make her look younger, it gives her more of a shiny, plastic Barbie face. Did I really just say that? How mean of me, hopefully, it wasn't out loud, and even if it was, she wouldn't have heard me over the noise of the chopper. Sad really, she genuinely has so much to offer if only she'd soften up a bit.

Happy to see a female pilot, we need more women in empowered professions, thankfully more and more women are tipping the balance, it's so important to have an equal footing with the male variety, they benefit immensely from our guidance.

"Is that the trash bag beneath your seat? Not you Lezzers, Jules."

Angy keeps pointing to the black bin bags under Jool's seat. There must be something in the bags she wants. Jools is nodding faster than a possessed dashboard bobble-head puppy.

"Here Angy, I can reach it."

"Thanks Lezzers."

What's this we have in here then? Oily, greyish brown fur, a glass eye with a deathly fixed leer, maybe a vintage fox stole that was all the rage back in the day roaring '20s, my grandma had one, they're illegal now, so it must be some recent road kill or other, maybe a duckbill platypus. I'm not sure why it's wrong to wear extinct animals, they're dead aren't they, you might as well put their lives on show so they didn't die in vain, maybe in pain, but not in vain. I don't think foxes are extinct yet, I do hope not, I have a penchant for their Glacier mints. Hold on, are you kidding me, that is NOT a flapper outfit, not even a slapper frock in sight, no, I am absolutely, categorically, am not fucking wearing this.

"Are you listening Jules? There is NOTHING that you can say or do that is going to persuade me that wearing that is a good idea. NOTHING I tell you. I'd rather trot to hell on a fast pony wearing a porcupine saddle."

"Relax Ange, he who shall not be named must have changed his mind about the theme that's all, or someone accidentally picked up the wrong bags, which is unlikely as I knew exactly where they were and told Nina nina's assistant, unless someone moved things around in the back of Gertie. Ange? They do look more like the costumes leftover from our performance of "The kangaroo King " and our pantomime "Winnie The Roo". Not to worry, put them on will you. Ange, relax, it was a great show, rave reviews, we'll be fine. Tell yourself that the kangaroo costume you're about to wear is a deer that's gone to the gym, now put it on please, we will land in 20 minutes. Here's your outfit Lesley, put this one on, we've been invited to a fancy dress party, the Great Gatsby meets the Outback. Next stop, Bondage Beach. Nina nina will land as close as she can, then we can hop in the surf, hop, skip and jump on the sand. Keep your heads low, and out of the way of blades, we don't want to land sliced and diced, Connie and Nina nina are going to head back to the helipad, we'll catch them later. Wish us luck. It's all in the bag, what could possibly go wrong."

"More like the Great Gadzthree, Jules."

I hadn't even noticed Bondi looming up on the horizon, caught up, literally, in putting on this costume Jools just handed to me. I'd recognise this panoramic snapshot anywhere, 1 kilometre of glimmering white sand, world-class waves, an easy aesthetic appeal as its width, gentle slope of sand, crescent shape, and plenty of room for everyone to enjoy. The beautiful shark-infested waters of the Pacific, welcoming swimmers, paddlers, surfers, and boogie boarders towards its salty glistening, treacherous spume. The beach is flanked by headlands which define the northern and southern points. Campbell Parade, the main promenade full of drag, or maybe it's drag promenade... no matter... is dotted with buzzing, trendy cafes, unique boutiques, and gift shops. I can see a group of people on the beach waving up at us, everyone is wearing beautiful retro, vintage 1920s outfits, there's an old man standing in the surf, even from this height, he looks very sexy in his trilby, waistcoat, braces, cravat, and pocket watch, spoiled marginally by the Daniel Craig sky blue budgie smuggler, speed knots he's wearing underneath. He's paddling in the surf, so it makes sense to wear dockers instead of trousers so that his formal attire doesn't get wet. What a sexy man, somewhat familiar in a way, but I can't really tell from this angle or without glasses, or see properly through these eye holes in this very scratchy, itchy costume I'm wearing. What kind of affair have they managed to get me messed up in ...again.

"I'm lost for words."

"Me too Lesley."

"No seriously, I'm lost for words. What was I saying? I think I'm ready to jump Jools."

"Don't jump yet Lesley, I'm not quite ready. Hold on, hold on, my tail is stuck between my legs. "

"Leave it Jules, it looks fine, looks like you have an unsparing hard on."

"Oh, that's right, this is Nigel's costume, it's designed this way. Come on girls, we're in this together, are we ready to take the plunge? Ready Ange? Lesley?"

"Yours doesn't look as bad as mine does Angy. I look more like a fat, hairy woolly granny pig, than a kangaroo, you still look chic and sexy in your roo drag, you not so much Jools, it must be your Channel shades that sets it off Angy. What kind of fancy dress party is this we're going to exactly? What's the theme again? Skippy?"

"Now that's where you're mistaken my dear Lesley, you attract your thought tennants, the rowdier they are, the more space they take up, besides, sexiness comes from a belief in yourself, not in a pair of designer shades or anything else for that matter, it helps, but if you don't feel, and I mean feel, not think of yourself as sexy, then those are the vibrational hula hoops you ripple out, best make sure you feel sexy beyond the acrylic marsupial jumpsuit you have one. I know I do, and I know how beautiful you are. Noone can make us think something we don't want to think, thoughts are only the choices we make, nobody has the ability to make our choices. We can't heal what we don't feel. Now, no time like our presence in the present, hold hands Laddies, we'll jump together on the count of three and lowp over the threshold directly into the centre of the next unknown moment. "All for one and One for All," ONE."

"WAAITT ....I'm not ready Jools, there's some costume jewellery in my marsupial pouch."

"Wear it like the one's I found in mine, or chuck it, come on, what's holding us back, all these thoughts we have can be sticky and when we touch them then they can bind us in misery for years, so let them go, say, "maybe so," that's one of my favourite things to say, "maybe so" Almost every great step we take in our lives, begins with a leap of faith, a shift into the unknown. Ready? Ange? Lesley? TWO."

"WAIT Up…I'm not ready either. I'm still working on my bucket list Jules, not ready to die just yet."

"Change the b to f on that list of yours and you'll feel better about it. We're all going to die Ange, but sometimes a small hop into the next deep, dark, uncertain cave of the next moment will lead us directly to the treasure we seek. When we carry fear, then with every cell in our taut body we are going to experience fear, or anger, or sadness, or whatever it is we're gripped to. Life is like jumping out of a helicopter, only without a kangaroo suit or parachute, only the last few seconds will kill you, but most people are terrified the entire journey getting there. Carry something wonderful instead, like excitement, joy, laughter, friends, and we'll all experience that etched on the cave walls of every moment.TWO and a half…I LOVE LOVE LOVE YOU Laddies. How much better does it get than this? When you laugh, I laugh, when you cry, I cry, when you jump off a cliff I yell, do a flip, now JUMP." "UGGGGHH You didn't say three Jules, I wasn't ready…aaaaaaggggghhhhhhhh. Oh, it's only ankle deep…"

A Good Friend Knows All Your Stories. Best Friends Help You Write Them

In a Nutshell

Jules

My face is firmly planted in the shallow waters of Bondage Beach, like one of those pinpoint impression needle art frames. The wet sand, sanding the skin down to the marrow, an innocent crustacean minding its own business, doing crab stuff in the surf, impaled by the candy floss tip of the kangaroo tail between my legs to the seabed, skewered by the rigid phallic symbol gripped between my flapping, furry thighs. The heavy, unnecessary costume jewellery stuffed in the pouch keeping me weighted down in the squall. I don't remember any jewellery in the shows, funny that. Thank the Lard I can reach it and offload it to the eager, hungry waves, ready to carry it all in its currents back to their watery grave. I'm quite sure our amateur dram society can afford some more artificial trinkets. Lesley is beside me, also facedown, body crawling through the surf, her pouch filling with wet sand with every drag of her belly. My key, who's wearing a black dress suit, bow tie, boater hat, and for some inexplicable reason, accessorised by a pair of baby blue Y fronts, clutching a box of chocolates, scoops her out like a drowned marsupial rat from the breakers, and all because the lady loves Milk Tray. Friends, family, and public beach onlookers temporarily leave the lit event tent, and the smorgasbord of appetisers, small bites, and desserts, including Lesley's famous homemade moist muffins, which My key's been squirreling away in friends' freezers across Sydney for months now. Everyone reaches the shore to greet and applaud the guest of honour as she's scooped out of the shallows like a drowned rat by her Shite in wining armour, her one true love. This celebration hasn't been done for the guests, My Key has done all this hoopla doodle, to show his love and devotion for his Lesley, his one and only, in the only way he knows how, and it's clear by the beam and glow radiating from her hairy headgear that he's nailed it.

"Knobber. Grab my paw Jules, I've finished laughing."

"You don't even look wet, how is that even possible Ange?"

"The night is young Jules, the night is young."
"I can see Richard waiting up at the cake stand, want to go to him?"

"Not yet, I need to take a minute to decompress from everything that just happened in the past few days. Let's sit by the water's edge and watch the sun go down. What do you say, Lezzers, want to join us? I have something I'd like to share with you both, and Bondage Beach seems like the perfect place to tell you both some really big news."

"You don't have to tell me Angy, I already know, I'm not as stupid as I look you know, I love Once Upon a Time fairytale endings, you and Richard must love each other very much for you to move here, so you have my blessing, and for what it's worth I am overjoyed to have you as my wicked stepmother in law. I'd love you to be part of our family...Slumsy."

"Once upon a time there wasn't a cheesy fairytale, romantic ending to the story Lesley, the the heroine decided to move to Sydney to take over the helm of her new company Badden- Minehards with her newly acquired deal-breaking Hermes bag, the matching twin to the one you own Lesley."

"Shirley not, you can't be serious Jools, I thought it was a knock off. Golly gosh all this time I thought it was one thing and it turns out to be something completely different. For what it's worth, I think you'd suit it on your arm Angy, I mean the handbag, although Richard would suit being on your arm also."

"You are always too nice and kind Lezzers, and sometimes that trait can be mistaken for weakness. I love that about you, you are anything but, carrying that battered, grubby, priceless, precious, timeless beaten up old sack around with you, like you own the joint, not giving a jot, not one fucking jot do you give as to whether it's a heifer or an Hermes, more power to you that's what I say. Not sure I could or would be able to do that."

"Och, fa's looking at me anyhoo Angy, if someone wants to judge me on my handbag or anything else for that matter, then that's a reflection of them, not me, and if that's your way of indirectly saying you love me Angy, I'll take it, and right back at you, spread the love, that's what I say."

"Speaking of spread, My key has put on a spectacular one just for you Lesley, he's been hoarding all your homemade muffins for months now, and I can see they're being wolfed down like there's no tomorrow. I managed to grab and scoff three down, and I know Ange had at least 2 before we got back down here to the shore."

"You're joking me Jools? Those are the special muffins I make for Mikey, the ones I told you about, the ones laced with viagra, and love potion, but you know what I'm thinking? If he's been stashing them, and …well you know…not eating them, then it's not the magic muffins that has put the pep in his step, the twinkle in his eye, maybe it's me.. well, blow me Mr McIvor."

"This is turning into the best and hardest day of our lives. You do know that Viagra won't make My key, James Bond Lesley, but it will make him Roger Moore."

"Fuck me, that's why they're so hard to swallow. Give me the platinum wine flask I spotted in your bag Lezzers, I don't know whether these viagra muffs are coming or going."

"You don't want this wine Angy, believe me, it's stale, warm, off. Seriously, I was about to pour it out."

"You're taking this really hard Lezzers, waste not want not, now be a good girl, and do as I say, give it to me, and let me decide whether it's palatable or not. Relax your grip girl, you're still a little stiff, let go of the flask. Lezzers, do as I tell you. What goes up, must go down my gullet."

"A little less conversation, a little more breathing Laddies."

"Give it here NOW Lezzers."

"If you insist Angy, don't say I didn't warn you."

"Thank you Lezzers, finally. You taking the piss? That's revolting, what the hell is this in the WINE flask, Cumboocha? I need a stiff drink, that's what I need."

"There are friends, there is family, and then there are friends that become family, so like it or lump it, I consider you both my family, my sisters from different misters, my glue to see me through, my fellow passengers on this terribly grand adventure, just look at the three of us. See no faecal, hear no faecal, speak no faecal. This is it, this is all we have, right here, right now."

"But one day it'll all be over Jules."

"Maybe so."

"Lezzers, think of all the life's sour pills we get to swallow, unlike your muffins. Viagra or not, we sure don't need a love potion to know that friends are like condoms, they should protect you when things get hard. When shall we three get the chance to meet again?"

"In thunder, lightning, or in rain? Or maybe at a water's edge."

"When the hubbly bubbly is done, and the battles of the Lesley's muffins have been lost and won.   Who came last, who came first. Come on, let's grab the chance while we can, and be together for the last few minutes of the setting sun one last time, before it slips easily and gracefully into the slot between sky and water, like a glistening coin being dropped into an empty piggy bank. Exiting backstage, entering stage left to the somewhat delighted, sleepy heads waking to their brand new day.

Hanging out with our Besties is a very rich place to be. Bring it on I say, life is way too short not to greet each moment with a spring in our step, a twinkle in our eye and a ready mischievous quiver on our lips. Come and take us on world if you think you're hard enough, we're ready. All I can be sure of is being here, right here, nowhere else to be, when I have you two by my side I laugh a little harder, cry a little less, and smile a whole lot more. We're like those three wise monkeys, see no shite, hear no shite, speak no shite. No wucking furries, and no prizes for guessing which monkey we relate to most. Now big breaths."

"Thank you Jules, when you know, you know, you know?"

"Hear, hear Angy. How much better does it get than this, bet there's not much that could change this moment."

"We may trip over the creases on our imaginary red carpet as it unravels, unfolds, and unrolls just for us, but when we do stumble, stick or fall, then pretend it's all part of the bigger picture, the once in a lifetime act that we're presenting for the live audience, get up, dust ourselves down, laugh and dance our way out of there straight into the next scene. Bring it on I say."

"Nothing is going to beat the past few days entertainment, nothing I tell you, other than my final decision, which one of you has spot on."

"Maybe yes, Ange, maybe not. When there are no preferences to outcomes, then anything is possible. We need to be still, yet open to be part of our reality as it is, as it really is. How much better does it get than being on an adventure with beloved friends, I cannot for the life of me think that there's anything that can top this moment."

Don't be afraid to share your Charm, Uniqueness, Nerve and Talent with the world - RuPaul

Is not dread of thirst when your well is full, the thirst that is unquenchable? - Kahil Gibran

To love and be loved is to feel the sun from both sides –

David Viscott

BREAKING NEWS: Seasoned criminal Connie Vikta in daring helicopter jailbreak. Still at large, accomplices sought. Reward offered for any information leading to an arrest. Contact - Chief Constable Cox 1 800-229-224 or 1 800-244-383

Happy to meet, sorry to part, happy to meet again - Bon Accord

終わり

Owari

La fin

An deireadh

That's all for now, friends.

Now, bog off and find something better or worse to read

THE END

Somewhere Deep In The Bush

DIRTY GERTIE

How to spik Scots and Doric wi Chummies. You can take the girl out of Scotland, but not Scotland out of the girl

A funcie piece and a fly cup - A Home bake and a cup of tea or coffee

Awa an' bile yer heid - I don't think so Wanker

Baw hair - hair of scrotum sack

Birl - dance

Besom - Rascal

Blether - Chat

Bop - Dance, or insult

Braw - Good

Feel - Numptie

Chuckies - small stones

Chuddy - chewing gum

Chuffed - quite pleased : delighted.

Cludgie - Toilet

Clammy- Warm and sticky

Clarty/clatty - Mucky

Clype - To tell tales

Crabbit - Grumpy

Deid - dead

Dirling - Throbbing

Dookers - Cassie - bathing costume

Dreich - Wet, miserable

Dreuth - Thirst

EEjit - Fool, idiot

Fizzog - face

Fouter - A tedious person

Galoot - an oafish person

Gaun - Going

Geggy - Mouth

Gie's a bosie quine - give me a hug lass

Glaikit - Feel

Greet - tears

Foostie - rotten

Hallyracket - Given to frolicking in a boisterous, thoughtless or foolish manner

Haiver - Gibberish

Haud yer wheesht an get oan wae it - Shut yer geggy and get on with it

Heebie Jeebies - Nervous, anxious, giving one 'the willies'

Heid - head

Lairy - British slang. : unpleasantly loud, confident, etc. When he drinks he gets a bit lairy

Lang may yer lum reek - A Scottish blessing

Laldie - Having a fee jee, going mad

Lavvy - Toilet, loo

Manky - Slovenly

Mauchit - Clarted, dirty

Numpty - Eejit

Peely wally- Off colour

Pished - drunk

Quine - Girl, lass

Rajin - Fuming, angry

Rowies -buttery, Aberdeen roll is a savoury bread roll originating from Aberdeen, Scotland.

Scallywag - rugrat - mischievous imp

Scrap - fight

Shewee - Extreme is the Original female urinating device.

Skree - Chuckies, loose stone chips

Sook - suck

Spaver - zip on men's trouser front

Stramash - Disturbance

Tootie - small

Wifie - lady

Sometimes confused with the Australian outback, **the Australian bush** is a colloquial term used among Australians to describe the backwoods or hinterland areas that are just outside the coastal areas of Australia. In fact, many Australians understand "the bush" as more of a feeling than a specific place.

How to speak straylian for the non Australians amongst us.

Arvo - afternoon

Footy - Football

Spewin - Angry

Barbie - BBQ

G'Day - Good day

Squizz - to look at something

Beaut - Great,

Good Onya - Well done

Strewth - Exclamation

Bruce - Bloke, Man

Grog - Booze

Too right - definitely agree

Bloody - very

Mate - Cobber

Tucker - Food

Bloody Oath - Very true

No Worries - Reassurance

Woop Woop - Region. Far far away..

Bludger - lazy person

Pint - large glass of beer

Dag - An unfashionable person

Liquor store - Offie

Flip flops - thongs

Brekkie - Breakfast

Pokies - poker machines

Cobber - Friend

Pot - 285ml beer glass

Crook - ill

Ripper –

Beaut Dip - Swim

She'll be right - It will all be ok

Dunny - Toilet

Sheila - Woman

www.mcpayne.com -

Menopause Madness

Hormones are racing through my BOD,making itchy, bitchy and slightly ODD.I'm happy then sad, & oh so sleepy,and in the blink of an eye, I'm suddenly weepy. I'm tired all day and awake ALL night,menopause Madnezz is just so shite.I'm hot , I'm cold and ALWAYS sweaty.I'm here, i'm there, and I often...what is it?...oh yes, forgetty.I open the fridge scrutinizing this and that.and just by looking, I get very fat.My life and home are completely chaotic,friends and family think I'm psychotic.There will be hot flashes, I can not deny,But hand held fans will get you by.Aside from the fans, there's always the wine,but it will only add to your facial shine.When there are days that you're feeling downjust put on your invisible menopausal crown.but a piece of advice before you enter this phase,

No One gets out in a matter of days.Copious amounts of tears WILL be shed,in the many, many, MANY years ahead.Settle in you're in for quite a ride,but soon you'll be saying with ultimate pride. "the menopause was such a breeze,I survived, wonders will never cease."But a word of warning....before you sneeze,you'll end up with wet panties

down to your knees.

BOOM BOOM   Kimberley Georgeson Cooper

www.ingramcontent.com/pod-product-compliance
Lightning Source LLC
Chambersburg PA
CBHW070736180626
46818CB00007B/2870